A DREAM SO WICKED

TESSONJA ODETTE

TESSONJA ODETTE

A DREAM SO WICKED

A SLEEPING BEAUTY RETELLING
ENTANGLED WITH FAE

PART ONE

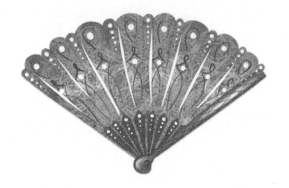

A
DREAM

1

This solitary dance will be my last. Each step shall seal my farewell to all the hopes I've harbored. There was a time I dreamed I'd get to spin and sway in a ballroom, my dance card full of names of eager suitors desperate to be my partner. But the closest I've come to the society balls I've fantasized about is this glade. For in this glade, I can live out my foolish dreams. My secret hopes can come to life.

One last time, at least.

My heart weighs heavy in my chest as I slip off my leather slippers and plant my bare feet reverently on the cool grass. The morning is mild, the breeze only somewhat chilly against the long sleeves of my plain gray dress. The rising sun peeks above the towering trees surrounding the glade, kissing the dainty white petals of the starflowers dotting the grass in hazy morning light.

With a deep breath, I gather the dew-scented air into my lungs. Country air. Air I'll never have the pleasure of enjoying again. Not in this exact way, at least. While I've only left my convent once since I was abandoned there nearly twenty years ago, I find it impossible to believe anywhere else will carry this same scent—the dew, the starflowers, the fields of Starcane sugar growing nearby.

It's strange how a place that felt like a prison for most of my life now carries such bittersweet nostalgia.

From my dress pocket, I extract a folded paper fan, tattered and faded after years in my care. On one side is a watercolor rendering of blue flowers. On the other, the illustrated steps to the quadrille. I memorized the dance long ago when I first found the fan discarded on the side of the road outside the convent, but I always take it out before I dance. It's tradition.

I fan myself once, twice, batting my lashes like a demure debutante. Then I tuck my golden-blonde hair behind my pointed ears—a shape that marks me as full fae—and imagine my tresses are styled in a fashionable updo, the kind popular amongst human society. Then, gathering a corner of my wool skirt with my free hand, I dip into a practiced curtsy. As I rise, I close my eyes.

And dream.

Images flash behind my closed eyelids, a hidden inventory of memories I've captured and filed away for later use. Since I've never been inside a true ballroom, I select one of my favorite dreamscapes to dance within—the night of last year's meteor shower, when stars fell over the Celesta Convent School for Girls. For a convent located in the Star Court and dedicated to worshiping starlight, a meteor shower isn't a rare phenomenon. But that one was special. The glittering shards of light illuminated the sky in radiant rainbow hues unlike anything I'd seen before. The shower so greatly enriched the Starcane sugar—a crop the convent is renowned for growing—that my three teachers took a selection of the older students to the city of Lumenas to celebrate.

That was the first time I left the convent.

The second time will be tomorrow.

With a slow exhale, I open my eyes and find the scene of the meteor shower frozen all around me. The morning sky has now been blanketed in black, specks of multihued starlight suspended midflight. While my toes still experience the soft grass beneath them, the ground no longer resembles a glade but the rooftop balcony above the convent. Acres of Starcane sugar fields span before me, surrounded by the towering trees of the forest beyond.

Unlike most other things in my life, this scene hasn't lost its luster. It still manages to spark awe, hope, and enchantment. I may have given up on dancing after today, but I'll always have this memory.

I tilt my chin in a distinct nod and the still frame comes to life, the meteors no longer frozen but soaring through the sky. With another nod, shadowed figures take their places around me, pairing up in twos to dance the quadrille. Unlike the memory, these figures hold no clear features. They are merely constructs of my mind, conjured to interact with me and my daydream. While I capture memories of scenes, landscapes, and groups of people on a regular basis, I never do so of a singular living person. Not anymore, at least. Only once did I frame a solitary figure within the bounds of my hands—thumbs and forefingers touching to form a rectangle around the person—and I'm determined never to do it again. For that gesture is what creates a permanent memory in my mind. Capturing a specific individual and conjuring their likeness to interact with my dreamscapes feels...wrong.

Not that it's stopped me from dreaming of that one person time and again. Unintentionally, of course.

Mostly.

Another nod and hazy music begins. I'm adept at recreating memories in my daydreams, but I've never been able to recreate music in quite the same way. It always sounds as if it's filtered through a closed door, the melody too intangible to grasp. But it's suitable enough for dancing, especially when no one else is around to hear the racket I've created. Only I can experience my dreamscapes. Anyone else who stumbled upon me would hear birdsong, the rustling of grass in the glade. They'd see the green clearing and a blue sky, not the nighttime meteor shower I've conjured. Once I begin dancing, I'll certainly appear strange to any onlooker, prancing around with my invisible partners, but that's what makes this glade so great; I'm the only one who comes here.

I close my fan and slip its beaded strap over my wrist. Then I curtsy to the featureless partner beside me. He mimics the gesture with a bow. I repeat the motion with the figure across from me. Then we follow the steps from the dancing fan, bypassing each other, circling, then bypassing again. We skip to the side in tiny hops, then circle around with the opposite partner. The dance is a complex yet joyful weave of movement, one that always puts a smile on my face. Soon my breaths are short and my temperature grows warm despite the cool breeze that brushes over my skin. I join hands with my imaginary companions and we skip forward, tightening the circle our bodies have made. With several backward hops, we widen it.

There's an absence of pressure where I clasp my partners' hands, something that can't be remedied in my dreamscape. That and the vacant shapes of my fellow dancers keep me from feeling fully immersed in the dance—lonely, in other words—so I close my eyes and follow the next moves from memory alone. I step, turn, reach for my partner's hollow hand. I skip, sway, and release the pretend hand. Then I weave through my fellow dancers, forward, then back. I reach for yet another weightless hand...

But the fingers that clasp my own are solid.

I stumble over my feet. My eyelids fly open to find a male figure dancing beside me. He isn't one of my shadowed partners, but a man of flesh and blood. I'm so startled, my dreamscape falters, returning me to the glade, but in the next beat of my heart, recognition settles over me. I note the man's piercing brown eyes, his dark hair that falls in tousled waves just above his shoulders. He's dressed in a stylish navy suit, his waistcoat brown, his cravat white to match his shirt. Black leather gloves adorn his hands, leaving only the flesh of his face exposed. My eyes widen as I take in the horns curling from the sides of his head, then the dark wings folded down his back. That's unusual. Considering he's fully human, he shouldn't have fae characteristics like these. I suppose that's the nature of dreams though. Even ones about real people.

My racing heart returns to a more manageable rhythm, and the glade falls back beneath the dark curtain of my meteor shower dreamscape.

I regain my composure, syncing my steps to the beat of the quadrille while the man takes the place of my former shadowed partner. He easily keeps up with me, which isn't surprising. He's merely a construct of my mind, after all, and we've done this plenty of times by now.

I give him a withering look. "I shouldn't be surprised you're here."

We step apart, then together. Apart, then together. He

tilts his head slightly, a corner of his lips flicking into an amused smirk. "Why is that?"

"Because I always manage to dream you into being."

"So you know who I am," he says.

"Of course I do." He's Thorne Blackwood, a man I've never met in real life, only seen from afar.

"And...you dream of me often?"

"I didn't mean to—you know what? I don't need to explain myself to you. You aren't real."

His smirk widens. "Because this is just a dream?"

"Exactly." Thank the All of All the real Thorne Blackwood doesn't know I dream of him like this. It truly was an accident that I ever did so in the first place.

Blackwood Bakery is one of the convent's most loyal patrons. They've been sourcing Starcane sugar from our fields for as long as I've lived at the convent school. While the bakery normally sends their buyer to fetch the sugar and load the wagon, one day Mr. Blackwood himself came to do the job. I just so happened to be taking lunch with a few of my peers in the fields when we spotted the handsome human from a distance.

This was about two years ago, before I'd ever left the convent for my weeklong stay in the city of Lumenas. Back then, my experience with gorgeous strangers revolved around a few stolen trysts with the occasional delivery boy. I'd yet to set eyes on a male creature so devastatingly beautiful as Mr. Blackwood. He wore spectacles then, his overlong hair swept off his forehead to reveal a widow's peak. That gave him a severe look that contrasted his open waistcoat and rolled-up shirtsleeves. I could have simply admired him from afar and left it at that, but he just had to take that moment to bend over and heft one of the heavy sacks of sugar like it weighed nothing. The most delicious thought occurred to me then: could he lift me over his shoulder as easily?

I was so entranced by his masculine beauty—the way his veins went taut in his forearms, the sheen of sweat that coated his brow—that I wasn't in my right mind. He released his burden onto the wagon and turned, giving me the perfect view of him in all his glory. That's when I lifted my hands and *framed* him. He glanced my way then, a furrow of confusion drawn on his forehead. I dropped my hands, breaking the rectangular gesture I'd made around his figure, but it was too late. I'd captured his likeness to dream of later. My very first solitary subject I'd ever framed. And the last.

"I was just starting to realize I had dream magic in the first place," I say, despite my earlier insistence that I didn't have to explain myself. It's not like I haven't already told him all this before, either. "I didn't know what I was doing. I hardly understand my abilities now. All I know is when I capture scenes or images with multiple people, the memories replay exactly as I recall them. I can watch these memories like backdrops, but I can't change them or speak to the figures. Conversely, if I create a frame around a single person as my focus, I can dream of and interact with them in an entirely personal way."

Sometimes too personal, I add to myself.

Out loud, I say, "At least, that's what happened with you, so I can only assume it would be the same with anyone else. I was so horrified when you started showing up in my dreams that I never dared frame an individual subject again."

I remember the first time he appeared before me. It was in this very glade, during a similar daydream. I was dancing the gallopade with one of my shadowed partners when suddenly Thorne Blackwood took their place. He stumbled and fell, blinking up at me in terror. I was so startled, my dreamscape disappeared at once, ending my daydream and all signs of Mr. Blackwood. The second time occurred a week later, in much the same way. I dipped into a curtsy in preparation for a daydream dance, but when I rose, he was there.

"This again?" he grumbled under his breath, and that was when I discovered we could speak with each other. Once more, my mortification was strong enough to dissolve my daydream. By the fourth time, however, neither of us were surprised by his appearance, and he even humored me with a full dance. From then on, he became a recurring dance partner of mine. A friend, almost, if you don't count the fact that he isn't real.

"I truly had no intention of dreaming of you," I say, "but fret not, because I won't do so as often from now on."

In a sudden move, he turns me toward him, placing his free hand at my waist. My shadowed dancers disappear as he leads me out of the quadrille and into a waltz. My make-believe music shifts to accommodate our new dance. "If I'm just a figment of your imagination," he says, "why would I fret about whether you dream of me?"

I'm unsettled by the unexpected direction my daydream has taken. This wouldn't be the first time a dream has veered off my chosen path, but rarely does one feel this real. The warmth of his palm seeps into my own, even through the thick leather gloves he wears. The hand at my waist rustles the wool fabric of my dress. I blink a few times, willing the dream to shift, but Thorne Blackwood remains as he is, devoid of his usual spectacles but with those strange horns and wings. Again, I'm perplexed that I'd dream of him with fae features. My eyes fall on his rounded ears. Could he be half fae, perhaps? While full fae have pointed ears, those with a mixture of human and fae blood have rounded ones. But no, that can't be true. Thorne Blackwood is a public figure, famous for Blackwood Bakery. Everyone knows he's the son of two humans—Edwyn and Alina Blackwood—a baker and a wealthy heiress, respectively.

Then again...what the hell am I thinking? This is a *dream*. The man before me isn't the real Thorne Blackwood, so what does it matter if I'm dreaming of him with wings and horns? I dreamed of him naked once, so this is hardly the strangest thing.

I shake the thoughts from my head, recalling the question I left hanging between us. "You may be a construct of my magic, but it still feels wrong to dream of a real person. To...make you do these things with me." I nod between us, at the sparse inches of space separating our chests.

He tilts his head. "What other things have you made me do with you?"

I scoff but the sudden rise of heat in my cheeks betrays my secrets. "You're not normally this crass," I rush to say. "Besides, most of the time we simply dance. For some reason, you show up most when I dream of dancing."

"Why is that?"

I shrug a shoulder as he turns me into a spin. "I suppose I crave a partner. One whose eyes I can hold while I dance." I do so now, catching his gaze. There's more depth in his dark irises than ever before. They seem to be brimming with questions, curiosity. And if I'm reading my own dream correctly, a dash of cruel amusement as well. I avert my gaze over his shoulder. "But like I said, I won't be dreaming of you as often anymore because this is my last dance."

He arches a brow. "That's a touch melodramatic."

I lift my chin. "It's true though. I leave the convent school tomorrow."

"Because...your parents have contacted you?" He states it like a question, but there's a wary note to his tone that I can't quite place.

Maybe he's merely reflecting my own emotions, the grief I've kept locked away after accepting that my parents were never going to come for me. It sparks now, a spear of pain and longing for the family I'll never have.

I bury my grief behind a contrived smile. "That's not it. I turn twenty today, which means the convent is required to turn me out. Unless I stay and take my vows as a sister, I must leave. So I've chosen the sensible route. I'm going to be a governess."

My heart falls. Becoming a governess will seal the coffin on all my dreams once and for all. Dreams that my parents might come back for me. That they might welcome me with open arms. That I might have the chance to enjoy at least one social season like women years younger than me already have.

But no. With neither parents nor a patron, I cannot enter society. The best thing a woman who's been abandoned at the convent can do is to leave as a governess. The school has plenty of connections for employment where that vocation is concerned.

"The life of a sister isn't for you?" he asks.

"Stars, no. I can only feign obedience so far. The sisters know my heart is too wicked for religion. Even one I admire."

"You? Wicked?" The curl of his lips turns seductive. Dangerous. "Now, that I believe."

He whirls me in another spin. As he returns me to his arms, I frown at him. Thorne doesn't normally ask so many questions in my dreams. Nor does he hold me so close when we dance. The inches of space we maintained when we first began our waltz have melted away, leaving the fronts of our bodies pressed together. His gloved hand drifts lower to the base of my spine. My pulse kicks up. I know I should push him away and reclaim the space we had before. No matter how many times we've danced, and no matter how many times he's entered my dreams that were of a more...*explicit* nature...I've been careful not to touch him—or dream of him touching me more than propriety would allow. It's the one boundary I'm determined to hold with him. The one line I won't cross with my imagined manifestation. Dream or no, somewhere on the isle of Faerwyvae, Thorne Blackwood is a real person. He deserves my respect, not my objectification. Not that I haven't objectified him before. Mostly at night when I have far less control over the content of my dreams.

I'm about to do the proper thing and take a step back when he pulls me even closer and lowers his lips to my ear. I shudder as his deep voice rumbles in his chest, reverberating against my own.

"Do you believe in fate, Briony Rose?" The question holds a note of jest, but that isn't what pulls my gaze back to his. He's never used my name before. I've never given it in any of my dreams, not even in the ones where we've spoken cordially like friends. When I don't answer, he speaks again. "Yes, I've finally put a name to the specter who haunts my dreams. Who leaves me waking with fleeting images of a girl I saw in person just once two years ago. And who would have guessed her name would be Briony Rose, a fae woman with a moniker so like my lifelong nemesis, Princess Rosaline Briar. You're the exact same age as she is too."

A chill runs through me at the shift in his tone. His

curiosity remains, but the cruel amusement I sensed earlier has deepened.

"I was never too keen on fate," he says, "but I do believe in curses. I'm starting to suspect curses are a lot like fate. Curses, like destiny, are determined to come to fruition. Wouldn't you agree?"

I plant my feet, forcing us to halt our waltz. What the hell is he talking about? Why would I dream of him saying these things?

Thorne releases me, but he doesn't step away. My dreamscape melts from night to day, leaving us at the center of the glade. I blink a few times, willing him to disappear, for the daydream to end, but he remains stubbornly in place.

"My mother always told me I was named for vengeance," he says. "Only recently did I understand what that means. Now, will you allow me to try something?"

"What in the name of the All of All is going on here? Why won't you disappear?"

His cruel grin widens. Then, tugging on the fingers of his gloves, he bares his hands. In a flash of movement, he closes the foot of space I created, his fingertips softly clasping my chin.

"Briony, darling," he says, his voice a dangerous whisper, "forget we had this dance."

2

The glade is empty. Wasn't there something here before? I stare at the grassy clearing, now fully illuminated by the rising sun. The heads of the starflowers bob in the breeze. A breeze that reminds me of whispered words.

Words...

What were they?

I shake my head to clear it, but there's a fog clouding my mind. I came to the glade to dance my final quadrille. To give up on youthful dreams and prepare for the practical life of a governess. I arrived at first sunrise, but the glade is now fully aglow. My fan dangles from its strap on my wrist. My feet are bare and my slippers lie in the grass a few yards away. I recall removing my shoes, extracting my fan, and... what happened after that?

I place my hand to my forehead. My skin feels warm, and my heart races like I've just recovered from some fright.

"Briony!"

I jump at the sound of my name, the voice calling me from a distance beyond the glade. With a calming sigh, I chastise myself for my flustered state. The voice belongs to Lina, a younger girl from the convent school. She's likely come to fetch me to return for my birthday celebration.

Though I'm not supposed to know, Sister Agatha has been planning my party for weeks. Of our three teachers, Agatha loves celebrations the most. She was the primary advocate for our trip to Lumenas after last year's meteor shower. She's also the teacher who allowed me to stay a week longer in the city to participate in a quirky bridal competition at the Church of Saint Lazaro. I lost, of course, for my heart had never been set on marrying Brother Dorian in the first place, and his affection had been captured by a selkie princess named Maisie. To me, the competition was less about securing a husband and more a means to an end. What I truly wanted from the extended visit was to sneak out after dark and watch as many kinds of dances as I could. By the end of the competition, I managed to catch four ballet performances and a burlesque show. It was time well spent.

The topic of dancing has my mind drifting back to its earlier confusion. I came to the glade to dance, and then...

"Briony Rose!" Lina calls again, her voice closer now. There's no use evading her. The students love Agatha's parties, no matter how quaint they are. If I don't come soon, every one of my peers will be scouring the fields and forest around the convent to drag me back just so they can eat a slice of cake.

My shoulders slump. I suppose it's better this way. Why bother with the sentiment of a last dance when I've already made the sensible choice? My days of waltzing in the woods are through.

~

I FIND LINA AT THE EDGE OF THE STARCANE FIELDS, CHEEKS red with frustration and her hands on her hips. She's dressed the same as I am, in a gray wool gown with long sleeves and a high-cut neckline, unadorned with lace or the other ornamentations that would grace more fashionable attire. Her brown hair is pulled into a tight bun, which shows off her rounded ears. Though both pureblood humans and human-fae hybrids have rounded ears, Lina is fully human. Unlike me, she knows who her parents are.

"Briony Rose," she says, eyes narrowing to a scowl, "you have some nerve leaving your bed before sunrise without permission."

I do my best not to laugh. She's about four years younger and a whole head shorter than I am, yet she delivers her reproach with zeal. Her efforts to prove herself a paragon of obedience have been quite exaggerated as of late. I understand why. Those very efforts have gained her parents' approval and permission to come home.

Not all students are left at the convent as babies like I was. Many are sent to the school for reform, etiquette, or as a respite in the wake of a recent scandal. Lina was sent for reform after her parents deemed her unfit to enter society due to her poor behavior. While the sisters' methods of schooling, training, and reformation are rather gentle and revolve around hours of tutelage in school subjects and manners, followed by chores and tending the Starcane fields, it's the boredom that truly inspires obedience in cases like Lina's. Now she's set to leave the convent next week, after which she'll make her debut in society.

I close the distance between us. Smiling demurely, I pat the top of her head—because I know she hates it and this just might be my last chance to torment the little spitfire. "You'll forgive me, won't you?"

She scoffs, pulling her head from under my hand and smoothing her hairline. "You'll make a terrible governess if you can't set a good example for your charges. My governess never would have been caught wandering our estate barefoot. Where are your shoes?"

I don't bother reminding her that her governess was let go due to Lina's bad behavior, but I do address my missing shoes. Lifting my hand, I show off my leather slippers dangling from my fingertips.

"You're barbaric."

I give her a sideways grin. "I'd be a little nicer if I were you. Otherwise, I won't share my cake."

"You aren't supposed to know about the cake," she says in a furious whisper.

"It's my birthday. Of course there's cake. There's always cake."

Her jaw shifts side to side. Some of her sternness fades from her expression and her voice takes on a note of pleading. "You *are* going to let me have some of your cake, right? It...it might be my last one. I leave next week, and Spruce made the cake this time. You know hers are the best."

She's right. Sister Spruce's cakes may be the ugliest but she certainly knows not to skimp on the sugar like Marsh or combine too many odd flavors like Agatha.

I pretend to ponder her request as I toss my slippers on the ground and slide my grass-stained feet inside. "Hmm. I suppose I can. Just pretend you found me in the washroom and I'll let you have the largest piece."

A wide grin splits her face, but she quickly smothers it behind a more modest smile. "I suppose I can do that."

We walk along the path through the plots of Starcane, the towering golden stalks emitting fine golden specks that float upon the morning breeze—a sign that the stalks have soaked up maximum starlight and are ready for harvest. Lina soon releases her austere façade and chatters away about the ballgowns her mother has purchased in anticipation of her return home. A pinch of envy strikes my heart. I once dreamed I'd find myself in Lina's position. That my parents would send for me. Or that I'd at least find some clue as to who they were or why they left me. Whenever I asked Sisters Agatha, Spruce, and Marsh, I got only silence and pitying glances. Well, I received the pitying looks from Agatha and Spruce. From Marsh, I got only the pursing of her thin lips. I assume this means my parents are dead. Or that they abandoned me with no intent to return.

As jealous as I am of Lina, I can't begrudge her a privileged future. She's the daughter of a human aristocrat, which means she'll get to experience everything I've craved: society balls, evenings at the opera, dazzling suitors. Maybe she can live life to its fullest for both of us.

The Starcane fields give way to a manicured lawn and the convent behind it. Though the Celesta Convent is run by fae who dedicate their lives to worshiping starlight and growing Starcane, the building itself lacks the lavishness often associated with fae architecture. There are no glittering marble statues, no impossibly high turrets, no walls of crystal. Instead, it's a rectangular building comprised of modest gray stone, its only adornment the rooftop balcony surrounded by a large yet practical balustrade.

We slow our steps as we approach one of the back doors to the convent, glancing side to side to ensure no one is around. Thankfully, we manage to avoid being spotted, as most of the sisters are either inside or praying at the sugar mill on the other side of the property. Not that we would suffer much if we were caught outdoors without permission. The worst forms of punishment students receive are either extra prayer sessions or taste-testing new sugar batches. The latter may not sound like much of a punishment, but after several dozen teaspoons of Starcane sugar in one's belly, a daylong sugar rush is inevitable. It's great if you don't like sleep. Which I do. Very much so.

We enter a quiet hallway and make our way toward the kitchen. Aromas of caramelized sugar, porridge, and potato leek soup reach me long before I catch a glimpse of the kitchen door. Once I do, I spot a small fae girl with fluffy white hair, bunny ears, and wide blue eyes peeking out into the hallway. As her gaze locks on mine, she scuttles back inside. Audible whispers follow.

I exchange a knowing glance with Lina, who mutters, "Act surprised."

We pause outside the door to give everyone time to get in their places. Then we cross the threshold to two dozen shouts of "Happy Birthday!"

I pull up short and let my mouth fall open in feigned shock. The sight around me isn't at all unexpected, as I've seen it hundreds of times by now, both as a party recipient and participant. Paper decorations hang from the rafters along with the bundles of drying herbs left by the cook. Half-melted candles are propped on the rough-hewn kitchen table where we students take most of our informal meals. Spruce's famously ugly cake sits at the center of it all, three lopsided tiers dressed in blindingly bright blue frosting. And then, of course, there are the students. Since the convent is run by fae, most of my peers are fae as well, but there are some human girls like Lina too. The students range in ages from five to nineteen, with age five being the youngest a student can leave the nursery to join class, and eighteen the oldest before graduation. Those over eighteen take on a student teacher role, like I've held the last two years. Now I'm the oldest student in the room, and I'm suddenly struck by how small everyone looks. How final this party is.

I've had twenty birthday parties of my own and participated in countless more for all the other students. But this one will be the last that is exactly like this. With these students. Within these walls. With our crooked kitchen table and Sister Spruce's even more crooked cake.

My lower lip trembles, compromising my well-crafted expression. Tears prick my eyes. "Thank you, everyone," I manage to say over the lump in my throat. My sudden change of mood is reflected in the eyes around me, as we all realize the same thing. This isn't just another birthday party. This is goodbye.

"Miss Rose," says a wobbly, high-pitched voice. I turn to find an aquamarine pixie fluttering beside me. It's Sister Spruce. In a flash of blue, a humanoid female takes the winged creature's place.

Most fae have two physical manifestations—seelie form and unseelie form—and our three teachers are no exception. While they appear as dainty winged pixies in their unseelie form, they take on a more humanoid appearance in seelie form. Spruce's seelie form hosts a petite body with pale blue hair done up in a messy bun, enormous aqua eyes, and slender limbs made for giving surprisingly strong hugs. She uses the latter to her full advantage now, wrapping her arms around me so tight it's hard to breathe. With a sniffle, she strokes the back of my hair the way she's done since I was small.

Damn it all, she's done it now. A sob builds in my throat.

"I'll miss you dearly," Spruce whispers.

"I'll miss you too," I say, my words dissolving into tears.

Several arms join Spruce's, pressing in around me and

my teacher in a group hug. Even Lina joins in, her cheeks wet as she lays her head on my shoulder. "You're so annoying," comes her muffled voice. "I didn't plan on crying today."

A throat clears, cutting through the sobs and sentimental goodbyes. The girls pull away one by one to reveal an austere-looking fae with moss-green hair and emerald skin. It's Sister Marsh, standing by the table with her hands on her hips. Like Spruce, she's in her seelie form. The two are dressed in the same long-sleeved, high-necked gowns the older girls like me wear, but with gray wimples covering the backs of their heads—a sign that they've taken lifelong vows to serve the convent.

"The day isn't over yet," Marsh says, tone chastising. "Miss Rose will be here until morning. There's no use getting all worked up ahead of time."

"She's right," Spruce says, wiping her cheeks as she frees me from her crushing embrace. "Besides, if we get too sad, we'll lose our appetite for cake."

That has some of the students—especially the younger ones—shifting back into smiles. As we crowd around the kitchen table, I force my lips into a wide grin, but it does nothing to lift my heart. Despite almost two decades feeling trapped here, dreaming of the day I'd get to leave with my family, only now do I wish I could stay. Not by taking vows as a sister. Just...here. The closest thing to home I've ever known.

Marsh begins slicing the cake, which further helps lighten the mood.

With everyone distracted by the prospect of dessert for breakfast, I take a step away from the crowd. From there, I lift my hands and press my thumbs and forefingers together to create a frame. I center it around the group of students bouncing on the balls of their feet. The stern Marsh, barely able to hide her smile as she divvies up the cake for her eager recipients. Joyful Spruce, clapping her hands and singing to entertain the youngest while they wait their turn. The quaint kitchen illuminated by the morning sun, the rays of sunlight swirling with dust motes. It's mundane. Simple. Beautiful.

I blink.

And the moment is saved.

This may be my last day at the convent, but at least I can return whenever I want in my dreams.

3

Nothing soothes a somber heart quite like cake. I insist on waiting until all the other students receive their plates before I accept my share from Sister Marsh. Then we crowd around the kitchen table, and I take my first bite. The sugary sweetness of the frosting melts on my tongue while the lemon chiffon paired with blackberry curd has a grin tugging my lips. Spruce's cakes truly are the best.

You'd think twenty years at a convent dedicated to sugar would make me tired of sweet treats. Instead, I reckon it's spoiled me. For every scraped knee, every apology, every reward, I've been given something sweet, something made with love and the kind of reverence only religion can inspire. Will cake outside the convent ever taste this good?

"You like it?" Sister Spruce asks, tone wary. Despite being the best baker of our three teachers, she's also the least confident in her talents.

"It's wonderful," I say.

A satisfied smile warms her face. "I'm so glad. I know it isn't Blackwood Bakery—"

I nearly choke on my next bite at her mention of Blackwood Bakery. Why would she bring that up? She can't possibly know about my secret crush on Thorne Blackwood. I'd never admit it to anyone. How could I? The only version of him that I've interacted with is a figment of my imagination. Which means I don't truly have a crush on *him* but a man I've constructed from my own desires. I could never confess to something so humiliating.

I cough a few times, which means I only hear the last part of what Spruce says.

"—but who can compete with Blackwood? Blackwood Bakery is the most popular chain of bakeries on the isle. Though I suppose *compete* is the wrong word. It's not like *I* own a bakery. Perhaps if I weren't a sister of the convent, I would have—"

"It's perfect, Spruce," I rush to say. Now that I know she's simply going on one of her anxious, long-winded musings, I can stop choking on my cake. "I would choose one of your cakes...a thousand times over." I originally planned on saying I'd choose her cakes over Blackwood's, but the words were stuck in my throat. Being full fae means I'm unable to lie. An inconvenience at times for sure.

Spruce, it seems, doesn't notice my need to correct course and smiles brighter. "Oh, I certainly am going to miss you, you little sugar sprite." She squeezes a fleshy portion of my cheek like she's done since I was small and gives an affectionate tug.

And now my eyes are watering again. Damn her.

A tiny hand taps my forearm, giving me a much-needed distraction. Tilly, the little fae with bunny ears, stares up at me with her adorable blue eyes, whiskers twitching. Though all students maintain seelie form indoors and save shifting into their unseelie forms for recess, some—like

Tilly—maintain many similar features in both forms. While she appears like a regular white rabbit in unseelie form, her seelie body hosts the same long ears, whiskers, and pink nose. Even her hair is more like fur than regular tresses.

"I want to sit in your lap," Tilly says, her little voice slightly lisped behind her adorable buck teeth.

"Be my guest," I say and scoop her up. She's so small, even for a five-year-old, that she's practically weightless. With a pleased giggle, she snuggles against me and proceeds to take dainty bites of her cake. I nestle my face in her soft hair and plant a kiss on top of her head. I know I shouldn't play favorites with the students, but I do. Tilly is by far my favorite.

"I suppose you won't be the worst governess," Lina says, claiming an open seat beside me on the bench. As promised, I had Sister Marsh cut Lina the largest slice of cake, which she's almost finished with. She glances at Tilly in my lap, and her dour expression softens. "You do seem to like children, after all."

"I've tolerated you over the last year, haven't I?" I say, tone coy.

She scoffs. "Are you calling me a child? I'm a woman grown, Miss Rose. I'll have you know I have every intention of being married by the end of my first social season and making my parents proud."

"Oh, I bet you do." Only the slightest hint of wistfulness colors my words, just a fraction compared to the vast yearning in my heart. Not for a husband, of course, but a social season. The love and approval of my family. Everything Lina will soon have.

Another girl squeezes in on my other side and offers a kind grin. Dorothy is my opposite, timid, quiet, and honest to a fault. Her hair is raven-black while mine is honey-blonde. She's short and as thin as a rail while I'm tall and soft around the edges. Despite our differences, we do share one similarity: we're both full fae but look mostly human, aside from our pointed ears.

Neither of us have animal characteristics like Tilly, nor do we shift into another form. That may be because neither of us knows of our parentage. Without knowing what kind of fae we're descended from, it's hard to tap into the magic that allows us to shift. I thought my dream magic would offer some kind of clue, but when I brought up my budding abilities to my teachers last year—without giving them any details about my dreams of Thorne Blackwood, of course— they only reacted with gentle amusement. None had anything to say regarding what kind of fae I might be, or whether I have the potential to shift forms.

Perhaps I can't shift at all. Not all fae can. Shifting is strange in that way, an unpredictable and ever-evolving magic. Even its origins are odd. Long ago, the isle of Faer- wyvae was inhabited exclusively by the fae. Back then, my kind were animals, spirits, or other beasts. After humans discovered the isle and began sharing their food, clothing, and language, faekind began to change. The most signifi- cant change was the ability to shift into a form that better resembled their new bipedal friends. Unfortunately, the first humans didn't remain friends with the fae for long. Two wars swept across the isle. While the first war divided the two people, the most recent battle united us under fae rule while smoothing out human-fae relations.

Dorothy pins me with a hopeful look. "You're still set on being a governess?" Her voice is so soft I have to strain my ears to hear her over the chatter around us.

I release an easy chuckle. "I leave tomorrow, Dor. What other choice would I have?"

Her cheeks flush. "You could stay," she whispers.

My heart falls at that. We both know what it would mean for me to stay. Every child over the age of five who enters the convent school makes a binding bargain that they will remain only until their twentieth birthday unless they take vows as a sister. Sisters dedicate their lives to the convent, tending the Starcane fields, praying for meteor showers, charting the stars to predict the ideal planting and harvesting days, paying reverence to the All of All, and teaching at the school. With little Tilly in my lap and a room full of laughter, I can't help wondering...would it really be so bad to stay?

The answer comes easily. I may love to admire a starlit sky and enjoy the taste of Starcane sugar as much as anyone else, but I don't feel the reverence the sisters do. I haven't an ounce of religious fervor in my body. Not like Dorothy. She's always been set on taking vows. And while my heart aches at the prospect of leaving, I can't forget the itch that has been my constant companion. A need to see the world outside these walls. The awe I felt during my short stay in the city of Lumenas. My craving for ballrooms, theaters, and fine clothing. As a governess, I'll at least get to enjoy these things secondhand. I'll get to teach my charges to dance, maybe even attend the ballet with them as their chaperone. And I do love children. They clearly love me back, as noted by the little bunny fae in my lap. So long as my pupils aren't terrible little shits like Lina was to her governess, I'll be happy wherever I'm sent. That simple freedom will be enough.

Within these walls, I'm content.

But contentment isn't the same as freedom.

I shake the thoughts from my head and give Dorothy an apologetic look. "I can't stay."

"No, she can't," Lina says, bumping her shoulder into mine, "because when I'm married with children, I'll be hiring Briony as my household's governess."

I snort a laugh. "We'll see about that. Agatha already has my first job lined up for me. At least she's supposed to. She still hasn't told me where I'm..."

Frowning, I trail off. Only now do I note the weight of our third teacher's absence. Agatha is the fondest of parties and oversees the planning and execution of each one. So why isn't she here?

I scan the room until my eyes lock on Sister Marsh. I raise my voice over the chatter so she can hear me. "Where's Sister Agatha?"

Marsh thins her lips while Spruce cuts a wide-eyed glance at the other teacher. Neither answers my question.

Dread fills my chest. They're hiding something, but I can't fathom what or why. I drop my fork to my plate. "Sister Marsh...is something wrong?"

Spruce shifts into her pixie form and flutters over to Marsh. Though she keeps her voice low, I manage to hear her frantic whisper. "Can't we tell her?"

Marsh shakes her head. "You know we're bound by our bargain. Try to speak the words; they won't come. We've done what we could. She's out of our hands as of tomorrow."

"But they might still...they were due to arrive last week."

"If they come for her, we'll tell them where to find her. That's all we can do."

My dread grows deeper, though winding through it is a thread of hope. One I haven't felt in years. They...they can't be talking about what I think they are, can they? With trembling limbs, I gently slide Tilly off my lap and rise from the bench. "What's going on?"

By now, the other students have noticed the sudden tension in the room. Silence falls, leaving only the occasional scraping of a fork on a plate and the buzz of Spruce's wings.

I'm about to repeat my question when the sound of a second pair of wings reaches my ears. A tiny pink figure zips around my head before the pixie shifts into seelie form. In a flash, the winged creature is replaced with a short, rotund female with pink candy-floss hair. It's Sister Agatha. She's dressed in the same gray gown as my other two teachers, but her wimple is so crooked it nearly hangs off her head. Her wide cheeks grow rounder with her growing smile. She gathers my hands in hers and gives them a squeeze. "He's here, Miss Rose," she says, somewhat out of breath. Or maybe it's excitement that strains her voice. "You aren't going to be a governess. You're going home."

"Home," I echo, the word ringing strangely against my racing heart.

Gasps and excited whispers spring up around me while Marsh releases a long, weighted sigh. "I suppose we can talk about it after all," she says.

Spruce lets out a tiny whoop before shifting back into her seelie form and racing to my side. "Oh, thank the All of All. I didn't think I could let you go without telling you the truth."

I blink a few times. This isn't a dream, is it? "What truth? I...I still don't understand."

"Your parents have sent for you at last," Agatha says. "They've been looking for you for years."

A wave of dizziness washes over me. After waiting to hear those words for almost two decades, I gave up on them. I came to terms with being an orphan. With being abandoned. With letting go of my dreams, no matter how badly it hurt.

Could this be real? After all this time?

My heart hammers so hard it sends ripples through my chest and down my arms. Logic. I need logic. I need to stay sensible or I'll lose my damn mind. "You said *he's* here," I manage to get out. "Who? My father?"

Agatha's expression turns apologetic. "No, dearest, your parents couldn't come. They sent someone else in their stead to take you to them."

"Who?"

Before she can answer, my gaze falls on the figure I hadn't noticed until now. He's no more than a shadow darkening the doorway until he takes a hesitant step across the threshold. My heart leaps into my throat as my eyes lock on Thorne Blackwood's.

4

Before I can think better of it, his name tumbles off my lips. "Thorne—" I realize my mistake at once, and it sends heat blazing in my cheeks. I can't call him *Thorne*. I shouldn't even be on a first-name basis with the version of him that lives in my dreams. And I'm not. I never use his name, and he doesn't even know mine. But in my head, I confess, I may have crossed a line. For there he exists as *Thorne*.

Whispers break out amongst the students, and I feel Sister Agatha's surprised stare burning into the side of my face. Even more heated might be the scathing look Lina gives me. I can't bear to meet her eyes. I'm sure she'd shoot daggers from her irises in a silent scolding for my slip in social decorum.

With a feigned calm that I'm sure doesn't hide my humiliation, I correct my mistake. "Mr. Blackwood."

"Miss Rose, I presume," he says, tipping his chin. His *I presume* embarrasses me further, proving that even greeting him with the confidence of his identity was too familiar.

He looks the same as he did when I first laid eyes on him

two years ago, with silver-framed spectacles perched on his strong nose, dark hair swept back from his forehead to reveal his widow's peak and the sharp planes of his face. Though, unlike the first time when I caught sight of his bare forearms, he wears a navy suit jacket over his fully buttoned waistcoat, and his cravat is neatly tied at his throat. Morning light catches on his lenses, obscuring his dark irises for a moment. When his eyes become clear once more, I note a hint of trepidation in them. A wariness. Or an unspoken question.

Something stirs in the back of my mind, and for a moment I picture him with wings and horns—

Wait...why would I think of that? Why would I picture a human man like Thorne Blackwood with wings and horns?

I blink, and the image flees my mind like it was never there to begin.

"Agatha!" Marsh's voice shatters the air with a frantic note. "What were you thinking letting a *man* this far into the convent? He shouldn't be beyond the parlor."

Spruce shoots Marsh a weighted look, as does Agatha.

When Marsh proves oblivious to both, Spruce steps in front of her with an exaggerated smile. "That's not just any man," she says, speaking slowly, pointedly. "That is Thorne Blackwood from Blackwood Bakery. Our most loyal patron."

"Oh!" Marsh's emerald cheeks deepen to forest green. Rarely ever does the rigid Marsh appear flustered. If this situation weren't so odd, I'd be amused right now. But I'm not amused, I'm...confused.

What in the name of the stars is Mr. Blackwood doing here? Better yet, what does he have to do with—

Stars above.

In my surprise at seeing the man from my dreams, I almost forgot the source of my previous shock.

My parents.

They've sent for me.

Before Thorne made his startling arrival, Agatha said my parents sent someone to fetch me. And that someone is... Mr. Blackwood?

"My apologies, Mr. Blackwood," Sister Marsh says, in an uncharacteristically sweet tone. "Forgive me for my rudeness."

"No, forgive me," he says, deep voice almost without inflection. "I should have known better than to enter this far into your sacred space."

A couple of the older students giggle, likely charmed by his baritone. Not to mention his looks. And his reputation. Blackwood Bakery's success has made him a household name, one I learned even before I first caught sight of him in the field two years ago. I'm not the only student with a crush on him, for he's considered one of the most prominent human bachelors on the isle. In a land ruled by fae where most young ladies dream of marrying fae princes rather than humans, Mr. Blackwood's popularity is impressive. Honestly, I'm surprised the room hasn't dissolved into fits and swooning. It isn't every day a gorgeous man strolls straight into the kitchen of the Celesta Convent School for Girls, much less one with wealth, fame, and status.

"If anyone is to blame, it's me," Agatha says, smoothing things over in her bright and bubbly way. "I was simply so excited to tell Miss Rose the news that I forgot to set him up in the parlor first. He must have thought I meant for him to follow."

"Well, we will remedy that now," Marsh says, gesturing toward the kitchen door. "Let us speak in the parlor."

Marsh shuffles into the hallway while Agatha, Spruce, and Mr. Blackwood follow. I try to do so as well, but my feet won't move. I'm still too overcome. Still half in doubt that I'm not dreaming.

"Go on, you dolt," Lina whispers, giving me a not-so-gentle shove. It's enough to shake me out of my stupefaction.

With a fortifying breath, I force my feet to move over the flagstones and follow my teachers into the hall. As soon as I cross the threshold, the kitchen erupts with a frenzy of giddy gossip.

THE ONLY THING LOUDER THAN MY TEACUP RATTLING IN ITS saucer is the thud of my heart. My teachers, our guest, and I sit in the parlor, a bleak room in varying shades of beige from the walls to the furniture. Even the landscape paintings of Starcane fields host this same bland color scheme. The brightest colors in the room belong to my three teachers, their pink, blue, and green features stark against their gray gowns and wimples. I can't even bring myself to look at Mr. Blackwood. His presence is as sharp as his namesake, constantly tugging at my awareness from the corner of my eye. There's something smug about his composure, some self-assurance that grates on my nerves. He sits at the far end of the room in a wingback chair near the hearth, leisurely sipping his tea as if he hasn't just upended a woman's life. The few glances we've exchanged have shown me nothing but his expressionless—albeit handsome—visage, but whenever I look away, I get the feeling he's smirking at me. But why? And why is he even here?

I'm about to look his way again but stop myself.

Thorne Blackwood isn't my primary concern. He's second to the reason we're gathered in this parlor.

My parents.

Their identity.

The impossible words Agatha spoke when she entered the kitchen.

You're going home.

Sister Nessie, a stout dryad with barklike skin and leafy hair escaping from beneath her wimple, finishes pouring tea into Sister Marsh's cup. Now that she's served tea to everyone, she makes her way to the door, her pace agonizingly slow. Though many fae appear ageless no matter how old they get, some fae seem elderly beyond their years. Nessie is like that. I know her to be a couple of hundred years old—young for a fae born before the isle was unified, whereafter fae began to reach maturity much faster—but she walks like she's on death's door. Every shuffling step might as well take an hour for how quickly my anxiety climbs.

My teacup rattles harder in its saucer, and I give up holding it altogether. I set it on the tea table beside my chair and face my three teachers, all of whom sit side by side on the faded beige-gold couch.

With a forced smile upon my lips, I say, "If someone doesn't start talking, there's a chance I'll lose my mind." Though my words are a clear exaggeration, using the phrase *there's a chance* circumvents my inability to lie. There's always a chance for just about anything to happen.

Sister Agatha's eyes dart toward the door where Nessie finally makes her exit. Once the door is firmly sealed behind her, Agatha releases a sigh. "Forgive us, Miss Rose. Your situation has always required great secrecy, due to your identity and the bargain we swore to."

I didn't think my heart could race any faster, but it does. "And...who am I?"

Marsh clears her throat and sets her tea on the table. "Your name is Rosaline Briar, and you were brought to us when you were a baby. We took a binding vow to keep your true identity—and that of your parents—a secret."

I swallow the sudden dryness in my throat. My next question is one I've yearned for an answer to all my life. "Who are my parents?"

Sister Spruce dons a placating grin, one I recognize from years of her soothing care. It does nothing to calm my nerves, for I know that smile means her next words will cause me distress. "Your parents are Horus and Divina Briar. Your father is the Seelie King of Lunar, and your mother is the queen."

I sit forward in my chair. "The seelie fucking—" I swallow my words at the horrified expressions on my teacher's faces. Under my breath, I try again. "The Seelie King and Queen of Lunar. You've got to be kidding me."

"I know this is shocking, dearest," Agatha says. Her eyes dip toward my hands, which are clenched so tightly around the armrests of my chair that my knuckles have turned white.

I loosen my grip and place my hands palm-down on my lap instead. "Does that mean...am I..." I can't even utter it out loud. It's ridiculous.

"A princess, yes," Marsh says, in her straightforward way.

I try to bark a laugh but all I manage is a strangled sound.

For the love of the stars, I'm...a princess.

An honest-to-stars princess with royal fucking parents.

I bite the inside of my cheek to keep my inner commentary from leaping off my tongue and appalling my poor teachers again. I'm almost of a mind to ask Marsh to repeat herself, just to be certain she was telling the truth, but of course she is. Pureblood fae can't lie.

And yet...how is this possible? Every young girl who enters the convent, particularly those who believe themselves orphaned or abandoned, dreams of being claimed by royal parents, discovering they're a lost princess, or being rescued by a dashing prince. I was no exception. I can't count the number of daydreams I've constructed to play out every one of those scenarios. But I gave up on them years ago, after reality became too solid to ignore. For if I had royal parents, then why...

With a deep breath, I finish my thought out loud. "Why did my parents wait so long to claim me?"

Spruce dons one of her placating grins again. "The king and queen arranged things so not even they knew where you were hidden. They did this to keep your location safe should someone try to force the information from them. To find you again, they had to go through layers and layers of protocol that they'd set in place, working through the agents they'd established between us."

A tangle of emotions writhe within me, bright hope mixed with cloudy shock, both smothered beneath a rising tide of something unexpected: anger. I narrow my eyes at my teachers. "You let me believe I was orphaned."

Marsh purses her lips, but when neither Spruce nor Agatha reply, she says, "We agreed to many things in the bargain we made when we took you in, all to ensure your safety. One of the terms we had to uphold was keeping the truth from you. We could only speak on the matter after confirming, over several weeks of authentication protocol, that your parents had sent for you and deemed our bargain fulfilled. Which is why we are talking about this now."

"But you...you let me participate in the bridal competition in Lumenas last year. If I'd won, I'd be married to Brother Dorian. How does that fit into the bargain you made?"

This time, Agatha answers. "We knew there was a chance that your parents wouldn't send for you before you were out of our hands, for we were told they would only do so *if* they found it safe for you to return. According to our bargain, we were to allow you to live as you chose, so long as during your time in our care, we protected you. If you'd married Brother Dorian, you'd have remained safe, protected by the Church of Saint Lazaro. Setting you up as a governess also would have fit the terms of our bargain."

"And if I'd taken vows as a sister?" I ask, my tone adopting a bitter edge. "I'd be stuck here. I wouldn't have been able to go home if they'd sent for me a day too late."

A look of hurt crosses my teachers' faces, which in turn cools my ire. I don't mean to take my frustrations out on them, but I'm still so confused. Hurt, even. All my dreams of being claimed by my parents were accompanied by joy and laughter. Not secrets, bargains, and dangers I don't understand.

"We never encouraged you to take vows, dearest," Agatha says. "We know you want more than what the convent can offer long-term."

I release a slow sigh. She's right. None of my teachers have ever prodded me onto the path of a sister.

"I do apologize for how last-minute this seems," Marsh says in her formal tone. "We've been in communication with your parents for weeks, and it's been difficult making anything official. Our bargain, as well as the safeguards your parents set up to protect both themselves and you, have made this a slow process."

I frown. "Why was such secrecy necessary? What danger was I in?"

My teachers exchange a glance. Spruce dons yet another conciliatory smile. "We must leave that for your parents to explain."

The way she says *must* suggests their silence is likely tied to their bargain. Perhaps not all terms have been fulfilled.

The sound of silver clanking against porcelain draws my gaze to Mr. Blackwood. He finishes stirring his tea, takes a sip, then adds two sugar cubes and stirs again. His presence almost fled my mind during my teachers' explanations.

"Pardon my rudeness, Mr. Blackwood," I say, trying to ignore the way my cheeks grow warm as I address him, "but why exactly are you here?"

He takes a long sip of tea before setting the cup on its saucer. The light from the fire catches on his spectacles as he faces me, his countenance as unflustered as ever. "I am here on behalf of your fiancé."

I inhale so sharply that I nearly choke on my own breath. "My...fiancé?"

"Yes."

"I'm engaged."

"Yes."

"To whom?"

"Monty Phillips, son of the Human Representative of the Earthen Court."

I stare blankly at him, for the name means nothing to me. The convent has very little to do with Star Court politics, even less so with those of other courts. The Human Representative of the Earthen Court and his son may as well be the shadowed figures of my daydreams for all I know of them. I suppose the same goes for my parents. While I'm well-versed in the history of Faerwyvae and know the names of every current and past monarch, I know nothing outside of what's stated in our textbooks.

Yet here I am, daughter of the Seelie King of Lunar.

This morning I thought I was a governess. Now I'm not only a princess but...engaged. To a stranger.

Another flash of irritation sparks inside me. How the glittering hell can I be *engaged*?

I turn my ire on Thorne, punctuating each word with venom. "What are you saying, Mr. Blackwood? You're here to fetch me for my new husband? To deliver me into a stranger's arms with no say in the matter? Am I to meet my estranged family at all?"

"Yes, yes, and yes," he says without giving any consideration to my obvious anger. "Due to your family's need for secrecy and my friend's...wariness of the situation, I've taken on the burden of acting as the go-between. I am to bring you to Mr. Phillips, as you've said, but I will take you to meet your parents first."

"Isn't that splendid," I say, not bothering to hide my sarcasm. "I get to meet the people who abandoned me for twenty years before they sell my hand to a man I've never met."

His lips quirk at one corner, like the ghost of a grin. The reflection of the hearth fire no longer masks his lenses, giving me a clear view of his keen eyes. Once again, I get the feeling that beneath his calm composure, there's a smug confidence, a bearing that doesn't quite fit this situation. Shaking his head as if to rouse himself, he averts his gaze and reaches inside his suit jacket. He extracts a letter but my eyes fall on the black leather gloves he wears. They tease at some lost memory. Or a dream? I can almost imagine him tugging the fingertips of those very gloves, baring his hands, and—

"Your mother wrote a letter that I think will explain things far better." His words have me meeting his eyes once more. He rises from his chair and passes a sealed envelope to me.

I study it, taking in the midnight-blue wax seal stamped with a crescent moon. Then, turning it over, I find an elegant script forming the word *Rosaline*.

My breath catches in my throat.

Rosaline.

Rosaline Briar.

That's my name. My *real* name.

I stare at each looping letter, which I can only assume was penned by my mother's own hand, trying to feel *something*. Some pride. Some sense of ownership in the name. Some giddy warmth at being closer to my mother than I ever have.

But I don't. I feel...nothing.

No, that's not true. I do feel something, but none of the feelings are pleasant. There's too much frustration, confusion, and anger clouding my heart to pay much heed to what might be buried beneath. But just because I don't feel any warmth doesn't mean it isn't there. Hope is something I've learned to smother, to shove aside in favor of sensibility when I'm really made for dreaming. Do I dare embrace that hope once more, after twenty years of disappointment? After I was certain I'd already given up?

The letter suddenly feels heavier in my hands, as if it contains the answer. Perhaps my mother's explanation will ease my anxiety, smooth my frustration.

There's only one way to find out.

I lift my eyes from the envelope and address my teachers. "May I have a moment alone?"

"Yes," Agatha says at once, "we can leave—"

"No, I'll go. I just…"

Spruce gives me a sympathetic nod that tells me there's no need to explain. She knows exactly what I require to process my feelings.

I nod back, clutch the letter to my chest, and flee the parlor.

5

Cake may be the best balm for a heavy heart, but there's something else I can trust to smooth my frazzled nerves. Music. But not just any kind of music. One song from one particular event in my life has become as precious as my glade. There's only one way to find such music in the convent, and I just so happen to be in possession of it.

I reach the door to the room I share with Dorothy. As the two oldest student teachers in the convent, we've been rooming together since the former eldest departed our company six months ago. I'm relieved to find the space empty. The others are likely still enjoying their cake in the kitchen. Perhaps more so now that the watchful Marsh isn't there to forbid any of the students from taking second helpings. I close my bedroom door behind me and lean against it, the letter still clutched to my chest. My heart thuds against the envelope, a frantic melody I know I must calm before I can read the note.

My *mother's* note.

Steeling my resolve, I push off the door and march over

to my bed. It's a narrow cot dressed in flannel sheets and a wool blanket. Dorothy's bed is barely more than an arm's span away in the cramped room—yet another *gray* room, I might add. The convent is almost entirely gray, from our clothes to our bedding to the simple stone floors. And when it isn't gray it's beige, like the parlor. The sisters insist on seeking the brightness of the stars and never outshining them ourselves.

From under my bed, I withdraw a small oak chest. Sitting cross-legged before it, I place the letter in my lap and remove the lid of the chest. Beneath it lies my most prized possession: a phonograph. The device is one of Faerwyvae's latest technological advancements, thanks to Star Court's cutting-edge innovation harnessing starlight. The phonograph utilizes crystal cylinders carved in minuscule patterns that manage to replicate sound when traced by a needle and amplified through a brass horn. It's a rare item, one I wouldn't have if a former student hadn't left it behind when she returned to her family. For a year, it remained untouched under my bed, for its previous owner hadn't left any musical cylinders to go with it. It wasn't until we took our trip to Lumenas that I was able to purchase a recording of the ballet we attended. It's still the only recording I own.

I pray to the All of All that my cylinder contains enough charge. The cylinders are fueled by starlight and only last about a dozen plays before requiring rest under the night sky for a handful of hours. In my current flustered state, I can't recall the last time I left it on the windowsill overnight. With bated breath, I lift the needle's arm and gently place it against the crystal cylinder. To my relief, the crystal tube begins to rotate, emitting a soft golden glow where the needle touches. Then comes the first strain of familiar music. Cherished music. A song from the first ballet I ever saw. Even though I managed to sneak from my lodgings and catch a few other shows during my visit to the city, the first performance holds a special place in my heart.

Because of that, I can always count on this song to set me at ease.

Once my nerves begin to calm, I rise from the floor with my envelope in hand and plop down upon my bed. My heart hitches as I scan the name scrawled over the front once more. Then, with a deep breath, I turn the envelope over, flick open the dark blue seal, and extract the letter within.

My dearest Rosaline,

First, please know I understand how shocking this must be for you and how sorry I am if any of this causes you pain. It must have been dreadful not knowing where you came from or if you were loved by those who left you where you've resided all these years. I promise you, Rosaline, you have been loved. For every minute of every day since your birth, your father and I have loved you. There was nothing I wanted more than you, long before your conception, and your birth was the brightest joy in my life. I never wanted that to end. Never. As you might have gleaned, though, your life was in grave danger. We thought we could protect you here, but we quickly learned our confidence was folly. Our only hope of keeping you safe was to spirit you away while we dealt with the threat. It pains me to say that the threat hasn't been fully eliminated, but I could not wait a moment longer before bringing you home. We have spent years trying to find you, my dearest Rosaline. Years. And I am so relieved that we have located you at last.

Now, let me write of happier things. You're coming home! Home, my love. I know I am but a stranger to you now, but my love for you has never grown cold. I cannot wait to be a true mother to you, if you will allow it. Though I suppose I must address something else you might have been told by now—your engagement to Monty Phillips. Darling, I do hope you can forgive me for springing such a surprise on you. The truth is, your engagement has been in the works for quite some time, as is customary for royals—you're a princess, Rosaline! Have your caretakers told you this? Anyhow, to put things bluntly, your marriage to Mr. Phillips will save our family. I know that sounds a bit ominous, and I will explain more once Mr. Blackwood escorts you home. Just know that you truly are my every hope in every way. You're the Briar family hero. Your father is reading over my shoulder and says I've just heaped an awful lot of pressure upon you. I hope you don't feel that way! You're already perfect as you are.

Oh, darling, I'm rambling now and I forget that you don't feel as close to me as I feel to you, considering you only just heard about me. So I will end my letter before you deem me annoying. Your father says I'm a little "too much" at times, but he does not truly mean it. He has me to thank for his throne, after all.

And I'm rambling again. I cannot wait to see you and hold you in my arms. Yes, I understand you're a woman grown, and not the baby you'd still be if fae children aged like they did long ago, but I do hope you will allow me to embrace you as I've dreamed of doing for so long.

My hope, my hero, my darling child. I love you. Eagerly awaiting your return home, Mother

P.S. If you don't want to call me Mother, that is fine. My name is Divina Briar. Did your caretakers tell you? Oh, this is rather strange that you don't know me, but we have time to remedy that! Even after you depart to meet your fiancé, I plan on taking a trip to the

Earthen Court to spend— All right, your father says I'm rambling again and is threatening to take away my pen

The letter ends with a slash of ink, which tells me my father truly did wrestle the pen from her. I find myself laughing even as tears stream down my cheeks. My anger melts away. Not entirely, of course, but enough to feel a flicker of my abandoned hope. I sink into that warmth, a feeling both sweet and terrifying at once. The tiny ember grows inch by inch until it shifts into a blazing fire in my chest. Fear accompanies it too, as does my rage over my shocking engagement. But those feelings are companions to my hope. To my joy. To my amusement over my mother's ever-rambling letter.

She was wrong about one thing: I do feel like I know her already, at least a little. Her effusive joy practically leaped off the page. Whether it's my imagination or some fae magic, I truly felt like I could hear her voice, a sound as comforting as the orchestral number that continues to stream from the phonograph.

I cannot wait to see you and hold you in my arms.

I've yearned for those words all my life. To feel like I belong. To know I'm wanted, needed, and worthy of the family who left me here. To finally have an answer to why I was left in the first place and the reason behind my prolonged stay. For so long I feared I simply didn't measure up to my mysterious parents' expectations, that their reasons for abandoning me were like Lina's parents'. Early on, I strove for excellence in my studies, tried to be obedient, but boredom made me weary. Jaded. Disenchanted.

I often wondered if I failed myself. If my parents would

have returned for me long ago if only I'd tried harder. Cared more. Forced myself to be sweet like Dorothy. Feigned obedience like Lina.

Now I know that isn't true.

You're already perfect as you are.

I may not know the details behind the danger that prompted my parents into hiding me, but at least I know I was wanted. That they've been seeking me out for years. I've been worthy of them all this time! Stars, what a relief it is to know that. I feel as if I've been missing a piece of my soul, my identity, my truth, and now it slides into place.

You're the Briar family hero.

I haven't a clue how my arranged marriage is meant to save my family, and I'm not willing to banish my fury over it. But if my parents love me as much as my mother claims, maybe I can convince them to postpone my engagement. At the very least, I should be allowed to meet the asshole before I decide if I'm willing to enter a betrothal with him. Perhaps my parents have a convincing reason as to why I must make a marital sacrifice to save them. At the very least, I can give them the benefit of the doubt. I can set aside my anger and let it hold hands with my hope.

Because I have a family.

The one thing I've wanted more than anything else.

And they're waiting for me to meet them.

With tender care, I refold the letter and return it to its envelope. I hug it to my chest again, and this time my heart beats not with anxiety but excitement. When the song streaming from the phonograph comes to its natural end, I leave my room and return to the parlor.

The room is exactly as I left it, with my three teachers quietly sipping tea on the couch while Mr. Blackwood does the same from his chair. The only difference being the broadsheets he's now reading.

I clear my throat and my three teachers leap to their feet. Marsh thins her lips while Spruce and Agatha wear tenuous grins. Turning to Thorne Blackwood, I say, "I'm ready to meet my parents. When do we leave?"

6

I've said many goodbyes during my time at the convent, some joyful, some bittersweet. All tinged with the congratulatory essence that comes with sending off a friend to a better life. I've sometimes wished to skip the farewells, the constant tug on my heartstrings, and often wondered if it wouldn't be easier to simply forgo the pomp and ceremony. Skip the cake, the hugs, the tears, and simply...leave. Perhaps that was just a theory I dreamed up to help me rationalize why my parents might have left me without so much as a note.

Now I know that goodbyes hurt whether they're given or not, and the one that cuts the deepest in this moment is the farewell I didn't get to say.

The coach rumbles with constant, steady motion, its interior dim, lit only by the sparse light coming in from behind the closed curtains. I cast a condemning glance at my fellow passenger, but Thorne Blackwood pays me no heed. It's his fault I had to leave the convent in such haste and secrecy, insisting I tell none of the other students what I learned today or even that I'm leaving. My peers have certainly gleaned by now that I was claimed by my parents and will no longer be taking the governess job Agatha had lined up for me, but they haven't a clue about my true identity or where I'm going.

I deepen my glare at the man, but it's no use. He's hidden his face behind the wide spread of his broadsheets, the third set of papers I've seen him peruse. Besides, I know my anger is once again misplaced. It isn't entirely his fault I had to forgo saying goodbye to my friends. According to him, he had to agree to a complex bargain before my parents allowed him to serve as my escort. It seems being a renowned public figure wasn't enough to earn the full breadth of my parents' trust. One of the terms he agreed to was keeping my identity and travel itinerary a secret from all outside sources until a predetermined time. He left that last part vague, but considering he's been tasked with taking me first to my parents, then to my fiancé, I can only assume his terms remain until I'm safely in Monty Phillips' care.

I suppress a shudder as I'm reminded that I've been promised to a stranger. The only thing that keeps a fresh wave of fury at bay is recalling my mother's letter, now stuffed in my skirt pocket.

You're the Briar family hero.

For whatever reason, my marriage to Monty Phillips is needed. I'm determined to figure out why and—hopefully— talk my parents out of it, but in the meantime, I remain fixedly not pleased.

I glance at Mr. Blackwood again but can only see the top of his head over his broadsheets. We sit across from one another on opposite sides of the coach, his papers acting as the only barrier between us. I know I should be nervous to be alone with him, but I'm more annoyed by his silence than anything. He hasn't said a word to me this entire time. I'm sure he's simply trying to be respectful, for our situation is hardly regular. In society, unmarried women do not travel alone with unmarried men. It's a known fact. My teachers nearly fainted when he showed them the letter from my parents that explained we'd be doing exactly that.

"I'm bound by a bargain neither to harm her nor touch her more than propriety allows during our travels," he explained, which only made Sister Marsh blanch to an unsettling sage-gray hue. "The trip from here to Nocturnus Palace is only a seven-hour coach ride. If we leave by early afternoon, we'll arrive just after nightfall."

They couldn't argue, for their own bargains kept them bound to my parents' wishes. Furthermore, none could confirm if he was telling the truth regarding any of this, for humans can lie. All my teachers had to rely on was the correspondence they received from my parents. Which did, thankfully, align with what Thorne conveyed. Still, if he wasn't such a well-known figure in society, I'm almost willing to bet my teachers would have refused to go along with such a preposterous plan, bargain or no.

Turns out, they had nothing to worry about, for Thorne might as well be a statue for all the companionship he's provided. While I appreciate him keeping his distance in such close quarters, he can't possibly intend to remain silent behind his papers for the entire trip, can he?

I angle my body toward him and sit slightly forward. "Mr. Blackwood."

He grunts his response from behind his broadsheets.

"What do you know about my fiancé?"

"He's a friend."

"Yes, you've said that, but it doesn't quite answer my question, does it?"

He says nothing.

I narrow my eyes at the wall of paper between us. The real Mr. Blackwood is so different from the man of my dreams. While dream-Thorne is a man of few words, he's normally at least quietly curious about my dreamscapes, amused by our dances, and amenable to light conversation. At least he was after we both adapted to his surprising appearances in my dreams. Dream-him grew so comfortable with our strange interactions that he was even a willing participant in...*that one dream*. That's how I refer to one particular dream when I had very little control over who was there or what was happening—but that's better left forgotten in the presence of Mr. Blackwood. Stars, if only he knew I've dreamed of him nude. My gaze dips below his broadsheets. I can't help wondering if he looks the same as he did in that dream. I recall black ink trailing over his skin in a pattern like scales. That and his massive—

I shake depraved memories from my mind and remind myself dream-Thorne and real-Thorne are two different people. Adopting as cordial a tone as I can, I say, "We can talk, you know. I doubt that conflicts with the terms of your bargain."

"Conversation is unnecessary."

I clench my jaw. Dream-Thorne is preferable indeed. Well, if he wants to be difficult, I can too.

"What if your silence hurts me?" I ask.

He turns down a corner of his papers to meet my eyes.

I give him a look of pure innocence. "You did promise not to hurt me on our travels, did you not? It would be a shame if you unintentionally broke your bargain."

Slowly, he folds his broadsheets and sets them on the bench beside him, holding my gaze the entire time. We both know what it means to break a fae bargain. Whether human or fae, anyone who breaks such a magically binding promise is subject to repercussions. Temporary breaches cause extreme pain. Permanent ones cause death.

His expression shifts, eyes narrowing, a corner of his lips quirking the slightest bit. Perhaps it's only my imagination, but I sense something akin to respect in him now. He removes his spectacles and a silk kerchief from his jacket pocket. Still keeping his eyes on mine, he wipes his lenses. "Were you born so wicked, or is this something you learned at the convent?"

I'm taken aback by the change in his tone. His voice is less cold and abrupt and more...soft, almost seductive despite his cutting words. The space between us no longer feels cold and vast but warm. And quite narrow indeed.

I lift my chin and try not to reveal how flustered I've become. "I don't do well with boredom, Mr. Blackwood. *That* is what I learned at the convent."

"Very well, Miss Briar."

"My name—" I'm about to address his butchering of my name when I realize he wasn't mistaken at all. I'm not Briony Rose but Rosaline Briar. Still, the moniker feels all wrong. "You can call me Briony."

He replaces his spectacles. "We aren't acquainted enough to be on a first-name basis. Besides, is your name not Rosaline?" Just like that, he's back to that cold, formal tone. I'm almost disappointed.

"I don't feel like a *Rosaline Briar* just yet. I've been Briony Rose my entire life."

"Then I'll call you Miss Rose. That is, unless my refusal to address you by first name causes you some...*pain*." His emphasis on the last word is barbed.

I pretend not to notice and bat my lashes instead. "It doesn't, but what does distress me is that I know nothing of my future husband. Distress is very much like pain, wouldn't you say?"

He releases an aggrieved sigh. "What would you like to know?"

"What is he like?"

"A wealthy, handsome human."

I scoff. Does he really think that's the kind of answer I'm looking for? He might as well be talking about himself. And a thousand other men on the isle. I suppose I'll ask more specific questions. "I recall you saying something about Mr. Phillips being wary of our situation, which is why you are acting as the intermediary between him and my parents. What exactly is the reason for his wariness? Why didn't he come for me himself?"

"I daresay he's about as keen on an arranged marriage as you are."

"Then why did he agree to it?"

"His father and your parents arranged it, as the match suits both parties. He had very little say in the matter."

An unexpected pang of indignation strikes my chest. Even though I'm annoyed at having been engaged without my consent, the thought that I'm unwanted by my future husband only increases my anger over the arrangement.

Thorne's jaw shifts side to side. "I do think he'd like you if he met you. You have...nothing to worry about." His tone is both conciliatory and begrudging. He could be lying, but I appreciate his effort.

"Do you have any idea how my marriage to Mr. Phillips might save my family?"

"I have some idea."

I arch my brow, waiting for him to elucidate.

He leans back in his seat, taking on a more casual posture. With one arm resting on the back of the bench, he props an ankle over the opposite knee. "Your family's reputation has been...declining."

"Why is that?"

He cocks his head slightly to the side. "Do you know anything about your parents' history? Not as your parents, of course, but as Lunar's seelie monarchs."

"I recognize their names from my studies. I know the year Horus Briar gained the seelie throne of Lunar." It was two years after the isle's unification. Before Faerwyvae was unified under fae rule, it was divided in half with fae living in the north and humans living in the south. After the war, the fae claimed rule over the entire isle and new territorial lines were drawn for the eleven fae courts—Spring, Summer, Autumn, Winter, Wind, Sea, Earthen, Fire, Solar, Lunar, and Star. To ensure both seelie and unseelie fae were given equal opportunity to live as they pleased, as well as care for the humans, two sovereigns were established in each court: seelie and unseelie. The unseelie monarch would oversee the wild fae and advocate for their continued way of life according to the Old Ways, while the seelie monarch would rule over everyday matters of life and finance, their subjects being the humans and the seelie fae who chose to live in modern society.

My history lessons never meant much to me, aside from a means to earn high marks in school, but now...I'm a part of that history. If my parents claimed rule two years after unification, then that was one year before I was born.

"Other than that?" Mr. Blackwood prompts.

I shake my head. "If you mean their personal lives, I've

heard very little royal gossip. I'm hardly aware of what happens in the Star Court, much less Lunar or elsewhere."

"So you don't know how Horus Briar claimed the throne? Or how he keeps it?"

A line from my mother's letter springs to mind: *He has me to thank for his throne.*

"I don't."

"Do you at least know what kind of fae your parents are?" His eyes sweep over me. "What kind of fae *you* are?"

My pulse races. Stars, I've yearned for that answer for so long. "I don't. Will you tell me?"

He studies me for a few silent moments, his gaze so piercing I find myself shifting in my seat. Finally, he speaks. "They're mahrts—dream fae."

"Mahrts," I echo, surprise mingling with a deep sense of belonging. My dream magic...there's a reason for it after all! I want to ask if he knows more about *my* specific type of magic, but I don't dare interrupt, not when I'm finally getting answers.

"Your father is an alp, a type of mahrt that feeds off the energy of dreams, but your mother is a particularly powerful dream fae. She's a succubus, capable of entering others' dreams or pulling them into hers. While her magic is at work, her victims are powerless, paralyzed until she releases them."

I bristle at the word *victim*. It's too dark a term for the sweet and flighty persona I met in my mother's letter. Though, if I'm being honest, I've only ever heard negative things about succubi. How they tempt men from their wives by forcing erotic dreams upon them, how they feed off arousal and abandon their targets once they've taken their fill. These may simply be rumors, of course. How could students at an isolated convent in the Star Court know the truth about a type of fae that never leaves the Lunar Court? At least I can take comfort in knowing I'm not *that* kind of fae. I only create dreamscapes and memories to interact with later. I don't have...victims.

Mr. Blackwood continues. "Your father won Lunar's seelie throne because your mother paralyzed his rival on the day the contest was held. He was unable to wake from his nightmare until after the agreed-upon time for the contest was over. That is how he's kept his throne ever since. Your studies have taught you how challenges to the throne are dealt with, right?"

I nod. Whenever a fae seeks to challenge a current monarch in hopes of gaining their throne, the challenger must make a formal decree and establish a date for the contest ahead of time. The contest itself is often a battle of strength, but there have been battles of wit, magic, and divine choice as well.

"Then you might imagine how Divina Briar has helped your father remain undefeated during his twenty-one years as king. And why they're losing the respect of their subjects."

I frown. His tone suggests he finds her methods to be unfair, but fae rules are far different from human ones. The fae respect brutal cunning. Though, I suppose the humans and seelie fae respect such traits far less—

Understanding dawns. "My father is a *seelie* monarch. The people he rules over don't respect my mother's...methods."

"That," Mr. Blackwood says, "and the fact that King Franco—the Unseelie King of Lunar—has gained a ridiculous level of popularity, thanks to his recent marriage to a charming human wife. Even the seelie people prefer King Franco over your father."

I puzzle over his words, matching them with what I learned in my studies. Only recently did Lunar's unseelie throne shift hands from Queen Nyxia to her younger brother, Prince Franco. No, he's *King* Franco now. Before he was king, my fellow students gushed about him the same way they do about Thorne Blackwood now. But as he's no longer considered eligible, thanks to the servant girl who won his heart, the students spend more time romanticizing his lucky human queen. It makes sense that such a marriage would draw the respect of humans and seelie fae, even if the king is politically unseelie.

The reasons behind my marriage to Mr. Phillips grow clearer. "Wait...are my parents trying to replicate King Franco's situation...with me and Mr. Phillips? They think my marriage to a human will gain them back the respect of their subjects?"

"Yes, and Monty Phillips isn't just any human," Mr. Blackwood says. "He's an aristocrat, the son of a Human Representative—the highest position a human can have in the government. And since he's from the Earthen Court, your family's influence will spread beyond their current sphere. More influence would result in fewer challengers to the throne, but if your mother's methods eventually fail and your father is dethroned, your marriage will ensure your family retains a respectable position in society thereafter."

I sit back in my seat, poring over this new information. I'm starting to understand why my parents would value such a marriage and why they consider it their salvation, but I never expected being the *Briar family hero* meant digging them out of a hole *they* dug.

Irritation writhes through me, but it's tempered by a wave of guilt.

Yes, I'm still furious over my unwanted engagement, and

Thorne's explanation hasn't lessened that. Yet I have no reason to believe Thorne knows the full story. Based on how he described my mother's magic, he's clearly biased. Until I meet my family and hear their explanation from their lips, I'll resist passing judgment on them.

I pose my next question. "Does my family's...*reputation* have anything to do with the danger I was in? Or...still am in?"

"Not exactly," Thorne says slowly. "That's a much more complicated tale."

"Will you tell me?"

"I doubt I have a choice. If I decline, you might feel *hurt*." This time there's a note of jest in his voice when he refers to my manipulation.

I give him my sweetest smile. "I might."

He emits a rumbling laugh, the first I've heard from him outside of my dreams. Then his expression turns serious. "Do you like stories, Miss Rose?"

"Sometimes."

"Only sometimes? Then what do you like more than stories?"

"Dancing."

"As in...you like to dance yourself or you're fond of watching ballet?" There's a keen glint in his eyes as if he already knows the answer.

"Both."

"Then you can consider this story a dance of sorts. A waltz between feuding families and curses. Would you like that?"

His tone has taken on that slow, soft quality again, and it isn't entirely comforting. Something tugs at the back of my mind. Some...memory that has me suddenly on edge. Still,

I'm desperate to understand more about my parents. "I suppose."

"There's just one condition. You will forget my tale once I've told it and will only recall it when I've allowed you to."

My heart leaps into my throat. "What—"

"Forget I've said that last bit as well."

7

My heart thrums at a rapid pace for some inexplicable reason. I blink a few times, clearing my mind until I can focus on Thorne Blackwood again. For the briefest moment, I catch him smirking at me. In the next blink, the grin is gone. Was it even there in the first place?

"Where were we?" Thorne says. "Ah, right. I'm going to tell you all about the threat that has plagued you from birth."

Oh, no wonder my heart is beating so fast. Mr. Blackwood is going to give me the answers my three teachers couldn't. I nod. "Please do."

He glances away from me, his eyes going distant. Thoughtful. "To explain that I'll first need to preface with a bit of history. For the last hundred years or so, two families have been bitter enemies: a clan of mahrts and a clan of banshees."

Since he already told me my parents are mahrts—dream fae—that must mean the banshees he's referring to are their enemies. Or...my enemies too, I suppose.

"The feud began in the Lunar Court, where both clans originated. Back then they had no surnames, for such a human practice had yet to be established amongst the fae. The two families fought over everything from land to mates to food sources. After seelie culture grew in popularity, the mahrts decided to take on seelie form as their primary manifestation and join Lunar Court high society. Little did they know, the banshees too yearned for the seelie lifestyle. They clashed once more, but this time their wars shifted from outdoor battlefields to quieter societal ones, coming to a head during a baby's birthday celebration."

I frown. That sounds like an odd setting for a war.

"This happened a handful of years before the isle's unification," Mr. Blackwood says, "so the mahrts weren't royals yet, just members of the fae elite. The matriarch of the mahrts, who by then had taken on the surname Briar, held a celebration for her firstborn, a boy."

My heart kicks up. If I assume the Mrs. Briar of his tale is my mother, then the boy he's talking about...could be my brother! Even if these figures are more distant relatives of mine, I'm struck by the realization that I have more than just my mother and father out there. I have a whole family! Siblings, maybe. Cousins. Uncles.

Thorne continues, stealing me from my racing thoughts. "Mrs. Briar invited all the important seelie fae, excluding only one: the banshee family matriarch, who had taken on a surname of her own, Lemuria. Feeling slighted, Mrs. Lemuria showed up anyway. As the banshee matriarch was equally popular amongst the seelie gentry, Mrs. Briar couldn't turn her away without causing a stir. So Mrs. Briar received Mrs. Lemuria with a cold welcome. Everything went smoothly. Until it was time to sing the birthday song."

"The birthday song?" I echo. If that's a well-known

custom, it isn't something we've participated in at the convent.

He nods. "A tradition picked up from humans. The guests gathered around the young child and began to sing, but the song turned to gasps of terror when the first guest noted the tears streaming down the banshee's cheeks."

He pauses and meets my gaze again.

It takes me a moment to understand the significance he's waiting for me to glean. I recall what I've heard of banshee lore. While I've never met one, as they are strictly Lunar Court fae, I know a bit about their magic. It moves through song. Banshees sing several types of magical melodies, but the one they're renowned for is their song of death. If a banshee cries while singing, death is near.

"Mrs. Lemuria predicted the baby's death," I say, my heart sinking.

"Indeed. The party ended abruptly, and all guests were sent away. Mrs. Briar's son died days later. While it's a known fact that a banshee's tears only predict one's death and don't cause it, the mahrts insisted the banshee cursed the boy. The Briar family retaliated by orchestrating the death of Mrs. Lemuria's firstborn, a boy who was still a very young child in fae years."

My stomach turns. I don't want to believe my family— my parents—could have killed a child. While I know Thorne can lie, I can't imagine why he would in this instance. The rational answer is that he's mistaken, repeating rumors and gossip. I'm almost of a mind to request a stop to his story, but he still hasn't explained how any of this directly involves me.

Swallowing my pride and my desire to defend the parents I've never met, I force myself to speak in a neutral tone. "What happened next?"

"Violence escalated from there until Queen Nyxia was forced to step in. Again, this was before your parents claimed the seelie throne, so they answered to her as their sole reigning monarch. Nyxia punished both clans with a curse. Its terms stated that if a member of one family draws blood from a member of the rival family, their own clan will fall into one hundred years of deathlike sleep. That way, whoever incites violence on the other family punishes their own. Of course, that didn't stop the violence. The families only found more creative ways to try and kill each other without drawing blood. But that wasn't the extent of Nyxia's punishment. To appease both clans and allow them retribution for their perceived grievances, she allowed each side to deal a final curse upon the other. The mahrts cursed the Lemurias' nextborn to never know his mother's face, while the banshees cursed Briars' nextborn to be bound by iron if it ever touches her flesh."

He gives me a weighted look.

A shudder runs down my spine. "Are you saying...I was the Briars' nextborn?"

"Yes. You, Miss Rose, are cursed."

Nausea churns in my stomach as I repeat the terms of the curse in my head. If iron touches my flesh...I'll be bound by it. Forever? And how? In a coffin? Shackles? It doesn't matter, I suppose. Iron is lethal to the fae. For pureblood fae, even touching the metal is excruciating. I can't imagine the torment of being physically bound by the substance. If prolonged contact didn't kill me, the pain eventually would. I'd...I'd go mad from it. I'd wish for death, beg for it.

My pulse quickens as my eyes dart around the coach. A blanket of dread falls over me, and suddenly everything feels dangerous. The edges of the cushioned seat, the hinges of the carriage doors, the buttons on my dress—

"Miss Rose."

The sound of my name has my eyes flashing open. When did I close them? I realize I'm trembling, my heart racing. Mr. Blackwood leans toward me, his gloved hand extended between us but not quite touching. Notes of concern etch his face, deepening the furrow between his brows and making him look completely unlike every version of him I've seen. He isn't curious like he is in my dreams. The stoic calm I've associated with the real him is gone, as is that rare seductive teasing. Right now he seems...open. Vulnerable, almost.

It's enough to clear my mind.

With a slow exhale, I settle back in my seat and remind myself that while I may be cursed, I'm safe. There is no iron lurking from the shadows ready to condemn me to eternal torment. Iron was banned from the isle of Faerwyvae upon unification. That was twenty-three years ago. I know from my lessons that the fae royals took severe measures to ensure every scrap of iron that remained in the south where humans once inhabited was discarded. There should be nothing left by now. Not even a splinter.

Mr. Blackwood withdraws his hand, but sits at the edge of his seat, elbows propped on his knees. His stoic mask has returned and he watches me through his spectacles beneath his dark lashes. When he speaks, his voice is quiet. Strained. "Are you all right?" He sounds almost angry. I can't tell whether he's forcing himself to voice his concern...or fighting against it.

"I'm fine," I rush to say. Now that I've recovered from my momentary panic, I'm embarrassed by it. "Please continue."

He slowly lifts his elbows from his knees and returns to his relaxed posture. Mouth pressed into a tight line, he studies me for an uncomfortably long beat, then averts his gaze to the shuttered window. "After the two families cursed each other's nextborn, both sides tried to avoid having another child for as long as possible, for they knew the other family would scheme to initiate the curse at their first chance. Yet both families did conceive. First Mrs. Lemuria gave birth to a son. Then the Briars had their daughter. You. Princess Rosaline Briar. Your parents had ascended to royalty, now the seelie monarchs of Lunar, which meant your birth was a widely known event."

"So, my parents sent me to the convent to keep the Lemurias from trying to initiate my curse?" I ask. "Was it not enough that iron had been eradicated?"

"You are twenty years of age, am I correct?"

"Yes."

"Twenty years ago," he says, "the isle was still adjusting to unification. Now and then, stores of iron were still found, particularly in the south. I can only assume your parents thought the safest place for you would be in a fae convent in a court up north where the land had never been touched by human metals."

"Why did my parents only send for me now? The isle has been free from iron for years."

"I can't speak for them," he says, a note of irritation lacing his words, "but I can tell you that even with iron being a rare commodity, they anticipate retribution by other means. While the banshee clan is no longer a threat as a whole, there is one left that they fear."

"What do you mean the banshee clan is no longer a threat? Are the Lemurias...dead?" Again, I don't want to ponder what that might suggest about my parents. Could they have used their royal influence to murder an entire family? And if so...can I truly blame them for it?

Yes, half my heart says, while the other insists that the

Lemurias were just as guilty of violence as my family was. I cling to the latter, recalling my determination to resist judging my family or take Thorne's tale as truth until I've met my parents. Heard their side.

"The Lemurias are no longer a threat," he says, "because they've since fallen under the curse Nyxia placed on both families—the sleeping spell that is enacted when one member of one clan draws blood from a member of the rival clan."

Relief washes over me. My parents aren't murderers, then. If the banshees fell under the sleeping spell, that means *they* initiated it by drawing blood from *my* family.

"But there was an unexpected caveat," he says. "The one who initiates the curse by drawing blood from the rival family is spared from the sleeping spell, which means there is one person left awake from the Lemuria family."

A shudder of apprehension writhes through me. "Who?"

"Mrs. Lemuria's husband—a moon dragon—has been spotted alive over the last several years, so one can only assume he put his bloodline to sleep. He may not have been born to the clan, but if he married into it, or if Mrs. Lemuria deemed him her mate, he'd still count as a member of the family. But since he's taken on unseelie form and sought refuge in the mountains on unseelie lands, he's under King Franco's protection now. Your parents can't reach him, even with their royal titles. Besides, they have more pressing matters to concern themselves with."

"You mean...their dwindling reputation?"

He nods.

"And my marriage that will supposedly save it."

Another nod.

"They waited so long because they feared Mrs. Lemuria's husband would try to hurt me," I whisper, more to myself than to him. "But they sent for me, despite the lingering threat, because they need me." I don't know how to feel about all this. If the banshee's husband is still a threat, then my parents are risking my life by bringing me home. And yet...if they're taking the risk now, they could have taken it long ago. Why didn't they?

We have spent years trying to find you, Mother's note said, and that softens some of the pain that tightens my chest. That's right. They've been looking for me for a long time. The only reason they didn't come for me sooner was that they had to go through protection protocols. And without access to iron, Mrs. Lemuria's husband can't hurt me through my curse. I'll be safe with my parents.

A nagging warning rings in the back of my head, reminding me of the darker parts of Thorne's story. How my family blamed the banshee for a magic she had no control over. How they reacted by killing her child.

I shake my head, reminding myself that Thorne might have been misinformed. What would a human baker know about such a personal fae saga anyway? If the feud was well known, it would have made it into my textbooks. If my parents were guilty of worse crimes than the Lemurias, they'd have been punished far more severely. No, Thorne can't know what he's talking about.

Yet the way he described my family's past...

I narrow my eyes as I take in his too-casual posture that contrasts the hard line of his jaw. The coldness in his eyes. The sharp edge that underlined his outwardly neutral tone when he explained certain parts of his story. "How do you know so much about my family, Mr. Blackwood?"

He slides his gaze from the closed window until his eyes lock on mine. A corner of his mouth flicks into a sad smile. "The story is over. It's time to forget, my pretty nemesis."

PART TWO

SO
WICKED

8

THORNE

I should have kept her from dozing off. I should have done whatever I could to hold her attention after I finished my story instead of falling into one of my brooding silences. Because now she's sucked me into a damn dreamscape, and I'm determined she doesn't find out these dreams hold truth. Not yet. Not until I've done what I need to do.

A quaint kitchen forms around me, focused on an old table upon which a crooked cake sits. Children bounce on their feet in slow motion, reaching for plates of cake with wide grins on their faces. I know this room. This scene. I entered this very kitchen this morning. While I may not have witnessed this exact moment, it's similar enough to tell me it happened shortly before I arrived at the convent. No, that is a lie. I arrived well before that moment. Miss Rose doesn't know that, and I plan to keep it that way for now, to use my ability to lie in my favor. Thanks to my human heritage, untruths slip from my lips with ease. Not that everything I've said to her has been a lie. Almost everything I've said is true.

Almost.

She'll learn the rest soon.

One hidden truth is that my appearance in the convent's kitchen marked my *public* arrival. My true arrival was in a small glade just beyond the Starcane fields, one I'd seen several times in the dreams I've been pulled into over the last couple of years. It was the third time in twenty-four hours that I'd visited the glade but the first that I'd finally caught her in the flesh.

Briony Rose.

Rosaline Briar.

My born nemesis.

She stands just before me in her dreamscape, watching the scene with a sentimental smile. If I knew how to leave the dream of my own volition, I would, but I've long since learned I'm trapped here until the dream ends, my physical body immobilized.

Dream magic. Sleep paralysis. The same power as her vile mother.

"Thank the All of All I'm not the driver," I mutter.

Briony bites back a startled squeal and whirls around to face me. Her blue eyes go from wide to narrow in an instant while distaste curls her upper lip. "Oh. You."

"That's the greeting I get?"

"I didn't invite you here. In fact, I never intentionally do. Regardless, I've had enough of you in all forms for the time being, though I must say I far prefer the dream version of you."

"What a compliment."

"Wait, what did you mean by *Thank the All of All I'm not*

the driver?" She says the last part in a deep and bumbling tone, a rather insulting impersonation.

"I mean, we'd be in a ditch right now."

"A ditch?"

I release a grumbling sigh. There's no point explaining. She hasn't a clue how dangerous she is. And it's better we keep it that way for now. "I thought you said you weren't going to dream of me anymore."

She furrows her brow. "When did I say that?"

I purse my lips. Of course she doesn't remember. I made her forget our exchange this morning. It had been a gamble whether it would work or not, but my bet paid off; she obeyed my demand and forgot our dance completely. After that, there was no turning back. My plan must commence.

"Never mind," she says with a shake of her head. "You're a figment of my imagination, so of course you know my inner thoughts. And it's true; I was sure I wouldn't dream of you quite so often anymore, for I'd given up on dancing. I'll have to take that back now that I know I'm a..." She pauses, her jaw shifting side to side as if she's sampling her next words before she speaks them. Once she does, she all but spits them out. "A princess. There, I've said it. I'm a princess, believe it or not. I hardly do myself. Though I'm not fully used to such a concept, I suppose it means I'll get to dance after all."

Her expression begins to shift. The annoyance my presence placed there gives way to awe. Excitement. A smile forms on her lips, and I can't deny it's a lovely grin. She may be my enemy, but that doesn't diminish her beauty. Her honey-blonde hair is half pinned up while the long ends tumble around her shoulders. Her blue eyes are framed with dark-blonde lashes, her lips as plump and curvaceous as her figure. Not even her dour gray gown can hide those ample curves. Besides, thanks to one naughty dream of hers, I've seen her naked.

"Stars above," she says, her words laced with a gasp. The sound rouses me from my thoughts. Finding my eyes have strayed to her hips, I lift my gaze. Thankfully, she didn't notice my inspection, for she's turned fully away from me. The kitchen dreamscape grows fuzzy at the edges, something I recognize as a precursor to a scene change. With her hands clasped to her chest, she twirls in place, stopping when she's facing me once more. "I'm going to dance," she says, her voice trembling with excitement. "Truly dance."

The glade outside the convent floods the space the kitchen previously occupied. The trees are blanketed in night while moonlight shines a single beam upon the clearing. Upon *us*.

Her shoulders fall and she casts a glare at our new surroundings. "Not now," she says to her dreamscape. It dims in answer, shifting into a hazy likeness. Night melts to day. She returns her gaze to me, and that look of distaste returns to her pretty mouth. "Not with...*him*. With a real partner. In real life. Soon."

"With your beloved fiancé?" I don't mean to say it with a hint of scorn, but I do. Monty Phillips may consider me his best friend, but I find him only tolerable at best. Half of the time. He's the most insufferable shit for the rest. Luckily for Briony, she'll never need to know his true nature, for she won't be making it to her wedding day.

Her eyes narrow to slits. "You're acting unusual. Is it because I've met the real you? Stars, I'd rather not invite *him* into my imagination. He's a moody piece of work, that one. Silent and disinterested one moment, then smirking like some storybook rogue the next. He's either ignoring me or studying me so intently I feel like his prey. Which is the real you, Mr. Blackwood?"

I try to hide my amusement over her observations of me. "Can a person not have two sides? Are you so single-faceted?"

"I've never pondered such a thing. I'm simply...me."

Tucking my hands into my trouser pockets—I should thank her for the fact that I am wearing pants in this dream, by the way—I take a step closer to her. "You're the dreamer who loves to dance and the sensible woman who was ready to give up on the life she wanted to be a governess. Those sound like two distinct sides to me."

She snorts a laugh, her mouth tugging into a sideways grin. "You truly are just a sliver of my imagination. The real Thorne wouldn't notice such things. He can hardly rouse enough interest to speak to me. I had to manipulate him into conversation, you know. Apparently, even that was so dull that I eventually nodded off." She glances around at her dreamscape, which has begun to melt once more. The glade transforms into a dark auditorium. Featureless figures comprise the audience while willowy dancers in flowing white dresses move gracefully across a stage.

The movement draws her attention. As she steps closer to the stage, a wistful sigh leaves her lips. "I suppose you're right," she says, her voice so quiet it's almost a whisper. "I do have two sides. A girl who dreams and a girl who's too scared to dream."

Something sharp tugs my heart as I study the awe on her face. The way her features light up as she watches the ballerinas dance. Is it guilt that plagues me now?

"What two sides do you have, Mr. Blackwood?" She glances over her shoulder at me. "Not outwardly, but within? What contrast lurks in your heart?"

The question catches me off guard, as does the genuine curiosity in her eyes. She's very much unlike the guarded version of her I've spoken with today. In this moment, she's open. Vulnerable. Real. I suppose I was the same way too when these dreams began—after I got over my shock, of course. Once I got used to them, I assumed they were nothing more than strange imaginings that struck me on occasion, taking over my thoughts at random times during the day or weaving through my midnight musings while asleep.

That was before I learned of her true identity. Before I understood the weight of the curse that binds us. Before I realized exactly what I was born to do.

I meet her gaze. "I am both a baker and a villain."

She scoffs. "You. A villain?"

"To you."

She rolls her eyes. "I don't hate Thorne Blackwood. He's just an easy target for my irritation. This whole situation has me on edge no matter how many times I remind myself that this is what I've always wanted, to be claimed by a family that loves me. To be needed. I never imagined an arranged marriage would come with all that, yet it's not Thorne's fault he's friends with my fiancé, nor that he was tasked with taking me to meet a stranger. What is his fault are his moody silences that I can't abide, but he's not so bad—"

"Don't get close to him." The words leave my mouth before I can stop myself. "Whatever you think we have here, in your dreams, do not confuse that with reality. You don't know Thorne Blackwood."

"I know," she bites back, cheeks flushing. Then, with a frown, she takes a step back. "You really are acting differently."

I clench my jaw. She's right. Ever since I learned the

truth of these dreams, I've tried my best to keep my composure when we meet in her dreamscapes, but I'm failing at that right now. It's more important than ever to keep up the charade. I don't even know why I uttered that warning. Wouldn't it be better if she did come to like me? Trust me? It would hurt her more when it comes time to enact my plan.

But that's just it.

I don't want to hurt her.

She may have been born my enemy, but she didn't choose to be. Before today, she didn't even know who she was.

Yet hurt her I must.

Hurt her I *will*.

Otherwise, everything my family fought for will be for naught.

Forcing my true feelings, my hidden darkness, to the shadowed places within, I feign the open curiosity I once had. Gesturing toward the stage, I ask, "What ballet is this?"

Her expression softens. "I've told you before, in another dream."

Yes, she has.

"But I'll tell you again. I love this ballet. I could talk about it for hours." She starts her tale about her trip to Lumenas, her first visit to the ballet, and the fascination with dancing it sparked thereafter.

I watch her animated gestures, her growing smile, knowing that soon I'll see that joy slip from her face for good. It's a prospect that fills me with far less satisfaction than I like.

I was born to do this, I remind myself.

I was named for vengeance.

My beautiful nemesis must lose everything I've already lost.

9

BRIONY

My eyelids flutter open, my mind heavy with dreams. The more I wake, the hazier the dreams become. However, I distinctly recall one that involved Thorne, which was followed by several less-memorable ones, none of which Mr. Blackwood paid any visits to. Still, even the easy-to-forget dreams leave my brain fuzzy, and for a moment I don't remember where I am. I blink at my surroundings and recognize the dark interior of the coach.

Ah, right. Now I recall.

I'm not sure how long I dozed off for, but it must have been long indeed for night has now fallen, as told by the open curtains and the inky sky beyond the coach's windows. I'm surprised to see the curtains open at all, for Mr. Blackwood insisted on keeping them shut for discretion's sake when we first began our journey. I suppose the veil of night can serve the same purpose the curtains did during the day.

I cast a glance at where my head had been propped

against the interior wall. How did I manage to nap in such an uncomfortable position for so long? Then I note the dark fabric clinging to my shoulder. I smooth it out, assessing it. It's a jacket, and not one of my own. All my excess clothing is packed away and stored on the luggage rack. My gaze moves to my traveling companion, hidden once again behind the wide expanse of his broadsheets. The view is enough to reveal he's no longer wearing his jacket. His forearms are bare, his shirtsleeves rolled up to his elbows.

I frown down at the article of clothing in my hands. Did he...prop this beside my face and neck so I could more comfortably doze?

He must have heard me stir, for he lifts his eyes above his paper.

I grin at him, an automatic response, but it's a gesture I regret as he pointedly ignores it and goes right back to reading.

With a roll of my eyes, I remind myself he isn't the man I spent my dream talking to. Dream-Thorne let me prattle on and on about the ballet I so greatly adore, watching me with rapt attention. A mental construct indeed. Though I recall he seemed far more Thorne-like when the dream began, which I'm sure is due to me having met him in real life. What a shame reality must color what was once a lovely fantasy.

But I shouldn't dream of him anymore. I never should have in the first place. While I have more control over my daydreams than I do over what happens in my mind when I'm asleep, I must find a way to rid myself of dream-Thorne. It was one thing to fancy a figment of my imagination based on a man I thought I'd never see again. It's another to maintain the charade when the real person has entered my life.

And if he's truly such good friends with my fiancé, he may be a fixture in my life for good.

Stars, what a nuisance that will be. I hope his demeanor isn't telling of the company he keeps. If my fiancé ignores me this much, I may have to flee before my wedding day. I scowl at Thorne's broadsheets and am startled when they suddenly come down. He catches my glare before I can hide it and gives me a pointed look.

"I can practically hear you thinking," he says through his teeth. "You don't like my silence."

I lift my chin and avert my gaze to the window, grateful it's too dark for him to see the blush that rises to my cheeks. "I don't like being bored."

"Well, I do. I like boredom and peace and quiet."

"You must live a rather uneventful life," I mutter.

"An uneventful life may sound dull to you, but for some, it's a luxury. Now, let me save us both from another one of your veiled threats and simply tell you what you want to know. We're almost to Nocturnus Palace. We'll reach the gates within minutes."

His response has my pulse kicking up. I sit upright and face him again. "Really?"

He gives me a curt nod before returning to his paper.

I tilt my head, realizing he's without his spectacles for once. "How can you read at night without your lenses?"

"My vision is better in the dark."

There goes my theory that he couldn't have seen me blushing. "That's unusual, isn't it? Especially for a human."

"Especially so."

"Then what makes you so special?"

"You shouldn't consider me special at all. That's hardly appropriate for a woman engaged." There's a taunting lilt to his voice that makes my cheeks flare with heat again. "Any other inquiries about my private life?"

He's clearly evading my question by distracting me with my own embarrassment. Well, it's working, that clever bastard. Which is fine. I don't need to get to know him anyway.

Dream-Thorne's warning echoes in my mind. *Don't get close to him.*

Forcibly wrenching my attention from Thorne, I scoot to the edge of my seat and study the view outside the window. A crescent moon illuminates the trees that surround the road, casting them in the darkest hues of blue and purple. Glittering stars decorate the night sky, but they look different than they do in the Star Court. Even though the convent is only a few hours from the border between Lunar and Star, the differences are noticeable. All eleven courts in Faerwyvae are like that, each hosting a different climate, terrain, season, or elemental affinity. In the Star Court, the stars are always more visible than the moon at night, showcasing an endless sea of sparkling shards in every hue. But here, it's clear the moon is sovereign, and the stars bask in her glow, not the other way around. Even the treetops seem to reach for that glowing crescent, eager to feel more of her silver light.

It dawns on me that this is my first time in a different court. No, I suppose that isn't true. I was born in Lunar. I just didn't know it. But this is certainly my first time leaving the Star Court since I entered the convent. Even though the city of Lumenas was so bright and boisterous that my time there made me feel like I was in a different land, this is truly my first journey away. And after I've met my family, I'll be joining my fiancé in another new location, the Earthen Court.

My elation drains at the thought. While my yearning for my family drives me onward and fuels my excitement, I still haven't reconciled the prospect of marrying a stranger. Nor has my fury over it waned. There's still much I don't know about the situation. When are we expected to marry? What kind of man is he? Will we have any kind of courtship? Will I get to debut in society and enjoy all the things I've wanted to experience? Is he a good dancer? How long do I get to visit with my family before Thorne takes me to meet Monty Phillips?

My heart races with all these questions, but it fully stutters when my eyes fall on a massive structure that has just emerged from the line of trees. As the coach proceeds, the structure becomes clearer. It's an elegant palace that shines violet in the moonlight, climbing high with towering turrets and walls topped with gilded crenellations.

"Nocturnus Palace," Thorne says, drawing my attention to him. He's put his broadsheets away and stares out the same window. There's something tense in the line of his jaw, though perhaps that's just the moody bastard's face. "You're home."

"Home," I echo and turn my gaze back to the palace. Our coach comes to a stop. I angle my head to find we've reached a towering gate of silver filigree. After a lengthy pause, the gate opens, and the coach proceeds. The scenery shifts from the dark forest road to an immaculate palace lawn dotted with bioluminescent mushrooms, slender birch trees dressed in tiny glowing orbs of light, marble statues and fountains, and perfectly manicured hedges and topiaries.

Finally, the coach enters a courtyard that circles a massive fountain and stops at the base of a wide staircase that leads to a pair of double doors.

"We are to wait here while the coachman delivers all

necessary paperwork to your parents. Then someone will escort us from the coach."

My heart beats faster. The coach jostles, and I catch sight of a figure darting from the coach and up the stairs. The coachman disappears behind the palace doors, leaving me nothing to study but the walls of the palace that take up the entirety of my view. Up close, I can see that they're constructed of amethyst. I shift anxiously in my seat, feeling completely underdressed before such elegance. Not that I had much of a choice. Everything I own is plain and gray.

That reminds me of the jacket I found when I awoke, which lies forgotten in my lap. I angle myself toward Thorne and find him studying me with that intense stare that so deeply contrasts his usual disinterest. "Thank you," I mutter, handing him the jacket.

He takes it from me and begins to roll down the sleeves of his shirt. I drop my eyes from his face to his forearms. As one cuff comes fully loose, I catch sight of black ink marking his inner forearm near its elbow crease.

My breath hitches. I've seen tattoos marking his flesh before, in *that one dream*. They trailed from his upper forearm and around his bicep, then across his back, a pattern reminiscent of a coiled snake, painting the hard planes of his body. His very naked and very...aroused body. My core tightens at the memory, for I can't help recalling exactly what we did after I saw him like that. The lust that sparked. The heat that drummed between my legs—

I bite the inside of my cheek to force the memory away. As it recedes, a question takes its place, one that douses my momentary fire in tepid water. I've always thought I imagined dream-Thorne with those markings for my own visual pleasure during that dream, but...they were real? My gaze snaps back to his, and I find his eyes have gone wide.

He blinks and his surprise is gone, as if it was never there to begin with. Perhaps I'd only been projecting my own. He angles the arm inward and draws both cuffs down to his wrists. "What?" he asks with a haughty scoff. "Am I being too quiet again?"

"No," I rush to say and force my attention back out the window. I'm too flustered to conjure a reply. What could I even say? *Oh, you have tattoos? I dreamed of you naked once and saw you had them then. What a fun coincidence! Tell me more!*

Thankfully, I'm saved by the opening of the palace doors.

A female figure emerges, backlit by the golden glow coming from within the palace. She pauses, shoulders heaving, then rushes down the steps. A slender figure races after her, a servant perhaps, and tries to assist her descent. She shakes him off, her motions giddy, and increases her pace. The nearer she draws to the base of the stairs, the clearer her features become. Moonlight glints off blonde hair arranged in pinned-up curls, a wide smile, and tears that stream down her chubby cheeks.

I don't need to guess. I don't need to wonder.

That's my mother.

And that joy on her face is everything I've ever hoped to see.

All that remains of my trepidation, my worry, my anger, my fear, dissolves at once.

Before I can even think to move, I'm already tumbling out of the coach, sprinting the rest of the way to her. My arms wrap around the female fae's shoulders while hers encircle my middle. She's shorter than me by at least a head, so I rest my cheek on her hair, my eyes wet with tears. I don't remember when I started to cry, but my shoulders are racked with sobs.

"My baby," she says, voice muffled against my shoulder. "My child. My love. It's you. It's really you!"

"It's me," I say, words strained with emotion. Then I voice the one thing I've longed to say. A word I thought I'd never get to utter. "Mother."

10

BRIONY

I wipe my eyes as my mother and I finally separate from our embrace. I've never considered myself the most sentimental or affectionate of people, but this is the second time I've cried during a hug today. My mother takes a step back but doesn't fully release me. She frames my shoulders with her hands and assesses me with glazed eyes. "You have my hair, my darling. And my blue eyes. Oh, and my physique. Look at those nice wide hips."

I blush at her words. No one has ever spoken about my hips like their girth is a good thing. Aside from one person, perhaps. The selkie princess I met at the bridal competition last year told me several times how cute my *blubber* was while wistfully gazing at my chest. My mother has an even softer form than I do, with plump arms, a curving belly, and pillowy breasts that nearly spill from her low-cut bodice. She's...beautiful.

Her smile takes on an approving quality. "Oh, but you have your father's height indeed."

"Do I?" Mention of my father has my eyes darting over Mother's shoulder, searching for him. All I see is the male who'd chased her down the stairs. He's a slender fae with overlarge black eyes, pointed ears, and a wormlike tail. Considering this is the Lunar Court, it makes sense there would be nocturnal rodent fae. The way he wrings his gloved hands, shoulders hunched with clear anxiety, tells me my first impression was correct—he's a servant. Not the King of Lunar.

"Yes, just wait until you meet him at the party!" Mother says.

"The party?" My eyes flash back to hers. That's the first I've heard mention of a party.

A throat clears behind us. Mother releases my shoulders, and we turn to face the coach.

Thorne now wears the jacket I returned to him. My mind shifts back to its previous musings over the sliver of ink I glimpsed on his arm. Though my shock remains fresh, I must be rational. If *that one dream* accurately depicted his tattoos, then it is simply because my magic picked up on them when I framed him in my hands two years ago. It was too far away for me to catch sight of any designs on his skin, but surely my magic could have been able to. Besides, there's no way to know if my dream depicted them accurately without seeing him naked in real life. Which I have no intention of doing. Ever.

Thorne bows at the waist. "Queen Divina," he says, tone respectful but without even a hint of reverence. I suppose that's because my mother isn't *his* queen. From what I know about the famous Thorne Blackwood, his estate is in the Earthen Court. Assuming the estate is also his primary residence, that must be the court he calls home. It also would explain why he's such close friends with Monty Phillips, son of the Earthen Court Human Representative.

Then another thought strikes me.

"Oh!" I whirl toward my mother. "Should I have curtsied? Or...or addressed you as—"

"Nonsense," she says with an indulgent grin. "You're my daughter and a princess. You must get used to seeing others bow in your honor. Mr. Blackwood, would you care to demonstrate?"

His jaw tightens, but his face remains impassive. I'm about to say there's no need for him to bow, not after we just spent several hours in a coach together, but I stop myself. My mother is right; I'm a princess now. As false and uncomfortable as that feels, it's the truth.

He narrows his eyes the slightest bit as he shifts his gaze to me. Then with a slow bow, he says, "Princess Rosaline."

His voice is as emotionless as it was when he addressed my mother, but I get the strangest sense he's mocking me.

My mother makes a sound of haughty satisfaction. "See, daughter? That is what you should expect from this point on. Now, Mr. Blackwood, I trust you were as discreet in your travels with my daughter as our bargain required?"

"I wouldn't be alive were it otherwise. That is the nature of bargains, Majesty."

Mother whirls toward me and lowers her voice, though not enough to avoid being overheard by Thorne. "He didn't touch you in an untoward manner or cause you any harm on your journey?"

Were I in a more playful mood, I'd bring up how cold and painful his silences were, just to see if I could make him sweat a little. But her question doesn't feel trivial. My mother may be a giddy creature, but she is a queen. One who—according to Thorne—has gone to great lengths to keep my father's throne safe. Who knows what she would do to Thorne if she took my jest too seriously?

"No," I say, "he kept his proper distance."

"Good. Normally I wouldn't trust humans due to their ability to lie, but Mr. Blackwood is a public figure, the face of the most popular bakery on the isle. His reputation demands propriety. Furthermore, in our family, we have more to fear from the fae."

I'm surprised by the disdain her voice held when she said she didn't normally trust humans. A seelie monarch's very duty revolves around aiding and protecting them. But then my mind snags on the last part. *We have more to fear from the fae.* Is she referring to contenders to the throne, due to my family's declining reputation? Or...was that about the mysterious danger I've been in since birth?

I frown, recalling how I asked Thorne to tell me about it earlier today.

Do you like stories, Miss Rose?

I answered him, and he shifted into that sultry, teasing persona of his, saying something about a waltz of family feuds and curses. And then...nothing. Why did he never tell the tale he'd tempted me with? I only remember silence after that, until I dozed off.

Mother speaks again. "I apologize for subjecting you to the indignity of traveling alone with a man. I know the rules of society forbid a young woman from being in such a precarious position, but I wanted as few people as possible to be involved with your retrieval. I had to stretch the truth a bit when it came to relaying information to your fiancé. He's under the impression you were at the convent doing volunteer work, and I didn't want him to glean otherwise. Thankfully, Mr. Blackwood agreed not to relay any classified intel to Mr. Phillips, for the less reason we give your fiancé to doubt the strength of the match, the better. Anyhow, fret not. You'll have a chaperone in attendance when Mr. Blackwood escorts you to the Earthen Court."

I blink a few times, almost dizzy from how much she spoke all at once. Not to mention how fast. My surprise turns to amusement as I recall her rambling letter. She's the very same in person.

Mother fully turns toward Thorne again. "You'll make my daughter's cake now, won't you?"

"I'd be delighted," Thorne says, though there's no delight in his tone.

Mother snaps her fingers, and her rodent fae servant approaches Mr. Blackwood.

I furrow my brow and ask my mother, "What is this about cake?"

"It's still your birthday, my love! For another few hours at least. We're going to have a dinner celebration."

My eyes go wide. "Tonight?"

Her shoulders fall. "Oh, I forgot you've traveled so long. Was the convent not nocturnal?"

"Some of the sisters kept nocturnal schedules, but not the school—"

"We aren't nocturnal either. For the most part, that is. Since we must hear petitions from the humans, we open court during the day. That's why we decided to host your party at night, when it will be the most private. Oh, don't worry, it will be only your close family and very little staff. Everyone is so eager to meet you. They're waiting in the dining room now! Besides, it's the only night you'll be home."

My heart drops to my feet. "It is?"

"Mr. Blackwood is taking you to Sandalwood Manor tomorrow. That's where your fiancé lives. Oh dear! I didn't add an itinerary to my letter, did I? I knew I forgot something, but your father insisted I was being too long-winded. For the love of the night, I've overwhelmed you, haven't I? If you want to cancel the party, we can." Her eyes turn down at the corners, lips pulling into a grimace.

"No, it's fine," I rush to say. The words grate against my tongue, tasting very much like a lie. But *fine* isn't *great*. Fine is tolerable, and I do think I can tolerate a dinner party if it means making my mother happy. If this is my one chance to meet my family before I leave, I want to take advantage of it. Yet through that joyous want writhes a spear of irritation. One night. That's all I'm being given before I'm pawned off on my stranger of a fiancé! Clenching my jaw, I swallow down my anger and force a smile. "I can at least get cleaned up and changed first, can't I?"

Mother beams at me, her face so bright it rivals the moon shining upon us. "Yes, my darling, I'll show you to your room."

With a more somber expression, she nods at her servant. "Virgil, show Mr. Blackwood the kitchens at once."

Virgil nods back, as does Thorne. Mr. Blackwood darts a quick, expressionless glance at me before following the servant up the stairs and into the palace. For a moment, I'm struck with a sense of panic at his departure, at watching the only familiar sight around me vanish from view. I chastise myself for the notion. The real Thorne is a prickly stranger. My dreams of him are folly. False. Nothing to be comforted by.

Mother laces her arm through mine and guides me up the staircase at a leisurely pace. "I'm so glad you're here. Oh, I have been waiting for this day for so long."

"Me too," I say, meeting her warm gaze. I'm struck by how young she looks. While she has the *feel* of a much older fae, she appears not much older than me. Fae aging is like that. Most cease aging after they reach maturity, though some can willingly age should they desire an older appearance. And then there are fae like Sister Nessie, the bark-skinned dryad from the convent, whose visage belies her relative youth.

As we reach the top of the staircase, two small foxes—fae in unseelie form—wearing black bow ties greet us at the doors, bowing low on all fours.

"Get her things from the coach," Mother says, and the foxes bound down the stairs. As we proceed inside, I'm overcome with awe at our surroundings. Moonstone walls stretch high to the arched ceiling, its beams strung with large orbs of light. An amethyst floor glitters violet beneath our feet. The occasional guard dressed in silver armor stands sentinel along our path, but the halls are mostly empty. Far more so than I expected from a palace. However, my mother did say there would only be close family and very little staff here tonight. Is my family always this secretive? Or is this again about the danger I'm in? I realize there's still so much more I need to know.

"Mother," I say, and my heart flips at hearing myself say that word aloud once more, "Mr. Blackwood told me some things about our family's...situation, but he never explained—"

"Situation? Oh, you must mean our reputation. It was futile to hope you wouldn't hear about that yet. Even Mr. Phillips knows about it, and it's why you must leave with such haste. The sooner your marriage takes place, the better, though I'm in agony that you must leave tomorrow. You must understand, my darling, that this marriage has been long in the making. I know it must be quite a shock to you, and if I could have sent word earlier to break such star-tling news, I would have."

"Yes, but back to what I was saying—"

"Right. Our reputation. Mr. Blackwood told you about my magic, didn't he? How I've used it to keep your father on the throne? I hope you don't blame me. And I swear, I don't intend to rely on such methods in the future! See? I said it out loud which means I'm being earnest. You must understand that times were volatile back then. After unification, Faer-wyvae was in chaos. Lunar needed a seelie ruler to balance the unseelie rule, and if we had to use underhanded methods to do what is right for our home court...well, you understand right? The mahrts weren't the only clan that sought to claim the seelie throne. We had to compete with the kitsune clan, the wisps, the banshees, the moon dragons—"

"Banshees and moon dragons." I don't realize I've said it aloud until I hear the pause in my mother's tirade. I'm not even sure why those two words stood out to me so much. It's just...I feel like someone mentioned those two types of fae recently, but I can't put my finger on when or what was said.

Mother's tone turns bitter. "Yes, our enemies, the Lemurias. Before unification, it was just Morgana—a wretched banshee—and her banshee ilk we had to contend with. But when we made our bid for the throne, she married a moon dragon and backed his contest against your father. Your father won, of course, thanks to me."

I say nothing in reply as my mind is still tangled in what feels like a forgotten dream. Something about her story feels familiar...

My mother must take my silence for disapproval, for she sidles closer to me, hugging my arm tighter. "My dear, I am trying to change. I hope you believe that."

I shake the thoughts from my head and don a reassuring smile. "I do! Mr. Blackwood told me as much."

She pulls her head back in surprise. "Did he? Well, it's true. But if we hope to stop relying on my...*methods*...then we must improve our reputation first. If we can secure the love and respect of our people, just like King Franco has, we will be as untouchable as he's become. Our rivals will be less determined to dethrone us, and the few who do will meet the scorn of our loyal subjects."

"And my marriage to Monty Phillips will help with that?" I try to keep the apprehension out of my voice. We turn down a smaller hall where the bright orb lights give way to smaller sconces lining the walls.

Mother's expression brightens. "Oh, indeed it will! Marriage is currency for respect when it comes to humans. Speaking of currency, that is another benefit. Your marriage will come with funds. Daughter, believe me when I tell you it is expensive to buy loyalty when one's reputation is in a ditch. Night above, we need that money and fast." She mutters the last part under her breath, then resumes her fast-paced speech. "Aside from that, your marriage will give us allies from the Earthen Court. *Human* allies. Irrefutable proof that we truly care about humans. Can you believe we've been accused of the contrary? And having allies in the Earthen Court will grow our societal influence across borders."

"But why me? Is there no one else in our family who could be married off in my place? Do I not have siblings?"

Her expression falls. "Dearest, you are our only child. In fact, you're the only child that has been born in our clan in decades. Pureblood fae don't conceive as quickly or as often as humans do."

"Oh." My heart sinks a little to hear I have no siblings. "What about my older relatives? Marriageable cousins?"

She shakes her head. "As a princess, you hold a title that makes you a prize for a husband, something your cousins and other relatives can't offer. And your fiancé is an equal treasure! His status will provide us a place of honor in society, even if we one day lose the throne. Night, we're so lucky to have secured the marriage. It's a miracle we did. Mr. Phillips is incredibly popular. His father, Lord Phillips, is Earthen Court's Human Representative, and the rest of his family deals in trade in every court. They might as well be nobility for the influence they have in society."

That's about as much as Thorne told me and still does nothing to paint a picture of the man I am to marry. I suppose that matters little when I'll be leaving to meet him tomorrow. Another spark of anger burns my blood.

My mother stops before a closed door. "We're here. Our bedroom is just at the end of the hall, so Father and I will be close to you tonight. It's a shame you'll only have one night to sleep here, as I've been eager to see you occupy this room for the last twenty years. It has always been set aside for you."

She pushes open the door to reveal a large space with pink moonstone walls and white marble floors. An enormous bed with posts of gold rests beneath a blue velvet canopy embroidered with silver stars.

My mouth falls open. It's ten times the size of my room at the convent and more elegant than anything I've seen.

The patter of feet reaches my ears, and a second later, the two bow tie-clad foxes race inside the room, my garment bag balanced across both their backs. They shrug off their burden at the foot of my bed, bow to me and my mother, and then scamper off as quickly as they came.

Mother guides me inside the room, her arm still linked through mine. "I hope you like it. I've redecorated it almost every year since you left, to accommodate your changing age. I've always hoped you'd be able to come home, and now you're finally here! Warm wash water is on your dressing table, and your wardrobe is there. I've stocked it with gowns mostly in the fae style, since they are less restrictive than human fashions. I would have had more modern gowns made for you, but I didn't know your size. The changeling we've had acting as your decoy in the tower the last two decades could only guess your frame so far."

"A changeling?"

"Yes, but don't worry. She's gone now and no longer wears your face, so we don't have to worry about that."

I was more worried that someone has been stuck in a tower all these years, but Mother speaks again before I can question her about it.

"I do hope something fits. We can't have you dressed like *that* to meet your fiancé. Oh! But for tonight, please don't feel you must get all dressed up after the long day you've had. It's better that you don't because the maid I've assigned to you won't be here until morning. After your bath, dress in whatever feels most comfortable. Like I said, tonight is just for family. A simple affair."

The ivory ballgown she wears says otherwise, but I'm comforted by her inability to lie. If nothing in the wardrobe fits, I'll have to wear one of my plain gray dresses from the convent.

Mother finally unlinks her arm from mine and faces me fully. She releases a slow sigh as she studies my face, her eyes glazing with tears. "You are so beautiful, Rosaline. I wish I could spend more time with you before you leave tomorrow. At least let me take a memory."

Before I can ask what she means, she steps back, lifts her hands, and forms a triangle with her fingers and thumbs.

She blinks.

Drops her hands.

"There. Now I can dream of you whenever I wish."

A shudder ripples through me, one of shock mingling with awe.

Mother's expression falls. "What's wrong, dear? Did you not want me to take a memory—oh! You might not know about my magic! That's how I—"

"I know it," I say, "because...because I do that too." I lift my hands to form my rectangular frame but find my arms trembling. All this time, I've known nothing about my magic. Everything I've learned has either been through instinct or accident. Little did I know, my mother does the very same thing I do.

"Oh, Rosaline," Mother says, voice choked with emotion. "This is the best thing I could have hoped for. You're a succubus like me!"

11

BRIONY

I stare at my mother in shocked silence for a long moment. "A succubus?"

Mother puts her hands to her heart and closes her eyes with a sigh. "I couldn't be prouder."

A ripple of revulsion moves through me, and I regret it at once. While I haven't heard the best things about succubi, I shouldn't be ashamed of being one—of being like my mother. If that's what I am. Which I don't entirely believe.

"I do have dream magic," I say, a note of trepidation in my voice, "which I don't yet fully understand, but I don't think I'm...a succubus."

Mother opens her eyes and her blissful expression drains. She blinks a few times, and I realize how plain I've made my distaste. The absence of her smile is like a splinter in my heart, sparking a desperate need to bring it back.

I force a grin to my lips. "It's just that I create dream-scapes. I don't...you know..."

Her countenance softens and she lets out a tittering

laugh. "Ah, I see what's making you apprehensive. I assure you, all that talk about seduction and arousal is highly exaggerated. It's far more impressive that we share dreams with our subjects, yet all anyone ever talks about is our erotic allure. Sure, succubi are beautiful, and it certainly doesn't hurt if my subject feels a...a tingle or two. But if they do, it's of their own accord. Even so, arousal only strengthens my magic, allowing me to keep my subject asleep for longer and with less effort, and makes the dreams more convincing. I don't rely on that aspect alone."

That provides some relief, but my pulse kicks up as I consider the implications if she's correct.

If I'm a succubus...

If I can do what my mother can...

"How many subjects have you framed?" she asks. "Do you have a favorite?"

I rouse myself from my growing panic. "I have a couple favorites. A meteor shower and a ballet—"

"Not scenes, my love. Individual subjects. People."

My anxiety quickens. "I've only ever framed one individual, and it felt wrong to dream of him."

Wrong.

Wrong.

The word rings through my mind, in sync with my pulse.

"It isn't wrong; it's your power. Any individual you frame becomes your subject to share a dream with later. You can do great things with this magic, darling. You can entice mates. Glean information. Or even just have a little fun. Have you struggled to keep your subject under?"

My stomach churns. "I don't know what you mean."

"Well, the strongest succubus can keep her subject from leaving the dream until she willingly ends it. However, some of the weaker succubi have struggled to keep their subjects under and find them rousing on their own, jolting awake and fleeing the dream in an instant." Her lips pull into a smug grin. "I've never had a subject leave a dream until I'm ready to awaken myself. That's how I've forced contenders to the throne to oversleep. I've had to slumber for entire days to ensure our rivals miss their appointments to contest the throne. Though, like I've said, I have resolved not to use my magic like that—"

"Mother," I cut in, my voice far sharper than I intend. My heart beats so hard that its frantic rhythm fills my ears. I force my question from my lips, half terrified of the answer. "You referred to *shared* dreams. Are you saying when a succubus dreams of her subject, he is having that same dream?"

"Oh, indeed!"

"And...are the subjects aware during these dreams? Do they remember them?"

Her expression turns thoughtful. "Every succubus is different. Weak succubi tend to share short, forgettable dreams with their subjects. Stronger succubi can alter the content of the dream, and that can influence whether the subject recalls it in the morning. Nightmares tend to give the subject more control to wake on their own and are harder to forget. Strange or curious dreams last longer and are easier to forget. Sexual dreams...well, those have the benefit of keeping a subject under for far longer, but they remember those."

Oh, this is bad. This is very bad indeed.

Heat crawls up my cheeks while an icy chill fills my blood. Vertigo seizes me, and I step back until the backs of my knees meet the plush mattress of my bed. I sink down on the edge of it, eyes unfocused.

"What's wrong, my love?" Mother crouches before me, but I can't meet her gaze. "You shouldn't worry, daughter. It doesn't matter if your subjects remember the dream or not, for it's merely a fantasy to them. Well, unless your subject knows you're a succubus, which is the unfortunate case with me and many of your father's rivals."

Stars, that only makes things worse.

The only solitary figure I've ever framed is Thorne Blackwood.

A man who's appeared in countless dreams, both intentional daytime imaginings and my uncontrollable nighttime ones.

It never occurred to me that they had anything to do with the real Mr. Blackwood. That he might be sharing the dreams with me. That he might be aware of them, able to recall them.

And he knows my family are mahrts. Dream fae. He knows my mother is a succubus.

Which means...

I squeeze my eyes shut as if that can lessen my panic. Breathing as deeply as I can, I seek any strand of logic that might aid me, that might banish my growing fears.

The first strand comes to me.

If my mother is right and I'm really a succubus, and if the real Mr. Blackwood is what she calls my *subject*, and if the dreams between us have been two-sided all along, and if Thorne just so happens to remember them *and* knows that I'm the cause...

Then wouldn't he have shown some sign of recognition when we met in the convent kitchen this morning? Wouldn't he be acting strangely around me?

The sight of him hidden behind his broadsheets comes to mind, but I try not to let that train of thought spiral out of control. Instead, I pore over what else my mother said, about every succubus being different. She said weak succubi create forgettable dreams while stronger ones can alter the content of them at will. While I can play around with daydreams, I have no control over what happens in my mind at night. Does that make me a weak succubus with forgettable dreams? Or no succubus at all?

Finally, I pry my eyelids open and meet my mother's worried gaze. Forcing as much calm to my voice as I can, I say, "You mentioned you've had to sleep for entire days to keep your subjects dreaming. Does that mean a succubus' power only works while she's sleeping?"

"Oh, yes. Falling asleep is the first step. After you've chosen a subject, that is. You must learn to dream lucidly during slumber, for that is how you forge a connection with your subject and enter their dream or draw them into yours."

"And there's no such thing as...let's say, a daydream succubus? Or one who draws subjects into dreams without trying to?"

She frowns. "I've never heard of a daydream succubus, and no, I don't believe I've ever heard of a subject entering a succubus' dream of their own accord."

I release a heavy sigh. Maybe I'm not a succubus after all. The children of fae don't always take after their parents. Some have been born with wildly different powers and physical characteristics. I have dream magic, but it could be a coincidence that Mother and I capture memories the same way.

"Why do you ask, lovey? Are you like this? Are you a daydream succubus?" There's a hungry gleam in her eyes, a chilling look that sends a shiver down my spine. It grows as she adds, "Can you paralyze a subject while you're awake?"

I shake my head and watch as her strange expression fades back to neutral. "I'm still learning about my magic, so I honestly don't know how it works, but I believe I only create dreamscapes. Are there any mahrts like that? Or ones who dream of a subject without sharing the dream with them?"

"Yes, I suppose," she says a bit absently, clearly disappointed in my refusal to accept that I might be a succubus. "Some mahrts create dreams only for themselves."

More relief courses through me. That sounds more in line with my magic. While dread continues to cloud my heart, at least I have the comfort of doubt now. The dreams I've had of Thorne might be nothing. My daydreams are clearly not the product of succubi magic, and my night dreams are devoid of control. Not to mention the fact that Thorne simply shows up. I don't forge a connection or summon his presence.

But still...

"Mother, is it possible to rid yourself of a subject so that you can't dream of them?"

"Oh, I never erase a memory. You never know when you'll need it. Every subject is an asset to you."

I lean forward and clasp her hands in mine. A mixture of fatigue and pleading strains my voice. "Please tell me how."

Her brows knit together as she studies my face. Then, with a resigned nod, she rises from her crouched position and sits next to me on the bed. Her voice turns somber, a tone I haven't heard her use. "While I'd prefer to teach you to strengthen your control rather than how to erase a memory, I must remind myself that you are a woman grown. You've had an entire life without me, with experiences and memories I know nothing about. You've had to sort out your magic all on your own, devoid of a proper teacher. So if there's a particular memory you're determined to relinquish, you can erase it."

I give her an encouraging nod, hardly daring to blink as I await her instruction.

She lifts her hands and forms her triangular frame, though she doesn't look through it. "You must frame your subject again, the same way you would if you were capturing a new memory, but this time you close the frame over your subject." Keeping her hands only as high as her chest, she demonstrates by sliding her fingers together until the triangular gesture disappears.

I feel as if an iron weight lifts from my shoulders, releasing my panic, my fears. "Thank you, Mother."

Her lips stretch wide and her giddy countenance returns. "Oh, I do love hearing you call me that! And don't worry, love, we have plenty of time for me to teach you more. There are a few techniques that might come in handy with your fiancé, should you need to secure his attachment..."

She prattles on, but I tune her out. I'm too busy feeling intense waves of relief. I may not be certain whether I'm a succubus or if my dreams of Thorne have gone both ways, but at least now I have a sense of control. A plan.

Tonight I'm going to erase Thorne Blackwood once and for all.

12

BRIONY

After my mother departs, I'm left to enjoy my beautiful new room in peaceful silence. I sit at the edge of my bed, the same position I've been in since Mother left. My party begins in an hour, which means I must enjoy this respite while I can. This is one of the rare occasions where boredom doesn't bother me. Perhaps it only ever has because I've been missing a mother who would talk my ear off. As charming as she is, she does make me appreciate silence. Is that how Thorne feels about me?

I shake thoughts of *him* from my mind, but not before reminding myself that his silences are sharp. This kind is soft. A much more enjoyable kind.

The only thing better than silence would be my phonograph, but the little foxes have only delivered my garment bag. I suppose the rest of my things will remain on the coach.

Since I'm leaving tomorrow.

To meet my fiancé.

The thought makes me want to punch my ruffled pillows and dive under the blankets to hide from tonight's festivities. My bones are weary, my mind and emotions even more so. It's no surprise considering the tumultuous revelations this day has brought. When I awoke this morning, I had an entirely different idea of how my day—and my life, for that matter—would go.

But no, I can't be selfish. Or perhaps it's selfishness that fortifies my legs and forces me to rise from the edge of my bed. As drained as I am, I *want* to meet my family. I want to see my father, my cousins, my uncles, my aunts—whatever extended family I have. I want to bask in their love. I want to hear how they've missed me. I want the validation that I was important to these people all along.

Selfish indeed.

But true.

I make my way over to a moonstone dressing table where I find a water-filled basin. Steam curls off the surface of the water and fills my senses with the aroma of jasmine. I dip my hands into the basin and splash the fragrant water over my face. The result is both soothing and invigorating. Once I've refreshed myself with my makeshift bath, I assess the contents of the wardrobe. Mother was right about stocking it with gowns in the fae style. While human fashions include layered skirts, corsets, and tight busts, fae clothing tends to be light, gauzy, and unrestrictive.

Growing up at the convent, my understanding of modern dress was limited to the fashion magazines some of the girls would sneak in. It wasn't until my trip to Lumenas that I saw stylish clothing firsthand. Since the city caters to humans and seelie fae, human fashions were most common, but I spotted many fae ensembles as well.

While I envied the latter then, seeing a wardrobe full

of sheer silks, crystal-speckled lace, and flowing chiffon has me feeling intimidated. None of the sensual dresses seem appropriate for meeting one's family for the first time.

With a sigh, I close the doors and retrieve my garment bag from the foot of my bed and prop it on my dressing table. One more night in my drab clothing won't hurt—

My mind goes empty as I open my bag.

A splash of color fills my vision where I expect to find only gray. I pull my head back, staring at the pink silk threaded with gold. Then, gingerly, I reach inside and extract the item. I anticipate something small—a kerchief, perhaps—considering my bag was already full when I finished packing. Yet the more I pull, the more that seems to be inside. First comes a low-cut bust lined with pale pink ruffles, followed by a bustled skirt decorated with silk roses. It's a ballgown, and one of the most beautiful I've ever seen. Once I have it fully out of my bag, I'm convinced it could only have been placed inside by an enchantment, for the gown is several times larger than my bag and has been stuffed with petticoats, a white-and-gold brocade corset, silk stockings, and a garter.

I turn the gown this way and that, then drape it over my bed. That's when I find the letter carefully pinned to the skirt.

My Dearest Miss Rose,

I've been working on this for you for months. Even when there was still a chance you'd leave us as a governess, I was determined to give this to you. I'll say to you now what I've been wanting to say to you for such a long time, for I know the secret yearning you hold in your heart.

You, Briony Rose, will dance.

All the best,

Sister Agatha

Tears prick my eyes. I can't believe Agatha made this for me. That she's been planning to give it to me for months. My only regret is that the dress is far too fancy to wear tonight. It's the kind one needs a lady's maid for. Still, the gesture along with Sister Agatha's kind words have a giddy sensation bubbling in my chest.

You, Briony Rose, will dance.

I note that she didn't refer to me as Rosaline Briar or Princess Rosaline, which I appreciate. To my teachers, I want to remain Briony Rose. Their student. The child they cared for. For twenty years, they and my peers were the closest thing to family I knew.

I cast one more wistful glance at the ballgown and return to my bag. Empty-handed, of course, for there's no way I'm getting that ruffled confection back inside. When I reach into it a second time, I discover yet another splash of color, pale blue. I shake my head in amusement as I withdraw yet another piece of clothing that had been magically forced inside my bag. It isn't nearly as large or ornate as the first, but it's still just as lovely—a chemise in a robin's egg-blue muslin. It's very much a human-style article with a lace-trimmed bust and bottom hem, but there's a sensual beauty to its low-cut neckline, the way the sleeves are meant to drape off the shoulders.

Something flutters to the ground, and I turn my gaze to the floor. There I find a folded piece of parchment. I set the chemise beside the ballgown on the bed and read my second letter.

My little sugar sprite,

Wherever you go and whatever adventures await, don't forget the value of a cozy night-gown. The secret is to call it a nightgown, not a chemise, yet wear it like the latter. That way, no matter how rough your day gets, you can always take comfort in knowing that beneath all your clothes, you're secretly wearing pajamas.

Sincerely yours,
Sister Spruce

I find myself laughing out loud, even as more tears prick my eyes. I'm only sorry the gift is yet another item I can't wear to the party. Not by itself, at least. I return to my bag, and this time I'm not the least bit surprised to find a third item that isn't gray. The color isn't as bright as the first two; it's mauve. As I pull it from my bag, I find a linen walking skirt. It's practical yet modern, with a fitted waist, a smooth front, and gathered pleats at the back. Beneath it is a simple white blouse, a black waistcoat, and a silk scarf. Marsh's letter is folded neatly just beneath the pile of clothing.

Miss Rose,

Since I am certain the other two will sneak something gaudy and impractical into your bag, I wanted to be the one to impart upon you the gift of sensibility. Whether you're a princess or a governess or something else that you choose to be, every modern lady needs a smart suit for daily wear. Yes, I too read the fashion magazines. I know the latest trends, whether I wear them or not. Don this ensemble for either professionalism, travel, or stylish comfort. Tie the black scarf around your neck in a bow, and you'll look like you jumped straight out of this week's fashion spread.

Forever your teacher (and from now on, I hope your friend too),

Sister Marsh

Marsh's letter has me tearing up even more so than its predecessors. Despite her stern demeanor, I've always known Marsh was hiding a soft interior, and this letter shows me a side of her I never got to see. As happy as I am to have been claimed by my parents, a pang of longing strikes my heart. I find myself yearning for Agatha's sweet enthusiasm, Spruce's comforting hugs, and Marsh's calm leadership. Furthermore, I regret how I spoke to them earlier today, blaming them for keeping secrets from me.

They know I didn't mean any of that, right?

My eyes fall on the new outfit draped in my arms, then on the chemise and ballgown strewn over my bed. A grin stretches my lips. Of course they know. They know what's in my heart.

A pang of longing remains as I dress—in Marsh's gift, of course—but I take comfort in the feeling. In the love of my three teachers. I carry it with me and don't let it go, not even after my hour of solitude ends and the two little foxes arrive to take me to the dinner party. I let that pang bloom and grow, let it bolster my courage with every step I take down the palace halls.

By the time I reach the ornate double doors that lead to the dining room, I'm a sweating mess. The realization that I'm seconds away from meeting an entire room filled with strangers-who-aren't-strangers makes my stomach roil with anxiety. How will they respond? Will they like me? Will I like them? I know it's folly to question such things when only a matter of heartbeats stands between me and the answer, but I can't stop my mind from spinning or my nerves from fraying.

My fox guides sit back on their haunches before lifting their upper bodies until their paws reach the silver door handles. The knobs turn, the doors open, and I'm met with music, laughter, and the heady scent of alcohol. I've only experienced the latter aroma once—in Lumenas when I snuck out to a burlesque show. It was held in a dark club that served fae wine, and I was sure to indulge. I recall the delightful buzz it filled my mind with, the warmth that flooded my belly. Ever since, I've considered myself thoroughly fond of wine and have been eager to drink it again.

A servant whirls toward me, startled by my arrival. She's in seelie form with white cat ears, slitted amber eyes, and long whiskers emerging from her cheeks. Her black hair is arranged in two braids that loop around her ears, each side pinned with a white ribbon. Her gown is black and trimmed in white ruffles. With her blocking my view of the room, I can't tell whether she's the only one who's noticed me, though the continued chatter tells me it might be the case. My gaze falls on the tray she's holding, one bearing flutes of some pale bubbly liquid.

"Princess Rosaline," she says, whiskers twitching as she sinks into a curtsy. "Would you care for a glass of Moondrop?"

"Please," I say and take a glass from her tray. I bring it to my lips and swallow a generous mouthful. The sweet and bubbly spirit tastes different from the wine I had in Lumenas, but it is delicious. Better yet, the calm heat it generates is twice as potent.

After another curtsy, the feline fae scurries away, giving me a full view of the dining room at last. It's an elegant space, dimly lit by a single chandelier comprised of a large orb surrounded by tiny, illuminated crystals. The way the light reflects upon the ceiling is reminiscent of the night sky. Dark velvet curtains are drawn shut over the tall windows that line one side of the room while the opposite side boasts gilded frames around portraits I can't quite see from this angle. I search the room for the source of music and discover an opalescent harp in one dark corner. Its strings vibrate, humming a gorgeous melody. At first, I think it must be enchanted to play itself, but then I note a shifting in the darkness, like shadow upon shadow. As my eyes further adjust to the dim room, I note semitransparent hands, a hint of a body. Is that one of my family members?

Finally, I let my gaze settle on the long table at the center of the room, around which nearly two dozen guests sit. I'm struck by an unexpected disappointment. Or perhaps it's shock. When Mother said I'd meet my family, I didn't expect there to be so few. Then I recall what she said about me being the only child born in decades. I suppose that would keep my circle of extended family rather narrow indeed. Then again, this might not be everyone. Mother did specify there would be only *close* family.

"May I present Princess Rosaline," says a baritone voice that nearly has me leaping out of my skin. I search for the source and find one of the foxes bowing on all four paws beside me. That's the first time I've heard either of the foxes say a word, and I certainly didn't expect such a deep tone from the cute creature.

Sounds of layered conversation cut off at once, and all eyes shift to me. A blonde head that I immediately recognize as my mother's pops up from the far end of the table. She lets out a cheery squeal as she rushes over to me and gathers my free hand in hers.

"Oh, my darling girl," she says. "Are you ready to meet your family?"

I swallow hard. I've been wanting to hear those words my entire life. My heartbeat slams against my ribs. I manage a smile, one I feel from the bottom of my heart, even through the rough edges of my nerves. I meet my mother's gaze and give her a nod. "I'm ready."

13

BRIONY

As Mother pulls me toward the dinner table, I down the rest of my drink in a single swallow. The feline servant scampers over and refills my glass while I walk. I'm impressed she doesn't spill a single drop. The guests rise from their seats and face me with awed expressions. I imagine the same awe graces my face as I look into the eyes of my family members.

I know all the Briars are mahrts, but since I only learned about dream fae today, I can't identify which kind of mahrt anyone is. Are most of them succubi? Incubi? I remember Thorne saying my father is an alp, but what other kinds of mahrts are there? My curiosity rises as I look from face to face. Most appear to be in seelie form, their visages human-like aside from their pointed ears. Then there's the shadowed figure, who has risen from the harp to approach the table. A few others have gnarled skin, elongated ears, and rather terrifying serrated teeth. All are dressed in fine dinner wear with dark suits and extravagant evening gowns, which makes me think I should have worn Agatha's ballgown after all. But no, I couldn't have donned that ensemble without aid.

"Rosaline," Mother says, fluttering her hand toward the table, "meet the Briars. Briar family, this is Princess Rosaline. She's a succubus like me!"

"Oh, I don't..." There's no use trying to refute her claim, for my words are drowned out by gasps of approval and the clinking of glasses. Sweat prickles behind my neck. While I'm thrilled to be so favorably welcomed to my family clan, I can't help but worry I might disappoint their expectations if they prove incorrect. I shift from foot to foot, a spike of anxiety burrowing in my heart—

"Rosaline." The voice has all others quieting in its wake. I turn to find a male figure standing next to my mother. He towers over her in height, but his frame is slender. He's one of the frightening-looking fae, his eyes beady and his nose bulbous. His skin is tinged with gray, his head bald and freckled. His ears are thrice as long as a regular fae's and are far more sharply angled, while his pointed teeth remain somewhat visible even when he closes his mouth. He's dressed in a suit of violet brocade, his bearing dignified. His lips pull wide while his brow remains furrowed. The result is a hesitant smile that somehow sets me at ease. "I've been waiting to meet you for a long time. I...I'm your father. Horus Briar."

"Oh." It's all I manage to say. While my relationship to my mother is clear in our similar features, I'm surprised my father looks so different. But as I've already surmised, fae don't always take after their parents. Realizing I'm being terribly rude, I sink into a curtsy. "I am honored to meet you, Majesty."

"No, none of that," he says, tone lighthearted. "If you

aren't ready to call me Father, please call me Horus instead. Though I do hope you'll perhaps one day call me Father. Or...Papa."

His eyes turn down at the corners, losing some of their hesitation. Then, with a sheepish grin and a blush that tinges his cheeks a deeper gray, he lifts his hand and pats the top of my head. The gesture is so awkward yet fatherly, I find myself warming to him at once.

I return his grin. "Very well, Papa."

His beady black eyes go wide, glossed with a sudden sheen. He puts a hand to his heart, his blush deepening further. "Oh, I do like that very much indeed."

Mother grasps my arm. "Will you call me Mommy, then?"

"Call me Auntie!" shouts one of the female fae at the table, and a couple others echo her sentiment.

"I don't mind being Unkie," says a male.

"I'm Cousin Kronald," says one of the fae who looks like my father.

"Call me Ralph," chimes a grumpy voice that I think came from a mustachioed fae with shadows for hair.

A series of birdlike clucks has my eyes darting to the middle of the table where a featherless rooster stands, pecking at a bowl of seeds.

Mother leans in and whispers over the voices still adding their preferred titles. "Oh, that's Uncle Bobbins. He's a lidérc and has quite a history of scathing dream-seductions. He got a bit murderous for a while, which was not at all good for our reputation, but we've reined him in. He's harmless in this form."

I haven't a clue what a lidérc is, but I'll take her word for it. And keep my distance from Uncle Bobbins.

"Come now," Mother says to the chattering table, "let us dine before the food gets cold."

Father offers me his arm with another sheepish smile. I don't know what it is about him, whether it's his scary appearance paired with his kind personality or something else, but I'm already feeling quite fond of the man. I place my hand at his elbow and he escorts me to the far end of the table. Once we reach the three vacant chairs, I expect Father to take the seat at the head. Instead, he pulls out the chair and nods for me to accept it.

"Shouldn't the king sit at the head?" I ask. This may be my first meal in royal company, unless I count my selkie friend from the bridal competition, but I know enough about etiquette to know that.

"No, daughter," he says, eyes crinkling at the corners. "It's your birthday. You are tonight's honored guest."

"Besides," Mother says, "this way everyone can better see your lovely face."

Heat flushes my cheeks, but I accept the chair. Mother and Father claim seats on opposite sides of me, and I take a moment to down yet another glass of wine. As if summoned by the empty bottom of my glass, the cat fae returns to refill it yet again. By now my head is swimming in a most pleasant way, aiding my efforts to keep my composure despite all the eyes staring at me with such adoration. Expectation. Awe.

I lower my gaze to the spread of serving trays boasting everything from fae fruit to steaming meats to fluffy bread. My mouth waters at the sight, and I'm painfully aware of how long it's been since I've eaten.

A female fae sitting beside my mother—and bearing a striking resemblance to her—leans in toward my end of the table and opens her mouth to speak. Before she can utter a sound, Mother holds up a hand. "Cecily, don't you dare bother her with a single question until she eats."

Cecily pouts but settles against her chair's backrest.

"That goes for all of you." Mother sweeps a glare across the table. My relatives chuckle in response. She shifts her gaze to me and gives me a subtle wink.

I smile back, moved that she must have realized how hungry I am. What a motherly thing to do.

"You heard the queen," Father says, an indulgent warmth in his tone. He reaches for the hand I have resting on the stem of my wineglass and gives it an affectionate pat. "Let us eat."

THE FOOD IS UNLIKE ANYTHING I'VE TASTED. THERE'S A richness to every dish that was absent at the convent. The bread drips with excessive butter, the fruit is stewed in herbed syrups, and the meats are smoked and tender. I hardly manage to sample a quarter of the different dishes before I'm bursting with fullness.

"Don't forget to leave room for cake," Mother whispers when she catches me clutching my stomach. It's taken all my restraint not to slump in my chair, though I did manage to loosen the top clasp of my skirt when no one was looking. Mother's mention of cake has my spine going rigid, and it isn't due to my desire for dessert; it's the reminder of Thorne. I haven't spared him a thought since I entered the dining room. Why would I with so much excitement around me, so many new faces, new names to learn?

Now that I'm reminded of him, my mind whirls back to its earlier panic. My debate over whether I'm a succubus. Whether my dreams of him were shared between us.

With a shudder, I take a generous swallow of wine. How many glasses have I had now? Three? I've yet to feel any ill effects, only pleasant ones, so I make no argument when the feline fae returns to refill my cup. While this is only my second time indulging in wine, it's a known fact that pure-blood fae are less sensitive to spirits, even those made from dangerous fae fruits. To humans, they can be hallucinogenic at best. Deadly at worst. Thank the All of All I'm fae and can enjoy glass after glass to my heart's content and feel only euphoria.

Mother speaks again. "Once everyone is finished, Mr. Blackwood will bring your cake. Oh, I've always wanted to bake you a birthday cake! If only the man had time to bake one large enough to make up for the twenty celebrations I've missed."

"I'm sure it will be more than adequate as is," I say.

"Oh, lovey," Mother says, puckering her lips and adopting a simpering tone. "You are the sweetest girl. I must write a thank-you letter to your teachers."

I'm glad she turns away before she can see my expression fall at her mention of my teachers. I never anticipated that I'd miss them so much. And it isn't just them. As I look down the table at my relatives who chat amiably, peppering me with questions now and then, I find myself wishing my friends were here. Dorothy. Lina. Little Tilly and the other younger girls. I know I couldn't have stayed at the convent. Even if my parents hadn't sent for me, I never would have chosen to remain. The life of a sister isn't for me. Yet a splinter of grief burrows deep in my chest, making me wish I hadn't spent so much time focused on getting out. Not when I could have simply appreciated more of what I had.

"This is the first time I've seen her smile on your birthday." My father's voice steals me from my thoughts. With a startled jump, I face him. His beady eyes twinkle as he gazes across the table at my mother. She's chatting with Cecily, who I've learned is her sister and my aunt.

"What do you mean?" I ask.

He turns his gaze to me, and there are notes of sorrow etched into his wrinkled, gnarled face. "Every year when your birthday came, she'd lock herself in her room and refuse to come out until morning. The next day, she'd be back to her usual self, but that day always stood out as a dark one, regardless of how much sunshine followed. Yours isn't the only birthday such a dark cloud fell upon. There's one other, and it remains a day of mourning for your mother."

I frown, feeling like I know the reason she grieves on another birthday. Yet no matter how I try to sift through my memory, the strand of thought doesn't come. "If you don't mind me asking, whose birthday—"

Father shakes his head. "I shouldn't have brought it up. It's too sad a tale for your birthday celebration. We'll save it for tomorrow."

"Don't I leave tomorrow?"

He releases a sigh that seems to carry no small amount of remorse. "Indeed, you do. However, I'll ensure we have plenty of time together in the morning."

I study Father's pained expression, weighing the density of that sigh. Does he have reservations about my hasty travels? Does he deem my marriage to Mr. Phillips as necessary as my mother does? Perhaps I can find an ally in him. A way to get out of this unwanted engagement.

"Papa," I say, and I'm not ashamed to admit I've infused my tone with a somewhat childish lilt. His eyes gloss over like they did the first time I called him that, and his expression looks akin to an adoring puppy. An ugly puppy, yes, but the kind that is so ugly it's cute. "Is it truly necessary for me to leave to meet my fiancé tomorrow?"

He sighs again, one that seems to pain him even more than the last. "I do wish it wasn't so, but I'm afraid it is. Your engagement has been in the works for years. It's been a challenge to keep Mr. Phillips content without allowing him to meet you in person. We couldn't reveal that we didn't know where you were, and we didn't dare let him meet your decoy instead. I'm not proud of the deceptive tactics we've used on your husband-to-be. While we certainly couldn't lie to him, we were able to convince him and his father that you've been sequestered at home this entire time. It wasn't until we located you that we led them to believe you were volunteering at a convent to prepare for your life of marriage and motherhood. After that, we were finally able to set a date for you to meet. A deadline we were dreadfully close to missing."

Disappointment weighs down my heart. Yet I can't give up that easily. "Is it truly so important that we meet this deadline? Could we not put it off a little longer?"

Father shifts in his seat. "Unfortunately, this is only the latest of the deadlines we've missed. The Phillipses are losing patience with us, and our declining reputation certainly doesn't help." He lowers his voice. "Furthermore, the crown is in debt. We must secure the financial award the Phillipses have promised. We have mere weeks before the collectors announce our debt both publicly and to the Alpha Council. If that happens, the Briars will lose everything. The throne, our status. *Everything.*"

I remember Mother saying something similar about needing money, but the way he puts it makes it sound far more serious. The Alpha Council is Faerwyvae's highest governing entity, comprised of every ruling monarch on the isle, and even if Father is a member of that very council, he is still beholden to its rules. I know from my studies that the council can force a monarch to step down if they run their throne into debt for too long. I assume a proclamation issued by a collector would denote *too long*.

He continues. "This marriage must take place before the Phillipses discover our financial situation. They cannot know we are so close to losing the throne, for our royal titles are what make the match admirable for the Phillips family. After missing so many previous deadlines to accommodate their demands in this alliance, they will not tolerate yet another. You must arrive at Sandalwood Manor in two days' time."

He doesn't elaborate on what might happen if I arrive late, and before I can ask, he speaks again.

"We *need* this alliance," he says, rubbing his brow. His shoulders sag as if weighed down with fatigue, his eyes going unfocused. "It isn't just about the debt. It's about our integrity. We can't keep ruling the way we always have. A seelie monarch cannot reign with fear the way the unseelie can, and we've never had a chance at Lunar's unseelie throne. Yet I've always known from the bottom of my heart that the mahrts deserved to be members of the ruling class. We are one of the few types of fae that reside exclusively in the Lunar Court. All the other clans we first stood against— wisps, moon dragons, kitsune—have other courts where they can belong. Dream fae belong in Lunar. This court is our pride. It pains me to think I could lose it all."

I'm surprised at how differently he speaks of his reign than my mother. Where Mother revealed fierce desperation in maintaining Father's throne, he shows a humble yet passionate reverence.

His gaze sharpens, and his eyes return to mine. "But I'm

willing to risk losing it if it makes me a better king. Which is why your mother will cease using her magic on contenders to the throne." He casts a brief glance at her, one that holds a mixture of love and long-suffering amusement. His lips pull into a wry grin. "I never wanted your mother to use her magic the way she does, but she's a stubborn creature. Luxury and status are things she's always strived for, even before we became mates. Her determination is formidable and she's unafraid of doing what it takes to get what she wants. For a long time, I was the same."

"But...you aren't anymore?"

He shakes his head, and there's something like guilt in his beady eyes. "I must admit, our family has its origins in activities that are similar to what humans nowadays call organized crime."

I try not to pale at that. Still, it's hard to imagine my gentle father and giddy mother as crime bosses.

"Before unification," he says, "our activities were respected by the fae, but things are different now. Where cunning, cruelty, and strength were the currency for respect back then, marriage, status, and propriety are today. We can't keep playing an old game and expect to win. We must form respectable alliances, act with fairness, and extend our reach as far as we can. You are our singular chance to do exactly that."

"Me," I say.

"Yes, you. Our daughter. Our princess."

Our pawn, some snide part of me remarks, but I keep that in my head.

"Did your mother tell you about our bargain?" he asks.

I tilt my head. "What bargain?"

"She has promised to cease using her magic on my rivals after your wedding to Mr. Phillips. After that..." He lifts his chin, inhaling a slow breath. "After that, I will fully rely on my own might to prove my worth as king. No more tricks. No more hiding. I've let paranoia make me a poor king to the humans and seelie fae, especially those in the north. Fearing my enemies has kept me too close to home, too trapped in the south. As a result, I've lost the respect of many of my people. If I can't win it back...well, then I suppose I don't deserve to be king. It's time I face that head-on, don't you think?"

Again, I'm struck by his humility. His honesty. His care. Perhaps he and my mother haven't protected his reign in the best way possible, especially for a seelie monarch, but I do believe he has the potential to be a better king.

"Besides," he says, and his kind grin returns, washing away the fatigue that had darkened his expression, "your marriage ensures that we retain a high place in society even if my reign ends. I know this must be a shock for you, and you might even resent us for the engagement, but I do hope you know how greatly we appreciate your role in this family. No, not just that. You, Rosaline. We appreciate *you*. We've loved you for so long."

I wince at the sound of my real name. It still feels... wrong. But what feels far more right is the satisfaction that surges inside me at hearing I'm appreciated. Loved. It buries my spears of irritation and my annoyance at being engaged to a stranger. It blooms in my chest in a way that feels far warmer than the effects of the fae wine.

Father reaches across the table and covers my hand with his. Holding my eyes, he says, "Can we count on you, daughter? Can you make this sacrifice for your family? Can you save the Briars?"

My lungs grow tight, and part of me wants to pull my hand away and run. But that's just fear, isn't it? I don't want to marry a stranger. Stars, I could never be all right with that. And I don't want to leave the family I just met. But they *are* my family. The one thing I've wanted all my life. They're depending on me. Something lies beneath that, a different kind of fear from the one that made me want to run. It creeps around my heart, whispering what I might lose if I refuse this engagement: I could lose *them*. If I rebel against this marriage, my family loses the alliance with the Phillipses. They lose their chance at improving their reputation with such a promising marriage. Worse, they could go bankrupt and lose the throne. They'll be left with nothing.

No, not *they*.

We.

I'm part of this family. If they fall, I fall. While I don't care much about being a princess, I retain the same material yearnings I always have—for ballrooms, fine dresses, and a place in society. If I lose my family, I lose all of that too. That, of course, pales in comparison to losing my family. If I become the cause of their downfall, lose them I will.

I could never live with that.

And now I realize there is something worse than marrying a stranger.

I swallow the dryness in my throat, so sharp it feels like knives. "I'll do what needs to be done."

The warm smile that spreads over his face is an instant reward, glossing over the tightness in my lungs, my throat. "You truly are a Briar."

The words thud against my heart. I'm a Briar. If I do this, I'm one of them.

"If only we could leave with you tomorrow," he says. "Your mother begged me to at least allow her to accompany you, but I don't trust her not to draw attention to herself. That's just how she is. She's too bright not to shine. And that, in turn, would draw attention to you. It's essential we keep your location a secret until you're safely with your fiancé. Even better if we can manage until your wedding day."

"Which will be when?" I ask, bringing my glass of wine to my lips.

He frowns, as if surprised I don't know the answer. "Two weeks from today."

I freeze, and I'm lucky I don't choke on my mouthful of wine. I blink at him a few times, then swallow my hearty sip. "Two weeks? I'm getting married in *two weeks*?"

Father stammers before speaking. "I...I told you we have merely weeks before the collectors announce our debt. The Phillipses will not release the promised funds until your marriage is final."

"Horus!" comes Mother's voice, tone edged with scolding. "You weren't supposed to tell her yet."

He shrinks down while I slowly turn toward my mother. "You were going to keep this from me?"

Her expression sinks with apology. She clasps my hand in hers. "Lovey, I was going to wait until tomorrow. This is your special day! I didn't want worries to cloud your thoughts."

My ire softens the slightest bit, but my lungs have grown tight yet again. My body moves before I can stop myself, legs straightening as I rise from my seat. The backs of my knees hit the cushion of my chair, forcing it back with a screech. My relatives take notice and cease talking to look at me. Smiles remain frozen on their faces, though their expressions have turned curious.

"Are you giving a speech?" asks a fae with a weathered face and slitted pupils. An uncle by the name of Joseph, I've learned. "You'll have to speak up, I'm hard of hearing."

I point toward the double doors. "I'm going for air."

"We haven't had cake yet," Mother says, batting her lashes.

"I'll be back in—"

"Then I'll come with you." Mother rises from her seat and reaches for my hand.

I take a step back, sending my chair screeching again. "No, I just need a moment alone." A moment to breathe. A moment to reconcile where my life is going. To assess the weight of my new position, my new responsibilities.

Mother reaches for my hand again, but Father's voice has her freezing in place. "Divina," he says, voice soft yet stern. "Give her some space."

Mother's face falls, and I ignore the way my heart plummets in tandem. Instead, I cast a grateful look at my father and rush toward the other end of the room. Realizing my wineglass is still in hand, I quickly drain it. As I reach the closed doors of the dining hall, the foxes push them open. Just then, the feline fae arrives like clockwork to refill my glass. This time, I find her presence grating. With a grin, she lifts her bottle from the tray and angles it toward my glass. Before she can fill it with a single drop, I wrench the entire bottle from her hand and march the rest of the way out of the room.

14

THORNE

I f only I had it in me to make a cake better suited to someone I consider my enemy. Something dry and hideous would suffice for tonight's purposes, for it's not like anyone will get a chance to eat it. Still, as a baker's son, I've inherited a lifetime of passion and pride in the craft, therefore I find it impossible to give anything less than my all when it comes to dessert. Besides, nothing calms the mind quite like the smell of vanilla buttercream. And I'll need to be calm, my conscience unfettered by doubt, to do what must be done.

Keeping my breathing steady so as not to disrupt the careful motions of my hands, I apply pressure to the cotton piping bag and dispense the perfect amount of lavender-colored buttercream to create an arched shell. I release the pressure, then start again. Again. Soon I've completed my circular border on the cake's top tier. I step back and assess my progress. My pride bristles at the cake's simplicity, but it's the best I could do with the time allotted. Two tiers, three layers each of vanilla sponge and apricot mousse, piped in a gaudy array of pink, teal, and lavender. I had no say in the colors, clearly. While the piping is neat and complex, I'd normally do far more intricate work. It's what Blackwood Bakery's celebratory cakes are famous for. Well, that and the taste.

But this will have to do. If I take too much longer, I just might lose my nerve.

I nudge the bridge of my spectacles, ensuring they're in place, and return to piping, this time with the pink frosting and the round tip. All that remains are the final details on the top tier. Then it's time to do what I came here for.

A shard of guilt spears my chest, but I breathe it away, focusing on the calming aroma of vanilla. Sugar. The feel of the piping bag in my hands. I'm grateful for the solitude, for the fact that the Briars were purposefully short-staffed and only halfheartedly offered the services of an assistant. Lucky for all of us, I work best alone. And while I prefer the comfort of my own kitchen—or any of the kitchens at the many bakery locations I'm in charge of—Nocturnus Palace's accommodations are more than suitable. The worktable is an enormous slab of black granite, large enough for several cooks and bakers to work at once. Since dinner is currently underway and all dishes have been served, I haven't had to share the space for almost an hour.

Which means peace for me. Silence. A perfectly calm and quiet—

"Oh!" The female voice has me nearly jumping out of my skin. Thank the All of All my reflexes are used to disruptions during my work, and I manage not to completely mangle my loop of frosting.

Gritting my teeth, I glance toward the kitchen door where Briony Rose has stumbled in. I say *stumbled* because she clutches the doorframe with one hand and a bottle of Moondrop wine in the other. She's dressed in a mauve skirt and black silk waistcoat. It's the first time I've ever seen her in anything but gray. Unless I count the time she was naked.

My heart kicks up a little at that. Seeing how she leans against the doorframe, hair slightly mussed, eyelids heavy, reminds me too much of a very specific dream we shared. One where she appeared out of nowhere, planting herself in one of my mundane dreams of my kitchen—yes, I dream about my kitchen often, and no I don't think that's strange— without a stitch of clothing. I noticed her first, startled to find her well underway in the act of pleasuring herself, then she noticed me. Then we both noticed I was equally as naked and...had developed a rather visible bodily reaction—

I intake a sharp breath, forcing my mind back to the present. To the fully clothed Miss Rose and the version of me who feels no desire for the girl interrupting my cake decorating. She straightens, blushing furiously, either from her overconsumption of drink, embarrassment, or...because she too has been reminded of that dream.

Clearing my throat, I focus my attention on piping the next loop of frosting. "Shouldn't you be at your party, Highness?"

She wags a finger at me. "I already told you once. You may call me Briony or Miss Rose."

I rephrase my question. "Shouldn't you be at your party, Miss Rose?"

"I'm getting some air." She pushes off from the door frame and squares her stance. She wavers in place, despite her obvious efforts to do otherwise.

"I didn't realize Moondrop had such high oxygen content."

She scoffs, but I'm almost certain there's a laugh tangled in it. "I'm overwhelmed, all right? You would be too if you were in my place."

"If I was in your place, I'd leave the baker to his business."

"You're such a sour bastard. Can you at least pretend to be as nice as you are in my dreams—" Her eyes go wide and her free hand flies to her mouth.

I know I should act surprised. She doesn't yet know that *I* know the truth of our dreams.

Before I can respond, she whirls abruptly around and starts to march out the door. But instead of exiting *through* the door, she collides with the doorframe. She emits a startled grunt, and her momentum propels her backward, forcing her to stumble over her feet—

I don't recall telling my body to move, but one moment I'm piping the cake, and the next I've discarded my tools and find myself behind her, my hands framing her shoulders as her back slams against my chest. She stiffens against me, frozen for a long moment. And a strange moment too, for it forces me to ponder why I'm here, why I did this, why I kept an enemy from falling on her ass when I could have let the drunk little idiot take a spill.

As if coming to her senses, she leaps forward and faces me on unsteady legs. Her cheeks blaze a fiery pink, lips pursed with indignation. "No."

I pull my head back but smother my confusion in an icy mask of indifference. "The phrase you're looking for is *thank you*."

"No. Just...no. I'm not clumsy."

"I never said you were."

"I'm not the type to fall or need rescuing from a big strong man." She rolls her eyes as she says the last part.

I huff a cold laugh. "Oh, you're not *that kind of girl,* is that what you're saying? Should I have let you fall then? Would you be happier with a bruised tailbone?"

"My...tailbone is none of your business."

"Then don't make it mine by stumbling into my work-place." I reach for the bottle of wine and wrest it from her uncoordinated grip. "Go enjoy your party, Princess."

I stride back to the table and set down the near-empty bottle of Moondrop with more force than necessary.

"You cold son-of-a-harpy." Briony charges after me, but her disequilibrium has her veering into the edge of the worktable. This time, I don't bother coming to her aid, and she's forced to catch herself on the edge of the counter. I take up my piping bag and try my best to pretend she isn't there, glaring at the table like it's at fault for her stumble. "What the glittering hell is in that wine?"

"It's Moondrop," I say. Apparently, my determination to ignore her lasts no more than three seconds. I resume piping my loops. "This is what it does. It's a particular variety of fae wine that tackles your motor functions first, then your emotions."

"But...but my mind feels clear."

"Your mind will soon fall beneath its effects as well."

"But I'm fae. I thought fae weren't as sensitive to..." She falls into silence. I'm about to thank the All of All she's finally gotten the good sense to leave me alone when I hear a quiet sniffle. Then another.

Gritting my teeth, I cast her a glance. My irritation wanes as I find her turned away from me, shoulders heaving. Here come the emotional effects of Moondrop. I know the repercussions of the wine very well because her dear fiancé, Monty Phillips, is overly fond of the drink, much to his downfall. I try to simply continue with my task, but my hands begin to shake. They *never* shake when I work.

Setting down the piping bag, I cross my arms and address the back of her head. "What's wrong?"

Her voice comes out strained. Soft. "I'm drunk, aren't I? I...I'm making a fool of myself. I thought I could drink as much as I wanted because I'm full fae, but...that was a foolish assumption. Hell, I...I feel like my lungs are going to explode. Like my heart is about to race right out of my chest." She slowly turns to face me, her moves careful and revealing only the slightest unsteadiness. Her cheeks are coated in a sheen of moisture, the whites around her blue irises tinged red. "Are those effects of Moondrop as well?"

What she's described sounds more like anxiety, but I keep that to myself. Instead, I release a grumbling sigh and make my way to the pantry. I familiarized myself with the layout of the kitchen and the ingredients I had at my disposal when I first arrived, so it doesn't take long for me to locate everything I need. A glass. Two teaspoons of Starcane sugar. One tablespoon of crushed bitterglass leaf. Two basil leaves. A sprig of rosemary. Lemon peel. Water.

I mash the dry ingredients together in a mortar and pestle, extract the larger pieces of herbs that remain, and pour the resulting flavored sugar into the water. Briony has stopped crying and watches me with a furrowed brow as I stir the beverage with a spoon. An aroma both sweet and pungent fills the room, overriding the vanilla scent of the cake.

"What...isssthat?" she asks, her words slow and slightly slurred. It's a sure sign the mental effects of Moondrop are starting to catch up to her.

I remove the spoon from the glass and push it across the counter toward her. "Drink this and it will counter the effects of Moondrop. You'll feel normal in about ten minutes, though you'll feel worse before you feel better."

She frowns down at the glass before picking it up and downing a swallow. Heaving a cough, she sets the cup back down. "Disgusting! What is that?"

"Bitterglass leaf. The faster you drink it, the better it will work. Don't taste it. Just drink."

"How do I know you aren't trying to kill me?" she mutters, yet she doesn't wait for a reply. Instead, she takes up that glass and downs the contents. Once empty, she releases a groan and folds her arms over the table, burying her face in them. "I think I'm going to be sick," comes her muffled voice.

"I told you. You'll feel worse before you feel better."

She stays like that for a few minutes, and I return to piping. If she wasn't half standing, I'd think perhaps she'd fallen asleep. After a while, she lifts her head. As expected, she looks even more inebriated than she did before. She blinks at me, her motions slow and sloppy. Her words are even more so. "Why are you...being...nice to me?"

I say nothing because I'm not. Letting the effects of Moondrop continue along their natural course would have been a mercy for us both, as would forcing her to forget what will happen by the end of the night, but we don't deserve mercy. We're enemies and this is a matter of revenge. Vengeance is merciless on both sides, which makes it fair. Making it easier to execute by allowing Miss Rose to amble haphazardly through it would only cheapen its justice.

She leans on her elbows, posture slumped as she watches me switch back to the purple buttercream with the star tip for the final border. We stay like that for a while. I'm nearly finished with the final arched shell when she speaks again.

"It's hard to forget you aren't really my friend sometimes." Her voice is less slurred, which means the bitterglass drink is starting to reverse the Moondrop's effects. Yet now we're back to the territory of emotional rawness. Either she'll start crying again...or speak too honestly. I think I know which direction she's already begun to take.

"Why are dreams like that?" she says with a wistful sigh. "Why do they fabricate emotions with the same ease that they conjure images and memories? It's a bit cruel."

"It is," I say.

With her elbows still propped on the countertop, she frames her cheeks in her hands. The result is a squishing of her cheeks that is both amusing and adorable—

No.

I shake the notion from my mind and force my eyes back to the cake. I turn it slowly, seeking any final corrections I need to make to my work.

"I'm going to erase you, Mr. Blackwood," she says, voice strained by the puckering of her lips, courtesy of her still-squished cheeks. "I'll never dream of you again after that, and I hate that it makes me sad. Thank you for being my dance partner. Now that I get to dance with real fellows, I wonder if you'll still be the handsomest man I've met."

My chest tightens at her words. At her unfiltered honesty.

"I won't," I say because I too can deliver honesty. "By the end of the night, I daresay you'll find me rather hideous."

She lifts her face from her hands, and her lips stretch into one of the brightest smiles I've seen her wear. "Impossible."

My pulse quickens as the warmth of that grin washes

over me. Stones, she's cute when she's drunk. And I can't even deny it this time.

I hold her gaze and let myself look at her as Briony Rose, the girl from my dreams, one last time. After this, we'll change and it will be impossible to go back. After this, we'll enter the dining room and she'll be Princess Rosaline Briar, the girl I was bred to hurt. And I'll shed the quiet safety that comes with being Thorne Blackwood, son of Edwyn Blackwood, inheritor of Blackwood Estate and Bakery, and one of the most respected gentlemen in Faerwyvae.

And I'll don my secret name, the identity I was born with.

Vintarys Lemuria, son of Morgana, last member of the banshee clan, and enemy of the Briars.

With a slow exhale, I harden my heart and remember who I am. What I was named for. The task I was born to do.

"Come," I say to Briony with stoic calm, my face devoid of emotion. "Let us return to your family. It's time for your cake."

15

BRIONY

Every step that draws me closer to the dining room brings a painful new level of sobriety. Almost as painful is my awareness of Thorne. He walks behind me, pushing my cake on a rolling cart. I offered to fetch a servant to do such a trivial task, but he insisted on delivering my cake himself and seeing that I return safely to the dining room. I'm glad he's chosen to trail behind and not walk beside me, for if he could see my face, he'd catch the color rising in my cheeks. I said some idiotic things to him just now, things I wish I could take back.

Thank you for being my dance partner.

I wonder if you'll still be the handsomest man I've met.

I slap a hand to my forehead, wishing I could beat the memory right out of my mind. "Stupid, stupid, stupid," I mutter before I recall that Thorne has a front-row seat to my every move right now. With a grimace, I cast a look over my shoulder, expecting to find the man smirking at me. Instead, his eyes are unfocused, expression hard. His forearms are taut, visible beneath his rolled-up shirtsleeves as he pushes the cart with a strange intensity. A stack of porcelain dessert plates softly rattles next to the cake and the sharp knife that rests at its base.

I return my gaze forward, confused over his shift in mood. He was almost kind in the kitchen. While I'd rather not remember how he caught me from my embarrassing fall, I'm grateful for the sobering tonic he made me. That, of course, brings to mind the way I cried and the idiotic things I said to him.

I shake my head and force the memories away. Unless Thorne brings it up or has the nerve to tease me about it, I'll pretend it didn't happen.

We come to the end of the hall where it intersects with another, and I glance down both directions. When I first left the dining room, I simply wanted to walk, to breathe, to give myself a moment alone, away from my family and their hopes and the sickening pressure of my too-soon marriage. The bottle of Moondrop helped distract me, but it also kept me from paying attention to where I was going. I remember turning a corner and then finding the kitchen at the end of that corridor, but which way did I turn?

The sound of the cart approaches and Thorne stops at my side. "Are you not ready to go back?" Though the question suggests some level of concern, his tone is cold and reserved.

"No," I say, echoing his formality, "I simply don't remember which direction the dining room is.

He points to the left. "Go on ahead. I'll enter in a few minutes."

I frown in confusion, but he doesn't meet my eyes. Instead, his gaze is fixated in the direction he indicated, his jaw set, his shoulders thrown back with quiet confidence.

"You could...come with me," I say.

"It would be improper for us to be seen entering the dining hall together."

I suppose he's right. A pinch of disappointment strikes my chest. For someone so annoying, I'm alarmed at how I continue to seek comfort in his presence.

It's the dreams, I remind myself. *The real him is no friend to me.*

Without another word, I turn down the hall. Sounds of music, conversation, and laughter meet my ears, telling me I am indeed going the right way. I catch sight of the correct pair of double doors, one still left ajar from when I fled, and am halfway to them when I hear Thorne utter my name.

"Miss Rose."

I halt and face him. He remains at the intersection where I left him, his expression as impassive as ever. I tilt my head in question.

Holding my gaze, he utters an emotionless, "You're welcome."

Heat flushes my cheeks, but I don't know what he's referring to. I don't get the sense that he's taunting me.

Then my own words echo through my mind.

Thank you for being my dance partner.

Glittering hell, I don't want to consider what this exchange means. I force a grin that probably looks as awkward as it feels and whirl away. At least now I'm one hundred percent grateful to return to the dining room.

Raised glasses and verbal cheers greet me as I approach the table. Either it's my sudden sobriety or the dinner party has grown more raucous in my absence. The scent of alcohol has intensified, as have the emotions in the guests. I pass two of my uncles who are locked in a heated debate over the rise of automobiles and whether they'll soon replace horse-drawn transportation. The next guest is one of my aunts, who sobs while downing a bowl of stew. Another aunt stands on her chair, swaying out of sync with the music. I notice then that the shadowed fae in the corner has switched from calm harp to jubilant piano.

I assess his writhing form as he taps the keys with impossible speed and grace. Mother explained earlier that he's a shadow mahrt and a cousin of mine named Remus. He doesn't consume any sort of physical matter for sustenance and only shifts out of his dark and misty unseelie form into his humanoid one when startled. While he seems sinister in the way he can enter through keyholes and cracks under doors, Mother explained he's a rather helpful creature. He seeks out nightmares, but he doesn't create them. Instead, he eats the ones he finds, which in turn leaves his subjects unburdened by frightening memories.

He catches me looking his way and offers me a friendly nod. I return it and am almost to my seat when Mother leaps from hers and crushes me in a hug. "My deeeeaaarest," she says, eyelids heavy. "I'm so sorry I made you sad. Are you upset? Are you feeling better now?"

She frees me from the hug and I smile down at her. "I'm all right."

"Good, good," Father says. He too has left his seat and stands beside me and Mother. "I...I never want you to feel burdened by your family."

My chest squeezes, but this time it isn't from panic. This time it's from warmth. From their love. They know this is new for me. They know it's a shocking adjustment. And they care. They need me, and they love me so much. Isn't that what I've always craved?

"Family isn't a burden," I say. "Meeting you, coming here, discovering I'm a Briar...it's a gift. Truly."

Father's lips stretch into another one of his bashful smiles, and he pats me on the shoulder. "Good, good," he says again.

"Oh look!" Mother points toward the doorway where Mr. Blackwood enters with his rolling cart. "It's time for cake."

My pulse jumps as I recall the exchange Thorne and I had in the hall.

You're welcome.

I lift my chin and remind myself that among my family, I am a princess. I have no reason to get worked up over *him*.

Thorne approaches the table, that intense expression still on his face.

Mother flutters a hand at him. "Just leave it, Mr. Blackwood. I'll have a servant cut the cake." She snaps her fingers, and one of the servants—of which there are only three currently in attendance—starts forward from his place by the wall.

A smile that doesn't reach Thorne's eyes forms upon his lips. "If you don't mind, Majesty, it would be an honor to serve your party."

Mother sniffs and returns to her chair, waving at the servant to return to his post. "Very well."

My father and I take our seats.

"Shall I serve the princess first?" Thorne asks, not bothering to look at me.

"No," I say, "please serve the others first." Why he wants to serve us at all is beyond me. Wouldn't he rather pass off his burden so he can be alone in a room reading his papers? Perhaps he's overprotective when it comes to his cakes. He is famous for them, and now that I'm sober, I can appreciate just how lovely it is.

Thorne pauses at the other end of the table and picks up the knife. With slow, deft movements, he makes a cut in the top tier, then another. Using the same knife, he lifts the portion from its base and plates it. Wouldn't a cake knife be more practical? My teachers always had an angled, shovel-shaped tool dedicated to serving birthday cakes. Surely the palace kitchen had one of those.

He hands over the first plate, then the next. Some of my relatives are more polite than others, accepting their plate with grateful grins, while others hardly spare him a glance. He may not be nobility, but he's a highly respected member of society. I'd expect more fawning over him, considering my family seeks to improve their reputation and gain more favor with the humans.

As he moves further down the table and I watch him cut piece after piece, my mind drifts back to this morning, to the first cake I was gifted. My eyes glaze over as I recall the tiny kitchen filled with laughter, the smiling children, my kind friends. Stars, I miss them, and it hasn't even been a whole day. I let my thoughts wander to the three gifted outfits I discovered in my bag—the ballgown, the nightdress, and the practical ensemble I wear now. My heart floods with warmth.

The sound of the rolling cart rouses me from my musings. Thorne has served over half the table now and has made his way toward my end. The top tier of the cake is gone, as is a quarter of the bottom. As swiftly and expertly as before, he slices the cake with his knife and hands a piece to a cousin whose name I forgot. Then serves a slice to Cousin Bergstrom, who has long black fluffy ears like a dog. Finally, he makes his way to Aunt Cecily, then Mother. He delivers the latter with a short bow and does the same for my father. Now it's my turn.

He wheels the cart directly beside my chair, lifts the knife, and plates the final piece of cake. "Princess Rosaline," he says, handing me the dish.

If we were alone, I'd remind him not to call me that, but this isn't the time or place. I imagine my parents' hurt should I confess I don't fully feel comfortable with my given name yet.

As I accept the plate, my fingertips briefly brush his. I try to stifle my sharp intake of breath, and he meets my eyes for the briefest moment. There's something like surprise or hesitation in his eyes. Then that moment is gone and he pulls away. Turning that false smile I spotted earlier to my father, he says, "May I have the honor of saying a few words?"

Father shifts in his seat, expression wary.

Mother speaks before he can. "We don't sing the birthday song, Mr. Blackwood, so I do hope you scrub that notion from your mind." Then leaning in toward me, she says, "I hope you don't mind, lovey. We discarded that human tradition long ago."

I'm about to tell her I haven't a clue what the birthday song is, but something nags at the back of my mind. I feel like I may have heard about the tradition recently. Why can't I remember?

"Very well, Mr. Blackwood," Father says with a nod. "We appreciate how you've aided our daughter's return. You may say a few words if you desire."

Thorne gives Father a gracious bow, then positions himself beside my chair, between me and Father. I can't bring myself to look at him, but from the corner of my eye, I see him place his hand on my chair's backrest. More than that, I can feel his presence. His nearness. A shudder runs down my spine and my breaths grow shallow.

"I don't know much about Princess Rosaline," he says, his deep voice carrying through the now-silent dining hall. Even Cousin Remus has gone quiet, his piano keys still. Thorne's voice shifts slightly, taking on the sensual lilt I've heard a few times now. "But I do know one thing. She loves to dance."

My heart leaps into my throat. I whirl around in my seat to face him.

"Princess," he says, his voice a chilling caress, "it's time to remember the dance we had this morning."

"Mr. Blackwood!" Mother exclaims. "What are you on about?"

Father rises from his seat, clawed fingers curled into fists. His lips peel back from his serrated teeth. "Step away from my daughter's chair."

Thorne does as told, holding up his hands and taking two steps back. He holds my father's gaze without wavering, and his grin has turned smug. Knowing. Calculating.

All I can do is stare.

And remember.

The sight of Thorne Blackwood cutting in on my daydream dance.

Curling horns protruding from the sides of his head.

An expanse of leathery wings behind him.

But his strange appearance isn't what stands out in the memories that bloom in my mind, vibrant in hue, crisp in sound. It's his words.

Do you believe in fate, Briony Rose?

I'm starting to suspect curses are a lot like fate.

Tremors rack my body as everything returns to me, including the last words he said to me.

Forget we had this dance.

My heart hammers in my ears, in my chest, as nausea writhes in my gut. I half tumble out of my chair, catching myself on the cake cart. Mother stands beside me, a protective hand on my arm, but I can tell she too is trembling.

Slowly, Thorne shifts his gaze from my father to me. A corner of his lips curls into a cold, cruel smirk. "Briony, dear," he says, "pick up the knife."

My eyes slide down to the cart before me. The knife, now clean of cake, rests just inches from where I brace myself. Some mindless urge forces my fingers to flinch. Then, against every ounce of my will, my hand closes around the knife handle.

My mother releases my arm and leaps back. "Wh—what are you doing, Rosaline?"

Terror splinters my heart as I stare down at the blade, at my hand acting of its own volition.

"Rosaline." Father's voice is strangled. I force my eyes away from the knife to find his face stricken with pain. Betrayal. Fear.

Those emotions aren't directed at Thorne.

They're directed at me.

At the knife in my hand.

"Hold the knife to your father's throat," Thorne says.

My legs obey, closing the distance between me and my father. I try to fight the motion of my arms, but in a flash, my hand flicks up and the blade kisses the gray flesh of Father's throat. I blink, unable to believe what I'm seeing. What I'm doing.

Thorne utters another demand. "Keep the knife there until I say otherwise."

"Daughter," Father says, "why are you doing this?"

A desperate sob escapes my throat. "It...it's not me. I don't want this! I'm not doing this!"

"Stop!" Thorne's shout makes me jump, and I hear a startled squeal leave my mother's lips. I don't know who he was talking to but sounds of shuffling movement cease. "If anyone takes a single step closer, she'll slice his throat, and she'll slice deep." To Father, he says, "Order your servants out of the dining room."

"Leave," Father barks, and I catch sight of the three servants scurrying out the doors. Then to the room at large, he says, "Stand down. She can't kill me. The blade isn't iron. If it were, I'd feel it against my skin."

My eyes move to my hand, to the way my thumb presses against the side of the blade, where the base meets the handle. If the blade were iron, it would be burning me right now. Father's right; as a pureblood fae, an iron-free knife is hardly a threat.

"It may not be iron," Thorne says, "but if she cuts the right artery enough times, you can still bleed out before your fae healing kicks in. The knife is sharp enough to cut bone. She could sever your head from your neck, should I demand it. Will you fight your own daughter? If you struggle against her, I'll have her cut her own throat instead. I assure you, she's just as much of a victim in this as you are."

Stars above, there goes my only thread of comfort. Tears stream down my cheeks as I try with all my might to pull away, but it's no use.

Father must see the effort in my eyes, for his shoulders relax the slightest bit. Taking on a diplomatic tone, he says, "What do you want, Mr. Blackwood? Is it money you're after? Did you trick her into giving you the power of her true name? That practice has been outlawed in every court. If you manage to leave this room alive, you'll be severely punished no matter where you try to hide."

"No such tricks were necessary," Thorne says. "And I have no need for your royal funds, for I'm quite a wealthy man as it is. Though I suppose I should introduce myself."

I expect him to speak again, but all I hear are gasps and frantic whispers. I can't bear to take my eyes off the place where the knife meets my father's throat, too afraid that if I do, the blade will sink into his skin. Not that I have control either way.

"The dragon," someone whispers from the table.

"It's him! Morgana's husband!" says another.

"No, not her husband. He's...he's..."

With bated breath, I manage to drag my gaze from the knife to Thorne. There he stands looking much like he did this morning during the dance I'd forgotten we'd had. Horns curl from the sides of his head, and dark wings splay out behind him. Features I never saw him have in any of my dreams. Not until this morning. Does that mean Thorne Blackwood is...fae? My eyes dip from his horns to his rounded ears. Only pureblood fae have pointed ears, which means he's at least part human. But how is that possible? Mr. Blackwood is supposed to be *fully* human.

My mind reels as I continue my assessment of him. His spectacles are gone, as is his shirt. I catch sight of the black ink I've seen in full only once before, in a dream I thought was fantasy. More and more, I'm losing the luxury of doubt. *That one dream* had to have been real, for the snakelike patterns trail over his skin in the same places they did then, looping over his upper arms, his shoulders, and dipping beneath the waistband of his trousers. I know for certain how they wrap around one thigh, ending just above his calf.

"You're Morgana's son," Mother says through her teeth. "Her wretched little boy, Vincent."

"You should be asleep with the others!" Father says. "How are you here?"

"That's not what's important now," Thorne says. "What's important is that Vincent is yet another pseudonym. My birth name will make everything clear for you. But first," he slides his gaze to mine, "remember what I told you today about the curse that was placed upon you."

A single memory begins to open, shrouded by hazy bits of conversation that remain lost to me. Only one sentence forms clearly in my mind.

The banshees cursed the Briars' nextborn to be bound by iron if it ever touches her flesh.

"My name," Thorne says, "is Vintarys."

More gasps and whispers erupt from around the table.

Dread strikes me before the truth does, but my comprehension isn't far behind.

Ancient fae language isn't a subject we spent much time on at the convent school, as the words are rarely in use in seelie society. But I learned a handful of terms, particularly those that held importance during the human-fae wars.

I remember *vintarys*.

I know what it means.

The word leaves my lips in a whisper. "Iron."

16

BRIONY

That dreaded word splinters through my mind, its resonance as painful as its ancient meaning.

Vintarys.

Vintarys.

Vintarys.

Iron.

An essential element in a curse I never knew was placed upon me. Not until today. Even after I learned about it... Thorne made me forget. But how? I try to recall what else we spoke of, but all I remember is him explaining my family's reputation, then taunting that he'd tell a tale of feuding families and curses. The only thing that stands out amidst the void in my memory is the explanation of my curse.

That I'll be bound by iron if it touches my flesh.

I'm desperate to know what else I've forgotten, but the lock on my memories won't give. So instead, I return to what I do remember. My dance with Thorne in my grove. The strange things he said. I recall what he did before he ordered me to forget our encounter. First, he took off his gloves, and...

Placed his bare finger under my chin.

He...touched me.

Vintarys—iron—touched my flesh.

And bound me.

To him.

He wasn't part of my dream. He was there in person, and it was the first time we'd ever touched, skin to skin. While I don't fully understand how it's possible that he's commanding me, I have no doubt that he is. Much like the outlawed magic of the true name bond, which gives a fae mastery over someone if their subject states the words *I give you my true name*, Thorne now holds full sway over me.

My knees tremble, and the arm that holds the blade to my father's throat begins to burn from maintaining the position. I try to pour all my will into lowering the hand, fighting the command Thorne gave me, but my limb won't obey.

A strangled wail comes from behind me. It's my mother. "No," she cries. "No, this can't be. After everything we've done to protect her."

My father bares his sharp teeth. "I ask again, son of Morgana, what do you want?"

Thorne takes a slow step closer and lowers his voice. "I want you to know that you haven't won. I want you to look into your beloved daughter's eyes and see that she is now my weapon."

Father slides his dark beady eyes to mine. His expression shifts, no longer hidden behind his mask of calm confidence, and the result feels like an iron spear to my heart. Where I've glimpsed so much kindness tonight, so much humble pride, I now see fear. Terror. Repulsion.

Of *me*.

"I want the queen to do the same," Thorne says, and there's a note like sorrow in his voice. I can only imagine it's in mockery of the true grief that grips me now. "Princess, keep the knife in place, but turn to the side and let your mother see your face."

Everything inside me rebels, but my body obeys in jittery motions. As soon as my eyes meet my mother's, the blood leaves my face. She recoils from me, stepping back toward her sister's chair. Aunt Cecily pulls her close in a protective gesture, stepping slightly in front of my mother.

A sob pours out of me. I shake my head, pleading with her. Begging her to understand. "I don't want to do this. I don't want to be his tool."

Mother says nothing, only stares at me with wide, terrified eyes. I'd give anything to wipe that look away. I'd marry Monty Phillips in a snap of my fingers with no complaints, no hesitation, no resentment, if only it would bring her indulgent smile back.

If only it would rid the sickening feeling writhing inside me now.

Father's voice draws my attention back to him. "What's your next move, boy?"

Thorne holds my father's gaze with narrowed eyes. "Now I'm going to leave this room, and you will let me. No one in the palace will attempt to stop me. Do you agree? Swear it, on behalf of everyone in this palace."

Father's jaw shifts side to side, his long fingers curling into fists. Then, with a grunt, he relents. "I swear it. On behalf of everyone in Nocturnus Palace at this time, no one will stop you from leaving. But that doesn't mean we won't come for you at once."

Thorne gives him a crooked grin. "I count on it."

Father's eyes flick to me, then back to Thorne. He lowers

his voice. "What do you intend to do with her?" The way he says *her* makes it sound like he's referring to a stranger. Not his daughter. Not the girl he so recently expressed fondness for.

"The question is, what do *you* intend to do with her? My weapon now lives among you. There's no way for you to know I haven't given her other orders to execute later. Will you chain her up? Lock her in the same tower you once kept her changeling decoy? Or will you be so cold as to end her life, like you've done to countless others who've stood in your way?"

I expect Father to deny such actions, to say he's a changed king. That he'd never resort to murder. He doesn't answer, which fills me with dread.

"Ah, I see," Thorne says. "It's a family decision. Well, I'll leave you to it." He takes a step away but pulls to a halt. Meeting my gaze, he says, "You can lower the blade now."

My arm goes limp at once, eliciting a gasp from me. I want to drop the knife, but my hand is curled too tight. So instead, I focus on the firm handle against my palm, the steadying comfort of a weapon in my hand. I've never wielded anything with deadly intent, but the rage that courses through me, mingling with the relief at being released from Thorne's demand, makes me feel like I could. Not just *could*. Would. Willing. Eager.

I burn Thorne with a glare. My toes flinch, my feet desperate to close the distance between us so I can plunge my blade into that bastard's heart.

My thoughts must be written clearly on my face, for Thorne wags a finger at me. "Perhaps you should think before looking at me with those murderous eyes, little nemesis. Your father swore on behalf of everyone in the palace that no one would stop me from leaving."

Would stabbing him in the heart count as stopping him from leaving? My eyes flick to his chest, to the tattooed skin that covers that treacherous organ. He did say the knife was sharp enough to cut through bone. Could I slide it between his ribs? My studies covered both human and fae anatomy. I know how to find the heart.

With a dark chuckle, Thorne stalks even closer. Father shifts his stance but says nothing as my enemy stops before me, staring down at me with a hateful, arrogant grin that makes him look so unlike every version of him I've witnessed before this moment.

I hate that I even know of another version of him.

I hate that I considered that version a friend.

I hate that I ever dreamed of him.

I hate that we danced together.

I hate *that one dream*.

I hate him.

Him.

Him.

My hatred burns hotter as he slowly leans closer. I clench my teeth, forcing myself not to flinch, not to show an ounce of fear as he brings his lips by my ear.

"Now tell me, nemesis. Was I right? Am I still the handsomest man you've ever seen?" There's no demand in his voice, no invisible pull that forces me to answer, only soft, seductive teasing.

I hate that if he wanted, he could command me to answer him. He could command me to say anything. Do anything. Hurt the people I love. The family I only just got back.

My rage builds into an inferno that writhes through my veins. A dark thought crawls into my mind, one so tantalizing I can't let it go.

Thorne can't command me if he doesn't have a tongue to speak with.

"You don't have to answer," he whispers. "Your dreams of me have shown me a truth you can't deny. I've been pulled into enough waltzes with you to know you want me. More than that, I've seen you hold my gaze while your hand slides between your thighs. I've heard you whine while you writhe with pleasure—"

The inferno takes over, fueling my muscles. I take a swift step back and plunge the knife upward, toward the underside of Thorne's jaw—

Too many things happen at once.

Warning shouts blare around me.

My blade punctures Thorne's skin.

The shouts cut off.

He lifts his head with preternatural grace and darts back, avoiding a deeper cut.

The clatter of plates and heavy thuds fill the room.

In that split second of rage-fueled action, chaos has fallen. But not the loud kind. Not the busy kind.

It's a quiet chaos, one so at odds with my whirling thoughts.

Thorne stands before me, hands behind his back, unperturbed by the blood dripping from the underside of his chin. His lips are pulled into a smug grin, like he expected my attack.

Like he wanted it.

And around us, in lifeless heaps, lies my family.

My breaths grow sharp, shallow. The knife slides from my fingers, clanging to the ground. I retreat a step back and nearly step on my mother's wrist, her limp hand flung over her head on the floor. Aunt Cecily is draped over her legs, a broken wineglass at her feet. My father lies crumpled on the other side of me, eyes closed, mouth parted. Everyone else at the table is the same. My cousins. Uncles. Aunts. The rooster. Cousin Remus lies at the base of the piano, no longer a being of shadow but a slender man with dark hair. I would have expected him, out of everyone, to have been capable of fleeing undetected, but I recall what Mother told me during dinner. *He only shifts into his seelie form when he's startled.*

Everyone...

My entire family...

They're...dead?

"Princess." Thorne's voice has me whirling to face him, my lips peeled into a snarl.

"What did you do?"

He shakes his head, his countenance no longer brimming with the self-righteous arrogance it bore before. "You did this."

"I didn't."

"You can remember everything now."

A sharp pain pulses through my mind at the return of my memories. All of them. Every word Thorne made me forget.

I recall his tale of the Briars and the Lemurias, the mahrts versus the banshees.

The death of the Briars' firstborn.

The revenge on Mrs. Lemuria's young boy.

The violence that escalated thereafter.

The intervention of Queen Nyxia, who oversaw the punishments of both clans.

The two curses placed on each family's nextborn.

And the sleeping spell that threatens both sides.

If a member of one family draws blood from a member of the rival family, their own clan will fall into one hundred years of deathlike sleep.

I'm granted only the slightest hint of relief at what this means for my family. They aren't dead, they're just...sleeping.

The one who initiates the curse by drawing blood from the rival family is spared from the sleeping spell.

Thorne is right. I did this. I drew blood from a member of the rival family and enacted the sleeping spell. My family shouted a warning just before they fell. They knew this would happen if I attacked him. I didn't know! How could I have known? How could any of us have known?

The memory of Thorne's voice as he whispered in my ear sends a shudder down my spine. My anger returns in full. "You tricked me. You wanted this to happen."

"I did," he said, tone as empty as his expression.

I'm tempted to retrieve the knife from the ground and try to finish what I started. What's to stop me now? My family will slumber for the next hundred years. I...I'm alone. Without them.

Again.

I did this.

I failed them.

I'm not the Briar family hero.

I'm their doom.

My grief is too vast, too unbearable. I summon my fury instead, funneling it toward Thorne. *He's* responsible for this. Planting my hands on my hips, I lift my chin and meet his gaze without falter. "What are you going to do to me? What will you order me to do next? In what other ways do you intend to ruin me?"

His shoulders sink and he averts his gaze, eyes distant. "I

have no more demands for you. All that's left is the cruelest thing I could do. I'm going to leave you alone."

Alone.

Alone.

Alone.

My bravado fails as Thorne spreads his leathery wings. I sink to my knees, eyes glazed with tears.

"If you seek your turn at revenge, you're welcome to face me. I won't hide. Goodbye, Briony Rose."

I don't watch as he departs, whether it's through a window or a door. Instead, I stare at my tears pooling on the dining room floor beneath me, mingling with the blood that had dripped from Thorne's chin.

I don't know how long I stay like that, whether it's minutes or hours, but eventually, footsteps rouse me from my grief. They begin at the far end of the dining room and approach ever closer, each step in sync with the thud of my grief-laced heart. A fire sparks inside me as I expect it to be Thorne. Did he never leave? Or did he change his mind and return? Of course he wouldn't be able to resist hurting me more. Commanding me. Bidding me as his weapon. My sorrow melts away beneath a far more welcome emotion: anger. I'd rather fight than cry. I'd rather face my enemy than be alone.

But as I pull myself to my feet, it isn't Thorne who approaches.

It's a slender female fae with short silver hair, skintight black trousers, and a white dress shirt, unbuttoned to the center of her chest, resulting in a style that is both sensually feminine and strikingly masculine at once.

Recognition dawns through the haze of my rage, sparking surprise next. I know who this person is. I've seen her portrait in my history books. Read about her legendary past.

She's Nyxia, former Unseelie Queen of Lunar, sister to the court's current unseelie monarch, Franco.

More than that, I know of her affiliation with my current situation. She's the fae who punished the two rival families with the sleeping spell all those years ago.

Nyxia crosses her arms over her chest and burns me with a withering stare. "For the love of the night, I'm retired. Let's get this over with."

17

BRIONY

I don't know if hope is the right word for the emotion that blooms inside me, for hope has no place in my current condition. Yet something like it lightens my heart, like a storm cloud parting to reveal a sliver of gray sky. Now that I have my memories back, I remember everything Thorne told me. About the curse and its origins. Nyxia is the cursemaker responsible for the sleeping spell. Does that mean she can reverse it too? Is that why she's here?

"Ah, good," Nyxia says, casting an unflustered glance at the bodies littered about the table. "It appears most of the Briars have gathered in one place. That makes things easier for me. You must be the initiator of the curse. Are you...the youngest Briar? The iron-cursed?"

Iron-cursed. I suppose that is me.

"Yes, I'm Bri—" I almost state the name I grew up with, but this isn't the time or place to deny my true identity. Training my features so as not to grimace, I say, "I'm Princess Rosaline Briar."

"I don't suppose you know which of your family members might be absent from this little feast?"

"No, I...all I know is that everyone here is close family."

She taps a slender finger to her chin and speaks in a muttered tone. "The clever ones have found ways to evade inclusion in the curse, but the prideful would have chosen to maintain such a high-ranking family affiliation over safety. I'll have to rely on reports of spontaneously dead bodies."

"But they aren't dead," I rush to say. My heart slams against my ribs. "Right?"

She looks me over with a furrowed brow as if suddenly recalling my presence. Then, with a sigh, she says, "Close, but no. They'll be sleeping for the next hundred years, though, so they can't stay here."

"You mean they can't stay...in the dining room?"

She pinches the bridge of her nose. "Things were different when I created the curse. A castle full of lifeless bodies sleeping under dust and cobwebs was charming then. Now property like this is a valuable commodity that can't go to waste. And I'm sure the next seelie monarch will want to take over Nocturnus Palace at once."

"Take over?" I echo. "This is my parents' palace."

She huffs a laugh. "Your father can't remain king if he's asleep. As soon as word gets out, the proverbial vultures will swarm and fight for who gets to take his place. So I must have everyone properly entombed in the catacombs before then. We have a facility for these sorts of issues nowadays. Oh, don't worry. The coffins are quite comfortable and were designed to accommodate still-breathing bodies."

Coffins.

Entombed.

Catacombs.

Facility.

None of those words do anything to encourage the sparse hope I first felt at Nyxia's arrival. I don't know what I was imagining when I pictured a hundred-year sleeping spell, but it certainly wasn't what the former queen has explained. Not that I had much time to picture such a horrendous fate in the first place because that winged bastard stole my memories, and my parents chose not to inform me of important matters—

I halt my thoughts, and my chest sinks with guilt. No, I will not blame my parents. I did this. I subjected my family to this horrible condition.

The frightened looks on my parents' faces when I held the blade to Father's throat flash before my eyes. I squeeze my eyelids shut, willing the images to fade. Breathing deep, I force their appalled visages away. In their place, I see my mother running down the palace stairs to greet me. Her happy tears. Her pride in me. Her hope. I see Father patting the top of my head. His bashful smile.

Stars, I can't fail them.

I open my eyes and find Nyxia strolling down the length of the table, head cocked as she eyes each body with a calculated look. Is she mentally measuring their coffins? The repulsive thought bolsters my nerves. "Can you reverse the curse?"

"Why would I do that?" she says absently, moving on to study the next sleeping body. "A curse is a curse. I'm simply here because the magic called me. As the original curse-maker, I maintain responsibility over the case. And all my prior cases. For the love of the night, I'm supposed to be done with politics."

"But I was tricked into initiating the curse."

She meets my eyes with a feigned look of surprise. "You

mean you didn't intend to curse your entire family and throw Lunar's seelie rule into complete chaos? What a revelation."

I bristle at her sarcasm but refuse to be cowed. She may be one of the most infamous fae on the isle, but she's no longer a queen. If I don't speak my mind, there's no hope for my family. "I didn't know about the curse. I wouldn't have... acted rashly if I had. More importantly, the Lemurias have been scheming for this moment ever since you punished both my family and theirs."

"Is that so?" Her tone is absent again, and she's back to assessing the sleeping bodies.

I march over to Nyxia, keeping my eyes on her and not the slumped figures around the table. "It is. When you allowed each family to curse the other's nextborn, the banshee clan had an underlying motive. They cursed me to be bound by iron, and then named their nextborn Vintarys. I'm bound to him. He can order me to speak or act and I obey against my will."

She chuckles. "Ah, that's clever."

Heat climbs up my neck. "You sound a little too impressed for someone who sought to end the violence between the Briars and the Lemurias."

She glances at me with a look of feigned innocence. "Who says I sought to end the violence? Had I wanted to do that I could have killed everyone in both families with very little effort."

"Then why—"

"Look, little Briar," she says, facing me with her arms folded across her chest. "You were born in a different era. A privileged one. This petty rivalry between the two clans stems from a different time. We weren't bound by propriety then. We didn't follow the same rules of justice we're expected to nowadays. We respected cunning. I punished your families to keep them from acting like animals in the seelie society they were so desperate to be part of. If they wanted to keep fighting, they could do so discreetly and cease bringing bloodshed to every public event."

My heart falls. I should have known better. My studies painted Nyxia as a ruthless ruler, clever, cruel, and respected in equal measure. She thrived during the age of the dangerous fae, back when humans lived in fear of fae compulsion, seductive glamours, and having the power of their true names stolen. Why did I think she came here to help?

"Oh, don't look at me like that." She rolls her eyes. "I'm not a monster. I have adapted to modern ways, and I do feel bad for you. A little."

"Then please tell me. Is there a way to break the curse? To bring my family out of slumber without having to wait one hundred years?"

"Of course there is. There's always a way to break a curse. That's the nature of curses."

The faint hope I felt earlier returns. My voice trembles with it as I ask, "Will you please tell me how?"

Her lips pull into a smile that is both cruel and amused, revealing the elongated tips of her canines. "Why should I do that? I don't simply hand out solutions to those I curse. And don't try to elicit any sort of sympathy over having been tricked. I know for certain your rival has been tricked by your family in equal measure."

Mention of my rival sparks my rage. My family couldn't have done something as devious as what *he* did. I open my mouth to say as much...but my words dry on my tongue. The truth is, I don't know the full extent of what my parents have done in the past, what lengths they've gone to protect not just me but themselves. All I know is that they're trying to do better *now*.

But what good would that argument do with Nyxia? There must be something I can say to sway her. She clearly values wit and cunning...

My gaze slowly slides over the bodies. A chill creeps down my spine, but an idea forms. More like an angle I can appeal to.

Folding my hands at my waist, I don more confidence than I feel. "I assume storing so many bodies in some facility must be taxing, both on your time and the court's coffers."

"My time being the worst of it, yes."

"And a battle for Lunar's seelie throne is sure to cause turmoil for the entire court, as well as for your brother, the Unseelie King of Lunar. He'll have to pick up the slack while the seelie reign changes hands, won't he?"

"It isn't something he hasn't already been doing," she says. "The humans prefer King Franco to your father. Especially those in the north."

I clench my jaw. Even my father admitted to as much. "Even so, such a sudden change can't be easy for the Lunar Court. Ever since the isle's unification, sudden shifts in power have caused long-standing repercussions on the local economy, as well as the overall well-being of the people."

She snorts a laugh. "You sound like a textbook."

My cheeks flush. She's right. I took the words straight from memory of my studies. "But I'm right, aren't I? Having two rulers in each court is relatively new. Ever since that practice was put into place, there has never been an instance where the current ruler was fully indisposed while contenders battled for the throne. There's no way to know how long the turmoil could last. What if the magic of the All of All refuses to grant a victor? What if my father is the truest monarch for the seelie throne—"

"Night above, enough already." She shakes her head. "You really are Divina's daughter."

I open my mouth but I'm not sure whether to thank her for the compliment or take it as an insult. Either way, I dare not press my case further.

"Fine," she whispers. Then she repeats it, louder this time. "Fine! I'll entertain the idea of telling you how to break the curse, but only if you can explain how in the pitch-black hell doing so will keep the turmoil you mentioned from spreading over the court."

My heart leaps with victory, but I keep it from showing on my face, for I doubt smugness will aid my cause. "If we break the curse, there will be no battle for the seelie throne. My father will awaken and keep his crown."

She gives me a patronizing look. "Breaking the curse won't be easy, and it won't happen overnight. It's going to take work, and not by me. You'll need to break it."

"Then I'll do it."

"And how do you intend to hide the fact that the seelie king is asleep while you do so? I know your family keeps the palace private, and from the empty state of this room, I assume there is only minimal staff on hand tonight. Still, you can't close court for long. Petitions will build up. Citizens will riot against being refused an audience with their king. Rivals will get suspicious. Sooner or later, the people will learn the truth and I won't keep it from them."

Desperation claws at my heart. I'm close. I'm so close to a solution. I can't give up now. "Just give me time, please. I'll do whatever I must to break the curse and bring my family back. It doesn't matter what it is." The last part grates against my throat, for it almost feels like a lie. While I'm determined to save my family, I must recognize that there are things I simply cannot do. What if I'm required to shoot rainbows out of my eyes or defeat a legendary beast that no longer exists? Aren't curses and countercurses usually something ridiculous like that?

I clasp my hands to my chest and bow my head. "Please, former Majesty, I'm begging you. Just tell me how to break the curse and I will try."

Silence stretches between us for several long moments. I don't dare lift my head until she speaks. Every second that she says nothing feels like a knife to my heart.

"You win," she finally says.

I lift my head, and my heart thuds with another spark of hope.

"I'll tell you how to break the damn curse, but only because I'm a kind sister and would rather not inconvenience my brother. He has enough on his plate now that his wife is with child. But I'm only giving you two weeks."

My shoulders tremble and I manage a shaky nod. "I'll do it."

"Now...I'll have to remember the terms. This stupid curse was so long ago..." Her eyes grow distant as she taps the side of her face. "Ah! I remember. To sever the curse, you must prove both families are no longer rivals."

"How do I do that?" My heart sinks. Both families *are* rivals. What could I possibly do to change that? To prove it?

"When I created this curse, I wove in very specific terms to allow its dissolution. Together with your rival, sacrifice your own wants in favor of the other family."

I pull my head back. "What does that even mean? What would that entail?"

She waves a flippant hand. "Basically, accomplish a task with your rival that neither of you wants to do yet that benefits the other clan. Only then will both families awaken from their enchanted sleep. And free up some damn space in the catacombs."

My blood goes cold. "Both families."

"You didn't think yours was special, did you?"

Shit. Of course that's how the curse would work. It would break for both families, not just mine. "And I have to do this task...with *him*."

"Yes, *him*. The only Lemuria who hasn't fallen under the sleeping spell. I assume you know who *he* is. I won't give away his identity. Your parents have been trying to coerce this information from me for years."

"Yes, I know who he is," I say through my teeth. "And I have to...accomplish a task with him? We have to work together?"

She nods. "Doing something neither wants to do but benefits the other family. Yes. I said as much. And no, the benefit cannot be the breaking of the curse. The task itself must have a unique benefit for the opposite family. Are we almost done here?"

I curl my fingers into fists. The last thing I want to do is work with Thorne Blackwood. Or Vintarys. Or whoever the hell that asshole really is.

And yet...this is the only way to break the curse.

Nyxia smirks. "I told you it wouldn't be easy."

Stars, she was right. But I've already committed. I have to see this through. I must save my family. I'm the only one who can. And if I have to ally with Thorne—

No.

I won't be allying with him.

I'll be *using* him.

Putting it that way smooths the edges of my ire.

"Remember, you only have two weeks."

Nyxia's words fill me with dread. Though she's already stated the given timeline, it means something else now that I know what I'll be forced to do. "But I...I don't know what task we can do—"

"Anything is fine, so long as neither of you wants to do it. And it benefits the other family."

I shake my head. "I have to do this with him, yet I don't even know where he is. How to find him."

"He's a public figure, little Briar. He shouldn't be hard to locate."

I want to argue. Maybe it isn't difficult for the average person to find a public figure, but I spent my whole life in a convent. I barely know how to navigate this palace, much less this city, court, or isle. If Thorne's gone into hiding—

The last words he said to me weave through my mind. *If you seek your turn at revenge, you're welcome to face me. I won't hide.*

I scoff. Right. Of course he wouldn't hide. He doesn't see me as a threat. Not even fae law can punish him for what he did, for he acted in his rights. Trickery and deception aren't illegal.

Still...

"It might take the entire two weeks to find him. Won't you give me longer? Or at least a hint of where I might find him?"

Her nostrils flare. "I'm already doing enough for you, and no, I cannot give you longer than two weeks. In three days' time, my brother is hosting a weeklong public celebration in honor of the queen's pregnancy."

"Oh, he is?"

Her eyes deepen into a glare. "He is now. Thankfully, the king has taken a liking to parties. I can get him to agree if it's in honor of his beloved. But two weeks is as long as I can guarantee the people will be distracted over the festivities. Any longer than that and citizens will start to suspect why the seelie court remains closed."

Surprise ripples through me. She's orchestrating this party...for my sake?

"Don't look so flattered. This benefits my brother, remember? Anyhow, I suppose I can offer you one piece of advice. If you want to find your nemesis, start with his bakery. He has an apartment built above his flagship store. I doubt he'll return to his estate before visiting. He's well-known for his frequent visits and the individual care he pays each of his shops."

I grit my teeth at her favorable commentary and focus instead on how I can use it as a clue. It still isn't enough information, but at least it's something. I bow my head. "Thank you, former Majesty."

"Former Majesty," she mutters. "You make me sound old. Well, I am retired, and this has been a rather unpleasant interruption in my night. If you and your nemesis fail to break the curse in two weeks, I'll be back with appropriate transport to take your family to the cata-combs. So don't waste my time, little Briar. Good evening."

She tips her head, and then she's gone. No, not gone. She's become a misty shadow, much like Cousin Remus but with a less-distinct shape, and shoots from the room faster than any storm wind. I stare at the open doorway for several long moments before I note the wide-eyed faces staring through it. The three servants who were ordered from the room when Thorne first made his threats are there, as is the feline fae and the two foxes. Did they hear my exchange with Nyxia? Do they know the full extent of what has happened here?

One of the foxes crosses the threshold and bows on his

front paws. "Princess Rosaline." Based on his deep voice, it's the same fox who announced my arrival at dinner. "As acting ruler, we await your commands."

I inhale a sharp breath. I'm...acting ruler? Stars above.

I look from the fox to the small handful of servants, then to the bodies of my family. Those I've failed. Those I've unwittingly betrayed.

Those I'll save.

Lifting my chin, I fold my hands at my waist and try to evoke the princess I'm supposed to be. "First, state your names. Second, tell me if any of you have human blood and can lie. Third, locate Thorne Blackwood's flagship bakery and gather all the resources I'll need to get there."

18

THORNE

R evenge isn't sweet. It's hardly satisfying. Revenge is necessary. Cruel. As sharp as the blade that made my vengeance possible. I knew it would be like this. I knew my actions wouldn't bring peace. I never expected them to. My father warned me it would be so.

Promise me you'll give up on revenge. If you continue down this path, my son, your hatred will burn you from the inside.

Then I'll burn.

Despite those bitter words uttered six months past, I feel more cold than anything. Not even the warmth of the kitchen ovens around me can rid me of this chill. I feel it every time I close my eyes. Every time I recall Briony Rose's stricken face when I left her three days ago. I thought I'd enjoy it more. I thought I'd relish the pain of someone experiencing the same terrors I've already felt. The same shock of being tricked. The same agony over bearing the responsibility for your family's forced slumber.

But I didn't enjoy seeing those echoes of my past in Briony's present. Because she was never my true target.

Her parents were.

She was simply the sharpest weapon I could use against them.

I shake thoughts of Miss Rose from my mind and pour all my attention into the dough beneath my hands. The first blush of sunrise lights the window over the sink, though the kitchen inside Blackwood Bakery's Gibbous Peak location is already bright from the electric bulbs that illuminate it. Thanks to the ley lines of fae magic that crisscross the isle, most cities in Faerwyvae utilize electricity. The town of Gibbous Peak, one of the most famous shopping and dining districts in the Lunar Court, is no exception.

The rich aroma of butter fills my worktable as I roll my triangle of dough into a crescent. Last night, I spent hours folding butter into this very dough, and this morning I'll get to see it come to life, rising into a delectably flaky pastry. Since Blackwood Bakery is known for cakes more than anything else, we only serve crescent bread in the morning. Even so, it remains one of my favorite things to make.

I fold each crescent with care, then line them up on the baking sheet with precision. The result is orderly. Pleasing. Perfect. A balm on my nerves. A slight thawing of my inner chill.

"Mr. Blackwood! Don't tell me you've been working all night."

I lift my eyes to find my favorite baker, Mrs. Fernly, shuffling into the kitchen from the still-dark storefront. Hearing her call me Mr. Blackwood serves as further comfort. It's a name free of scorn and hatred. A name that has provided me a quiet life for the last fifteen years. Mrs. Fernly doesn't know I ever went by any other name. No one in my life does, nor do they know I'm half fae. To them, I've always been Thorne Blackwood, son of Edwyn and Alina Blackwood. No one knows that one of my parents holds no blood relation to me. That half of me owes allegiance to a different family. A different name. That I carry a past tinged with blood and darkness.

Mrs. Fernly wags a finger at me. "I'm right, aren't I? You did work all night."

I don't bother confirming her suspicions, but she's right. Sleep has eluded me. Or perhaps I've eluded it. All I know is dreams are the last thing I want right now.

I nudge the bridge of my spectacles and cast a warm grin at the baker. "Are you trying to insult me, Mrs. Fernly? You must be hinting that I look like yesterday's leftovers. Meanwhile, you look as bright and lovely as the dawn."

She scoffs as she ties an apron around her wide hips and burns me with a look of mock scolding. "Don't think for a moment flattery will make up for you taking over my job. You know crescent bread is my specialty, and you already stole three cakes from me yesterday. I get paid by the hour, Mr. Blackwood, and I like to earn my wage. I don't appreciate being forced to have idle hands."

With a chuckle, I lift the tray of buttery crescents and set them on the rising rack. "It almost sounds like you don't want me here."

"No one wants the boss here. How are we supposed to gossip freely with you sulking about?"

"Sulking. You think I'm sulking?"

She arches a brow. "You've been in a state ever since you showed up out of the blue, and you never did tell us why you're here. You don't normally arrive unannounced or without a purpose."

"You know the Gibbous Peak bakery is my favorite.

Besides, how do you know I didn't come just to see your bright and sunny face?"

She gives me a glare that is anything but bright and sunny, yet somehow carries as much warmth. "I've already told you, flattery will get you nowhere with me. Nor will it hide your brooding state. I've known you since you were a boy, Mr. Blackwood, and I've seen all your moods. Don't you dare touch that oven!"

I halt mid-step, halfway toward the oven in question, where the previous batch of crescent bread bakes.

Mrs. Fernly swats my shoulder with her oven mitt as she brushes past. "I'm serious. Stop taking my job. This work is beneath you, anyway. You're one of the wealthiest men on the isle. You don't need to do grunt work anymore."

She may be right, but *grunt work* is what I miss. I enjoyed working in the kitchen as a child. The smell of butter. The feel of flour. The joy of shaping chaos into orderly perfection. Other than the occasional elite client whom I bake for, most of my work is done behind a desk at Blackwood Estate. Every chance I get to work with sugar and dough is one I'm eager to take.

"Either tell me what's put you in such a dark mood or leave me be," she says. "I can't work around those sullen eyes."

I release a sigh and lean against the counter but say nothing. I can't tell her why I'm here. What I did. That I decided to remain in the Lunar Court for a few days to see how the repercussions of my actions would unfold. Will the seelie throne fall under chaos? Will Briony confess what I've done? I'm prepared if she does. In fact, I'd almost be relieved. What would it be like to finally live as both identities? Thorne Blackwood *and* Vintarys Lemuria. I'm sure my name will fall under scrutiny and scandal, but the fate of the seelie throne will be enough to ensure it doesn't last long.

So why haven't I heard anything yet?

I clear my throat and adopt a nonchalant tone. "Have the morning papers arrived?"

Mrs. Fernly extracts the tray of freshly baked crescent bread from the oven and sets it on the cooling rack. "Ah, indeed they did. I brought them inside and left them on the storefront counter if you fancy a look. The news on the front page is sure to put everyone into a frenzy of talk today."

I swallow hard. "Is that so?"

"Yes. Queen Ember is with child, and King Franco is hosting a public celebration at Selene Palace starting tonight. All citizens are welcome to attend all week long. Night above, what a hectic event that will be. I'll be happy to avoid setting foot anywhere near Selene Palace, though I do wonder if the celebration will result in slow business."

I frown as I ponder her words. No news of the sleeping seelie royals, yet plenty about King Franco's party. Surely the king must know what has happened by now. It's been three days. His sister would have felt the initiation of the curse she placed. Nyxia would have come to Nocturnus Palace to take the bodies to the catacombs, just like she did with my family.

What does it mean that there's no such news?

An unexpected spark of panic strikes me.

If word has yet to get out...

If Briony has kept mute about my actions...

The sight of her grief-stricken face, her rage, her agony over my betrayal fills my mind. I did what I needed to do. I knew I'd have to hurt her to complete my plan, and I did so willingly.

But what if it was too much for her?

What if the pain sparked not a fiery rage like it did in me fifteen years ago, but a well of sorrow too vast to traverse? What if my cruelty left her without a will to live? What if word about my true identity has been kept out of the papers, not because of Briony's discretion...but because she...she...

No, I won't let my mind take such a dark path. I may not know everything about my nemesis, but I believe she'd rather fight than end her life.

But if I'm wrong—

"There's that melancholy mood again. Get out already, Mr. Blackwood, or you'll make the bread taste bad."

I rouse myself from my thoughts and push off the counter. "Maybe you're right and it's time I took my leave. I've been away from Blackwood Estate for over a week now."

"That's a sensible boy."

I give a halfhearted chuckle at the word *boy*. I'm six-and-twenty. She has known me since I was eleven, so I suppose I'll always be a boy to her.

"Go on, now." She waves me off with a glare, which is as good as a farewell hug coming from her. Would she act so brashly with me if she knew the truth? Would she speak so freely if she learned I've acted against my father's last wish and sought revenge instead of the peaceful quiet life he gave me? Perhaps it truly is best that I return home before I get a chance to find out.

I exit the kitchen to the storefront, where a half-fae male counts moonstone chips—Lunar Court's currency—in preparation to open the bakery for the morning. He gives me a nod that is so deep it's almost a bow. "Good morning, Mr. Blackwood! We've been so honored by your presence."

I suppress a laugh. Not everyone is so determined to get rid of me. Or perhaps the young cashier is simply eager to kiss my ass. I retrieve my jacket from where I draped it over the counter this morning and stroll out the front doors. The sun has risen over the horizon, casting the streets of Gibbous Peak in a hazy glow. Even at full light, the Lunar Court is never quite as bright as other courts. The light is always filtered through an enchanting haze, like that of a partial solar eclipse. Yet it's still too bright for me to see well without my spectacles. Only dim rooms or nightfall improve my eyesight. I nudge the bridge of my lenses—more out of habit than necessity—and stroll past my bakery's front window.

Despite the early hour, the streets around me are busy with activity, as most shops will be open within the hour, and this particular street is famed for its breakfast goods. In a matter of minutes, a line will form outside Blackwood Bakery full of hungry patrons craving fresh crescent bread or those picking up cakes for later in the day.

The bakery is located on the corner at one of the busiest intersections in Gibbous Peak, with cafes, inns, and restaurants clustered together. I round the corner and head toward the back of the building where the entrance to my apartment is located, shrugging my jacket over my waistcoat as I go. But I manage only a few steps before a figure crosses the street and merges onto my path.

Angry blue eyes meet mine.

Briony Rose squares her shoulders and plants her feet in a wide stance, fingers curled into fists. She wears the same outfit she had on when last I saw her, though her hair has been expertly pinned in an elegant updo, a small black hat with a mauve ribbon and pink peonies perched stylishly upon her head.

My heart leaps in surprise at seeing her, but I hide it from my face. Training my words beneath a mask of disinterested calm, I stare down at her through narrowed eyes.

"So you came for revenge after all. Make your first move. I won't stop you."

"I came to talk," she says, her words slow. Even. Not an ounce of fear on her face. "Unless you want me to make a scene, we'll speak in private."

I almost laugh. How foolish I was to think she would have succumbed to sorrow. I extend my hand toward where I'd been traveling. "We can speak in my apartment. It is just inside and up the stairs."

She scoffs. "I think not, Mr. Blackwood. We'll speak privately but in the open. Come." She whirls on her heel and marches away from me, in the exact direction I just offered to take her.

Clenching my jaw against the irritation that courses through me, I follow her into the alley. She stops just behind the bakery, several feet from the door that leads to my apartment. Does she not realize where we are? That this is my territory? My bakery? My second home? Shaking my head at her foolishness, I halt before her, leaving ample space between us. I haven't a clue what she has planned for me, whether she's concealed a weapon or is simply here to threaten my reputation—the latter of which I've been anticipating for days. While I'm willing to meet her fury, I won't take her turn at revenge lying down. Better I don't get too close.

I fold my arms and wait for her to make her move.

And yet...

All she does is stare, studying me through slitted lids.

I arch a brow. "So...what did you come to talk to me about?"

She stares at me for a few uncomfortably long beats more. Then, with a sigh, she briefly closes her eyes. A smile stretches across her lips as her eyelids flutter open. She takes a small step closer. "You, Mr. Blackwood, are going to do exactly as I say. We are going to make a bargain and you are going to agree to every term."

I huff a laugh. Then another. "I think you have our roles reversed, Miss Rose. It is I who can command you to do whatever I wish. With one word, I can have you forget you were ever here. I can order you to leave. To dance naked in the streets, should I wish it."

She tilts her head to the side. "Do you wish to see me naked again so badly? Shame on you, Mr. Blackwood. But no, you won't be making any demands with the bond you've forged between us. If you utter even a word of command, you'll find yourself on the wrong end of a knife, and this time, the blade won't miss. I've surmised enough to know you have some fae blood, but if I cut the right artery enough times, you can bleed out before your fae healing kicks in. Remember those words? You see, I learned a thing or two about sharp knives when we last met."

"Yes, but I let you cut me then," I say, scanning her figure for any sign of the weapon in question. Her hands remain curled at her sides, empty of any such knife. I lift my eyes to hers again. "I'll do you the honor of wounding me, but I won't allow you to strike a killing blow."

"You won't have a choice."

"How so?"

"Because you can't move."

I take a step to the side, proving otherwise. My lips curl at the corners, but hers do as well, sending a spear of doubt through me. She's far more confident than she should be. She's almost giddy with it. A thought blares in the back of my mind, but it couldn't be true.

Could it?

"Oh, did you not realize?" Her expression shifts into one of false sympathy. "You're asleep."

The blood leaves my face. Only now do I notice the eerie quiet, the lack of footsteps passing by the alley, the morning light that's a touch too dark for how high the sun must be by now.

Truth dawns like a punch to the gut.

I'm in a fucking daydream.

19

BRIONY

Watching Thorne's smug confidence melt away before my eyes is the most glorious sight. It's enough to make this reckless plan worth it. Laughter bubbles in my chest, but I suppress it. I won't be foolish like Thorne and let my arrogance get the better of me. There's still much I must say and do. I can't allow my plan to fail now.

With a steady breath, I will a window to appear in my dreamscape, just large enough to allow me a glimpse at the scene outside my daydream. The alley looks almost exactly as it does in my illusion, except Thorne is standing slightly off to the side, body immobile, eyes wide and sightless. Before him, a slender fae male with russet hair presses a dagger to his throat—the very same Mr. Blackwood forced me to wield three days prior. The fae holds the blade steady, lips peeled back from his teeth in a way that makes him look very much like the creature I first met him as—the deep-voiced fox servant. He's now in his seelie form, which boasts a thin mustache, a black suit, and the same black bow tie he wore as a fox. I was surprised that he didn't balk when I proposed this part of my plan, but seeing how confidently he holds the knife makes me wonder if he's used to such violent requests from my parents.

I blink, and the window snaps shut.

"How are you doing this?" Thorne's voice holds only bored curiosity, and the shock in his expression is gone. I'm disappointed with how quickly he's recovered his composure.

I snort a dark laugh. Does he really think I'll answer his question? Reveal just what a gamble this plan was?

"It's all thanks to you," is all I say.

And it's true. He told me enough to convince me our dreams have been real. Shared. That I've pulled him into my dreams or entered his, leaving his body paralyzed all the while, just like my mother does to her subjects. Even though Mother insisted that she's never met a daydream succubus, I know that's what I am. Or...more that my magic works whether I'm asleep or awake, and that I have far more control during daydreams. Before this moment, there was a chance I was wrong, but I was willing to bet I was right. My plan hinged upon it. And I executed it exactly as planned.

Step one: create a daydream. Step two: maintain eye contact long enough to distract him while I cast my dreamscape. Step three: draw him in as my subject. That gave me some anxiety, as he normally enters my dreams without my permission. But all it took was my intent, my slightest wish, and there he was, trapped in my dreamscape. I assume that's how my magic has always worked. My wish for a partner lured him into my dancing daydreams. My arousal pulled him into *that one dream*.

I force the latter from my mind.

The most important part of my plan was choosing a location I knew I could lure Thorne to and framing it every hour of every day, so that I could create a convincing scene when my opportunity came. That was yesterday's task. A tedious one, but it paid off.

He releases an irritated sigh and tucks his hands in his trouser pockets. "You said you wanted to talk. Then you threatened me with a knife I can't see and a bargain without terms. Why are you here?"

"Oh, our bargain has terms. And just because you can't see the knife doesn't mean it isn't there. I assure you, my new friend Mr. Boris is holding a nice sharp blade to your throat as we speak. While you can't move, I can. This is a daydream for me, which means Mr. Boris can hear everything I'm saying now. See everything I'm doing. With a single gesture from me, he will cut your throat."

His eyes widen the slightest bit. He knows I can't lie.

"Now, let's get to the important bit. Our bargain. We're going to break the sleeping spell on both our families."

I'm rewarded with another look of shock.

I bat my lashes and tilt my head to the side. "Oh, did you not know there's a way? Perhaps if you weren't so busy ruining my life, you'd have figured it out for yourself."

He opens his mouth, but it takes several long beats before he utters a word. "How do you know there's a way?"

"Nyxia told me. The former queen and I had a rather informative chat. She told me exactly what it will take to break the sleeping spell. You and I must join forces to complete a single task that neither of us wants to do yet benefits the opposite family. If we do, the curse ends, and both of our families awaken."

His jaw shifts side to side. I can practically see the struggle in his eyes, his desire to appear unflustered despite his burning curiosity. "Why would I agree to do anything with you?"

"Don't you want your family to wake up before their hundred-year term ends? Or is hurting me your only goal in life?"

"I might be willing to entertain the idea," he says through his teeth, "but what task would we—"

"That's already been decided. You're going to help me secure my marriage to Monty Phillips." The words sear my tongue, making me bristle at my own proposal. But this is what I have to do.

"Why the hell do you need my help?"

"I need you to lie for me. You're going to take me to Monty Phillips, exactly as you were supposed to, and tell him everything is fine. That my parents are well but indisposed and that our wedding should proceed as scheduled, regardless of their absence."

"This is the task you chose? Couldn't something simpler suffice?"

"It must be something that benefits the opposite family," I say.

"Breaking the curse benefits both families. We could do anything together that we dislike for the sake of breaking the curse for the opposite family."

I shake my head. "Nyxia already addressed that. She said the breaking of the curse cannot be the sole benefit. The task itself must uniquely benefit the rival family."

"Any activity could be paired with enough logic to make it a benefit." His lips curl into a sly grin, and his voice deepens. "I know of one activity we could do together that neither of us would enjoy."

Heat floods my cheeks as I realize what he's suggesting. "Absolutely not."

"Why?" He takes a step closer. "Ah, it wouldn't work, would it? Because you wouldn't truly find that act between us unsavory at all, would you?"

My fingers curl into fists and I narrow my eyes. "I'm not here to jest, Mr. Blackwood. Our task has already been decided. I chose it because it fulfills every purpose. I don't want to marry Monty Phillips. I'm guessing you don't want me to marry your friend. But if you aid me in this task, you benefit my family by improving our reputation, financial situation, and position in society."

"And how does your role in this benefit my family?"

My pulse quickens as I prepare to confess the next part. It feels like a betrayal to my family to share it, but it's the best bait I have. "My parents made a bargain. Once I'm married to Mr. Phillips, Mother will cease using her magic on Father's rivals. Doesn't your family want a fair shot at challenging my father to the throne?"

I remember what my mother said when she briefly brought up Morgana, Thorne's mother. How she married a moon dragon and backed his claim to the throne when he challenged my father. How he lost due to my mother's magic. I can only assume this moon dragon isn't Thorne's father, considering Thorne is part human. Regardless, I'm willing to bet he'd rather see this moon dragon on the throne than my father.

Thorne runs his hand over his jaw. "I'm starting to see how this task of yours has mutual benefits."

I hold his gaze, trying to hide the fact that there's a deeper reason I've chosen our mission. If I can break the curse and marry Monty Phillips in the same breath, I'll regain my parents' love and respect as soon as they wake. I won't have to see fear in their eyes when they look at me. Instead, they'll be proud of me for making the sacrifice that saved them, not just from the curse, but in every way they described. My wedding will earn them the respect of their human subjects and provide them the funds they need to wipe away their debt before the collectors out them for it. They'll be so impressed with what I've done, they'll forget they were afraid of me.

That is, assuming my bond with Thorne breaks along with the sleeping spell.

Thorne releases a slow breath. "What are your terms, nemesis?"

My heart races with victory. I've got him!

"You will escort me to Sandalwood Manor and remain my companion and advocate until my marriage to Monty Phillips is finalized, which must take place in less than two weeks' time." I swallow the irritation that crawls up my throat. The fire that rages against my own terms. "You will lie for me when I tell you to. You will cast me and my family in a favorable light at all times. You will act as my patron and provide everything I may need—"

"Your patron? As in you expect me to financially provide for you?"

I cut him a glare. "It's not like I have anyone else to do so at this time, and Monty Phillips must be convinced there's nothing amiss with my family. I might need clothing. Ballgowns. A wedding dress. Anything Lord Phillips expected my father to provide."

"Your parents have their own coffers, you know."

"I'm not going to take money from them while they're asleep." A sharp pain strikes my heart, and I rush to say, "More than I already have, that is." The relief at correcting my almost-lie is instantaneous. Technically, I didn't take anything from my parents. Mr. Boris *gave* me a small purse from the royal funds, but only enough to get me to Gibbous

Peak and provide food and lodgings. But when it comes to fae magic, intent and belief are key, and there's a part of me that believes accepting the funds was akin to stealing.

He rolls his eyes. "Aside from playing matchmaker, babysitter, and financial provider, what other terms do you insist on?"

"The final term is that you won't use our...bond, or whatever it is, to make demands of me. You won't force me to do anything against my will."

"Ah, but that takes all the fun out of our relationship."

"We don't have a *relationship*. We will be nothing but allies."

A corner of his lips quirks as his gaze sweeps over my form. "So do you always pleasure yourself in the company of men you aren't in a relationship with? I won't judge. I'm just curious."

His words send such a violent shock through me, I almost lose hold of my daydream. How dare he bring up *that one dream*! I dig my nails into my palms to anchor my control. My cheeks flush, but I manage to bark a cold laugh. "Don't act like I was the only participant that night. I watched you come undone before my very eyes. I heard your strangled words as you begged to touch me. Watched your lips part as you studied the play of my fingers between my thighs. I've seen just as much of you as you've seen of me, Thorne Blackwood. Vintarys. Whoever you are."

Can he hear the tremble in my voice?

Can he see the sweat beading on my brow?

"I've seen all you have to offer." I want to say it wasn't impressive. That it was laughable. But stars above, that would be untrue. I may be mocking him now, but I'd been just as aroused by his actions in that dream as he was by mine. The heat of that memory burns inside me, almost hot enough to reveal my bluff. I don't trust myself to speak again, to say anything even close to a lie, so I let my expression do the deceiving. Let my lips curl into a disgusted snarl as I look him over like he's dirt. When my eyes return to his, I expect to find anger in his expression. Embarrassment. Something other than the seductive heat in his gaze.

"When you put it like that," he says, "I'm more in favor of the task I proposed. I do enjoy a hate-tryst." He runs his thumb over his bottom lip and watches me from under his lashes. "I could...*come undone*, as you put it, while your fingers play with me this time. Or, if you'd rather, while your hands tighten around my throat. I think we'd both like that."

My breaths sharpen as another flash of traitorous heat pools between my thighs. I bite the inside of my cheek, begging my body not to betray me with the shudder that teases the base of my spine. I swallow hard. "Stop trying to change the subject. Agree to my bargain. Need I remind you of your lack of choice?"

The reminder serves me well too, for I'd almost forgotten we had an audience. Thank the All of All Mr. Boris can only hear my side of the conversation. Not that it hasn't been condemning enough.

His expression hardens as he averts his gaze.

"Do we have a bargain, Mr. Blackwood?" My heart thuds as I await his answer.

"Fine," he mutters like a curse. "We have a bargain. I agree to your terms."

I let my lips stretch into a smile, but I rein in my full mirth. "Good. We leave for Sandalwood Manor at noon by train. Buy our tickets. I'll meet you at the station."

With that, I release the dreamscape. The alley brightens and sound crashes around us, a rumble of horse hooves, wagon wheels, and distant conversation. Thorne abruptly stumbles back, freed from my daydream. Mr. Boris pockets the knife and takes a protective stance beside me. Without another word, I brush past Thorne and cross the street, Mr. Boris close to my side. I feel Thorne's burning glare with every step I take, but I don't dare look back at him. He's likely trained his features into that smug confidence again, and I'd rather leave feeling like the singular victor.

We reach the building across the street—a cafe at ground level with an inn above it. Mr. Boris escorts me inside a door beside the cafe. We enter the tiny lobby of the inn, then up the stairs to the room I've stayed in the last two days. He opens the door to reveal a modest living space. It isn't much larger than my bedroom at the convent, but it is clean and decorated with the most modern of touches—an elegant tea table set with porcelain cups, a couch uphol-stered in blue brocade, and a velvet wingback chair. Most importantly, it provides the perfect view of my target, cour-tesy of the window that showcases the intersection, Black-wood Bakery, and the alleyway behind it.

The feline fae from Nocturnus Palace turns away from the window. Her white cat ears perk upright at the sight of me, and her long white whiskers twitch, as she asks, "He agreed to the bargain, Highness?"

I nod, releasing a sigh of relief at the same time. "Thank you for keeping watch, Minka."

Minka is the only other servant aside from Mr. Boris that I brought with me. Everyone else remained behind with tasks of their own. Hiding my family's fate. Guarding the dining room. Closing court. Ensuring only trusted staff who are essential to running the palace are allowed entrance. Everyone else was given a surprise two-week holiday in honor of my upcoming nuptials. Thanks to the only servant with human blood who attended that fateful dinner, we were able to spread a lie that my parents are traveling to the Earthen Court for that very celebration.

"Is there anything else we can do for you, Highness?" Mr. Boris asks in his deep and rumbling tone.

Minka extends her hands toward the table. "Tea? Wine? Cookies?"

I shake my head. With my bargain with Mr. Blackwood secure, there's only one thing I want to do.

I excuse myself from my two attendants and enter the singular bedroom included in our temporary accommodations. My luggage rests at the foot of the bed, including my phonograph. I'm almost tempted to play my favorite song, but fatigue pulls at my limbs, my mind. Sinking onto the bed, I let myself relax for the first time in days. Sleep has been fitful at best, as I've been terrified of dreaming of Thorne. Of giving away my location, my plan. But I can forget about that now.

I can sleep.

I can breathe.

With slow motions, I extract my paper fan and a folded piece of parchment from my skirt pocket. I lay the fan over my chest, just to feel the comfort of something cherished and familiar, then unfold the letter. A lump rises in my throat as I take in my mother's words. Sorrow and hope battle within me, but I focus on the sentence that encourages more of the latter.

You're the Briar family hero.

I don't feel like it yet, but I will be. I'll save my family. I'll save our reputation, our finances, and our future. I'll break this curse and be the hero they wanted me to be. All I have to do is sacrifice my heart and marry a man I don't love.

Pressing the letter to my chest, I close my eyes and fall into dreamless slumber.

PART THREE

A

LOVE

20

BRIONY

I t may have been my idea to leave Gibbous Peak by train, but I underestimated the shock of traveling at such great speed. I've only ever traveled by coach, and even those instances were few enough to count on my fingers. At least the rumbling motion and view of the Lunar Court countryside rushing past the window serve to distract me from the aggravating presence of my companion. Even without looking at him, his proximity feels too near, our enclosed compartment too small. We sit on opposite benches on opposite sides, yet my hatred for him has me bristling as if he were pressed beside me.

Mr. Blackwood's posture is annoyingly relaxed, one leg crossed over the other, his upper body hidden behind his broadsheets. He looks much like he did on our coach ride to Nocturnus Palace. Mr. Boris sits beside him in his fox form, his body as stiff as a statue. Though I've learned the fox was one of numerous footmen at the palace, I've deemed him my personal butler for the duration of our task, a promotion he accepted with much stammering thanks. He's taken his duties so seriously that he's begun acting more like a bodyguard than a butler, threatening Thorne's every subtle motion with the baring of his teeth.

Minka sits beside me, fiddling with the hem of her ruffled black dress. She too received a reclassification of duties and will be acting as my lady's maid. While she seemed grateful for the honor, she's been extra silent and fidgety ever since I told her she need not ask to refill my beverages every five minutes. I also told her noon was too early for wine when she insisted on bringing an assortment of bottles to the station, but I'm starting to regret that. Perhaps if I had wine, I wouldn't be so on edge.

I try to focus on the beauty of the landscape, the thick forests that flank the tracks interspersed with the occasional city or town. Once our train reaches the southern edge of the Lunar Court, it will take us down the coast of Spring and Wind before finally entering Earthen. I'll get to witness the weather and terrain of courts I've never been to, plus the sea. The prospect should excite me, but I'm finding the journey far more boring than I expected. Or perhaps it's the silence. The tension in the air.

I shift my gaze from the window to Thorne. He's dressed the same as he was earlier, without any sign of those wings and horns I've glimpsed twice now. During my two days of spying on his bakery, I spotted him several times but never saw him with those fae features. If I assume the horns and wings comprise his unseelie form, then I must also assume he rarely shifts from his seelie form. It makes sense, I suppose. To public knowledge, Thorne Blackwood is fully human, and shifting forms would shatter that image at once. I still don't fully understand his parentage, and I'm desperate to ask. Yet I doubt he'll respond well if I simply blurt out my question. It would serve me better to warm him up to conversation first.

As he turns the page of his broadsheets, I angle myself toward him and clear my throat. "Mr. Blackwood, how long until we reach our destination?"

He folds his paper with more force than necessary and reaches into his waistcoat pocket. The light from the window catches on his spectacles as he glances down at a brass pocket watch. "Ten minutes," he says through his teeth.

I pull my head back in surprise. "Really? I had no idea trains traveled so fast."

"No. That's how long the quiet lasted. Let's make it an hour next time, shall we?"

Heat rushes to my cheeks along with a spike of rage. It grows as he opens his broadsheets once more. Mr. Boris growls in my defense.

"I'm serious, Mr. Blackwood. How long until we arrive?"

"You're the one who insisted on taking the noon train. Did you not bother looking at the arrival times?"

"Would I be asking if I had?"

He says nothing for several long seconds. Then finally, "We'll arrive tomorrow morning."

I nearly choke on my gasp. "Tomorrow? We aren't arriving until *tomorrow*?"

"We disembark at the Jasper City Station. That's a twenty-hour trip at the very least. Hence tomorrow."

"Where the glittering hell are we supposed to sleep? Will we move to a sleeping car in the evening?"

"This is a sleeping car."

"This?" I glance at the cramped space, the lack of bed. "How is this a sleeping car?"

He peers over his broadsheets to give me a patronizing

smile. "I thought I was here to secure you a husband, not inform you on how trains work."

With a huff, I turn to Minka instead. Lowering my voice, I repeat my question to her. "How is this a sleeping car?"

She shrugs, her whiskers twitching. "This is my first time on an overnight train."

"If I may, Princess," Mr. Boris says, and I give him a grateful nod. "In the evening, both seats fold out to be slightly wider. Overhead, bunks have been built into the walls that can be lowered into two more makeshift beds."

My lips pull into a grimace. "So we have to share this room...together."

"There's a partition that unfolds to divide the room in half," Mr. Boris explains. "This train was designed with human propriety in mind. You and Minka will have your own private quarters. Besides, I don't plan on sleeping. I shall keep watch and ensure you rest easy. Nothing untoward will occur." He says the last part with a fierce glare at Thorne.

I nibble my bottom lip. The idea of a partition provides some comfort, but I'm still disturbed at the thought of sleeping so close to Mr. Blackwood. "Surely there's a more suitable room. Sharing a sleeping compartment with an unmarried man can't be good for a princess' reputation."

"No one knows you're here, much less that you're a princess," Thorne says. "I'm a public figure, Miss Rose. I know a thing or two about traveling discreetly. I paid enough moonstone chips to ensure this journey will remain unremarkable."

I suppose I can be grateful for his foresight. But still. "I would have preferred a separate compartment, Mr. Blackwood."

"You insisted on the noon train. This was the only compartment left."

I clench my jaw. "How do I know you aren't lying? You are part human, aren't you? Or are those rounded ears of yours a glamour?"

He casts an incredulous look at me as he drops his paper to his lap. "I am half human, yes, but why would I lie about this being the last compartment left? Do you think I want to be stuck here with you? Do you not realize I'd rather be anywhere else where I don't have to hear your insufferable voice and be inundated with your questions?"

His insult stings worse than I care to admit. I give a haughty sniff to hide my hurt. "You should be thanking me, you know."

He barks a laugh and refolds his broadsheets with agitated motions. "Thanking you? Really?"

"If it weren't for me, you wouldn't have a clue the curse could be broken in the first place, am I right?"

The tightening of his jaw is answer enough. I expect him to return to his papers. Instead, he lowers his voice to a tone of poorly concealed interest and asks, "How did you get the information out of Nyxia anyway?"

I purse my lips, my refusal to answer more out of spite than anything else, but Minka speaks for me.

"She threatened King Franco!" the feline fae says, her amber eyes as bright as her smile.

I open my mouth to argue but she isn't wrong. Nyxia didn't sympathize with my cause until after I brought up the troubles my family's fate would cause the unseelie king. I am, however, surprised that Minka knows of this. While I suspected the servants had listened in on my conversation with the former queen, I hadn't been sure just how much they'd gleaned.

Thorne's expression goes blank. "You threatened Nyxia's brother to her face and live to tell the tale?"

"I threatened him *nicely*," I amend. "Like I said, you should be thanking me. How long has your family been asleep? Five years? Ten?"

"Fifteen," he says under his breath.

"Why aren't you asleep with them, anyway?" I recall my family's shock over his identity. They expected him to be Morgana's husband at first, not her son. Thorne told me himself that the moon dragon was the only member of the Lemuria family that remained awake. Was that a lie?

He looks from me to Minka, then averts his gaze. "Family matters are private. They're none of your concern."

"They are my concern," I bite back. "They involve me. My family. The reason I was sent to a convent for twenty years. I deserve an explanation."

"My family kept secrets to save as many people from the curse as possible. Why would I share that information with you?"

I give him a pointed look. "We're in the process of breaking that very curse. Once we do, these efforts your family went to need no longer apply. Besides, whatever truths you're hiding could compromise my safety. You told me my parents feared retribution from Morgana's husband, yet they were flummoxed to find you'd escaped the sleeping spell. If there are others who managed to escape, I could be in danger."

"The only person you ever needed to fear was me, and look how swimmingly we get along."

His reluctance to explain has my curiosity shifting to annoyance, then to fury. I lean forward and bat my lashes. "Mr. Blackwood, if you don't answer my questions, I'll keep asking. And asking. And asking. I'll ensure you spend the next twenty hours of our trip hearing my voice—"

"For stones' sake, woman."

Mr. Boris clears his throat in a way that sounds more like a growl. "*Highness*, not *woman*."

Thorne shakes his head. "I'm not calling her *Highness*."

"You aren't calling me *woman* either," I say. "We've already established that I prefer you call me Miss Rose. Now, as I was saying, the best way to get the peace and quiet you seek is to answer a few of my questions. Afterward, I promise I won't bother you for the rest of our trip. If you refuse—"

"Fine. Just stop talking."

I curl my lips in an innocent smile.

Thorne removes his spectacles and pinches the bridge of his nose. "I'll answer your damn questions, but only if we speak privately."

"I think not," Mr. Boris says.

"Yes, why should our conversation require privacy?" I say. "My companions already know everything about our situation. The only benefit I can see to them leaving is that you may get away with lying to me easier. Or slandering my family without anyone around to correct you."

"You don't know a damn thing about your family."

"Oh, and you do?"

"Yes, I do. Maybe you would see the truth if you weren't so obsessed with impressing these people who are no better than strangers to you."

Rage floods from my chest and surges down to my fingers and toes.

Obsessed.

Impressing.

Strangers.

His words dig under my skin until I want to fly at him. Slap him. Claw him with my nails. I curl my fingers to keep from lashing out. It takes all my restraint just to keep my voice calm. "How dare you act all high and mighty. How dare you act like the victims lie only on your side. Your family cursed me before I was born, and schemed to give you a name that would hurt me."

He barks a humorless laugh. "Aren't you forgetting something? Your family cursed me before I was born as well, that I would never know my mother's face. To this day, I haven't a clue what she looks like, for she wore a veil to circumvent whatever unexpected effects the curse could have. I only ever looked upon her without the veil once, and only because your cousin Ned thought it would be fun to trick a five-year-old."

"I don't know Cousin Ned—"

"My eyes melted out of their sockets. It was as painful as it sounds. I was blind for a year."

My retort sticks in my throat, my rage replaced with disgust. I blink a few times, seeing his spectacles in a new light. Is that why he wears them? Because his curse melted his eyes? The thought of that pain, especially for a child, sends my gut roiling.

And yet...

I release a slow breath. It clears my shock, and I find my ire returning. This time, I manage to keep my composure with very little effort. "Mr. Blackwood, I'm not responsible for anything my family has done. I've never even met this cousin—"

"That's because he's dead, thanks to me."

"You killed him?"

"No, but his death is on my hands."

I'm tempted to inquire more about that, but I still haven't

finished my prior train of thought. "Regardless, I'm not responsible for the past. For the people I didn't know at the time. I can only claim the burden of my own actions, and the same goes for you. *You* took vile actions against me. *You* plotted. *You* deceived."

"I did what I had to do."

"All for the sake of revenge? You could have left us alone. You could have given us peace and kept your own."

"Your family doesn't deserve peace after everything they've done."

"And yours does? At least my family is trying to change!"

He snorts a laugh. "Are they really?"

"Yes!"

"You're so certain."

"I am."

"Is that why they've been trying for the past six months to burn down the catacombs?"

His question empties my mind, smothers my words, dampens my anger.

He speaks again. "My family isn't the only one there. There are others, and not just the sleeping and the dead. There are vampires, unseelie banshees, and a multitude of unseelie fae creatures who've been granted a safe haven in the catacombs, yet your family has sought to burn them down twice now. They would have tried again. They were already planning to."

I swallow the sudden dryness coating my tongue. "That...that can't be true."

"Ask your companions," Thorne says between his teeth. "You're the one who wanted them here to ensure I don't slander your precious parents."

My shoulders tremble as I turn toward Minka.

She shakes her head, her slitted amber eyes wide with worry. "I don't know anything about this, Highness."

Slowly, I shift my gaze to Mr. Boris. His head is lowered, his fox ears so low they're almost flat. "Is what he says true?" I ask.

"I'm not high enough in rank to be privy to the king and queen's secrets, but...there were rumors."

I lean back in my seat, eyes unfocused.

"But Highness," Mr. Boris says, "I would never condemn your parents' actions. Everything they've done has been for the greater good. If they sought to end the lives of their enemies in such a way, then I will trust the ends justified the means."

I want to believe him. I want to trust he's right about my parents. But all I feel is disgust. A hole in my heart. A gaping chasm of betrayal almost as vast as the one caused by Thorne's hideous actions at the dinner. From its hidden depths echoes the word Thorne said earlier.

Strangers.

Strangers.

Strangers.

Thorne was right. My family are strangers to me. There's so much about them I don't know. Darkness in their past. Present actions I can't condone. Yet despite that, I continue to feel a pulse of affection for them. It grows stronger as I recall my mother's letter. Her exuberant chatter. My father's frightening appearance paired with his kind personality. His gentle pats on the head.

Perhaps I've woven a fantasy around them, as false as my dreamscapes, but that doesn't mean I don't yearn for them. That my desire to be loved by them has grown any less. And based on the ways I've manipulated Thorne thus far— forcing him to talk to me during our coach ride, threatening him to answer my questions now—maybe their darkness simply runs in our blood.

Whatever the case, my emotions have leveled. Disgust. Rage. Sorrow. Betrayal. Hatred. Grief. It's all the same now, each feeling as sharp as the last but not any greater or lesser. The result is calm. Neutral. Or maybe empty.

I avert my gaze to the window where more of the Lunar Court countryside speeds by in shades of green, brown, and hazy blue. "Mr. Boris, Minka, you may give us privacy."

Minka places a hand on my arm. "Are you certain, Highness?"

"I can wait outside the door," Mr. Boris adds.

"There's no need," I say, my gaze still trained on the view. Thorne won't hurt me more than he already has. And now I know he can use the truth to do it. Minka and Mr. Boris are no shields against that.

After a stretch of silence, the bench shifts, followed by footsteps and the pad of paws. My two companions exit the compartment, leaving me alone with my cruel nemesis.

21

THORNE

I hadn't planned on telling her about her parents' plans for the catacombs. It was the truth, but an unnecessary one, for it serves to lessen my guilt over what I did to her. I don't deserve a lessening of guilt, for I could have found a thousand other ways to stop her family. A thousand other ways to initiate the sleeping spell. Stones, I could have done it without setting foot inside Nocturnus Palace. I could have done it the morning I met her in the glade.

But I chose my scheme.

My motives may have been somewhat honorable, but I followed the path of vengeance my mother set out for me from birth in a way that would hurt the Briars the most. I wanted to see the terror on their faces when they realized they'd lost. I wanted to hurt them in the sharpest possible way, to make their last waking moments a living hell.

And I used Briony to do that.

I study her now, the way she slumps against the backrest

of her seat, the way she stares out the window but sees nothing. The single tear that trails down her cheek.

My heart squeezes at the sight.

I shift uncomfortably on the cushioned bench, half tempted to say something to spark her ire. She's an inferno when she's angry, equal parts aggravating and beautiful. It was almost painful to watch that light go out. To witness her shock turn to hurt. Then to apathy.

I could apologize, but I won't.

Though if she kept me here instead of ordering me out with her servants, I suppose she intends to finish our conversation. I open my mouth to say as much, when I find myself transported to a rooftop balcony beneath a night sky. Unlike in the alley, which was an impressively subtle shift from reality to dreamscape, the startling change of scenery makes it obvious I've been pulled into a daydream. The illusion is a familiar one, a canopy of black streaked with falling stars in every shade of color. Briony sits beside the rooftop's balustrade, her posture the same as it was on the train, the bright hues of the meteor shower reflecting off her face.

I glance back up at the sky. "One of your favorites," I say before I can think better of it.

She cuts me a glare so sharp it pierces my chest. It relays what she doesn't say: I have no right to act so familiar with her. No right to reveal that I know she created this daydream to soothe her mood—something she does when she's upset. I shouldn't know that about her either.

But I do.

Regardless, I have no right to show it.

I lost that right when I hurt her. Now, our days of dancing beneath this dreamscape belong to the past. To an earlier time when we were both innocent. Unwitting.

The loss of that innocence is palpable. I almost miss the

days when I thought my dreams of the pretty fae girl were nothing but imaginings. What would it be like if I never learned the truth?

If Monty Phillips hadn't bemoaned his unfortunate engagement to Princess Rosaline...

If I hadn't used my friend's disdain for the marriage to scheme my way into acting as an intermediary between the Phillipses and the Briars...

If the Briars hadn't been so desperate to hide their unsavory past from Monty that they decided to trust me, a man they thought was simply a harmless upstanding human citizen...

If they hadn't sent me to retrieve her from the convent...

Where would we be if I never solved the riddle behind my name and understood the power it yielded?

There's no use asking. It was almost like the curse wanted to be carried out. It wanted to bring us together.

Curses are a lot like fate.

I shift to the side and prop myself upon the balustrade. The contact between my backside and the rail lacks the pressure it should have if this setting—or my body—were real. But it isn't. This body is just my dream form and this dreamscape is an illusion.

Briony's gaze dips down to my stomach, then quickly away. "I'm not responsible for that."

It takes me a few moments to realize what she's referring to. Then I discover I'm shirtless. Not only that, but I'm in my unseelie form, my wings draped on either side of me. All it takes is a slight turn of my head to feel the weight of my horns. My spectacles are gone too. Now that she's seen my unseelie form—and remembers it—I suppose she can dream of me this way. Still, since she can't lie, I must trust she didn't choose for me to show up shirtless.

"Your eyesight," she says, staring at the meteor shower again. "Is it because of...of what happened when you were a child?"

"Yes. Being half fae allowed me to heal from it, but not fully. Had my eyes been completely severed from their sockets, they wouldn't have grown back at all."

"But you can see better at night?"

I nod. "My mother—the banshee Morgana, as you've likely surmised—is a creature of the night. I inherited that from her."

She turns her head to assess me fully, brows knitted together. "You're only half fae, which means your father was human."

"My father was Edwyn Blackwood." My heart clenches at the word *was*. Six months hasn't been nearly enough to reconcile the loss of him. "I truly am his son, just like everyone thinks."

"Yet your mother isn't Alina Blackwood."

Another name that tightens my chest. Like my father, she too is no longer amongst the living. It feels like a disservice to answer her question honestly. "No, she was not." What I don't say is that while Alina may not have been my mother, she was family. She treated me like a son and claimed me as her own. She held no grudge against her husband for siring me before they met.

"What about the dragon, Morgana's husband?" Briony asks.

Yet another complicated family relationship, but this one causes me less pain to explain. "Trentas was a father figure to me from birth, but he was never my mother's husband or mate. I lied when I referred to him as such. He was her ally, nothing more. Their relationship was a front to hide the identity of my true father as well as the sires of my siblings. My mother didn't want to bring her lovers into our family curse, but she desperately wanted children, especially after the loss of her firstborn."

I don't bother mentioning her family's guilt in that loss, how they orchestrated my brother's death long before I was born, all to get revenge on my mother for crying at that fateful birthday celebration. After what I confessed about her family and the catacombs, I'm sure she can recall their other crimes on her own.

"If you're not part dragon, then why does your unseelie form look like this? Your horns, your wings, your..." She flourishes her finger in a swirling pattern. "Your inky scales?"

"My *inky scales* are tattoos to honor Trentas. He may not have been of my blood, but he helped raise me. After my family fell under the sleeping spell, I was turned over to the care of Edwyn Blackwood in secret. When I was a child, I was constantly glamoured to appear to have pointed ears so everyone would assume Trentas was my father. But after I went into hiding with my birth father, I had to do the opposite, to convince the world I was fully human. I was never able to shift into my unseelie form in public. No horns. No wings. I understood why, but it infuriated me that I had to hide my true self. So when I came of age, I got these done to remind me of who I really am."

She arches a brow. "You still haven't explained the wings and horns. Unless those are...banshee features?"

"You know not every fae child takes after their parents."

Her glare returns. "Of course I know that. I'm not an idiot, Mr. Blackwood. I scored high marks in fae biology."

I suppress my grin, though I'm secretly pleased with the return of her haughty fire. I'd take a shouting match over watching her cry any day. To my relief, the tear I glimpsed earlier has dried.

Shifting my seat on the balustrade, I prop one leg upon it and watch the falling stars. I steel myself, preparing to confess something I never have to anyone. Not even my family talked about it more than a time or two, for our ruse over my parentage required far too much discretion. "I am a type of fae humans have always feared, ever since humans first came to the isle a thousand years ago."

Briony says nothing, but I can feel her gaze on me.

"I'm a demon."

More silence.

Then finally, "A demon?"

I nod.

Briony's tittering laughter has my gaze shooting back to her. Her laughter builds until it catches on a snort. "A demon. You! It's just so fitting."

My jaw tightens. "I'm glad you find my heritage so amusing."

She sobers from her mirth, but her smile remains on her face. "As much as I believe you a devilish creature, what are you really? You can't be an actual demon. Demons belong in the biblical texts of human religions."

"That may be true," I say, "but the name was given to the fae long ago, particularly to one the first children born of human and fae relations. Back then such intimacies were taboo, even more so when a woman gave birth to a baby with horns and wings, resembling neither parent. The child was called a demon, and humans feared all human-fae hybrids would be born as such."

"But the humans were wrong," she says. "That child was never truly a demon as they understood the word to mean."

"And yet the fae kept that name for what I am, as not

everyone found it offensive or frightening, particularly the wild unseelie. I may not be the servant to some dark lord of the underworld, but I am the same kind of creature who first earned that name. The humans were right about one thing too: demons are only born from human-fae relations. But only one kind of fae can contribute to such offspring —banshees."

She tilts her head. "Really? Just banshees? Is that why I've never heard of a fae demon before?"

"Yes. The Lemurias are the only banshee clan currently in seelie society. Or they were before the curse put them to sleep. The other banshees are firmly unseelie and prefer relations with their own kind. Morgana is the only banshee who has mated with a human in centuries. That makes demons incredibly rare."

"But what exactly is a demon? What can you do?"

Part of me wants to keep the answer to myself. I feel like I'm baring too much. Yet I did agree to answer her questions if she sent her companions away. "Horns and wings mark our unseelie forms, though some of us are beautiful in appearance while others are grotesque. We are persuasive without using compulsion. And since we are part human, we can lie. All of those things combined make us frightening. Dangerous. You can see why we were aptly named."

"I suppose," she says. Then, "How did your family fall asleep?"

This is what I least want to tell her. Not because I fear her having the information, but because this story hurts me the most. And it won't just pain me. It will add another layer of darkness over the bright fantasy she's turned her parents into. I suppose that makes it fair.

"Fifteen years ago," I say, "the feud between our families was mostly fought between gangs formed to defend each clan. Rarely did our parents or family members interact face to face. Only your cousin Ned refused to be swayed. He enjoyed the fights and wanted to be part of them, despite the risk to his life or the curse."

Briony curls her hands around the railing she's sitting against in her illusion of the rooftop balcony, her jaw set as if she's fighting not to defend her unknown family member. Or perhaps she's trying to steady herself for what I'm about to say.

"Ned was a nightwind," I explain. "He was born long before the isle's unification, so he aged slowly like the fae of long ago. Despite his hundred or so years, he was more like a teenager, and just as rebellious. While he didn't have the power to invade dreams like most of his relatives, he had his own unique traits and was desperate to prove himself worthy as a Briar. He could send icy air into the slightest of cracks and freeze people in their sleep. He could control wind and air pressure. That was how he tricked me into seeing beneath my mother's veil, lifting it with the wind from afar while I smiled up at her.

"One day, my mother's secretary was captured, tortured, and forced to reveal Morgana's whereabouts. Ned took the opportunity to attack her directly. She was at the modiste with my two young sisters. I was eleven at the time, an ornery child. I would have no part in a dressmaker's shop, so I made Trentas take me to the confectioner. I managed to give him the slip afterward and went off on my own with a bag full of sweets. When I finally deigned to return to the modiste, I could hear their screams. My mother's. My sisters'. The dressmaker's. The other shop patrons'. The shop was surrounded by people trying to get in, but a violent wind pushed everyone back, sealing the doors on both sides, preventing anyone from breaking the windows.

One of the nearby spectators whispered that they saw a young man throw a cylindrical object inside the shop before darting away. A bomb, they assumed."

Nausea turns my stomach. I focus on the falling stars and try to say the next part with as little feeling as possible.

"But I knew what it was. I'd heard about Ned's grenades. They were filled with powdered iron, a substance your cousin could only have obtained under illegal circumstances. A substance he risked his life even to experiment with. But experiment he did, on my clan's gang again and again, and now finally on my mother and sisters themselves. His previous experiments had been fatal, the iron circulating through his chosen space with his control over air, invading his fae victims' lungs, eyes. The iron burning. Choking."

I intake a sharp breath, failing at my determination to remain detached from my story. For a moment I feel small again. That same eleven-year-old boy, listening to the sounds of my mother, my two little siblings, crying for help. Gasping. All I could do was stand there.

The dreamscape falters, the night sky flickering to reveal the train compartment. It shocks me out of my emotions, giving me a chance to reel them in. To breathe. To gather my composure. I feel a slight tug on my form, a loosening of Briony's control over the daydream. Should I want to, I could wake up. Leave.

Instead, I stay in place.

After a few more flickering beats between the two scenes, Briony regains control over her dreamscape. A blanket of night spreads above us once more, the rooftop balcony beneath it. The meteor shower resumes and stars fall once again. My gaze dips to her, but her face is averted. "Go on," she whispers.

I swallow hard before I can find my voice. "I knew there was only one thing I could do. One way to save them. Ned had to be close by, particularly somewhere he could witness what was happening at the shop, where he could keep people back with his gusts of wind while ensuring the pressure on the exits remained fixed. I darted across the street and found Ned in one of the alleys. I didn't hesitate. I leaped upon him and slammed my skull into his nose. Blood splattered my face and I heard my mother's and sister's screams cut off, but I didn't stop hitting him. I struck and struck, drawing more and more blood. Trentas found me then, hauled me off the body, and finished what I'd begun, severing your cousin's head from his neck to ensure the boy's silence. After that, Trentas took me to my father and let everyone believe I'd fallen under the sleeping spell with the rest of my family and that *he'd* been the one to initiate the curse."

Briony turns her face slightly toward me. I catch sight of her lower lip wobbling before she speaks. "Your mother and sisters, are they…"

"I don't know. The sleeping spell could have saved them, allowing them to heal in painless slumber for the last fifteen years. Or it could be prolonging the inevitable. They could already be dead." My voice is barely above a whisper when I say the last part. So badly do I hope it isn't true.

"Damn you," Briony utters between her teeth. Then louder. "Fucking glittering hell, I hate that you've made me feel bad for you." She swipes at her cheeks where fresh tears have begun to stream, reflecting the multihued stars falling in her dreamscape.

"Don't," I say, tone firm. "That's not what this is about. I told you the truth because you asked. Because you wanted to know if there was anyone left who would do you harm. The answer is no. Trentas seeks the throne, not your death."

A flash of guilt weighs down my stomach. At first, I think I just feel bad for flinging a threat to her father's throne in her face, but it's more than that. My mind shifts to a letter I sent just before we boarded the train, one I penned in secret to Trentas. I haven't seen him in person since the day he brought me to my father, but we've kept in contact. He maintains a vast network of spies, which is the reason we learned about the Briars' attempts on the catacombs. The letter contained a brief and coded message informing him that he'd have a chance at defeating Horus Briar and taking the throne after the princess' wedding. I penned the letter almost mindlessly, automatically, as we've regularly exchanged updates and intel over the last fifteen years. Our relationship isn't as warm or as strong as it was when he was posing as my father, but I still respect him. He's still my family's ally.

So why do I feel so guilty for having sent him that letter? Shouldn't I feel guiltier that I didn't say more? That I purposefully avoided mentioning anything about our bargain or that I succeeded at putting the Briars to sleep?

Yes, I most certainly should feel guiltier about that, for Trentas deserves to know everything. Besides, Briony told me about the bargain her parents made. She willingly gave me the information that would ensure our task benefits my family—an essential component in breaking the curse.

Still, I get the strangest feeling that sending that letter was a betrayal. What the hell is that about?

She sniffles, then wipes more aggressively at her eyes. "And after we break the curse? Will anyone in your family seek to hurt me? Will everything go back to the way it was before the Lemurias fell asleep? Gang wars, blood in the streets, children suffering?"

I give her the answer she deserves. The truth. "I don't know."

She glowers at me. "This task of ours is supposed to prove to the magic that fuels the curse that we aren't enemies anymore."

My lips curl into a smile I don't feel. One that only makes my chest feel tighter. Heavier. "Perhaps by the time our bargain is complete, we won't be."

"Doubtful," she says.

"Doubtful," I agree. Yet somewhere deep inside, a crack forms, a splinter in stone. I've known this all along, but this is the first time I'm ready to admit it out loud. "I'd rather you weren't my enemy."

She rises to her feet and plants herself before the railing I'm perched upon in her dreamscape. Her expression is closed-off. Cold. Her countenance betrayed only by the sheen still coating her eyes. Extending her hand, she says, "Then let's settle for false friends. For two weeks, at least."

I give her an equally cold nod and clasp her hand. It feels so small in mine, warm even though we're not really touching. It is only my dream form that interacts with her now. I squeeze her palm tight in mine. "False friends."

Briony releases my hand. The dreamscape melts away, and I find myself blinking into the light of the train compartment. She sits angled slightly away from me, her gaze fixed out the window like it was before the daydream.

I retrieve my broadsheets and hide behind them with what I intend to be a relieved sigh. Against my will, it turns wistful, the warmth of Briony's momentary touch still pulsing inside my palm.

22

BRIONY

There's only one word I can use to describe the Earthen Court: lush. No matter which window of the coach I peer out of, verdant hills span all around, a majestic backdrop to the busy city streets of Jasper. Even the architecture is a sight to behold, with elegant stonework, storefronts draped in trailing vines, and sidewalks edged with topiaries, tiny trees, and shrubs. I feel like a child as I take in every sight, my nose nearly pressed to the coach window.

"Sandalwood Manor is located in the Sagemoss District," Thorne says, "which is just a few minutes from downtown Jasper, which is where we are now."

I acknowledge him with an affirmative sound but nothing else. After what he told me yesterday, I can't help feeling awkward around him. He saw me cry. He saw me looking weak. Even though he said he hadn't meant to make me pity him, I did, and I admitted as much to his face.

Worse than that was what happened after he said those unexpected words to me: *I'd rather you weren't my enemy.*

He said it with such grief, such regret, that I believed him. I believed him so much that I shook his damn hand and called him my false friend. Why did I do that? Why did I touch him? I regretted my actions when he immediately drew up his broadsheets with impressive haste. He's hardly looked at me since. Or maybe I haven't looked at him.

The storefronts give way to elegant brick townhouses, then to larger manors. My heart lurches, and my awe over our surroundings melts into a bubbling cauldron of anxiety. I pat the sides of my hair, which Minka styled for me this morning, then adjust the brim of my hat. It was one of the few purchases I made in Gibbous Peak while staking out Thorne's bakery. There was a milliner just down the street with a hat on display that so perfectly matched the outfit Sister Marsh gifted me.

"You look lovely, Highness," Minka says, picking up on my fidgeting. "I wouldn't be surprised if Mr. Phillips fell in love with you at first sight."

My stomach turns. What kind of idiot would fall in love at first sight? I've fallen into lust at first sight—with Thorne, regretfully—but I certainly don't need love or lust from my fiancé. Our match is a political one. A necessity. A salvation for my family in more ways than one.

And yet I'm overcome with a sudden spike of self-consciousness. Though I'm quite proud of my new hat, I've been wearing the same ensemble for days. I didn't dare bring more than what I already own on our journey and left all the gauzy dresses stuffed in my wardrobe at Nocturnus Palace behind. Considering all those gowns were of the far more provocative fae style, I figured they would do more harm than good, for I highly doubt a peek at my bodily assets beneath the sheer silks would impress my human in-laws. But with our hasty travel plans taking precedence, I haven't had a chance to set foot inside a dressmaker's. My current outfit will have to do for a first meeting.

Shifting away from the window, I force myself to look at Thorne. I nearly choke on my own breath as I find his eyes already on me. "Remember the terms of our bargain," I rush to say.

He narrows his eyes. "I recall them just fine."

"You must do all the lying," I say, ignoring his last statement. "Cast me and my family in a favorable light. Do everything you can to ensure my wedding to Mr. Phillips ensues on schedule."

"I know, Miss Rose."

Mr. Boris whips his face toward Thorne. My butler is in his seelie form today, his russet hair brushed back from his forehead to reveal the pointed tips of his ears, his slim mustache twitching as he bares his teeth, canines as sharp as they are in his vulpine form. "You should get used to calling her *Highness*."

Thorne shows no sign of intimidation. "I seem to recall the princess insisting I don't."

Mr. Boris looks to me.

I lift my chin. "You should address me properly in any situation where formalities are expected, Mr. Blackwood. But in casual situations, you may call me Miss Rose, as I've requested. It remains the name I prefer most, as it blends my two identities. I'll even allow my fiancé to call me Miss Rose, as it will be a name that denotes familiarity."

Thorne arches a brow. "So you want us to appear...familiar? Even in front of your fiancé?"

A blush creeps up my cheeks. "We should appear to have become cordially acquainted. As allies in this bargain, we'll need to spend time together and communicate without going through secret means. So, yes, Mr. Blackwood, you may call me Miss Rose even in front of Mr. Phillips."

Minka's amber eyes brighten, her fluffy white ears perking up. "Can I call you Miss Rose too?"

"No," Mr. Boris says. "You will call her *Highness*, *Princess*, or *my lady*."

"It's really all right," I say. "I understand most fae aren't as particular about honorifics as humans are. We'll need to show my in-laws that we maintain the expected formalities, but the two of you may call me whatever you wish outside of those events."

"Highness," Mr. Boris says at the same time Minka says, "Miss Rose!"

I nod. "Yes, those are both fine."

"We're here," Thorne says, and my pulse kicks up.

I turn my gaze back out the window just in time to see our coach pull into a gated driveway. Tall trees and perfectly kept shrubs line the property, creating ample privacy despite being so close to neighboring manors. As we proceed, I catch my first sight of Sandalwood Manor. It's only a fraction of the size of Nocturnus Palace, but it's a gorgeous building nonetheless. Red brick contrasts elegant white columns, cornices, and window casings. It boasts several balconies and one charming turret.

"Miss Rose!" Minka says with a squeal. "This will be your home!"

My admiration over the manor turns sour. "My home," I echo and feel no warm resonance in my heart.

"Not exactly," Thorne says, tone edged with a hint of irritation. "As far as I know, a separate property will be purchased for the two of you by your parents."

Stars above, my mind has been so wrapped up in simply

breaking my family's curse, I haven't given much thought to what comes after. I've bargained to marry a man I'm about to meet. If all goes to plan, we'll be wed in less than two weeks. After that...

I'll have to live with him.

As his wife.

I suppress a shudder and focus on the more pleasant aspects of my bargain with Thorne. My parents awakening. Their throne kept safe. Their trust in me restored.

The coach rolls to a stop at the end of the circular drive. A middle-aged human woman rushes down the stairs, looking mildly flustered. From her plain yet neat state of dress, I assume she's a high-ranking servant.

Our footman descends the coach and opens the doors for us. Mr. Blackwood exits first and stands outside the door with his gloved hand extended. I stare at it for a few beats before I realize he expects me to take it. I suppose that's the gentlemanly thing to do for appearance's sake. I place my palm loosely over his, grateful for the lace gloves I wear, and step from the coach. He releases my hand as soon as my feet touch the ground, then approaches the woman. Minka and Mr. Boris exit next and take their places just behind me.

"Mrs. Donahue, it's lovely to see you again," Thorne says in a startlingly kind voice. "May I present Her Highness, Princess Rosaline Briar. Highness, Mrs. Donahue is the housekeeper at Sandalwood Manor."

She gives me an awkward curtsy, a grimace on her lips in place of a smile. "I must admit, Your Highness, we weren't expecting you."

"You weren't? I...I was scheduled to arrive two days ago." I glance at Thorne for affirmation, but his brows are knit together.

"That's just it," the housekeeper says. "When you didn't

arrive, we assumed you weren't coming at all. We haven't heard any word since Mr. Blackwood departed to fetch you."

"I'll take the blame for that," Thorne says. "We ran into several unforeseen delays. I was so preoccupied that I didn't think to write."

Mrs. Donahue wrings her hands as she glances from him to me. "I'm afraid Lord Phillips isn't here to receive you, Your Highness. He's out of town on Human Representative business until next week."

"What about Lady Phillips and Monty?" Thorne asks. "Lord Phillips wouldn't have left without ensuring a proper host was left in his place, and Monty was supposed to be here to meet his fiancée."

"My lady and her son are both here, but I daresay neither are expecting the princess either."

"A single day's delay shouldn't have been enough to convince them she wasn't coming at all."

Mrs. Donahue lowers her voice and speaks only to him. "You know how the situation has been, Mr. Blackwood. This is only the latest of delays."

"Well, she's here now. You may take her to her room to ready herself to be received by Mr. Phillips. Is my guest room available? I'll be staying until the wedding."

Her lips stretch into another grimace. "It will take some time to ready your rooms. Mr. Phillips is hosting an impromptu garden party, and there are several guests staying over."

Thorne curses under his breath. "Monty, you stone-headed fool."

"I will arrange the best rooms for you at once," Mrs. Donahue says. "In the meantime, you may wait in the parlor. Unless you'd prefer to join the party."

Thorne's gaze turns to me, and I realize he's allowing me to make the choice.

"Garden parties are lovely," Minka whispers beside me. "They usually host a wide variety of delicious beverages."

At the same time, Mr. Boris says, "A party with strangers is no place for a princess."

While he might be right, meeting my fiancé in public sounds preferable to a private introduction in the parlor. "We'll join the party."

Mrs. Donahue gives me an anxious smile, then escorts us inside the house. Minka accompanies me while Mr. Boris stays behind to deliver my bags to my room. The inside of the manor is just as lovely as the outside, with rich mahogany wainscoting, stylish furniture, and walls papered in cream-and-silver damask. The housekeeper leads us past a grand foyer, then into a bright solarium filled with potted orchids. Beyond it sprawls a sunlit lawn crowded with guests. Sounds of raucous laughter and giddy voices ring through the tall glass windows that line the room.

"Stones, I hate Monty's garden parties," Thorne says under his breath.

Mrs. Donahue reaches the door that leads outside but pulls up short. She whirls around with a too-wide smile. "I think it's best you wait in the parlor after all. I shouldn't spring a guest upon Mr. Phillips so suddenly."

Thorne groans while I narrow my eyes. The housekeeper steps toward us, ushering us back, but I cast a glance over her shoulder at the scene beyond. The guests appear human and around my age or slightly older. Men and women mingle with ease, their attire elegant yet relaxed. While the women wear day dresses and hold lace parasols, they laugh unrestrained, wineglasses full to the brim. The men wear fine suits, but many have their cravats loose or jackets discarded, top hats perched crookedly on their heads.

My eyes move to the center of the gathering where much of their amusement and attention is fixed. There, a man with curly blond hair sits on his knees in the grass, his cravat undone, his sleeves rolled sloppily up to his elbows. His head is thrown back, lips parted wide, as a woman pours wine directly into his mouth. The liquid overflows over his cheeks, and he rises unsteadily to his feet, spraying his guests with stray droplets as he attempts to swallow his mouthful. His guests laugh at his antics and join him as he lets out a whoop of a cheer.

Terror strikes my chest. "Please don't tell me that's my...my..."

"That's Monty Phillips," Thorne says.

At the urging of his guests, he gets back on his knees and opens his mouth for another round of force-fed wine.

My shoulders sink. "But he's..."

Thorne releases a long-suffering sigh. "An idiot."

"An idiot," I echo with a solemn nod.

"You really should wait in the parlor," Mrs. Donahue says, her voice edged with hysteria.

"No need," I say. "I'll meet him now."

The housekeeper's face burns beet red as she proceeds to open the door and lead us out to the crowd. The scent of alcohol clashes with the clean breeze and the fresh aroma of cut grass. Monty rises to his feet again, eliciting another cheer from his guests. His expression goes blank as he notices our arrival but quickly breaks into a dimpled grin.

"Thornyyy!" he says, drawing out the last syllable far too long. His gaze slides to me. "And you must be..."

"Her Highness, Princess Rosaline," announces Mrs. Donahue, head bowed low in either deference or shame.

The guests go quiet as all eyes lock on me.

"Right," Monty says, the mirth leaving his tone. He gestures toward me with a sloppy wave. "Everyone, meet my fiancée. Or she would be if..." He halts on a hiccup. His lips pull into another wide, dimpled smile, and something sly dances in his glossy gray eyes. "If our engagement hadn't been broken."

23

BRIONY

My heart leaps into my throat. I blink at the man who is supposed to be my fiancé. "What do you mean our engagement was broken?"

Monty gives an exaggerated flourish of his hand. "It means...what it means."

"Monty," Thorne growls, a sharp warning in his eyes. With a string of muttered curses, Thorne strides over to him, whispering something I can't hear. After some back and forth between Thorne looking angry and Monty looking like a giddy fool, my fiancé finally has the decency to wipe the shit-eating grin off his face. With a somber nod, he slinks over to an empty chair and drops himself into it. The guests resume chattering, but the mood is much more subdued.

Thorne's jaw is hard as he leaves his friend. He's about to brush past me when I stop him with a tug on his sleeve. He freezes in place, his gaze landing on where my gloved finger-tips meet the navy linen of his jacket. I release his sleeve and speak through my teeth. "What does he mean our engagement is broken?"

"I'll take care of this," he says. "Don't talk to him until I return."

With that, he marches away and into the solarium.

Minka puts her hand on my arm. "Your fiancé may not have meant what he said, Miss Rose. Everything might still be all right."

I purse my lips, unsure of what to say. What to do. Thorne told me not to talk to Monty until he returns, but what am I to do until then? I've never been to a garden party before, and I don't particularly want to talk to any of these strangers. Even if I did, none of them seem partial to speaking with me. Whether it's due to their own dislike, Monty's chilly reception of me, or respect of royal protocol, I know not. Some look at me with sideways glances as they sip their wine while others ignore me entirely.

Mrs. Donahue approaches me, wringing her hands. "I deeply apologize for such a chaotic introduction, Highness, and I am sorry to say Lady Phillips is not available to receive you at this time." She glances to the side, toward a nearby tent. Beneath it stands a table of concessions as well as a divan. Upon the divan, a fine-dressed woman naps with a fluffy brown dog in one arm and an empty wineglass in the other. Lady Phillips, I presume. "Shall I make any other introductions for you, Highness?"

"No, Mrs. Donahue, but thank you. I'm...fine." The last word nearly refuses to escape my lips, for it's almost a lie.

She gives me a gracious nod and shuffles away, a grimace tugging her lips with every step. Poor Mrs. Donahue. And poor me! *This* is the family I'm supposed to marry into? *This* is the family that's supposed to save my own's reputation? I glance from the snoring Lady Phillips to Monty sunk low in his chair, head tipped back, eyes closed. I'm starting to think the best this family has to offer mine is their wealth. Considering what Father told me about the collectors announcing his debt in a matter of weeks, it makes sense he'd be desperate. And why Lord Phillips might be equally as desperate to marry off his idiot son.

After an uncomfortably long stretch of merely standing, staring at the crowd, and doing nothing, Minka leans into my line of sight, whiskers twitching. "Shall I get you a glass of wine, Miss Rose? I'm not certain they have Moondrop or Midnight Blush like we favor in Lunar, but they likely have the Earthen Court specialty, Oakmead."

My fragile nerves say *yes please give me wine at once*, but as I glance around the party, which is once again growing rather rowdy, I'm not sure I want what they're having. "I'll take tea instead."

She flounces away toward the concessions tent, and I immediately regret having dismissed her. I feel even more awkward standing alone. Before the feeling can grow too strong, a firm touch alights at my elbow. I expect to find Minka, but instead, it's Thorne. He stands beside me, a heavy clay cup in hand—not one of the delicate porcelain ones from the party. His gloves are gone, as is his jacket, and his shirtsleeves have been rolled to his elbows. His dark hair has been tied back from his face in a style I haven't seen him wear before. It shows off his widow's peak more than when he wears his tresses down, but there's a messiness to it that gives it a roguish air. His spectacles somehow tie the look together in a surprisingly dashing way.

"I'm sorry I left you," he says, voice low. "Give me ten more minutes, and I'll fix this."

Before I can react, his hand leaves my elbow and he strides over to Monty, thrusting the clay cup at the man.

Monty rolls his eyes as he accepts it, downing its contents in a long gulp. He makes a disgusted face as he returns the empty mug to Thorne.

I think I know what's in that drink and the reason for Thorne's hasty exit from the party, but my mind is more wrapped around what he said to me.

I'm sorry I left you.

He...apologized to me. That was unexpected. I find myself clutching the part of my arm where Thorne touched. The contact had been firm, considerate, and oddly attentive. At least, that's how it had felt to me. Almost...friendly. Like he used to seem in my dreams. Thorne was clearly too distracted by his annoying friend to realize he was being nice to me. And I'm annoyed that I even care.

"Your tea, Miss Rose." Minka's return startles me, but I accept the porcelain cup, grateful to have something to do with my hands. I return my attention to Thorne and Monty. The former stands with his arms crossed, staring down at the latter, who continues to sulk in his chair.

I narrow my eyes on the empty cup in Thorne's hands, remembering the tonic he made for me at my birthday party. He helped me sober up from the disastrous effects of Moondrop. My chest tightens. That was one of the last moments between us before he betrayed me. Before he ruined everything. A strange tangle of emotions writhes through me, rage dancing with something softer. Sadder. The grief of something lost. I expect that loss to be my parents, but it isn't. It's...

My gaze lands on Thorne's profile, the sharp cut of his jaw on display thanks to his hair being tied back.

Thank you for being my dance partner.

You're welcome.

I shake my head and wrench my eyes from Thorne. My

determination to look anywhere but at him aids in my discovery of a small body of water beyond the crowd. It's a pond encircled by a well-kept path. Thorne said to give him ten minutes, which means we have time to kill. "Come, Minka, let's take a stroll."

TEN MINUTES LATER, THORNE AND MONTY JOIN ME AND Minka on the path around the pond. Thorne still holds the empty cup in his hands, which he seems to notice at the same time I do. He frowns down at it as they stop before us.

"Shall I take that for you?" Minka asks Thorne. "Can I get anyone wine? Tea?"

Though she's been promoted to my lady's maid, she can't seem to shake her preoccupation with serving beverages. I shake my head, as I left my teacup behind at the party, and before Monty can say anything, Thorne says, "No wine," and keeps the clay cup in his hand.

"No wine," Monty repeats grudgingly. Then, after an elbow to the ribs from Thorne, he bends into a deep and steady bow. When he straightens, I find his cheeks are still ruddy from drink and his curly blond hair is in disarray, but he appears far more sober than before. I know firsthand the power of Thorne's miracle tonic, so I'm not surprised.

"Forgive my ungentlemanly behavior, Highness." Monty speaks slowly, carefully. His words are probably rehearsed. He steps closer and offers me his arm. "May I escort you around the pond?"

I've already circled it five times, but I accept, placing my hand in the crook of his elbow. I expect a flutter in my chest, for I don't exactly have a long-standing history of formal courtships, but I felt far more flustered when Thorne touched my arm earlier. My schooling was thorough in etiquette, so it's not like I haven't practiced this exact scenario with my peers. And I suppose my dances with Thorne haven't hurt in that regard either.

Or maybe—and this is by far the most likely—I simply despise my fiancé and am incapable of feeling a single flutter for him.

We proceed with our stroll in tense silence for a few moments until the sound of a clearing throat shatters the quiet. I cast a glance behind us and find Thorne and Minka following in our wake. Thorne stares daggers at the back of Monty's head. As if he can feel the invisible threat, Monty releases a resigned sigh and gives me one of those dimpled grins I glimpsed earlier. "I am most pleased to meet you in person, Highness."

If I wasn't so on edge regarding our supposedly broken engagement, I'd laugh at how feigned his enthusiasm is. But I'm not at all amused.

"Let us drop the pretense, Mr. Phillips," I say. "What did you mean when you said our engagement has been broken?"

His expression turns more casual as does his posture. "If you aren't already aware, our parents have spent years arranging our betrothal. I was supposed to meet you long ago, but for whatever reason, you were unavailable. Then it happened again. And again. And again. It became a bit of a game to me. A bet if you will. The latest of which resulted in today's party, my self-gifted prize for winning the bet."

I furrow my brow. "Because you expected me two days ago and I didn't arrive?"

He nods. "Since our betrothal has been constructed by means of a fae bargain—thanks to your parents' fae nature —it is bound and broken by conditions and rules. Your late arrival has severed the bargain and voided our engagement."

Panic pulses in my chest. Had I received this news the night of my party, I would have been thrilled to hear our betrothal had come to an end, but I need this engagement now. My bargain with Thorne depends on it. The fates of our families do too. "Surely we can fix this. I know we've missed several prior deadlines, but our parents have renegotiated each time. Why can't we do the same now? I'm finally here."

His expression brightens with a sly grin. "Ah, that is because I made a bargain myself. My father agreed that if our betrothal bargain was broken one more time, I would get to choose my bride thereafter. A luxury for someone in my position, I know, but one I'm eager to have."

"You don't want to marry me?" Thorne already said as much, but he made it sound like it was due to my family's declining reputation. Perhaps I'm vain for this assumption, but I thought meeting me would assuage any such reservations.

He chuckles. "I don't know you well enough to want to marry you. Can you not say the same? Do you want to marry me?"

No, of course I don't, but I don't say so out loud.

Thankfully, he doesn't wait for my answer. "Besides, my father won't be home for a week. Even if I wanted to proceed with our wedding, he won't be here to renegotiate the terms until then."

Stars above, he's right, and I need this wedding to proceed on schedule. Nyxia only gave me two weeks until my family will be moved to the catacombs, a deadline that aligns with my original wedding date. At this point, there are only ten days left of the two weeks she gave me. Ten days until my wedding *must* occur. Desperation propels my next words. "Perhaps if we spend the week getting to know one another until your father returns, you'll find our arrangement amenable, and we can proceed with far fewer reservations."

He runs his free hand over his jaw, expression thoughtful. "A princess shouldn't be forced to win her prince's affections. Isn't that the opposite of how most love stories go?"

I bristle at his words. I said we should get to know each other, not that I'd win his affections.

"But I do like the sound of that." He stops in place and whirls to face me. "It's like a reverse fairytale romance. You'll spend a week trying to win my heart."

A thread of irritation winds its way around my chest. It takes all my effort to keep a false smile on my face. "I can't tell if you're jesting, Mr. Phillips."

He claps his hands. "Let's make it a game."

"Monty." Thorne says his friend's name with a growl of warning as he and Minka stop beside us on the path.

Minka bounces on the balls of her feet. "Oh, I love games."

"A game," I say. "You want our betrothal...to be a game."

He casts a withering look at Thorne. "Did you not tell her how much I love games? Stones, Thorny, what are you good for if you didn't talk up my best points?" He turns back to me with a crooked grin. "I bet he said nothing to you the entire time you were together. He can be as dour as a slug when he wants."

Monty isn't wrong, but he's taken our conversation off course. I clear my throat and try to speak with as much calm as I can. Even so, my words are half hissed between my teeth. "About our betrothal. I don't think we should make light of it."

He waves a dismissive hand. "I don't mean that I'm not taking it seriously. In fact, I can't think of a better way to fall in love with you than through a game. Bets, bargains, and games are my love language, for I do enjoy the thrill of a risk. I'm halfway in love with you already, for I tend to fall in love at first sight." He says the last part with a wink.

Stars above, I might punch him.

"How about this?" he says, oblivious to my growing ire. "If you can win my heart five times over the next seven days, I will beg my father to reinstate our betrothal agreement. Beg. On my knees. I swear it."

Thorne's voice comes out sharp. "You're talking to a princess, Monty. You can't proposition a royal like this."

Monty shrugs. "She's more than a royal. She's my potential future wife. For the first time, I've been granted permission to choose the woman I spend my life with. I'm not going to pretend to be someone I'm not just to please the bride that was chosen for me." To me, he says, "If you don't like how I am, we should just call it off now."

Yes, let's do that! my insides plead. This man is insufferable and clearly dislikes our arrangement as much as I do. Perhaps more, considering I at least need the marriage to fulfill my bargain with Thorne and break the curse on our families. If we'd met before our union became so necessary, I'd find him to be a kindred spirit. The rebellion he shows now is the same I felt when I first learned of my surprise engagement. No matter how it irks me in this moment, I understand it. Understand him. But what he's proposing is humiliating.

Thorne steps closer to me. "Say the word and I'll punch him for you."

"No, Thorny," Monty says with an easy laugh. "The last time you punched me, you shattered a rib."

"Let's make it two this time," Thorne mutters.

Monty leans in with a loud whisper. "This one I don't like playing games with. He really doesn't know his own strength."

Thorne's fingers curl as if he's truly preparing for that punch. I feel bad for the clay cup he still holds, which is surely being strangled in his grip. "This isn't a game, Monty."

"Oh, but it could be."

Minka lifts a finger, head cocked to the side. "The terms are hazy, though. How exactly will Her Highness win your heart?"

"You're right, kitty cat, a game should have clear rules. We'll have seven activities total. Drinking, dining, dancing. That sort of thing. If I find Her Highness pleasing—judged beneath the lens of becoming my future wife, of course—I'll reward her with a kiss by the end of the day to show she's won my heart."

"Stones below, Monty." Thorne runs a hand over his face as if he's truly embarrassed. Or is he simply worried our bargain is about to unravel?

Monty gives me a playful pat on the arm, a far-too-familiar gesture. "What say you, Princess? Are you up for a game? Do you think you can win my heart in seven days?"

Minka's grin stretches wide. "Oh, I think she can!"

My stomach roils. I've done this before. I've competed for a man's heart and lost. I wasn't invested in the bridal pageant I participated in and was rooting for my rival the entire time, but this situation is different. I *need* this marriage—

Wait. Yes, things *are* different this time. I'm not alone. Thorne knows Monty. He can help me act however I need to act, be whomever I need to be, to satisfy his friend. At this point, it's our only hope. For now. Once his father returns, I can appeal to him myself, as can Thorne. This marriage is happening. It must.

You're the Briar family hero.

The reminder of what's at stake bolsters my nerves. I can do this. Donning a pleasant smile, I say, "I agree to your game, Mr. Phillips."

He thrusts his fist in the air in a victorious gesture, then closes in on me so fast, I'm not at all prepared for the kiss he plants on my cheek. Keeping his face next to mine, he whispers, "You've already won your first round. Four more to go."

I almost don't hear the last part, for a sharp sound like something breaking splinters the air nearby. Monty pulls away, then saunters back toward the party, whistling a jaunty tune.

I'm so caught off guard by that exchange, I almost forget to seek the source of that breaking sound. Then I see it. Two halves of the shattered clay cup in Thorne's tightly clenched hand.

24

THORNE

My blood boils as I watch Monty stride away, hands in his pockets. How dare he turn his engagement into a game? He's always been one of the most irritating human beings I've ever had the displeasure to know, but he's reached a new low with this.

Monty waltzes past his guests, only some of which had been spying on the exchange by the pond, and heads for the solarium. I start after him. Maybe I can talk some sense into the bastard. I can't count on Lady Phillips to intervene, for she's never cared what Monty does. Lord Phillips will be outraged when he returns, but he can do nothing while he's away.

A sharp pain pulses in my palm just as I reach the cluster of guests crowding the lawn. I glance down at my hand and find a stream of crimson beneath two halves of shattered clay. Right. The broken cup. I don't know what came over me, but when Monty shoved his idiotic face so close to Briony's and kissed her cheek, I nearly throttled him. He's lucky I only broke a cup and not his nose.

Some of the party guests call out to me as I move through the crowd, for many are my acquaintances as well, though I can't say I like any of them. I ignore them all, setting the broken cup in the middle of a table and eliciting startled gasps from its patrons, then proceed after Monty. As I near the solarium, I untie my cravat and wrap it around my bleeding hand. My half-fae heritage will ensure rapid healing, but for now, I might as well staunch the blood flow.

I find Monty sprawled on a divan in the solarium beside a cluster of potted orchids. He absently plucks one of the blooms between two fingers and brings its short stem to his lips like a cigarette. His expression brims with a combination of arrogance and carelessness as I stop before the divan, arms crossed over my chest.

He mimes smoking the orchid bloom, then perches it between his lips and rests his arms behind his head. His voice comes out slightly muffled around the stem. "I told you not to bring her back if she was ugly, so I can see why you ensured her safe arrival."

"You're making a mockery of your betrothal."

"Her family has made a mockery of it ever since it was forged."

"Is this really how you want to start your marriage? With a game?"

He takes another pretend puff of his orchid and flicks it away. "I like to start everything with a game."

"You're showing her that your love must be earned. Won."

He looks me over with narrowed eyes. "Why do you care? If she wants me to choose her, she should choose me as well. Besides, I wouldn't want to play with her so badly if I didn't think I liked her."

"She isn't a toy, Monty. She's a person."

"You're awfully protective over my fiancée. Is there something you want to tell me, old pal?" He gives a pointed look at my bandaged hand. "Interesting wound you have there."

His words have my own sticking in my throat. Why *am* I being so protective? I want to believe it's because of my bargain with Briony. Because Monty's idiocy is jeopardizing it. That's certainly part of it, but there's more to it than that. Outside of our families' feud, Briony is a wonderful woman. Before I discovered the truth of her identity, I cherished my dreams about her. When we aren't fighting—stones, even when we are—she's undoubtedly beautiful. Strong. Fierce. A prize for any man. Yet Monty is treating her like an inconvenience. A pawn on a game board. She deserves so much better than this asshole.

"By the way," Monty says, "we're going to your house tomorrow."

"My house?"

"Yes, for I'd rather not play our game with so many spectators. I'm already tired of them. I told my guests they could stay until my father gets back."

I speak through my teeth. "Then make them leave."

"I can't do that, Thorny boy. That's plain rude."

"And inviting yourself over to my house isn't? What about leaving your guests? That isn't well-mannered either."

Monty chuckles. "They won't even know I'm gone. Come on. You promised Angela you'd host a country party when she came back from boarding school. She'll be home tomorrow and she'll be giddy if I tell her we're going to Blackwood Estate."

My heart softens the slightest bit. Angela is Monty's

younger sister and has always felt like a sister to me as well. And he's right. I did promise her I'd host a small—*very* small—gathering at Blackwood Estate this year. But still. "This isn't the time or the place, Monty. You need to prepare for your wedding."

He waves a flippant hand. "There's nothing to prepare. Well, hardly anything. The date is set, our appointment at the church still stands. And I was telling the truth about what my father said. He was quite angry when my future bride failed to arrive on the promised date two days ago. He said, *Monty, you charming and most handsome son of mine, I will finally allow you to choose your wife. Make sure she's well endowed.*"

"Your father didn't say that."

"No, maybe he said something about a dowry. Well en-dowry-ed. That's probably it."

Stones and soil, my head might explode if I have to hear more of his nonsense.

"I'm going to your house whether you meet me there or not," Monty says. "I've already written ahead, and your butler was more than amenable. You know Mr. Hartshire loves me."

I remove my spectacles and pinch the bridge of my nose. "You wrote to my butler already?"

"Indeed I did. As soon as the first guest arrived for my party, I immediately regretted having said I'd host one at all."

"Why the hell did he agree to receive you while I'm away?"

"Why wouldn't he? I always stay at your house when you're off on business. Did you not know?"

Of course I didn't know. If I had I would have doused my manor in Monty repellent, which would include one part responsibility and one part tact. And perhaps fired all my female staff to ensure there was no one he'd be tempted to harass.

Monty sits upright on the divan but his posture remains slumped. Lazy. He stares out the wall of windows with a crooked smile on his lips. "She is nice on the eyes, I'll give her that."

I follow his line of sight and find Briony out on the lawn, not too far from the solarium. She stands away from the crowd next to Minka, sipping from a porcelain teacup. Damn. I left her alone again. I was so preoccupied with following Monty that I didn't give enough thought to how awkward she must feel amongst all these strangers. Though one wouldn't know she feels uncomfortable just by looking at her. She's always had a regal air about her. The way she stands. The way she speaks. The haughty way she lifts her chin. It's been apparent since the first dream I had about her. And now, with the afternoon sun glinting off the loose tendrils of golden hair that spill beneath her hat, she looks every inch the princess she was born to be.

My resolve hardens as I'm reminded why we're here. What's at stake.

She's Princess Rosaline Briar, and I'm Vintarys Lemuria. We have a bargain to fulfill and a curse to break.

I followed Monty to try to convince him to discard his idiotic game, but I realize now the game is exactly what Briony and I need. The anger we feel over it will ensure we remain fixedly opposed to the wedding. That's the only way we fulfill the terms required to break the curse. The task we undertake *must* be something neither of us wants to do.

It dawns on me how everything might have unraveled. Had Monty pulled his head out of his ass and acted like a proper gentleman, had he taken one look at Briony and realized how lucky he'd be to have her, he might have ruined everything. Briony might have liked him. She might have *wanted* to marry him, voiding the terms required to break the curse. Likewise, I could have been happy for them, voiding my side of the effort required as well.

As things stand now, Briony likely rues the thought of marrying Monty, even more so than before she met him. And on my side...

Stones, the very thought of them marrying, of Briony being stuck with my asshole friend for the rest of her life, sends spears of rage through my chest.

I clench my teeth.

This is how it should be.

It's the only way our bargain will work.

The only way to awaken our families from slumber.

One question remains, one of shadows and thorns that dampens all thoughts of victory: will it be worth the cost?

Monty rises from the divan with a stretch. "If Princess Rosaline wants to play with me, she'll meet me at your place tomorrow afternoon. I'll head to Blackwood Estate after Angela gets home." With a dismissive wave, he tucks his hands back in his pockets and exits the solarium to the main part of the manor.

I glance back out at the lawn. My eyes lock on Briony's, then slide to the side of her face, where Monty laid that impertinent kiss. I lift my gaze back to her eyes and give her a nod, wordlessly conveying that I'm here. I'll help her. We'll do what needs to be done.

And I'm going to hate every second of it.

25

BRIONY

The next morning, I enter a department store for the first time in my life. I pull up short in the foyer, stunned by the marble floors, the enormous reception desk, and the curving staircases that lead four stories up. After seeing Nocturnus Palace, I didn't think a clothing store could impress me, but I was wrong. Bartleby's is a sight to behold, even amongst the other grand buildings in downtown Jasper. Unlike a modiste, which I've at least read about and seen in passing, Bartleby's is several times larger and hosts ready-to-wear fashion. There are no wait times like those associated with custom clothing, which means I'll be in possession of new ensembles in a matter of minutes.

Thorne stops beside me, assessing the interior of the department store with far less enthusiasm. "I can't believe we have to put up with this farce."

"I heartily agree," Mr. Boris says. He's in his humanoid form today and has been rather cross all morning. Though I daresay his sour mood began yesterday when I briefly relayed the events of my first meeting with Monty Phillips. He lifts his chin. "Mr. Phillips is lucky I was preoccupied yesterday. I might have torn out his throat with my teeth."

I give him a placating smile. "I don't think my parents would have appreciated that, Mr. Boris, considering I'm doing this for them."

Minka links her arm with mine. "At least we get to go shopping. And with Mr. Blackwood's funds!"

Thorne nudges the bridge of his spectacles. "Are you sure this is necessary?"

"You saw the note," I say. "Of course it's necessary."

Thorne mutters a string of curses but doesn't argue. He knows I'm right. After a blessedly uneventful rest of the evening yesterday, I got a good night's sleep for once, and a dreamless one at that. I awoke more refreshed than I've been in days and was even feeling somewhat positive about the newest developments in our scheme. But all those good feelings fled when I received a note this morning that read:

Second game. Dress pretty for me.

I was momentarily puzzled over the *second game* part. What happened to the first game? Then I recalled what he'd said when he'd kissed my cheek. *You've already won your first round.* I was glad to find he'd been serious about that since it means I only need to win four more games to fulfill our agreement, but I was more enraged than anything.

Dress pretty for me.

Like he has any right to demand such a thing!

Thorne was equally annoyed when I showed him the note over breakfast this morning. Since Monty was nowhere to be found, we were left to figure out what to do about the game on our own.

Hence shopping.

"Come along, then," Thorne says, tone begrudging. "Women's clothing is on the second floor." He starts off toward one of the staircases, leading our party past the reception desk. Two fae females in simple black dresses welcome us with enthusiastic grins. As soon as we pass the desk, I catch a snippet of whispered conversation.

"That's Mr. Blackwood!" says one of the receptionists. "Oh, he's so handsome. I can't believe he's yet to be married."

"Yes, but who is the lady with him?" the other asks. "I've only seen him here with Miss Phillips."

We reach the staircase, and I'm no longer able to overhear the conversation. Thorne shows no sign that he heard the receptionists gossiping, and simply strides up the stairs with the confidence of a king in his court. My curiosity gets the better of me, and I quicken my pace to reach his side. "You're certainly popular here."

He gives me a sideways glance. "Blackwood Estate isn't far from Jasper. When I'm in town, I do my shopping in the city."

My pulse kicks up as I ask, "Who is Miss Phillips?"

"Monty's sister."

I gathered that much already, considering they share a last name. "Are the two of you close?"

"Yes."

I open my mouth, determined to find out just how close they are, when we reach the top of the staircase. My words stick in my throat as I'm suddenly distracted by the splendor around me. The second floor expands fully around the building in a circular shape, with a view of the first floor below at its center. The walls of the ladies' department are papered in blush-pink brocade, the ornate coffered ceiling boasting crystal chandeliers. Countertops line the perimeter of the room, spread with ribbons, jewelry, vials of perfume, and hats. Velvet curtains enclose what I assume are private fitting rooms, where I see shopgirls delivering garments. Chairs, tables, and divans are interspersed between displays of evening dresses, ballgowns, daytime clothing, and even underclothes, giving off a comforting air. It begs one to stay and shop with leisure, and from the way several ladies sit and chat amongst their bags and boxes or newly purchased goods, shopping at a department store seems as much a social event as it is a practical one. I look from one end of the space to the other, unsure of where to start.

Thorne's voice pulls me from my stupor. "Have you never been to a department store before?"

"Of course I haven't. I've never even picked out my own clothing."

"Truly?"

I meet his eyes with a pointed look. "I grew up at a convent, remember? Everything was chosen for me. What I'm wearing now is the first thing I've worn that wasn't gray, and it was a gift, not something I chose for myself."

A furrow forms between his brows. Is that pity in his eyes? He shakes his head, and the expression is gone. "Let's start with daytime attire. You'll need clothing for the week, not just today's game."

SHOPPING IS FAR MORE WORK THAN I EXPECTED IT TO BE. First, there's a whole sizing chart to get used to. Then I have to try everything on to ensure a good fit. After an hour, I've selected two new skirts, three blouses, and a day dress. Only then do I realize I've yet to find a single outfit for today's game. Thorne told me about Monty's insistence that we meet at Blackwood Estate, so I assume the game will commence after he arrives.

Minka and Mr. Boris wait with my bags while I locate Thorne. He gave me a purse of emerald rounds—Earthen Court's currency—and then kept his distance while I browsed and tried on clothing. But now I need his expertise. I find him leaning against a marble column near one of the staircases. His arms are crossed over his chest, one knee bent while his foot is propped on the pillar. The posture would look lazy on anyone else, but as I approach him, I'm struck by how intimidating he'd be if I didn't already know him.

Not only that, but...stars, he's gorgeous. His dark, almost shoulder-length waves. His intense brown eyes. The cut of his perfectly tailored navy suit that hugs his frame like a second skin. And I'm not the only one dazzled by his appearance. Nearby, a trio of human women stare at him from one of the many sitting areas, whispering amongst themselves and hiding their giddy smiles behind their hands. I wonder how they would feel if they knew he was half fae. If they saw him in his unseelie form. Would they be more attracted? Less?

I stop before him, feeling slightly self-conscious before our audience, and am careful to keep a respectable distance between us. "I need you now."

He straightens, his eyes going momentarily wide at my statement.

My cheeks flush. "I need your advice, Mr. Blackwood," I amend.

"About?"

I cast a sideways glance at our three spectators. One pouts as she stares daggers at me, but after a sharp glare from Thorne, the woman pointedly looks away and sparks up conversation with her companions. I feel oddly smug about his cold reaction to his admirers, but I admit he was quite rude. How would I feel if a handsome man glared at me just for looking at him?

Still, I can't find it in me to feel bad for the women. I really do need his advice.

I lower my voice so as not to be overheard. "I need you to help me pick something to wear for today's game. When will Mr. Phillips arrive? During the day? The evening?"

"This evening, I assume, as he's waiting for his sister to return home before they head to my estate."

"Oh, he's bringing Miss Phillips?"

"He is."

For some reason, a strange sinking feeling hits my gut. Maybe I simply don't want an audience for Monty's game. Or maybe it's what those receptionists said.

I've only seen him here with Miss Phillips.

I can't help wondering if Thorne has a romantic connection with Monty's sister. Not that it's any of my business.

I shake the thoughts from my head. "What kind of clothing does he find attractive? What are his favorite colors?"

He shrugs. "I haven't a clue."

My mouth falls open. "What do you mean you haven't a clue? You're supposed to help me win his stupid game. Have you ever met someone he's attracted to? Was she modest? Daring? Confident? You must give me something."

He rubs his brow. "I suppose you can rule out modest. The women Monty associates with tend to be..."

"Sexy? Alluring?"

His jaw shifts side to side. "You might say that."

"Fine, that's a start. Now come help me choose something." Before I can think better of it, I lace my arm through his and drag him toward a display of evening gowns nearby. I release him as soon as we reach it and assess the four headless mannequins, each wearing the same dress but in four different hues. "What about this?"

He studies the display without interest. "It's...nice."

"Yes, but would Monty like it?"

"I told you, I don't know what he does and doesn't like. What matters more than the dress is how it looks on you."

"Then I suppose I'll have to try a few on." I make a note of the name of the gown so I can inform one of the shopgirls of my intent to try it on in my size later, and move on to the next display. Thorne shadows me, offering nothing helpful whatsoever. His posture is tense, expression closed off, as if he can't stand being forced to shop with me. Well, if he isn't going to be helpful, I suppose I can make the experience worse for him.

"Are you sure you don't know Monty's favorite color at least?"

"I don't."

"What about his favorite food? His favorite music?"

"I've never cared enough to ask."

We move on to the next display, which features a gown in indigo spider silk with a plunging neckline and a skirt that flares out beneath the mannequin's hips in a waterfall of chiffon. It's a slightly more modern style than the others we've looked at so far, blending human fashion with a hint of fae flair. I haven't a clue if Monty will like it, but if I could choose something for myself, this just might be it.

I glance at Thorne, ready to ask for his opinion despite knowing full well he won't have one, when I'm distracted by him running a hand through his hair. His dark tresses fall in tousled waves around his face, and I'm reminded of how it looked yesterday when he brought Monty the tonic.

Thorne catches me staring and narrows his eyes. "What?"

I avert my gaze. "You had your hair pulled back yesterday."

"I tied it back when I made the tonic," he says. "I don't normally mind having my hair down, but if I'm working on a time crunch, I can't stand it near my face."

"Wasn't my birthday cake rushed? Your hair was down then." My chest tightens. Why did I bring up my birthday? While our encounter in the kitchen had been cordial, what followed was a nightmare.

Thorne glances away from me and gives the skirt of the indigo gown on display an absent touch, as if sampling the feel of the chiffon. His tone takes on a tense quality despite his neutral words. "A bit, but I knew I had enough time."

I'm determined to lighten the mood for both of our sakes. In a teasing tone, I say, "I wonder if that cake was any good. You ruined my life before I got a chance to try it."

He huffs a halfhearted laugh. "Perhaps I'll make your wedding cake then."

Mention of my wedding sours my mood once more. Then a startling realization dawns. "Wait...should I be shopping for a wedding dress?"

"No need," Thorne says. "I spoke to Lady Phillips this morning. She wants you to wear her wedding dress and will have it altered before your nuptials take place. That is, if Lord Phillips agrees to resume your contract." He says the last part between his teeth, then mutters, "Damn Monty."

Meanwhile, my mind is stuck on the part where he said I'd be wearing Lady Phillips' wedding gown. I still haven't met her face to face, and my only impression of her was when I spotted her napping during the garden party. "Will it even fit?"

"I don't see why not."

"You say that, but are we even remotely the same size? I'm not exactly slender, you know."

His eyes meet mine. "You're perfect, what does it matter if you're slender?" His delivery is so dry, so matter of fact, he almost sounds annoyed.

My breath catches, my cheeks growing far too warm.

He blinks rapidly behind his spectacles as if he only now realizes he gave me a compliment. Or...was it a compliment at all?

You're perfect.

What a strange thing to say.

The energy between us grows taut, an awkward air stirring in the intervals between our too-quiet breaths. I force my attention back to the indigo dress and try to pretend I feel nothing amiss. "What matters, Mr. Blackwood, is that the dress won't fit, regardless of alterations, if Lady Phillips is significantly smaller than me. I'm not short either."

He clears his throat and studies the gown on display with far more interest than necessary. "Quite right."

I nearly laugh at his overly formal tone. He's truly flustered. Despite my efforts to shake the uncomfortable tension, it's grown. There's only one thing I can think to do now.

Turning to face him, I angle my head and bat my lashes. My lips curl in a coy grin. "So, you think I'm perfect, hmm?"

He blushes—actually *blushes*, like a damn schoolboy—for one glorious second. Then his mouth mirrors mine, a sly smile that has my stomach flipping. His posture eases and he tucks his hands in his pockets. Then he leans in close, eyes locked on mine. I hitch a breath, but I force myself not to flinch back. I know what he's doing. He's trying to turn the tables on me, to make me flustered as revenge.

Well…it's working.

He inches incrementally closer, and my heart nearly gallops out of my chest. Still, I keep my chin lifted, back straight, as he stops with his face mere inches from mine. He speaks, voice low, his breath warm as it brushes over my skin. "I think you're a nuisance."

He steps back, and his confident demeanor returns. It makes me wonder if I imagined his moment of bashfulness all along. He gives the skirt of the indigo gown another brush of his hand. "I like this one."

I can do nothing but stare after him as he strides away. When he's out of sight, I press my hand to my chest, feeling the pound of my heart, still racing after his nearness.

Damn.

Thorne and I may not be the ones playing a game, but he certainly won that round.

26

BRIONY

Six hundred emerald rounds later, I'm a whole wardrobe richer. Evidence of my spoils packs the interior of the coach, for Thorne's and my travel bags are already taking up the luggage rack. I never knew it could be so satisfying to spend someone else's money—or any money, for that matter—on myself, but it is. Though I suppose my satisfaction comes less from spending money and more from tormenting Thorne. I took great joy at how wide his eyes grew when he saw the final tally of bags and boxes filling Mr. Boris' and Minka's arms. He muttered about how dreadfully I was using him under the terms of our bargain, which was less satisfying, for it seemed more talk than true annoyance. Yet I had to take pleasure in some sense of revenge after he made my heart race earlier.

It's impossible to forget our exchange with him sitting so close to me in the coach. With the opposite bench so cluttered with my purchases, Mr. Boris and Minka insisted I claim the more comfortable seat beside Thorne. I tried to bully Thorne into sitting with Mr. Boris and my bags, but he would have none of that. So instead, I stare pointedly out the window and try not to recall the warmth of his breath on my face.

Thankfully, the scenery is stunning enough to distract me. After leaving the department store, we began our journey toward Blackwood Estate, which lies just outside the city of Jasper in the countryside. Here the towering emerald mountains loom even larger, while the landscape that flanks the road alternates between forests, farming fields, and wildflower meadows. The Earthen Court truly is a lush and gorgeous place.

We turn off the main road and make our way through a lightly wooded area. Just beyond it, I glimpse a field brimming with long grass and purple flowers. Just looking at the verdant carpet makes me want to kick off my shoes and run through it. Longing pulses in my chest as I'm reminded of my grove outside the convent, my private sanctuary I used to dance in. I always considered my grove as a consolation, second-best to the theaters and society balls I couldn't attend. While I still yearn for the latter experiences, I find myself regretting that I didn't appreciate that beautiful grove more. There was beauty in my solitary waltzes. Or even the ones with Thorne, when I thought he was a dream.

Now all that awaits in my future are dances with my unwanted husband. If he's even one for dancing at all.

My heart sinks, a regrettable thing considering how awed I was a moment before. I rouse myself from my unpleasant musings and focus again on that plush field, imagining the tickle of grass on my bare ankles, the scent of mountain air—

A sudden jolt of the coach has me lurching in my seat. I fling out my arms to brace myself as I'm propelled forward. I manage to catch the wall beside me, but my gloved hand slips. As for my other flailing hand...

A strong palm takes mine, while another grips my waist, pulling me back into my seat. The coach lurches again, but this time, I remain rooted in place. After another much smaller jolt, the coach rolls to a stop. Catching my breath, I assess the scene around me. My bags and boxes have tumbled off the opposite seat, some spilling their contents. Mr. Boris—still in seelie form—frantically reaches for the nearest one, stuffing loose stockings and silk underwear beneath layers of now-crinkled tissue. For a moment I fear Minka has somehow tumbled out of the coach, for I see no sign of her. That is, until I catch sight of the black-and-white cat perched on the backrest, claws digging into the upholstery, body arched in feline terror. I'm taken aback, for I've never seen Minka in her unseelie form, but my surprise is quickly surpassed when I feel a squeeze to my palm.

I whip my head to the side and find Thorne far closer than I expect. Not only that, but my hand is clasped in his, inches above his lap. He must have caught it when I reached out to brace myself. I'm suddenly aware of another grip, one firm and warm on my waist. He holds me tight, arm behind me.

"Are you all right?" he asks. The sides of our bodies are pressed so tightly together, I can feel the rumble of his deep voice.

I pull my hand from his and scoot several inches away. He releases my waist without argument. "I'm...fine," I say. Thank the stars for that word, for how often I've come to rely on it to mask what I'm really feeling without lying. I am *fine*, for I'm feeling neither terrible nor great, but I'm also unnerved, discomposed, disquieted, and all sorts of other things that I care not to admit out loud.

Thorne exits the carriage just as the coachman descends from his perch. I peek outside the door, watching as Thorne rounds the back of the vehicle. He curses under his breath. My curiosity is too strong to keep me inside, so I exit after him. It doesn't take long to see what transpired; one of the rear wheels has broken. The footman is already assessing the damage while the coachman addresses Thorne. "Mr. Blackwood, we will have the wheel replaced with the spare as soon as possible."

"I'm grateful," Thorne says in a voice far kinder than I expect. He turns from the wheel, frowning when he notices I've left the coach. Mr. Boris and Minka funnel out beside me, with Minka still in her feline form.

"Wait here," Thorne says. "I'll walk to my manor and send alternate transport."

I furrow my brow. "You're going to walk? Is it far?"

"We're already at Blackwood Estate," he says. "My manor is just a short walk from here." He starts off toward the field of lush grass. A pinch of envy strikes me.

I follow after him. "I'm coming with you."

"There's no need. I'll have a wagon sent to retrieve you in no time."

"Yes, but I want to walk."

He halts and glances over his shoulder. "Forget what I said. My manor is far."

I scoff. "You won't dissuade me that easily."

"You should stay with your belongings instead of leaving six hundred emerald rounds worth of clothing unattended."

Mr. Boris gives a proud sniff. "I will wait with Her Highness' purchases. If you're suggesting we have reasons to fear bandits, then the princess should not remain."

Thorne hangs his head and rubs his brow. "That's not what I was implying."

"Then I'll walk with you," I say, closing the remaining distance between us. "You know I don't do well with boredom."

He lifts his face, his mouth quirking at one corner. "Instead, you'd rather be alone with me? In the woods?"

I know he's trying to get me riled up like he did in the department store, but I refuse to fall for his ruse this time. "Instead, I'd like to *walk*."

Something soft brushes my leg. I nearly jump out of my skin before I find Minka slinking around my ankles, rubbing on the hem of my skirt in a very catlike manner. "I'll chaperone," she says, though her mouth remains closed when she speaks. Not all fae utilize their lips and vocal cords when talking in their unseelie form. Some simply utter the words, carried by fae magic. "The princess won't be alone. It's been years since I've taken a walk in this form."

I meet Thorne's eyes with a triumphant grin. "See? You can't argue now."

He emits a string of grumbled curses. "Fine, but I won't slow down for you."

THE FIELD IS AS LOVELY TO STROLL THOUGH AS IT APPEARED from the coach window. My only regret is that I can't take off my shoes. Well, I suppose I *could* take off my shoes, but then Thorne would be annoying about it. He's already reached the edge of the field while I'm still at its center, and if I dawdle too long, I'll lose sight of him completely. I've already lost Minka. Despite her offer to chaperone my walk with Thorne, she immediately grew distracted by pouncing about and batting rustling grass with her paws.

I quicken my pace and discover the field ends with a

curving hill. Thorne waits on its crest, hands in his pockets. I reach his side and nearly gasp at the sight before me. More green fields stretch out at the base of the hill before the wild land gives way to an elegant garden. A manor twice as large as the Phillipses' lies beyond that, with rich forest and towering green mountains as its backdrop.

I knew Mr. Blackwood was a wealthy man, famed for his well-loved bakeries, but I never realized he was this well off. I face him, and find him smiling down at his property, a gentle expression on his face. It's almost enough to make me want to keep quiet, to let him enjoy whatever he's experiencing right now. The key word being *almost*. My curiosity is far greater than my kindness.

I narrow my eyes at him. "How in the stars did a baker come to own all this?"

He gives me a withering look, but there seems to be humor in it. "Marriage."

The word makes my pulse kick up. "What do you mean, marriage? You...you haven't been married, have you?" Surely society would have been all over that news.

"No, not my marriage. My father's. His first occupation was as a baker, and he still was one when he had his short-lived dalliance with my mother. When she got what she needed from him—me—they cut their ties. Soon after, he won the heart of a wealthy heiress, Alina Mayes. By then, he'd become more than just a baker and had gone into business with Lord Phillips. So he had just enough status to appease her parents. They married. She died a year after I came into the picture."

I'm surprised at the sorrow that laces his tone.

"I wish I'd gotten to know her longer," he says. "Alina was kind to me. Accepted my existence and all my secrets without question, which tells me my father had already confided in her long ago. She claimed me as her own, going so far as to pretend she and Father had conceived me in secret to keep me from her family's battle of heirs. By the time Trentas thrust me upon my father and his wife, Alina was in full possession of her family's fortune. After she died, my father inherited it. Then after he died..."

His lips tug into a frown. I dare not utter a word, dare not shatter this moment no matter how my curiosity begs me to. It's so rare I get to hear him speak candidly about his past, and this time I didn't have to coerce him into doing so.

"The bakery was for her," he says. "She's the one who first fed me sweets, to cheer me up after the loss of my family. She encouraged Father to dabble in his former trade and bake us cakes, even though we had ample staff to do so. After her death, baking was the one thing that saved Father from his grief. The one subject I could get him to talk about, and soon he taught me the craft, purely for the sake of bonding. That led to us opening Blackwood Bakery. We didn't need the additional income, but making cakes together brought us joy. It kept Alina's memory alive."

I swallow the lump in my throat. "You've known a lot of loss in your life, haven't you?"

His expression hardens, jaw tight. "I told you not to pity me. Were I deserving of it, I wouldn't have sought vengeance on your family. I would have honored my father's dying wish and left revenge in the past. Come. Careful down the hill." Without another word, he begins his descent.

My feet won't follow, as I'm busy reeling from what he said. From the tender vulnerability he showed me.

"I caught this." Minka's voice makes me jump. She sets something small and brown in the grass at my feet. Is that a dead mouse?

"Oh—um, that's...great job?"

She blinks up at me with her amber eyes. "Do you want it?"

"No, thank you," I say, then proceed down the hill, one careful step at a time.

She saunters beside me. "Do you mind if I stay in this form a little longer? I am quite enjoying myself. I haven't felt a mouse struggle beneath my paws in years. It was almost as enjoyable as sorting wine by vintage, variety, and alphabetical order."

If she wasn't full fae and unable to lie, I'd wonder if she was being sarcastic. "You like beverages that much?"

"I do. And while I appreciate the promotion to lady's maid, I hope you'll allow me to return to my previous position once this is all over."

"Of course," I say, spreading my arms for balance as I traverse the decline. "If that is what you wish. And yes, you may remain in unseelie form as long as you like. But why have you spent so long in seelie form if you enjoy being a cat so much?"

"I once spilled a glass of wine at dinner when I tried to pour it with my paws, so your parents forbade me from shifting into my unseelie form in their presence thereafter. I understand now that paws and glasses don't go together unless your objective is to line them up in a neat row and knock them down one at a time from a high place, but I only do that on my days off."

"I see," I say, trying not to laugh. Her tone is earnest, so I wouldn't want her to think I'm making fun.

I reach the bottom of the hill where Thorne waits by a rushing stream. Arching my brow, I say, "I thought you said you wouldn't slow down for me."

He ignores my comment. "We'll have to cross here. It rained recently, so the stream is unrulier than normal."

I assess the body of water in question. It's about a dozen feet wide, and while it appears to be shallow, it would be impossible to cross without getting my feet wet. Thorne walks downstream a ways, then stops before a row of large rocks that protrude from the water—a makeshift bridge of sorts.

Minka scampers to the first rock and hops to the next with ease. In just a few graceful motions, she reaches the other side, then proceeds to rub her body in the grass.

Thorne crosses to the first rock, then stretches his long legs to reach the second. Shifting toward me, he extends a hand. I stare at it, remembering how that very palm felt as it gripped my waist in the coach. Unlike me, he wears no gloves. The quickening of my pulse hardens my resolve. Or perhaps it's stubbornness. "I can cross on my own, Mr. Blackwood."

"Very well," he says and finishes crossing the stream.

I'm almost disappointed that he didn't argue. I shake the thought from my mind and hop to the first rock. The second is a challenge, for it's spaced farther than the first. Two more await. The next is perhaps the farthest away, but I'm undaunted. I might even call this fun. I perch one foot at the edge of my current rock and prepare to leap to the next.

My other foot meets its mark.

"Careful, Briony."

I'm so caught off guard by the sound of my name—my *first* name—leaving Thorne's lips that I lift my gaze to his and lose purchase on the rock entirely. I fling my hands out, much like I did in the coach, but this time Thorne doesn't catch me. With a startled cry, I land on my backside, icy water soaking my skirts and chilling my legs. I'm too surprised to move. To stand.

A shadow falls over me, and I look up to find Thorne's

smug face staring down at me from the rock I slipped from. He crosses his arms. "I seem to recall you claiming not to be clumsy. Do you remember? You were drunk on Moondrop, and if my memory serves me, your exact words were 'I'm not the type to fall or need rescuing from a big strong man.' Yet you've required my aid twice in less than half an hour."

I glower up at him, pursing my lips. I can't tell him I fell because he called me by my first name. It's bad enough that *I* know the truth. He's only called me Briony once before, when we danced in the glade, right before he stole my memories. Even though I've since given him permission to address me by first name, it was a fully unexpected sound.

Thorne extends his hand, eyes dancing with mirth, lips pulled in an infuriating smirk. "Will you accept my assistance now?"

I feign humility and grasp his hand. As his fingers tighten around my palm, I tug with all my might—

He doesn't budge.

A burst of laughter escapes his lips. "Did you...did you just try to pull me in?" His continued laughter tells me he's amused at the concept. "I'm stronger than you. It will never work."

Pouring all my strength into the move, I attempt to drag him down once more. But my tug is countered by his own. Before I realize what's happening, I'm hauled to my feet. The momentum sends me crashing into his chest. Not wanting to fall again, I clutch the front of his jacket.

"Satisfied?" he says, voice low. I lift my eyes to meet his, our faces nearly as close as they were when he teased me in the department store. "Now you've got me soaking wet too. Can we carry on?"

He doesn't give me a chance to answer and just leaps to the next rock, tugging me along after him until we reach the other side. My heart pounds with every step, still tangled in that moment when I collided against him. And then before that, in the carriage, when he caught me with such a firm and protective grip.

Finally, we reach the walkway that leads to the garden and the elegant manor beyond. With every step I take, I can't help feeling like I just lost yet another unspoken game.

27

BRIONY

I feel guilty for dripping stream water all over the shining marble floors in Thorne's foyer, but it can't be helped. My skirts are thoroughly soaked, as are Thorne's trousers, courtesy of him pulling me against him. I'm grateful I hadn't changed into any of my new clothing before we began our journey here, but that's only a small consolation. I can't change into a clean ensemble until my belongings arrive.

"I'll show you to your guest suite and have my butler fetch your things," Thorne says. "I assume you'll want a warm bath."

"Please," I say. The thought of a warm bath would sound lovely even if I weren't drenched in freezing water.

Minka gives us a wide berth to avoid the puddles we leave behind and proceeds to prance ahead, investigating corners and peering under furniture. Perhaps looking for mice. Thorne leads us further into the foyer, providing a more thorough view of the manor at large. The ceilings are high, bedecked with crystal chandeliers that rival the ones at the department store, while the walls are papered in ivory-and-sage damask. Tall windows invite plenty of natural light and provide glimpses of the emerald hills outside. It may not be as large or as grand as Nocturnus Palace, but there's something cozy about it—if a manor can be called cozy—in a way Monty's city manor lacked.

"Mr. Hartshire," Thorne calls as we reach the nearest staircase, one constructed of rich dark wood and intricately carved balusters.

A short man with a heavy build and neatly combed gray hair shuffles out from a corridor. "Mr. Blackwood! I deeply apologize for not greeting you at the door. I didn't see your coach. And—" The butler's eyes fall on the puddles of water at our feet, his nose wrinkling in distaste. "Stones below, what happened?"

"The carriage lost a wheel by the southern meadow, so my guest and I proceeded on foot. On our way here, we... had a spill."

"Oh dear. I'll send out a wagon to retrieve your things."

"Please do."

"And..." Mr. Hartshire glances at me, a puzzled look on his face. Only briefly does he wrinkle his nose once more at the growing pool I'm creating. "Who might your guest be?"

"This is Princess Rosaline Briar. Monty's...fiancée." He says the last word with a bitter edge. Now that I've met Monty in person, I can't tell whether Thorne's bitterness is reserved for the fact that his friend must marry his enemy... or that I have to marry Monty.

The butler's eyes go wide. "Oh! Your Highness, I am pleased to meet you." He bends at the waist.

"And I you, Mr. Hartshire."

His cheeks redden as he rises, lips curled in a bashful

smile. What an adorable old man. Facing Thorne again, he says, "Your guests have been eagerly awaiting your arrival."

Thorne pulls his head back. "My guests? They're already here?"

"Yes, they arrived an hour ago."

Thorne and I exchange a glance. We must be thinking the same thing—that I need to get changed before Monty sees me. It's highly aggravating that I'm even considering catering to the whims of that insufferable man, but neither of us knows for certain how this game will work. Monty's letter only said *Dress pretty for me*. If our courtship were a normal one, I'd assume he meant on our first formal date, but Monty Phillips has proven himself to be abnormal indeed. There's a chance he could judge me by his next glance.

"Damn you, Monty," Thorne mutters. "Where are they now?"

"Miss Phillips is taking tea in the back gardens while the other two are out riding."

Thorne goes still beside me. "What do you mean, other two?"

"Mr. Phillips and Miss Dervins."

"He brought Cosette?"

I shoot Thorne a sharp look, but he doesn't meet my gaze. Who the hell is Cosette? Or...Miss Dervins, as the butler referred to her.

Mr. Hartshire shrinks down slightly. "Was she not an approved guest?"

Thorne releases a long sigh, then gives his butler a warm smile. It doesn't reach his eyes, but Mr. Hartshire seems placated by it. "It's fine. Please arrange for the retrieval of Her Highness' things."

Mr. Hartshire bows and leaves the foyer.

Thorne faces me. "Take off your shoes and stockings."

Heat flushes up my neck. "Excuse me?"

"Take off your shoes and stockings. The stairs were freshly polished, and your skirts are going to drip every step of the way. The least you can do is remove those potential hazards. Otherwise, you're going to slip, and I'm going to have to save you again." His lips quirk into a devious grin. "You wouldn't like that, now, would you?"

"Perhaps you simply need to stop concerning yourself with me, Mr. Blackwood."

"Had I less concern for you and more for the carpets you're about to drench, I'd make you take off every sodden article before setting a single foot upstairs."

My breath catches. "You wouldn't."

"Not if you do as you're told. We're in my house, Miss Rose. If you won't make this one compromise, I'll carry you upstairs. And not in a nice way. I'll throw you over my shoulder like a sack of flour."

My heart tumbles at the visuals he conjures. Even though he said it as a threat, I don't find the concept entirely unpleasant. I've never been thrown over a man's shoulder, and the fact that Thorne thinks he can carry me up a flight of stairs with such ease almost makes me want to dare him to try. But I've already suffered enough humiliation in his presence today. "Fine, but at least turn around."

"So I don't see your bare ankles?" He lowers his voice to a whisper. "It's a little late for modesty between us, don't you think?"

Despite his words, he turns away. I'm grateful for that, for I can't bear to have him look at me now. Not with *that one dream* haunting my thoughts and mingling with my fantasy of being carried by him. A traitorous thrill heats my core.

Keeping my head low to hide my reddened cheeks, I

take a seat on the bottom step and set about removing my shoes and stockings. Minka scampers from wherever she'd been investigating to rub against the balusters beside me. "I like it here," she says. "Or maybe I just like being a cat."

I huff a laugh. She does seem to be enjoying herself, even though the shift has made her a less adequate lady's maid, as evidenced by how she makes no effort to aid my undressing. Not that I need her help. It also fills me with a sense of secondhand guilt. She's been kept from her unseelie form by my parents due to a single mistake. It seems a bit cruel.

"Finished?" Thorne asks over his shoulder.

I ball my stockings and stuff them into my shoes, then rise to my feet. As I open my mouth to answer, a figure enters the foyer. She appears to be a few years my junior with a pretty, round face, curly light-brown hair, and a slender figure. Her smile stretches wide as she locks eyes with Thorne. She lets out an excited squeal and rushes toward him.

"Angie," Thorne says as she throws her arms around his waist. His expression holds surprise at first, but soon it warms into a genuine grin. He returns her hug with an ease I find startling.

A strange tightness balls in my chest. Perhaps I'm unused to seeing people embrace with such familiarity. I may not have much experience in society, but I know public signs of affection are taboo, especially between opposite sexes. Maybe I'm also just taken aback at seeing Thorne treating someone so kindly. This tight feeling couldn't be jealousy. That would be absurd.

The two separate, and the girl beams up at him. "I've missed you so much, Thorne!"

"And I you. I trust school is going well?"

"It is! I've gotten high marks in every subject." She steps back, and her eyes find me. Her expression brightens further. "You must be Princess Rosaline!"

Thorne clears his throat, facing me. His smile remains warm as he introduces us. "Princess Rosaline, this is Angela Phillips, Monty's sister. Angie, this is—"

"I've been dying to meet you!" Angela rushes over to me and takes my hands in hers. "You're going to be my sister-in-law."

"Angie," Thorne says, a light reprimand in his tone. "I thought you said you received high marks in school. How are you meant to greet a fae royal? Also, be careful. The floor is wet."

"Oh, right! Forgive me, Highness." She releases my hands to sink into a curtsy. As she straightens, she notices Minka weaving around her ankles and picks her up at once. She holds her up to look at her, eyes dancing with glee. "Thorne, did you get a cat?"

He lifts a hand in warning. "No, that's—"

"Pet meeee," Minka says, her voice laced with a purr. With a yelp, Angela releases the cat. Minka lands on all fours, but unfortunately sticks her landing at the dead center of a puddle. She skitters away and frantically races for me. Before I can stop her, she claws her way up my skirt and into my arms. "She dropped me in a puddle!"

Angela brings her hands to her mouth, eyes turning down at the corners. "I'm so sorry! I was startled. I didn't know you were fae."

With a huff, Minka shifts in my arms so that she's facing away from the girl. Not knowing what else to do, I hug Minka to my chest and run a soothing hand down her silky back.

"I think we've had enough excitement for the time

being," Thorne says, his voice both calming and authoritative at once. "Angela, please give Her Highness some privacy. As you can see, there has been an incident, and the princess requires some rest."

Angela gathers her composure and backs away with a nod. "Of course. I apologize for making such a poor first impression, Highness. I look forward to getting to know you more." She glances at Thorne, who gives her an approving nod. With that, she scurries out of the foyer.

Thorne makes his way to me, a dark laugh leaving his lips. "What kind of chaos have I let in through my doors?"

With Minka still pouting in my arms and my skirts still dripping, I can't help but agree. Chaos is the only thing I can think of to describe our current circumstances. Not just the foyer, the excited girl, and the terrified cat, but the game, my engagement, and our bargain too. This is all so ridiculous. A disaster. Nothing has gone the way I thought it would when I came up with my plan. That should make me anxious, but instead, it sends giddy mirth bubbling in my chest. It escapes in a bark of laughter.

Thorne narrows his eyes at me, but there's mirth playing around his lips too. "Why are you laughing?"

My laughter grows until I'm doubled over. Minka flees my arms and races up the stairs on her own. "Sorry, just give me a moment."

When I manage to sober from my laughing fit, I feel oddly light. Maybe a little levity is what I needed. Straightening, I find Thorne on the stair above me, arms crossed with a poorly concealed grin twisting his mouth. He arches a brow. "Are you finished?"

"I am," I say, my cheeks sore from my laughter.

As Thorne leads me up the stairs, I allow my mind to

return to more serious matters. An important question snags my mind. "Who is Miss Dervins?"

"Trouble," he says under his breath.

"But who is she *really*?"

He doesn't answer, and his silence tells me plenty. She must be Monty's lover. Or perhaps the girl he wishes to marry. Guilt swarms in my chest. I'd never once given thought to Monty's wishes and feelings. His awful personality made them easy enough to dismiss. But what if he's preferred another woman all along? What if she's his first choice, the person he intended to choose when his father promised he'd have his pick of bride if our betrothal contract was broken?

Dread and relief war inside me. I can't...compete with another woman. I don't want to. If Mr. Phillips is truly in love with someone else, I can't stand in the way.

"Miss Rose." Thorne's brow is knitted with concern as he studies me from several steps up.

I realize I've come to a halt, my mind so tangled with my thoughts. "Does Monty...does he love this woman?"

Thorne's expression sinks with sympathy. "No, it isn't like that," he says, tone gentle.

"What is it like then? Why is she trouble?"

He descends the steps until he stands before me. "Cosette Dervins is a friend of Angela's. Monty and I have tried to discourage the friendship, as have Lord and Lady Phillips. Cosette has...an unfavorable history with Monty, and anyone with eyes can see she's using Angela to remain close to him. Angela is too kind to see through her friend's ruse."

"So Cosette is in love with Monty?"

"Yes, and..." His jaw shifts side to side before he continues. "I admit, Cosette and Monty once courted. While she clings to her feelings for him, he has no serious interest in her. He will never marry her and has told her time and time again. I assure you, it's true. But because of her feelings, I anticipate she may try to come between the two of you."

My guilt abates. At least I know my actions aren't compromising a true love match. I resume climbing the stairs and this time Thorne keeps pace with me.

"I won't let her interfere," he says. "I will keep my part of the bargain and do what I can to ensure your wedding commences as planned." That same bitter note I heard when he introduced me to his butler as Monty's fiancée returns, sharpening the edges of his words.

Perhaps we could use a change of subject, but there's only one other thing at the top of my mind. I keep my tone casual as I say, "Miss Phillips seems like a lively girl. The two of you are very close."

"I said as much."

"Yes, but..." I bite the inside of my cheek. His relationship with her is none of my business, but for whatever reason, I'm desperate to know if they are romantically involved. I'd like to say it's my burning curiosity, but there's something darker lurking in my interest. A simmering anxiety.

"She's like a sister to me," he says, answering my unspoken question. "She's the same age my youngest sister would be now if she were awake. When I befriended Monty —at the behest of our fathers—I befriended Angela too. We've been as close as siblings ever since. She considers me a second brother as well."

Relief uncoils inside me and that dark feeling dissipates. We reach the top of the stairs where Minka grooms her lower belly, one leg stretched toward the sky. She freezes mid-lick and shifts into a more refined posture. The second floor is lined in plush ivory carpet, and I'm once again sorry for my sodden state, cringing at every drip my skirt makes. Thorne's taunt about forcing me to undress before coming upstairs seems somewhat practical now. He guides us away from the stairs and down a hall lined with tall windows on one side and mahogany doors on the other. We stop at the second to the last door. "This is the second-largest suite in the manor. You have a private bath, a separate bedroom, and a full living space. My suite is at the end of the hall."

I glance at the last door, a mere dozen feet from mine.

"Take your time getting ready," he says, hands in his pockets. His posture has grown slightly tense. Perhaps he too has realized our sleeping quarters are side by side. "I'll keep Monty at bay and send word for you as soon as I know when and where we are to commence this game of his."

"Thank you."

"I'll leave you to it." He proceeds down the hall toward his own room. I'm about to turn the handle and enter my suite when he pauses halfway toward his door.

"It was a nice sound," he says, back facing me.

I blink a few times. "What was?"

"Your laughter." He glances at me over his shoulder. The light from the windows catches on his lenses and obscures his eyes. "I hope after all of this is done, you can do that more."

28

BRIONY

Three hours later, I stand before the closed doors to the parlor, gathering my nerve to enter. Mr. Boris pauses with his fingertips on the handle, awaiting word that I'm ready. I can at least say with some confidence that I meet Monty's *dress pretty for me* terms. I'm in the indigo spider silk gown Thorne suggested. Well, *suggested* might be too generous of a word, but he said he liked it, so I had to assume it would do for tonight's game. It hugs my curves perfectly, the low V-shaped neck revealing just the right amount of cleavage to keep it in the realm of human fashion. The back dips low too, then gathers at my waist in flowing pleats. The way the skirt rounds my hips before flaring out above the knees creates a pleasing hourglass effect on my figure.

Minka arranged my golden-blonde tresses to perfection —while she was in seelie form, of course, for she quickly learned paws had no place in hairstyling. The top half of my hair is piled on top of my head in dainty curls while the bottom half cascades over my shoulder. Human propriety favors full updos for formal occasions, but Minka insisted I try the style. Once I looked in the mirror, I couldn't resist keeping it.

But now every inch of me stands to be judged by my future husband. And whoever else might be in the room. This isn't at all how I wanted my debut in society—however private—to go.

It's for my family, I remind myself. *I have a bargain to fulfill. A curse to break. A throne to save before Nyxia's promised time is up and my sleeping family is taken to the catacombs.*

The reminder serves to harden my heart and steel my resolve all over again.

Mr. Boris arches a russet brow, fingers flinching on the door handle. "Highness?"

I inhale a deep breath, then force a well-practiced smile on my lips. "I'm ready."

Mr. Boris opens the door, and we stride inside.

The parlor is a large yet cozy space, with dark wood floors, several seating areas, and a pianoforte. The curtained windows reveal a setting sun, dipping behind the towering hills. Two girls sit on a couch facing away from me, their heads close together as they exchange animated conversation. One I recognize as Angela Phillips, which means the other must be the infamous Cosette Dervins. I can't see her well from here, but she appears to be tall, pretty, and slim with black hair and an enviably long neck. I assess the other side of the room. A fire roars in the hearth, before which Thorne sits, reading his papers in his usual manner. Upon my entrance, he lowers his broadsheets and begins to fold them, expression impassive.

Then his eyes lock on mine.

He freezes mid-fold, and his face goes slack. Behind his

spectacles, he blinks once. Twice. Then he sweeps his gaze down the length of me. My breath catches at his assessment, my skin heating under the weight of his stare. As his eyes reach mine once more, his lips flick in the slightest hint of a smile. A soft one. A desirous one. An arrogant joy brightens in my chest as there's no doubt *I* put that smile on his lips. Or the dress did. Whatever the case, I feel like I've won a round of *who can make the other flustered* at last.

I lower my eyelids slightly, shifting my grin into a sly one, so he can see that I *know*. That I'm fully aware of my victory.

His eyes narrow in response, his lips pulling up at one corner. A silent conversation dances between us—

"Oh, Rosey, you're here." Monty saunters into my line of sight. I hadn't noticed him when I entered, but the tumbler of amber liquid in his hand suggests he came from the drink cart. His blond curly hair is as messy as it was when we met at the garden party, and his state of dress is not what I expected. While I wasn't sure how our meeting in the parlor would go—for I'd only been delivered a note from Thorne an hour ago stating I should meet Monty there once I was dressed—I at least assumed this would be something like a date. The kind of formal meeting one expects from a new courtship. But now, seeing Monty dressed down to his shirt-sleeves, his waistcoat open, his shirt buttons crooked, I realize even my barest assumptions were wrong.

Mr. Boris folds at the waist and addresses the room at large. "May I present Her Highness, Princess Rosaline Briar."

His introduction feels several seconds too late, and my confidence slips. Gone is the triumph I felt at having momentarily stunned Thorne. Mr. Boris backs out of the room and closes me inside with my spectators.

The two girls cease conversation and rush to their feet, dipping into elegant curtsies. Once they rise, Miss Dervins assesses me with a cold stare while Angela rounds the couch, hands clasped to her chest. "Highness, you look absolutely stunning!"

"Yes, let me get a look at her," Monty says. He eyes me over the rim of his glass as he takes a hearty swallow. With a wink, he lowers his tumbler and flashes me a dimpled smile. "Well, you certainly dressed pretty."

"Thank you, Mr. Phillips." I do my best not to speak through gritted teeth. My gaze slides briefly to Thorne, who gives me an encouraging nod. "So, Mr. Phillips, shall we—"

"What should we play next?" Monty says before I can finish asking if he'd like to converse with me on the couch.

"Pardon?"

"What game should we play next? That one was over too soon. I'm already bored. Let's go straight into another."

My gloved fingers curl at my sides. "You proposed seven games over the next seven days."

"Yes, but that doesn't mean we have to play one game per day. Let us at least add a second one for today. Just think! If you impress me enough tonight, I'll reward you with two wins. Only two more to go after that."

"Shouldn't I be given ample time to prepare?"

He wags a finger at me, and I get the urge to snap it in half. "If you want to be my wife, you'll have to get used to spontaneity."

Everything inside me wants to tell him to take his spontaneity and shove it up his ass. I purse my lips to suppress my retort. For all I know, *this* could be the next game—accepting or refusing. I keep my tone as pleasant as I can. "Very well, Mr. Phillips."

"Ah, I knew you were a good sport." Monty downs the

rest of his beverage and strolls over to the drink cart laden with tumblers, bottles, and decanters.

A lilting melody weaves through the room, and I find Miss Dervins sitting at the piano bench. She plays beautifully. It makes me wonder why Monty wouldn't want to marry such a refined and lovely woman. Unless, perhaps, her parentage is unfavorable. She glances up from the keys to give me another icy stare.

Angela steps closer to me and clasps one of my hands in hers. "I hope whatever we play, it will help me get to know you better."

I offer her a kind smile. "I'd like that."

"I hope your cat doesn't hate me," she says, lips pulling into a grimace. "I feel so bad about dropping her."

"She isn't exactly my cat; she's my lady's maid. And I doubt she'll hold a grudge for long."

"Oh good. I love cats. I don't know if I could survive if one hated me."

Thorne comes up beside us. "Don't take too much of the princess' time, Angie. This evening is for her and your brother to get to know one another."

"You're right." She releases my hand. "After you're my sister-in-law, we'll have all the time in the world to get acquainted. First, you have to win over my awful brother." She glares at Monty as he joins our group, his glass refilled to the brim, but there's more teasing than ire in her scowl.

"Don't be too cross with me, sister," Monty says. "I'm setting a precedent in our family. Don't you want to be allowed to choose your husband once your time comes? This game is the one freedom I ask for."

My annoyance softens the slightest bit. However insulting Monty's treatment of me is, he's acting from the same emotions I've felt. The same anger at being trapped in a pairing he never asked for.

Monty flourishes his free hand. "Now for our next game! I need ideas."

A soft and sultry voice raises over the music. "What about piano?"

Monty glares over his shoulder at Cosette.

She holds his gaze with a coy smile. "Your wife should be accomplished in the feminine arts. Let her take my place at the pianoforte."

Angela's expression brightens. "Do you play, Highness?"

The blood leaves my face. Piano was by far my worst subject in school. A sad irony, considering how much I enjoy music. I simply have no talent for playing. But I can't admit that out loud. "I can play," I say, adding *badly* to myself to ensure my words hold no lie. Playing badly is still playing.

"I'm not a fan of piano," Monty says, loud enough for his words to carry across the room. Cosette's lips tug into a pout. "But if my prospective fiancée thinks she can impress me..."

Stars above, I'll lose for certain. I cast my gaze around the room, seeking some inspiration for an alternative, something that will sway Monty far from the idea of me playing music for him—

"Dancing," Thorne says, and my eyes lock on his. There's a kindness in his gaze. Had he noticed how flustered I grew just now? "Your next game should be dancing. Judge her by how well she moves."

My muscles uncoil, and my earlier confidence returns. Dancing I can do.

Monty utters an unenthused, "I suppose. Cosette, play us a waltz."

"No," Thorne says, tone sharp. He approaches the pianoforte and states the last thing I expect. "I'll play."

Cosette's song cuts off and she relinquishes her spot with clear reluctance. Thorne settles in her place and starts to play. I'm immediately impressed with his skill, for it surpasses that of even Miss Dervins. But that pales in comparison to my next surprise—I recognize the melody. It's from my favorite ballet. But how...

Oh, right. The dreams. He's watched me gush about the ballet numerous times. While I struggle to replicate sound during my daydreams, he must have recognized it anyway.

Something warm melts in my chest and with it, my confidence grows even more. I can waltz to this. I know this song, as well as my own heart. My feet would never betray that passion. My only regret is that I don't have my dancing fan. Taking it out before a dance is a tradition. This time, I'll have to do without my comforting routine.

Monty sets down his drink and extends his hand, expression thoroughly bored. I place my gloved palm in his ungloved one, and his other hand moves to the middle of my back. His fingertips settle on the skin exposed from the low back of my dress, and I suppress the urge to flinch. We fall into the rhythm of the waltz and move through the parlor. My moves are stiff at first, but soon I feel more at ease, focusing on the melody I adore—

"No, no, no." Monty releases me and steps back. "This is all wrong."

Stars, what did I do? Am I a worse dancer than I thought?

Thorne's playing cuts off and he burns his friend with a glare. "What the stones are you on about? She danced perfectly."

"That's just it, Thorny. I couldn't *see* how she danced, nor could I enjoy it. You know I hate dancing."

His words cut like a knife. He...hates dancing? My future husband is not only a despicable untamed animal but *hates* dancing. I don't think I've ever been so crushed.

He waves a hand at Thorne. "Come. Take my place. Angela, you play this time."

Angela squeals with joy, taking her seat at the pianoforte before Thorne has even risen. He and I exchange a questioning glance.

"You want us," I say, pointing between me and Thorne, "to dance together."

Monty folds his arms and gives me a sideways smile. "There's something you should know about me, Rosey. I like to watch." With that, he backs away, retrieves his drink, and slumps onto the couch.

Thorne's shoulders are tense as he approaches me with a stiff bow. "May I have this dance?"

I return it with an equally stiff curtsy. "You may."

He takes the same hand Monty discarded, his grip firmer, warmer. His other hand softly lands on the naked flesh of my back, sending a shudder up my spine. I bite the inside of my cheek to keep the shiver at bay and meet Thorne's dark eyes. His chin dips in a nearly imperceptible nod, yet another silent exchange between us, a wordless reminder that we've done this before. We've danced more times than we can count. Why should this be any different just because it isn't a dream?

"All right, you two," Monty says between sips of his drink. "Impress me."

Angela starts a waltz, one I'm not at all familiar with.

Thorne and I begin to dance. He's an excellent lead, and I trust him to guide me around the room, careful of running into furniture. We make it only halfway around the parlor when Monty calls out, "Pull her closer, Thorny. No man in his right mind would keep that much distance with such a pretty partner."

"Then perhaps you should have taken your own advice," Thorne snipes back.

Monty chuckles. "That wouldn't do. You're an excellent dancer whereas I am not. My pleasure in this game lies in the fantasy. In watching. Now pull her close so I can imagine myself as you."

Thorne's jaw tics at the corners, but he does as his friend suggests, turning me in a graceful spin before gliding me back to him, much of the distance we first maintained now closed. My chest brushes his, and his hand slides lower down my back. This time, I can't hide the shiver that crawls up my spine. A quiet gasp parts my lips.

"Relax," Thorne whispers, so quiet only I can hear. "You're doing perfectly."

That brings to mind his earlier compliment. *You're perfect.* Warmth dances over my palm, my back, my chest, everywhere our bodies touch, no matter how slightly. Contrasting that is the chill that remains where we don't touch, thickening the air between our stomachs, our faces, our arms. It's a palpable cold, one that begs to be warmed. Caressed. I've never felt this way when we danced. I suppose that's because this is only the second time I've danced with his true body and not his dream form. The only other time was when he tricked me in the glade, but I hadn't been aware he was real then.

Now there's no denying he's real. Touching me. Holding me. In my dreams, physical contact between us lacked the right firmness that should be there in reality, whereas now it's all I can feel, his palm holding mine like an anchor. The hand bracing my back as protectively as a shield.

He spins me again, then brings me back to him, even closer this time. My eyes lock with his, then fall to his lips, to his soft smile. I find myself grinning as well, and my heart pounds a rhythm with the waltz.

This is what I've always wanted.

A dance. A real dance with a real partner. Someone to smile at me when I move. Someone to lead me with ease, our moves in time with the beat, allowing me to enjoy my most favorite activity of all.

I may not be at a society ball, but *this* is a dance.

A shadow falls over us. Lifting my eyes to the ceiling, I find a wash of black melting above us, bedecked with multi-hued falling stars. "Shit," I mutter.

"What is it?" Thorne keeps his voice to a whisper. His gaze flashes up, but he shows no sign that he sees what I do.

"I'm conjuring a dreamscape." I try to keep half my focus on the dance while the rest battles the ever-spreading illusion. This hasn't happened before, where a dreamscape forms against my will. Not during the day, at least. When I sleep, I lose all control, my mind taking my dreams wherever they want to go. My daydreams, on the other hand, are normally intentional. Except when it comes to summoning Thorne, that is. Maybe that's why this is happening. In the past, I've conjured Thorne against my will when I'm dancing. Maybe now that he's here and I'm getting swept in the dance, my magic is taking control in a new way. I feel it tugging at my will, begging to be freed.

"That's all right," Thorne says. "If it helps you feel more at ease, let the dreamscape fall. I can't see it, so no one else can, right? I'll lead you. Just don't pull me into the dream or we'll both look like idiots."

A laugh escapes me as I picture what he means. If I use my magic to pull him into the dreamscape with me, he'll fall under sleep paralysis, while I'll continue the dance with an invisible partner. That was fine in my glade, but here...

I release a breath, giving my dreamscape permission to remain, but only halfway. The tug of my magic lessens, as if placated by my acceptance of it. The dreamscape stretches over the ceiling but doesn't melt down the walls. A perfect compromise.

We finish our dance without further incident. My dreamscape disappears as Angela's song slows to a stop, and my heart sinks with it. Thorne releases me, and I'm struck by the urge to pull him back, to ask for another dance. How I wish our waltz could have continued far longer, for I've never felt so much joy—

Something dark clouds my heart, my gut. Guilt. Embarrassment. Or is it shame? As Thorne and I step apart, I remind myself who he is. He may be responsible for my momentary elation, but he's also liable for every awful thing I experienced at my birthday dinner mere days ago.

Thorne.

Vintarys.

The man who tricked me into putting my family to sleep.

He gives a formal bow, and I'm grateful for the opportunity to look away from him. To distance myself from the emotions our dance conjured. They were false, just like my dreams have always been. A lovely side effect of dancing, but nothing more.

I plaster a too-wide smile on my lips as I face Monty. He sits at the edge of the couch, elbows braced on his knees. I expected to find disinterest on his face, but he seems thoroughly impressed after all. The only one who seems displeased is Cosette, who sits beside him on the couch with her nose in the air.

He rises to his feet and claps his palms in slow applause. "You were a vision of perfection, Princess Rosaline, just like Thorny said."

"Thank you, Mr. Phillips."

"No, Rosey dear, we might soon be married. You'll call me Monty."

I bite back my urge to tell him *not* to call me Rosey, and I somehow manage to smile instead. "Thank you, Monty."

"Let us end our game here, for I don't think anything else could top that lovely dance. I'll bid you good evening." He takes my hand in his and brings it to his lips, where he plants a single kiss. I expect a second to follow, but it doesn't. Instead, he drops my hand.

"Just one kiss?" Angela says from the piano bench. "Surely you're forgetting we played two games today, brother."

"I'm not forgetting anything. The dance was lovely, but the dress..." He gives me a piercing look. "The dress wasn't for me."

He exits the parlor, leaving his last words ringing in my head. I could trust he simply didn't like the dress, despite admitting I looked pretty. And yet...why do I get the feeling there's a double meaning hidden between the lines—one that asks, if the dress wasn't for him, who was it for?

29

THORNE

The next morning dawns, bringing with it a sharp pain pulsing behind my eyes. Half of it is due to the morning sun streaming through my bedroom window and searing my eyelids, while the rest is simply a side effect of having a house full of guests to contend with. And yes, four people is more than enough to denote *full*. This, of course, makes me loath to leave my room. Not knowing where Monty might be, whether he's in the drawing room, dining room, or wine cellar, makes me want to avoid my entire house for now. My patience is thin this early in the morning, even for the sweet yet overly talkative Angela. Until I've had my morning tea and a plate of sweets, I'm better left alone.

I take my breakfast in my private study—a room located within my personal suite—while I sort through the documents and correspondence that have piled up in my short absence from the estate. There are contracts to renew for the bakery, employees to pay. I find a recent letter from Trentas, asking me to expound on the brief missive I sent three days ago. Specifically, he wants to know if I managed to succeed in my plan to put the Briars to sleep.

Guilt crowds my heart from every side, both from the fact that I sent the previous letter at all and that I haven't shared more with Trentas. He must be anxious to find out if he'll finally have a shot at the throne and why I told him to wait until after Briony is married. As far as he knows, her marriage to Monty was never supposed to happen, for putting the Briars to sleep would have put an end to the alliance. I've never kept anything from Trentas before, but I can't risk his interference. I doubt he'd approve of me teaming up with Briony, regardless of how it benefits my family, but I'm already committed to my present course. Trentas, my first father figure and a man I respect more than any other now that my birth father has died, will have to wait.

Another pinch of guilt strikes my chest.

Cursing under my breath, I shove Trentas' letter in my desk drawer and slam it shut. I'm not at all in the mood to deal with the inconvenient emotions warring inside me, so I pore over the other letters I've received. The rest are of a far more bearable nature, but I read three of them before I realize I haven't comprehended a single word. Thoughts of Trentas aside, my mind remains wrapped up in yesterday's games, as well as my dread for whatever today's will bring.

With a sigh, I set down my stack of letters and lean back in my chair. I extract a silk kerchief from my waistcoat pocket to idly polish my spectacles, my mind drifting to yesterday's events. The dress. The dance. Stones, that dance. It was different from any we've had before. Maybe because both of us were truly there. She moved even more beautifully than she does in her dreams, and she *felt* so much more real. My palm against hers, my fingertips grazing her bare back, her body nearly flush with mine—

I clench my jaw and force the memories away. I shouldn't harbor these thoughts about her. These...sparks of desire. Less because she'll soon marry my idiot friend and more because I don't deserve to crave her after what I did. I don't deserve to dance with her like we once did, under the enchantment of our unwitting ignorance. I don't deserve to touch her with any sort of familiarity. But touch her I did. Smile at her I did. Stepped too close. Held her eyes. Caressed her figure with my gaze. When the dance came to an end, I feared we'd gotten carried away and revealed the strange history between us that Monty would be better left unaware of.

Yet when it came time to award her a kiss for her wins, he only gave her credit for the dance. The dress—that stunning, curve-hugging, sin-inducing dress—he said wasn't for him.

Fool.

What game is he playing at? I know his type. I know he can't tell a gown from a garbage bin. So long as it graces a female form, he's attracted to it. So why the stony fuck did he reject her dress?

A knock sounds at my study door. My muscles tense. For a moment, I fear it's Monty, and I still haven't had enough tea to deal with him. Then I remind myself he wouldn't have the decency to knock. To my relief, it's Mr. Hartshire with a note from Monty. Which is almost as bad as his actual presence.

All the note says is: *Game four. Stables. We ride at noon.*

Some of my dread lessens. So today's game will be riding. At least I now know what to expect. Yet I can't shake the feeling I'll be getting more than I bargained for.

AT A HALF HOUR TO NOON, I FINALLY EMERGE FROM MY sanctuary, outfitted in my riding clothes. I stop outside Briony's door, hesitating for a long breath before I knock on it. At first, there's no answer. Then the jiggling of the handle on the other side. Once. Twice. Three times. The door opens a crack, and Minka's feline form nudges it the rest of the way open.

"Would Miss Rose care to accompany me to the stables for Mr. Phillips' game?"

She blinks up at me with her slitted eyes. "She already left for the stables. Mr. Boris accompanied her."

I'm taken aback by that. I assumed Briony would want me to escort her so we could go over any questions she may have about impressing Monty. Not that I'd have a damn helpful thing to say. Monty isn't exactly an expert equestrian, at least not when it comes to judging others in their skill. Still, I fully expected Briony to hound me with a flurry of questions like she normally does.

Could she be avoiding me? She barely looked at me after our dance yesterday, her demeanor shifting from warm to cold in the wake of our waltz, and she left the parlor soon after Monty did. I checked with Mr. Hartshire to ensure she received dinner, but now a spike of panic lances through me. Did my desire show through when we danced? Did she come to the same conclusions I have—that I have no right to grin at her like a friend? To hold her as close as a lover?

I shake the questions from my mind and bid Minka farewell. It's too late to dwell on any mistakes. What matters is that I see our bargain through.

Once I reach the stables, I find I'm the last to arrive. Everyone but Briony has mounted, and it's no surprise that

Monty has claimed my favorite horse, a stallion named Biscuit. Cosette and Angela sit sidesaddle upon my calmest geldings, chattering away, while Briony strokes the neck of—

My heart leaps into my throat. I burn Monty with a furious glare. "You can't be serious. You have her paired with Betty?"

The party ceases conversation as they note my approach. Briony pauses her petting of the sleek black mare and shifts to face me. She's dressed in one of her new ensembles, an emerald-green riding habit and matching hat. Her expression holds surprise at first, but it quickly melts into one of confident ease.

Monty guides his horse toward me. "Of course I'm serious. Betty is your finest mare. There's no better horse for my lovely potential fiancée."

The way he emphasizes *potential* grates on my nerves, for his intent is clear—to remind me that we're here on *his* terms. Briony's betrothal hinges upon his acceptance of it. Therefore our bargain does too.

I speak through my teeth. "She may be my finest mare, but Betty is an asshole. You know this."

Monty shrugs. "I want to see how she rides, and it certainly won't hurt if her mount is a little feisty. It might tell me much about my future mate."

"It isn't safe. She should ride Periwinkle."

"Oh, maybe she should," Angela says, her expression brimming with concern. "I don't want Her Highness to be hurt."

Cosette sniffs. "I'll ride Betty, then."

"No one is riding Betty," I say. "The princess will ride Periwinkle, and that's that."

Monty groans. "Periwinkle is boring. It will tell me nothing about Rosey's skill."

"You wouldn't know skill if it slapped you in the face."

He grins at the insult. "Which is precisely why I need her to ride a challenging mare. If she sits that horse as well as she strokes it—"

"This isn't a game."

"Oh, but it is."

"I mean her safety." My voice rises nearly to a shout. "Toy with us all you like with your events and activities, but—"

"Mr. Blackwood." Briony's words sever my own. She meets my gaze with a look of smug defiance. "I'm perfectly capable of making my own decisions."

I open my mouth but I don't know what to say. She's right, of course. I'm sure she's fully aware that *this* is likely part of the game as well. Knowing Monty, whether Briony rides Betty at all may be the deciding factor of her win. But she doesn't know what she's getting into. Betty is fast and rarely obeys new riders.

My eyes dart to the saddle on Betty's back, and my anxiety darkens. "You can't ride her sidesaddle."

"I can." Briony's lips pull into a smirk.

"You'll need more control—"

Holding my gaze, she climbs upon the mounting block, plants one boot-clad foot in the stirrup, and swings herself gracefully onto the saddle. The skirt of her riding habit drapes perfectly around her. Eyes still locked on mine, she repeats, "I can."

Monty chuckles. "It seems my blushing bride is a stubborn mount too."

My face whips toward Monty, the fury of a thousand

suns heating my blood. "Did you just call her a fucking mount?"

"And start!" Monty snaps Biscuit's reins, and the stallion takes off at a gallop. The three ladies follow suit, leaving me to scramble for the only remaining saddled horse. Looks like I'm the one riding Periwinkle today.

Thankfully, Periwinkle is almost as fast as Betty and is a hundred times more obedient, so I catch up to the others in no time. The party has slowed to a leisurely canter as they make their way toward the northern edge of my property. I draw my horse beside Briony's, opposite Monty who rides at her other side. Her back is straight, posture refined. Despite my fears, she clearly knows how to ride. As long as the rest of our journey remains uneventful, she'll be fine.

She meets my gaze with a glare. "What's wrong with you?" she whispers. "Stop looking at me like I'm made of glass."

I keep my voice low enough so as not to be overheard. I can't give Monty any bad ideas. "Whatever you do, don't bring Betty to a gallop."

She scoffs. "I know how to ride. My education was thorough, trust me."

"I trust you," I grind out through gritted teeth. "It's him I don't trust."

Monty remains oblivious to our conversation, a cocky smile twisting his lips. Briony outpaces me, and Monty pulls ahead to join her. The two fall into amiable conversation—at least I assume it must be, for Briony only clenches her jaw twice.

Angela passes me to ride beside Briony, while Cosette's horse sidles next to mine. "Do you think he'll choose her?" she asks.

Her voice is like razors against my eardrums. Not

because her tone isn't pleasant; we've simply never gotten along. I suppose that's because she's partially to blame for why Monty is the way he is.

"He certainly won't choose you," I say, not bothering to hide the ire in my tone. "You had your chance and you threw it away."

"That was so many years ago," she says, her tone devoid of emotion. "I regret rejecting him, and I've told him as much. I've done everything I can to show him how I feel."

"All you've done is plague him with your presence, reminding him of the woman who broke his heart. What are you doing now? Why are you here?"

"You know why I'm here. I'll win him back."

"You won't," I say with somber certainty. Monty may be a frivolous rake, but he will never be soft enough to forgive her. He may take her to his bed, simply because she's already been there and he feels no guilt in refusing a deeper intimacy, but he will never marry her.

I'd feel bad for her if she hadn't been so cruel to him all those years ago. Her family fell to ruin shortly after she rejected Monty—her long-time beau—to accept a wealthier man's proposal. After her family lost their fortune, he called off their engagement, which further destroyed her reputation.

"I understand your desperation," I say, for how is it any different from my own? From my need to fulfill the vengeance I was born to enact? "But you need to let him go. Winning him back won't prove anything. It won't magically make your life like it was before. It won't make *him* like he was before. You made sure of that."

She purses her lips, the only sign that she's listening at all.

"Don't interfere with them." I nod toward the riders ahead of us. "Don't get in the way of their betrothal."

She bares her teeth in a vicious grin. "Why would I do that, *Thorny*, when I can leave it to you?"

I bristle at her use of Monty's irksome nickname, but as she races ahead to ride beside Angela, her words crawl under my skin. She'll leave what to me? Did yesterday's dance reveal too much after all? Does she have the wrong idea about my feelings for Briony?

I refuse to acknowledge the train of thought that lies just beneath. That maybe—just *maybe*—her suspicions aren't entirely off base.

30

BRIONY

We reach the northern edge of Thorne's property, which ends in a white picket fence that separates Blackwood Estate's rolling fields of green from a similar expanse of land dotted with fluffy sheep. There we pause atop our mounts and take in the view. The slight elevation of our current location provides a look at the land we traversed. It truly is a stunning property with ample farmlands, gorgeous woods, and even a lake. The sun is high, but with the wash of fluffy white clouds painting the sky, it isn't overly warm. Or perhaps the Earthen Court's climate is always like this. The perfect weather to enjoy the outdoors.

My mood is further amplified by my success in reaching our destination with none of Thorne's worries materializing. Betty has proven to be a perfectly obedient horse, never once fighting against the reins or compromising my position sidesaddle. My thighs burn slightly, as it has been months since my last riding lesson at the convent, but other than that, I'm perfectly unscathed.

"You're a lovely girl," I whisper, stroking Betty's silky neck. I glance up to find Thorne's gaze locked on me. I meet it with a smirk. *See?* I silently convey. *You were wrong and I was right.*

His only reply is a narrowing of his eyes.

"I hope you aren't too disappointed." Angela's voice draws me from my battle of stares with Thorne. I tilt my head at her question, and she shakes hers as if reconsidering her words. "Not in Blackwood Estate, but that our manor isn't quite as impressive as this. We do have other houses, though, and one has a particularly lovely view. Besides, I believe you and Monty will have a place of your own once you marry."

My stomach tumbles, a sour roiling that I try to keep from showing on my face. I glance at the back of Monty's head. His horse is several feet from mine and Angela's, and he doesn't seem at all aware of our conversation, as engrossed as he is in droning on about the rising cost of imported Brettonish liquor to Cosette. I applaud her for pretending to care about a word he says, the only evidence to the contrary in the way she blinks in rapid succession, as if trying to keep awake. I'd think he was purposefully annoying her, but he and I held small talk on our ride, and I can safely say he is not an engaging conversationalist. Enraging, yes. Boring at best.

Stars, I can't imagine living with this man, much less marrying him. Panic slashes through me, and I'm struck with a sudden desperation to get out. Get away. Call this off. I...I can't do this—

This is how it must be, I remind myself, halting my anxiety with a steadying breath. I have to dislike him. I have to continue being averse to our union, otherwise marrying him will cease being a sacrifice. And I'll be unable to break the sleeping spell.

My panic is simply a sign that my plan will still work.

As much as it sinks my heart and ties my stomach in knots, I accept it. Then, gathering my resolve and molding it into a smile, I face Angela. "I'm sure my future dwellings will be more than adequate." Vague words for a contrived truth. Anything more direct would be a lie.

Angela beams. "I'm so glad you think so. I know we don't know each other well yet, but I feel a fondness for you, Highness. I've always wanted a sister."

Her kind honesty reminds me of some of the students back at the convent. Not Lina, of course, for her honesty always grated. Angela is more like Dorothy and many of the other girls I've had to say goodbye to over the years. I can see myself growing fond of her in the same way, and it would be nice to make a friend I won't have to lose.

My grin turns slightly more genuine at the thought. Perhaps one good thing can come from my marriage.

"Oh, I do wish we brought a picnic basket," Angela says, tone wistful. "Is this not the perfect hill for a picnic? I saw a field of strawberries on the way. Thorne's aren't nearly as delicious as the famous Davenport Berries, but you must taste them anyway. Do you love strawberries as much as I do? If not, what is your favorite fruit?"

I open my mouth to answer, but Monty interjects, turning his horse to the side. "No, dear Angie, those are not the kinds of things I care to know about my future bride."

She casts him a good-humored glare. "We weren't even talking to you, brother."

"Yes, but I was in earshot, and I'll not tolerate such boring conversation." This, of course, coming from a man who readily complains about the cost of liquor and his least favorite breed of dog for minutes on end. He waves a dismissive hand. "Favorite foods, colors, fragrances—none of that will tell me whether Her Highness will make an acceptable bride."

"And what will?" Thorne asks, his expression devoid of amusement.

"Our game, of course. I want to see how well she rides." He says the last part with a wink for me. I'd like to stab him in the eye.

"You've seen," Thorne says. "Now award her the win and let's get on with our day."

Monty taps his chin. "Hmm. No, I don't think I will. My future wife must do more than simply enjoy a smooth ride. She must keep up with...a rapid pace."

My gloved hands tighten around the reins as I catch the meaning behind his words. That insulting son-of-a-harpy—

"Stones below, Monty." Thorne's voice is as deep as a growl. "If only murder weren't illegal..."

"Then I daresay you'd have done me in years ago." Monty chuckles. "Unfortunately for you, we are bonded by a love as deep as brotherhood. But if you'd like to take things further, I'll award a kiss to the first person who reaches the southern meadow. That includes you, Thorny-boy."

Angela clucks her tongue. "Well, it certainly doesn't include me, brother. I've no need for a kiss from you. And I don't race."

"*No one* is racing," Thorne says, but at that very moment, Cosette snaps her reins, and her gelding takes off.

"A kiss for you would be another win," Monty says to me, then he too races away.

I blink after them, torn between my need for another win and the rage that lingers in the wake of Monty's irksome innuendo. Every inch the riders gain on me is another chance at a loss. As much as I want Monty's lips nowhere near me, I need to earn another kiss. Another win.

Angela starts off at a trot, grumbling to herself about how a picnic would be much better than a race.

I'm about to follow and outpace her, but Thorne's horse darts before mine, making Betty sidle away. He holds my gaze with a sharp warning. "Don't you dare. Remember what I said."

If he wanted me to forfeit this game, he shouldn't have said that. My lips curl at one corner.

"Briony!"

The sound of my name shocks me, not just because it's the rare use of my first name but because it bears a subtle crushing weight. A prickling of my skin. My hair stands on end.

Magic.

He's about to use his power over me.

To command me.

I bare my teeth. "You can't. We made a bargain." And we both know what would happen if he were to break it. Excruciating pain. Maybe death.

He opens his mouth as if to do it anyway, then his expression turns slack, defeated. Edged with something like fear.

Maybe I should take that fear to heart, but I don't.

Instead, I snap Betty's reins. She takes off, and I urge her faster. Faster. We outpace Angela with ease and close in on Cosette. Despite her head start, she's already fallen behind Monty. Soon Betty passes Cosette's horse, then approaches Monty's too. Stars above, she's fast. My hat flies off my head, taking several hairpins with it too. Tendrils of loose hair whip into my eyes. Betty's speed rumbles throughout my entire body, leaving my blood, my bones, and my heart thrumming in concert. I clench my thighs around the pommel of my sidesaddle, determined to appear as composed as possible as I outpace Monty. I catch the briefest flash of his wide smile, but I can't pay him any more heed than that. Betty's speed increases, and despite my tug on her reins, my attempts to get her to slow down now that we've bypassed Monty, she only goes faster. Faster.

She races down the next hill, jostling me so hard I can hardly see our surroundings. I lurch in my seat, careening off the side. The burning in my thighs increases tenfold as I struggle to stay in my saddle. Stars, if I fall off my horse at this speed...

The fear I glimpsed in Thorne's eyes when I stubbornly took off now fills every inch of me. Shouts ring out behind me, but I can't move. Can't turn my head. I can do nothing but pour all my focus into remaining on Betty's back, even as the sharp wind stings my eyes, drawing tears from them.

Betty veers off to the left. I may not be familiar with Thorne's property, but I know we're no longer following the path we took to reach our destination. She heads for a cluster of trees, the start of the dense woods that lie to one end of the estate. My heart leaps into my throat. If she enters the woods at this speed...

Deadly branches reach out at me from my imagination. Falling logs requiring reckless jumps. A tumble on the lawn could mean grave injury. A tumble in the woods—I can't risk it. There are some wounds not even pureblood fae can recover from.

As we speed toward those trees, I consider the only recourse. Trembling, I shift in my saddle, preparing to force myself to fall. My skirt is designed to break away from the trousers beneath if it gets stuck while I dismount, but that doesn't stop visions of being dragged to my death from flooding my mind.

With a deep breath, I loosen the grip of my thighs...

Lean to the side...

Betty chooses that moment to decide she no longer cares for me as a rider and bucks. I lurch from the saddle, certain my fall will be met not with the ground but with a kick of hooves—

Arms circle my waist, while something warm and leathery cradles me, pressing me tight against a firm body. My momentum doesn't slow, however, and I tumble, turn, tumble, turn, until I finally roll to a stop.

My surroundings are dark as I remain encompassed by flesh and whatever has folded around me like a cocoon. The sharp rising and falling of the surface beneath me paired with the rapid rhythm that pounds in my ears tells me I'm against someone's chest, my front flush with theirs. We stay like that for several moments, catching our breath. Then the leathery blanket shifts and slides out from behind me. Sunlight replaces the dark cocoon, and I blink into the sudden brightness. Lifting my head, I find Thorne beneath me, sweat coating his brow, his neck. His large membranous wings splay out on the grass on either side of him, while his horns curve from his head. His eyes are closed, lips parted to emit sharp breaths.

I try to slide off of him, but every attempt is infused with pain. His palm comes to my back, and his eyes fly open. Slowly, he raises us both up, keeping my back supported all the while until we're both upright. My cheeks flush as I realize I'm straddling him. I scramble to shift my weight and find a seat in the grass beside him but only manage to get one leg from around him. The other remains sprawled over his hips as he closes the distance I created and takes my chin between his thumb and forefinger.

I freeze, fully aware of how close we are. How my skirt has torn away exactly as designed, leaving my lower half in nothing but form-fitting trousers. How his palm remains splayed on my back, ensuring I can't pull away from him.

My eyes dip to his mouth, the slight baring of his teeth. Then I meet his furious gaze. He brings his face closer to mine, tone as dark as a storm cloud. "You've got to be fantastically stupid, little nemesis."

31

BRIONY

I tug my chin out of his grip and slam my palms into his chest. He releases me and I clumsily scramble to my feet. Holding my gaze without wavering, he rises in a far more fluid motion. His horns shrink back into his skull, leaving no sign that they were ever there, as do his wings. He's still dressed in his riding ensemble, his wings having manifested without any impact on his clothes. Fae who can shift forms can do that, altering their bodies and their clothing as one.

My chest heaves as I stare at him, the man who saved me, the man who called me stupid. My anger outweighs my gratitude, but mostly because of the shame filling my heart. Betty is nowhere to be seen, which means she reached the woods by now. It also means Thorne was right.

Glittering stars above.

He was *right*.

As he glares at me—eyes devoid of his spectacles—

hands on his hips, I imagine he's waiting for an apology. Or a *thank you*, perhaps.

My jaw shifts side to side as I prepare to speak through my rage, my shame, my guilt, and say the words that burn like razors on my tongue—

"Let's call it off," Thorne says before I can utter a sound. "The bargain. Let's call it off."

I'm too dumbfounded to reply. He wants to...call off our bargain?

He shakes his head, jaw tight. "This is getting dangerous. You could have died, Briony. You could have been stomped to a pulp, leaving no part of you intact to heal, regardless of the fae magic in your blood."

I manage a scoff. "Careful, Thorny. I might start to think you care."

His expression darkens and he takes a menacing step closer, the move so sudden I flinch back. "Don't you fucking dare suggest I don't. I'm clearly the only one who does."

My heart hammers an echo of his words, of the rage in his eyes—rage that isn't reserved for me. Or maybe it is, but not in the way I originally thought.

He speaks again. "I don't know what game Monty's truly playing, but he doesn't have your best interest at heart. Whether he's trying to scare you away, force you to lose the game, or simply play with you without a care in the world, you can't participate anymore. It's only going to get worse from here. Let's call it off."

There's that phrase again. *Let's call it off*. As if it can be so simple. "We can't do that. It's the only way to break the curse—"

"Like hell it is. We can do something else. Find another task that fulfills the terms. Anything is better than this. You can't lie, not even to yourself. You know what I say is true."

My stomach sinks, but it almost feels like relief. What would happen if we gave up? We could sever our bargain. As the creator of its terms, all it would take is for me to state out loud that I release him from our bargain and consider every term null and void. How would I feel if I let my plans go? If I stopped catering to Monty's whims? If I not only forfeited his game but refused to marry him?

I inhale a deep breath and feel my lungs expand, feel the tension leave my muscles. Stars above, I want that. So badly do I want that. I want...freedom. I want to never see Monty's face for the rest of my life. I want to choose who I love. Who I marry. I want—

The dining room at Nocturnus Palace flashes before my eyes, filling my mind with the sight of my family lying lifeless on the floor, limbs limp, eyes closed in deathlike sleep.

My relief hardens into remorse. It's my fault my family fell under the sleeping spell. Thorne may have been in control, but my hand swung the blade. My hand drew his blood. My hand put my father's throne in jeopardy.

I turn partially away from him. "The bargain remains."

"Then let us at least alter it. Leave room for another task. As our bargain stands, it isn't fulfilled unless you marry Monty."

"Which I'll do."

"Why?" Thorne's question is edged with iron. His eyes bore into the side of my face but I refuse to meet his eyes. "Why are you so determined to see this plan through?"

"You know why. We need to break the curse on our families."

"Yes, but why your marriage to Monty? Why is that the only task you're willing to consider?"

I assess my words before I speak, careful to state only

truth. "Because it suits our purposes. It benefits both families and fulfills the terms required to break the curse."

"Perhaps, but there must be something else we could do—"

"No." I face him once more, hands balled into fists. "This is the task that will save them. The timeline fits. We'll be married in time to awaken my parents before Nyxia has them sealed in the catacombs. She gave me only two weeks —of which we only have eight days left—and if we fail to break this curse by then, the seelie throne will be in peril. My father will lose his place as king and others will fight to claim what is his."

"Maybe your father should lose his throne."

I narrow my eyes to a glare. "Keep your personal opinions of my family to yourself."

Thorne lifts his chin, eyelids lowering into a squint. I'd think it was due to his poor eyesight without his lenses if it weren't for how keenly he studies me. He takes one slow step closer. Then another.

I keep my posture straight, even as the space between us shrinks to mere inches. There's a penetrating quality to his dark irises, as if he's staring into my very soul. "There's another reason," he says, voice barely above a whisper. "Why are you *really* holding so tightly to your betrothal with Monty? And don't you dare use that fae deception on me. Tell me the truth."

I hold my ground, my countenance unwavering. "Why should I?"

"I saved your life. Consider it payment."

A flash of warmth lights my chest. He did save my life. Or, at the very least, he saved me from being grievously injured. And despite his annoying perseverance in trying to get me to end our bargain, I can't deny that he's doing it because he cares, at least partially. In some twisted way, he's come to care for my well-being. For *me*. His enemy. Admitting as much has my knees trembling, making me feel even more naked before him than I was in *that one dream*. Perhaps it's that vulnerability that prompts me to speak. "Because it will make my parents proud. If they awaken to find I've broken their curse and married the man who will save my family's reputation, I'll regain all the respect I lost when I enacted their curse."

His eyes widen the slightest bit. Then his throat bobs. His hands open and close at his sides as if he's not sure what to do with them. Finally, they curl into fists and he speaks, his voice a soft yet deep tone that rumbles in the air between us. "You don't have to do anything to earn their love. You are enough exactly as you are."

The warmth in my heart grows, but it's a sharp heat, painful in how violently it clashes against the anger I hold for Thorne, the rage I still feel over what he did. How dare he say something like that! How dare he look at me like he wants to reach for me, touch me, shake my need for my parents' approval out of my bones. The fact that part of me wants him to sends my fury rising like a tide.

"You don't understand," I say through my teeth. "You didn't see how my parents looked at me when you controlled me. When you made me hold a knife to my father's throat. You didn't see the fear in his eyes or the disgust on my mother's lips, because you were too busy feeling victorious."

He flinches back as if I slapped him.

"If you understood—"

"I do," he says. "I do now and I did then. I know exactly what I did, and I know it was despicable. That sin is mine to bear, but it doesn't negate that the sacrifice you're trying to make for your family is far greater than they deserve. Your efforts are wasted on them."

My mouth falls open with a scoff. "You dare talk about *my* family. My sacrifice. My efforts. What about you? You admit your actions were a despicable sin, yet you did them anyway and speak about them as if your regret is vast. Why did you even do it?"

"I did what I was born to do, a plan laid out in the name I was given."

I throw my hands in the air. "Don't you see how wrong that is? You say my family doesn't deserve me, but you weren't born to be a tool, Thorne. If that's how your mother saw you, then *she* was wrong."

Anger flashes in his eyes, in the tightening of his jaw. "Don't talk about my mother."

"Then don't talk about mine."

He leans in closer, voice rising almost to a shout. "Has it still not registered in your brain that you don't know your parents as well as you think you do?"

I refuse to be cowed. "Has it still not registered in yours that maybe *both* our families were corrupt? Cursing someone else's nextborn. Killing another's child. Gang wars in the streets. Plotting to enact each other's curses. Naming your child for the sole reason of hurting someone else someday in the future. None of that is okay!"

My words ring in the silence that follows. Not even I expected to say what I did, but now that I have, I can feel the full truth of it. It sears my soul as much as it soothes, for even the darkest confession can act as a balm. From the depths of that darkness comes a softer truth. One that doesn't negate what I admitted but settles alongside it.

I put the truth to words. "But none of that matters because I love them," I say, voice trembling. Tears pool in my eyes. "They may be bad people, but I think they are good people too. Most importantly, they're my family. There is nothing more important to me than them. It doesn't matter what they've done. I will sacrifice for them. I will marry Monty. Don't act like you're better than me. We're the same, Thorne."

His breath catches and his expression softens. He takes a step back. Then another. Averting his gaze from mine, he nods. "You're right. We're the same."

Exhaustion weighs down my shoulders. Whether it's due to my disastrous ride or my argument with Thorne, I know not.

He releases a heavy sigh and stalks away from me, eyes on the ground. I watch him, unsure of what he's doing or if I'm to follow until he crouches down and retrieves something from the grass—his spectacles. He must have lost them when he saved me.

He places two fingers between his lips and emits a loud whistle. Several moments later, a brown horse trots over one of the small hills. It's the horse he was riding earlier. What was his name? Periwinkle, I think. The one Thorne had originally wanted me to ride. I now regret not having listened to him.

My gaze slides to Thorne's back where his wings had sprouted for just a short time. If he saved me in his unseelie form, does that mean he flies faster than a speeding horse? Impressive.

Periwinkle trots the rest of the way to Thorne, and he swings into the saddle with ease. Then, facing me, he extends a hand. My eyes widen as I stare at the space in front of Thorne. A space he clearly intends for me to occupy.

"I...I can't ride astride. It's unladylike."

"Fuck unladylike. You're getting on."

Not wanting to argue any more with him today—and more than that, not wanting to walk the rest of the way to the manor—I grudgingly accept. As I approach the horse, I try not to focus on the slim cut of my trousers or the way Thorne's eyes briefly dip to my hips. Despite my best efforts, my cheeks blaze by the time I take his palm. He hauls me up, first by the hand, then with a firm grip around my waist, and settles me before him. I stifle a gasp. The front of him is pressed against me, chest to shoulders, stomach to back, pelvis to backside. And without my skirt, there is very little fabric between us.

Thorne takes the reins in one hand and steadies my hip with the other. His palm splays evenly over my side, making me think I'm the only one of us aware of our proximity.

For several minutes, we ride without talking, our pace slow.

Thorne breaks the silence first, and I'm startled at how close his voice is to my ear, how I can feel the rumble of his words deep in his chest as it reverberates against my back. "What about your curse?" he asks, tone neutral if not a little careful. "The one...with me? Your parents will never trust you so long as they believe I can control you."

I frown. "You don't think it will break alongside the sleeping spell?"

"No. The nextborn curses were delivered separately from the sleeping spell."

Anxiety cuts through me. Regaining my parents' trust hinged upon my assumption that my bound-by-iron curse would break too. I angle my head to meet his eyes over my shoulder. "Then...then after we fulfill our bargain, we'll make a new one. You'll promise never to command me again."

He meets my eyes but says nothing.

Panic laces through me. "Thorne, tell me you agree."

"All right," he says, and even though his human blood allows him to lie, I believe him. At least I want to. "We will."

My alarm abates. I'm about to face forward again when his hand leaves my hip to land softly on my jaw. Gently, he angles my face even more, bringing us eye to eye. My pulse thrums.

"I'm sorry," he whispers. "I'm sorry for what I did to you, Briony. I'm sorry for taking away the one thing you cared about the most. I promise to do whatever I can to get your family back for you."

I swallow hard. Making a promise to a fae is dangerous business, even for someone like Thorne who can lie. Fae promises often take the form of binding vows, as unbreakable as a formal bargain. "Thank you," I say once I manage to find my words.

He lifts his hand from my cheek to my forehead, where a wayward lock of hair has crisscrossed my face. With slow, intentional movements, he sweeps it off my face and tucks it behind my ear.

As soon as his hand slides back down to hold my waist, I shift my gaze forward again and lean against him. My heart hammers a rapid beat, but its stuttering rhythm makes me think mine isn't the only one I feel thrashing against the cage of its ribs.

32

BRIONY

That night, I stand before my open wardrobe in my borrowed bedroom, confronted by silk, lace, and the richest of wools, yet my eyes glaze over, seeing nothing. I'm supposed to be selecting my outfit for tomorrow's game. A letter arrived with my dinner—which I took alone in my suite—stating: *Game Five. Gallery after breakfast.*

The last thing I want to do is play another one of Monty's games. It doesn't matter that he deemed me the winner of today's, sealed with a kiss on the back of my hand after we reunited with the rest of our party at the stables. I don't feel like I've won at all. It feels more patronizing than anything. And that's without considering everything that happened with Thorne. His annoyingly valiant rescue. His wings encircling me in a protective cocoon. Our argument. Our too-close ride on the shared saddle. His apology.

Stars, that apology.

I wasn't expecting that.

It rings through my head, even hours after sundown,

mingling with the other things he said before that, about how we should end or alter our bargain.

Let's call it off.

Even though I explained myself and we came to a tense understanding of one another, those words have continued to plague me all evening, rising to my mind despite every distraction I try to find. Not even my phonograph, which blares my favorite song for the fifth time tonight, manages to drown out his voice in my head.

You don't have to do anything to earn their love. You are enough exactly as you are.

With a frustrated groan, I slam closed my wardrobe doors only to fling them open again. Right. I need to select tomorrow's outfit. I assess my clothing once more, forcing myself to truly *look* this time. It's all I can do to rebel against Thorne's wishes. I'm not entirely sure why I want to rebel, only that I do. Perhaps I want to prove him wrong. Prove that I'm as certain as I said I was. Prove that I truly believe my family is worth saving with this sacrifice.

My confidence flares, and I rifle through the wardrobe, eyeing each article of clothing. While Monty's letter suggested our next game is simply a rendezvous in the manor's gallery, I know better than to expect anything to be simple with him. If his previous tendencies are anything to go by, then I must assume *I'll* be on display, competing with the art lining the walls. And since I'm still quite sore about losing the *dress pretty for me* game, I'm determined to impress him with my state of attire.

My gaze slides down to the far end of the wardrobe, where a pink gown takes up nearly a third of the space all on its own. It's the ballgown Agatha had magicked into my bag when I left the convent. While no one at Nocturnus Palace knew how to enchant it back into such a small carrying case, I had Boris pack it for me in a separate garment bag when we left anyway. Even after my shopping trip with Thorne, the ballgown remains my most extravagant piece of clothing.

I remove the gown and hang it over the front of the wardrobe so I can study it fully. Stepping back, I assess the lovely pink fabric threaded with gold, the ruffled bodice, the bustled skirt decorated with silk roses. It's far too ostentatious to wear so early in the morning, but it is daring. Spontaneous. Monty likes that. And it's very different from the dress he said *wasn't for him*. Pale pink to the other gown's deep indigo blue. Wide and flowing instead of curve hugging.

If I am to be presented as a work of art, this ballgown just might do it. It's a risk, of course. He could laugh at me. He could claim his future wife must be more aware of the proper state of dress for every time of day.

Still, there are only three games left, and I need to win two of them.

I need to take a risk. One on my own terms.

The music flooding from my phonograph begins to lag, the lilting melody taking on an eerie quality. My heart sinks. I know what that means. The cylinder is losing its charge.

I glance over to where I've set the phonograph upon a round ivory-and-gold table. Sure enough, the cylinder's golden glow has faded to a flickering murky yellow. The glow dies completely as the needle halts over the now-frozen cylinder. Shoulders slumped, I cross the polished wood floors, carpeted in plush floral-printed rugs, to the table. With practiced care, I lift the cylinder from under the needle and bring it to the nearest window. Throwing back the mauve velvet curtains, I look out at the night sky, the deepest indigo dotted with glittering lights. The stars look less plentiful than they do in the Star Court, yet the sight sets me at ease. There's something about starlight that will always feel like home.

I set the cylinder on the windowsill where it can soak up the glittering illumination and be back in working order by morning, then prop my arms beside it. Leaning my forehead on the glass, I stare down at the scenery one floor down. A labyrinthine garden spans below, one I've yet to visit, only seen from my window. It's wilder than the manicured garden out front, its hedges taller, its flowers larger, its trellises overgrown with ivy. Shadows gather at its center while fireflies—or perhaps some sort of sprite—flit about, lighting paths with their passing.

Yearning burrows deep inside me, the same I once felt for my glade. For solitude in nature. For an unseen dance. It grows, lighting a fire in my heart. I assess the garden with a keener glance, seeking any sign that it's occupied. It's near midnight now, and both Minka and Mr. Boris have already retired to their own rooms. I can't imagine many others are awake. The only reason I am is because my mind wouldn't let me sleep.

My argument with Thorne resurfaces, making my fingers curl into fists. I need a better distraction than any I've attempted tonight. I need fresh air and the night sky. I need the feel of earth beneath my bare feet.

A soft smile warms my lips as I pad back to the wardrobe and extract a long silk robe from inside. I drape it over my linen chemise, securing the tie at my waist. I consider donning more appropriate clothing, including shoes and hose, but that would defeat the purpose. What I need is a sense of freedom. Solitude. Connection with nature.

On bare feet, I slip from my suite and into the hall. It's dark, the sconces dimmed to a pale glow. As quietly as I can,

I descend the stairs and make my way through the manor, relieved when I pass no one. Thorne doesn't seem to keep the largest staff at the manor, and with dinner having been served many hours ago, I imagine not even the kitchen remains active this late at night.

With the manor so dark, it takes me several tries to find the door that leads to the garden beneath my window. I have to circle back to the main foyer twice before I gather my bearings and locate the part of the manor that is just beneath my suite. Finally, I locate a drawing room with a pair of doors that let out to the tall hedges I've been seeking.

My excitement grows as I step onto the path, breathing in aromas of mountain air, rosemary, and spruce. I cross beneath the first trellis, brushing my fingers over the tangled ivy that weaves through it. After a fork in the path, I turn to the right, where the hedges grow taller, thicker. High enough to block the sight of the sleeping manor, my only company the stars overhead. Peace falls over me. I wind through the paths with no agenda, no destination in mind, only mindless comfort.

A giddy urge climbs up my chest, flooding my arms, my legs, my toes. It begs me to dance, or at the very least, skip. So I do, grinning as I leap from one paving stone to the other, then circle in a graceful spin. If anyone could see me now, I'd be embarrassed by my frivolous moment of play. But I'm alone. Free to act as wild and unrestrained as the ivy that serves as my silent companion—

"This is rather childish, don't you think?"

The words have me halting in place, nearly tripping over my feet. My heart races as I whirl in the direction of the voice—Monty's—but I see no sign of him. It's only when he speaks again that I realize how far away he must be.

"Asking me to meet you at midnight? We aren't the love-struck youths we once were, Cosette."

My shoulders sag with relief. He hadn't been talking to me at all. From the sound of his voice, he must be on a different path on the other side of the dividing hedges. But my relief is soon replaced with a twinge of discomfort. Monty is alone with Cosette. At night. While jealousy or anger would be an acceptable reaction to one's fiancé meeting another woman, that isn't what unsettles me. It's more that I feel I'm invading their privacy. Whatever follows isn't meant for my ears.

Cosette's voice comes next. "I wanted to be alone with you. I knew you wouldn't come to my room nor let me in yours."

I bite the inside of my cheek. Shit. I'm right.

Monty's reply, however, surprises me. "You need to give up. I'm never going to love you."

"Then why did you meet me tonight?"

"I was bored."

The sound of shuffling footsteps.

"You say you'll never love me," Cosette says, "yet you always let me touch you."

A male gasp. Then...a low groan.

My hand flies over my mouth. Stars above, this is *definitely* not something I'm meant to overhear.

"This is the last time," Monty says, voice slightly strained.

"Why? Because you're getting married?"

"No, because I'm tired of you."

"You don't *feel* tired."

Another deep sound from Monty. "I've never been particular about sex, Cosette. You know that. If you're offering, I'll take it. But I will never return it. I will never, *ever* give you what you want. My feelings for you are less than dirt."

"You're cruel, Monty."

"Less so than you." There's no amusement in his tone. No teasing. No seduction.

I slowly begin to back down the path, careful to keep my steps quiet. My stomach turns over having been privy to such an intimate conversation, as well as...whatever they're doing now. And with that comes a heavy dose of disgust for the man that is supposed to be my future husband. The anger I didn't feel when I first overhead them now comes to a boil, but it isn't from hurt or envy. It's something fiercer. Bolder. The knowledge that I deserve better than this. Stars, even Cosette deserves better than this.

A feminine gasp pierces the air and my bare toe snags on the edge of the next paving stone. I lose my footing with a hiss of agony and fall. I catch myself on my palms, but one knee slams into stone, sending a sharp pain through my leg. I bite back a cry, and the muffled sounds of the two lovers cut off.

"Did you hear that?" Cosette whispers.

"Hear what?"

I remain crouched in place, not daring to move. Warmth trickles down my shin; my knee's collision with the paving stone must have broken skin. My heart hammers so loud, I fear they'll hear it. I can't let them find me. I can't face them, not until I've gathered my bearings, my composure. I can't let Monty humiliate me one more time.

The muffled sounds resume, each audible kiss fueling my anger. I try to stand, but my leg is still lanced with pain. So instead, I close my eyes. Cover my ears. And try to think of anything else. Be anywhere else. Hear anything else.

Hands close over my shoulders, but the touch feels too light. Too insubstantial. I open my eyes and find Thorne hovering before me, my meteor shower dreamscape all around us. Damn it! How did this happen? Thorne's presence is hardly better than the company of Monty and Cosette's midnight tryst. I nearly curse out loud.

He shakes my shoulders again, and I know it's his dream form, for his grip is all wrong. Weak where it should be strong. Cold where it should be warm. "What's wrong? Where are you?"

Clenching my jaw, I seek my unruly magic, trying to untangle whatever thread summoned him here, but it's too enmeshed with my rage, my annoyance, my desperation to be anywhere but here.

Thorne crouches before me. "Tell me where you are."

I shake my head, unable to speak for fear of being overheard. Found out. Pitied by Monty. Smirked at by Cosette. I can't show him the garden either, for it isn't an image I've framed. With us in separate locations, he won't be able to see my true surroundings even if I lower my dreamscape.

Placing his forefinger under my chin, he lifts my eyes to his. Through his teeth, he speaks. "Tell me where you are."

I give in, mouthing *garden* as clearly as I can.

He nods. "End the daydream."

If I weren't already so enraged, I'd be even more so at his demand. Yet I do as he says, blinking hard and relinquishing my control over the dreamscape. Both Thorne and the meteor shower disappear. I keep my hands over my ears, not wanting to hear if the activities on the other side of the hedge have escalated. I stare sightlessly ahead until a shadow blots out starlight. By the time I glance up, there's nothing. Then a startled female cry rings out, loud enough to make it past the palms over my ears. I lower them and hear Monty's voice.

"Fucking stones, Thorne, where the hell did you come from?"

Thorne's voice is a deadly growl. "Get. Out. Of. My. Garden."

Silence. Then Monty's tone turns light. Easy. "Gladly. It's not like I was enjoying myself here. This was a mistake. As all things are with you, Cosette."

"Monty!" Cosette's voice is edged with desperation. Two sets of footsteps pound the stones, growing more distant with every beat. Only one remains. Slow. Soft. Drawing near.

Soon Thorne stands before me. He's dressed in dark trousers and a cream linen nightshirt, the collar open. I remember the shadow that passed overhead, just before his presence startled the trysting couple. He must have flown to find me so fast, but there's no sign of horns or wings. He extends a hand. "Come on."

I shake my head. I hate that he had to save me. *Again*. "Just...go. I can find my own way back."

He releases an aggrieved sigh and crouches beside me. Before I know what's happening, he snakes one arm beneath my knees and the other behind my back. In one swift movement, he hefts me in his arms and rises to his feet. Without thinking, I instinctively encircle his neck with my arms.

"What are you doing?" I ask.

He says nothing, only carries me down the garden path. Despite my anger that he keeps playing the part of my rescuer while I've only come to look increasingly foolish, the weight off my injured leg is a comfort. Perhaps even more so is the warmth of his arms. For just this moment, I let myself settle into him. Let myself be carried. Comforted. His aroma —a medley of clean laundry mingling with something sweet like burnt sugar—invades my senses.

Thorne pulls up short. I lift my head to find Monty and

Cosette at the entrance to the gardens. Monty stares down at her, lips curled in disgust, while she grips his collar, expression pleading.

"Why are you still here?" Thorne's voice ripples with rage, chest heaving against me.

Monty's fingers circle Cosette's wrists and force her hands from his collar. "We were just leaving. And Cosette will be departing at first light."

"You can't mean that!" she shouts.

That's when Monty notices me cradled in Thorne's arms. He straightens, eyes wide, face pale. I've never seen him so discomfited. "Princess, you...you were in the garden?"

I purse my lips, refusing to say a word. I'm not ready to deal with him.

Thorne proceeds forward and brushes past them. "She's hurt."

"Where? Is she all right?"

"Fuck off, Monty."

"The poor girl," comes Cosette's simpering tone. I glance over Thorne's shoulder and find her pleading expression gone, replaced with cold triumph. She must know I came across them. Heard them. Her lips curl in a cruel grin.

I may have admitted that she deserves better than Monty, but I still deserve better than both of them. Than all of this.

Thorne halts and turns to face her. "You fuck off too, Cosette. Get out of my manor. Not at first light. *Now*."

That wipes the smug look off her face. Her eyes meet mine, and I return the wicked grin she gave me. Thorne whips back around, and I settle into him once more, my face nestled against his collarbone.

33

THORNE

Briony's breath warms my neck in a way I find all too pleasant. Or perhaps I'm simply enjoying that she isn't fighting me for once. She's letting me help her without argument. I find it oddly appealing. Not that I would find it any less so to have her curving form draped against me like this while she tried to claw out my eyes. Some twisted part of me likes helping her. Holding her. Touching her. Yet the farther we get into the manor and the more distance we put between ourselves and the garden, the stiffer she grows in my arms.

It comes as no surprise when she says, "You can put me down now. I can walk."

"No," I say, mostly because I know it will annoy her.

"Why?"

"I made a bargain to lie for you. Monty and Cosette could catch up to us at any time. If I put you down now, it will look suspicious." There's hardly any truth in that statement. What a boon it is to have human blood. I glance down and meet her eyes. "Besides, you're hurt."

"I'll heal, Thorne." A spark flickers in my chest at the sound of my name on her lips. When did we start calling each other by first name?

"Then I'll at least clean your wound." We round the next corner and reach the hall that leads to the kitchen.

"I can do that myself."

I lower my voice. "Just shut up and let me tend to you. I know you're hurt in more ways than one."

She blinks at me, her blue eyes going wider. Her throat bobs. "Fine."

As we reach the kitchen, I stride inside, heading straight for the worktable. The room is dark, lit only by the moonlight filtering in through the small windows and the flames that flicker in the stoves. I prop her on the counter, which elicits a surprised gasp from her.

"Sit," I demand, then head for the cabinet that contains items for first aid.

"You're awfully brusque tonight. How can you see a thing—oh, right. Your eyesight is better in the dark. I just realized you're not wearing your spectacles."

"Yes, I can see clearly right now," I say a bit absently as I seek what I need. I return to her with antiseptic and a clean muslin cloth. Glancing down at her legs, I find both knees are covered beneath the folds of her robe. "May I?"

Her eyes deepen into a scowl, but she grudgingly parts the skirt of her robe to reveal the wounded knee. Then, crossing her arms over her chest, she says, "Go ahead. If you're so determined to tend to me."

"I am. It's my form of revenge." I step closer to her, holding her gaze as I soak the cloth in antiseptic. With her fae healing, plain water would likely suffice, but I am a creature of cleanliness and habit. Injuries happen in kitchens, and there is a specific way to clean them.

She scoffs. "Revenge? For what?"

"For so rudely interrupting me while I was baking. If you hadn't dragged me into that daydream, you'd be free of my attention right now."

"I had no intention of drawing you into that. It just—wait, you were baking? Is that what that smell is?" She breathes in deep. "What did you make?"

"Chocolate cake," I say, softly gripping her calf as I lean over her knee. With gentle motions, I dab the wound with the soaked cloth. She doesn't hiss or wince, which tells me the lesion has probably closed already. I apply slightly more pressure, focusing my efforts on cleaning the blood. I glance up at her, ensuring she shows no sign of pain, and find her staring down at me with a questioning look.

"You baked a chocolate cake at midnight?"

I return my gaze to her leg, running the cloth down the length of her shin where rivulets of crimson have dried. "I couldn't sleep."

"You bake cakes when you can't sleep?"

"Of course I do. What do you do when you can't sleep?" My eyes flick to hers, and I lift a corner of my mouth. "Oh, wait. I know the answer to that."

Her nostrils flare as she realizes what I'm referring to. She aims a kick at my shoulder, but I grip her ankle, softening an already weak blow. Her jaw tightens as I hold the ankle in place, her heel pressed to my bicep. I lean slightly forward, forcing her to fall back. She catches herself on her forearms, blinking at me in surprise. "Careful," I whisper. "I could get into this."

Her chest heaves, and the way she's half sprawled on the countertop, eyes dancing with anger, her leg nearly thrown over my shoulder, has my mind going to places better left unexplored. I give her another smirk, then release her ankle. She sits upright, cheeks blazing as she burns me with a glare. With a huff, she reaches for the cloth and yanks it from my hand.

"I'll finish tending to myself, thank you." Crossing the wounded leg over the other, she picks up where I left off.

"Oh, I know you will. I've seen you do it."

Her gaze is murderous as she speaks through her teeth. "Will you stop bringing that up?"

I chuckle and saunter over to the stove, where the scent of chocolate has grown to a mouthwatering degree. Oven mitt in hand, I open the stove and remove the tray of four ramekins. Then I set it on the wooden worktable to cool while I retrieve plates and forks.

"That doesn't look like chocolate cake," Briony says.

I return to her with two plates in hand. She's finished cleaning her leg, though it remains bare, crossed over the other in a tantalizing display of smooth flesh. I force my gaze back to the ramekins. "It's not the kind of cake you're thinking of."

"What kind is it?"

"You'll see." I count off the seconds in my head, just long enough to ensure the cakes cool slightly. Then I place a plate over one of the ramekins and flip them over together. With the mitt, I lift the ramekin from the plate, leaving its delectably dark contents perched upon it. I hand it to Briony along with a fork. "Molten chocolate cake. The perfect cure for a broken heart."

She gives me a withering look. "My heart isn't broken."

"Well, then. I suppose you won't need this." I start to take the plate away, but she grasps it with her fingertips.

"I still want cake."

With a grin, I release the plate and tend to my serving. I lean against the edge of the counter and taste my creation. It's perfect. Rich and slightly crisped on the outside, warm and melted on the inside. One of my favorite things to make when sleep eludes me.

Briony releases a soft moan, one that reflects her enjoyment of the cake but has my mind flashing back to when I had her ankle in my grip. I smother the thought in another bite of cake.

"This is really good," she says.

"I'm glad," I say, not daring to look at her, for if her face reveals as much pleasure as her voice does—I shake my head. "It's one of the first things my father taught me to bake. He always made it to cheer me up."

"You and I have similar upbringings." Her words are muffled, and I hear her scrape her plate for another bite. "The sisters at the convent were always baking things. I can't help but associate sugar with comfort."

"Then I suppose it's a pleasant coincidence that I just so happened to be baking cakes while you were...distressed."

She says nothing for a few more bites. Then, "I meant what I said about not being broken-hearted. I'm not hurt in the way you think."

I finish my final bite and face her, careful to keep a few feet of space between us. Between the pleasure of sugar on my tongue and the sight of her perched on my countertop, robe still draped open over that leg, I find it impossible not to desire her. It's not like this is new. I desired her when I thought she was nothing but a dream. But our current subject calls for candor. As much as I like to taunt her, flirt with her, and tease her, she deserves to get whatever is plaguing her off her chest. Despite what she says, *something* hurt her. It was clear in the way she was crouched in a ball, eyes squeezed tight, hands pressed over her ears. I thought my heart would burst in my chest when I found her like that, suddenly pulled into her daydream.

Keeping my voice nonchalant, I ask, "Then what happened?"

She takes another bite of cake, eyes distant. "I'm...not even sure myself. At first, I was simply embarrassed to have caught a private conversation, but once things escalated..." Her cheeks flush and her expression turns sour. "I shouldn't have had to hear that, you know?"

"No, you shouldn't have."

"I've had my share of lovers, but clearly not as many as he has. I never expected us to be a love match, nor do I care who he takes to bed, for I have no intention of ever inviting him into mine. And he technically isn't my fiancé until his father reinstates our betrothal, but..." Her words dry up.

I finish them for her. "But any man in his right mind would stay true to you, regardless."

She scowls. "That's not what I was going to say."

"Yet it's true."

Her blush deepens, and I wonder if she's forgotten how well I can see in the dark. "Maybe I'm naive," she rushes to say. "Maybe this is childish to admit, but...I...I've never had to overhear sounds of pleasure like that. It made me unsettled. Angry. Embarrassed."

"You have every right to be angry. No one would feel easy about that situation. It's not childish."

She lifts her chin as if bolstered by my words of validation. "Thank you, Thorne."

"Besides," I say with a wicked grin, no longer able to stop myself from teasing now that she's said her piece, "I know full well you're no stranger to sounds of pleasure when it comes to your own."

She nearly chokes on her next bite of cake. "Why do you keep bringing that up?"

I take a step closer, tucking my hands in my pockets to keep them at bay. "Maybe it's time we talked about it. It won't feel so taboo if we do."

Her breaths grow sharper. Keeping her eyes on mine, she finishes her bite of cake and sets the plate off to the side. "I suppose."

"It's fitting, considering this is the very location that dream happened in."

She glances around the room with renewed interest. "Stars, is it? Wait...now that I understand what my dreams really are, I know I must have entered *your* dream that night. Why were you dreaming of your own kitchen?"

I shrug. "I have baking dreams often. That was the first one a naked woman stumbled into, though." I remember it now, the way her nude form appeared out of nowhere, leaning against my doorway, head thrown back in pleasure as she worked her fingers between her legs. It wasn't until I cleared my throat that she noticed my presence. Then it was my turn to be caught off guard, for I was suddenly as naked as she was.

I inch closer. "What had you so...worked up that you entered my dream like that?"

"Does a lady need a reason to get *worked up*? I'm privy to the same sexual urges you are. Besides, I wasn't in control. I never am at night, only during daydreams. Even then undesirable things tend to pop up."

I'm guessing that means me. "Yes, but what had you feeling so out of control? What had you so on edge that dream-you wasn't put off by a naked man showing up in your fantasy?"

"Oh, I was put off at first." Her eyes dip down to my waist. "Then I saw your body's response."

A similar tightening in my trousers forms now as the memory of the dream builds in my mind. I can't count the number of times I've replayed that dream in my mind for my own enjoyment, the heat of it carrying me through many lonely nights. My voice is thick as I say, "And you...stopped your activities. Walked up to me. Then sat on my counter. Just like this." Stones, she was so daring then. So eager to finish what she'd begun, even with an audience.

Her breaths grow even sharper as her eyes sweep over me. "And you stood just like that."

"No," I say, closing another foot of space between us. My stomach tightens. "I stood right here."

Her throat bobs. Once. Twice. "You asked to kiss me. Then to touch me. I said no."

"And you told me to touch myself."

"You obeyed."

"Eagerly."

We stare at each other for several long moments. I note the way she curls her fingers over the edge of the counter, arms quavering. My own grow tense in my pockets, begging to reach for her. What would she do if I planted them beside her, stepped between her legs, leaned in...

Punch me, most likely. And I can't say I find that unpleasant.

Gritting my teeth, I take a deliberate step back. Then another.

Briony releases a slow exhale, her grip on the counter's edge loosening.

My heart slams an uneven tempo as I force myself to move even farther away, to take her plate and stack it upon my own. I'm about to tell her we should go to bed—separately, of course—when she speaks.

"You flew tonight when you found me, didn't you?"

I release the two remaining cakes from their ramekins so I can store them for tomorrow. "I did."

"Can I see it?"

"See what?" My gaze shoots to hers, my mind still lost in treacherous waters. Seductive ones.

"Your unseelie form."

I run a hand through my hair, wondering if this is wise. Why is she lingering? I know why I am, but...

With a resigned sigh, I seek the magic that allows me to shift, a warm tingling that's always alive in my blood. With a shudder, the magic ignites, and my wings sprout from my back while my horns curl from the sides of my head. My eyes dart to the partially open doorway and the dark hallway beyond. Spreading one wing out wide, I extend it behind me, then thrust it forward. A gust of wind funnels through the room, closing the door the rest of the way.

Briony jumps at the sound. "Why did you do that?"

"No one in this house has seen me like this. Alina and Father knew about my fae heritage, but no one else. Not the staff, not Monty. No one."

Her brow knits together. "Just me?"

"Just you."

Her eyes rove over my wings, my horns. "Does it ever get exhausting hiding your past?"

"It does."

"What will you do after we break the curse?"

That's a question I've had to ponder myself lately. And I don't have all the answers yet. "Once I'm reunited with the Lemurias, I won't be able to hide my history. The Blackwood name will fall under scrutiny, and I'll certainly have a scandal to deal with."

"Will you discard the Blackwood name after that?"

The question sinks my heart. "I don't know. I am Thorne Blackwood just as much as I am Vintarys Lemuria. Maybe more so. Blackwood Bakery and Estate have become my life. I don't know how things will be for me after my family awakens."

Her expression turns sympathetic. "You thought you had to wait one hundred years to see them again."

I nod.

She tilts her head to the side and studies the length of one wing. I extend it farther to give her a better look. My chest tightens at her scrutiny. I feel bare like this, with her seeing the parts of me no one else has. Her lips curl into a pout. "How unfair is it that you have an unseelie form when I do not?"

"You don't think you can shift?" It's not unheard of for a pureblood fae to be unable to shift. While most fae can—even those with only some fae blood—there are types who have only one physical form. I never considered that a bad thing, but the wistfulness in her face tells me she considers it to be so.

She shakes her head. "If I'm a succubus like my mother, I don't think I can shift into another form. My magic is tied to dreams. I think my dream form *is* my unseelie form. And I look the same in both dreams and reality."

"You don't need another form. You're already overwhelming in this one."

Her eyes lock on mine. "I can't tell if that's a compliment."

"It is."

With a soft smile, she splays her hands out on the countertop just behind her hips and leans back slightly, posture relaxed. It does terrible things to my imagination. She kicks out her legs in a playful manner. "I don't hate you tonight, Thorne."

My chest tightens. Whether with guilt or desire, I'm not sure. "That's unfortunate," I say, holding her eyes. "I was hoping we could have that hate-tryst I suggested a few days ago."

She tenses, legs ceasing their lighthearted kicking. For one moment, I can't tell whether I've enraged her...or enticed her. The former had been my intent, but if it's the latter...

I swallow hard, waiting for her reaction.

Finally, she rolls her eyes and hops off the counter. "I've changed my mind," she mutters and strides from the room with her arms folded over her chest. Her exit seems to take all the warmth from the room with her.

I release my hold over my unseelie form, and my wings and horns vanish. Closing my eyes, I turn around and slump against the edge of the counter, relief and remorse swarming inside me. I'm glad she left. She had to leave. Otherwise, I have the deepest, darkest feeling we may have done something we'd come to regret.

34

BRIONY

I wake with a start, sweat drenching my body. It's the third time I've woken like this, my mind filled with images of naked skin and breathless sighs. Thorne is to blame, and maybe eating chocolate so late at night has contributed to my restless state as well. All I know is that every time I close my eyes, I see him. Hear him. Feel him. And I'm terrified that I might unwillingly invite him into my dreams. Dreams that will surely divulge the truth—how badly I wanted him to touch me last night. How badly I want that still.

Lifting my head, I squint toward the windows. The heavy velvet curtains block out all light, so it's impossible to tell how late in the morning it is. Minka is supposed to wake me up before breakfast, but she obviously isn't here yet. Is it folly to try and go back to sleep?

I toss on my side, my legs tangled in bedsheets. Why do the sheets have to be silk, of all things? They practically beg for sensuality. I squeeze my eyes shut, seeking calm thoughts, but my mind fills with images of Thorne. The way he lifted me in his arms in the garden. The way he cleaned my wounded leg with the tenderest care. The cake he made. The way he listened when I talked. The way he taunted and teased, got me to talk about *that one dream*.

An ache builds between my legs, one that hasn't fully ceased since sitting on Thorne's counter last night. It started the moment he caught my ankle in his strong grip, leaned in slightly, and sent me half falling back. I was caught in madness then, convinced he was about to climb upon the counter on top of me, or perhaps bury his lips between my thighs—

I squirm in bed, tossing to the other side now. The warm pressure builds at my core, and I don't know if I can stop it. But if I let myself release it the way I want...stars, I don't trust my magic. I just *know* it will bring him here.

And yet...fucking hell, I can't stop this feeling. This need.

Giving in, I turn onto my back and slide my fingertips over my aching center, determined to sate this fire as quickly as possible. I can already feel my magic sparking around me, and when I open my eyes, I catch sight of it breaking apart the ceiling with a vision of a night sky, then stage lights from the ballet, then the meteor shower. I bite my lip trying—and failing—not to think of Thorne. But there he is in my mind's eye, running a cloth down my bare leg. Then he's standing before me, his length gripped in a fist, in a reenactment of our shared dream. And now he's hovering over me while we fall upon his countertop, and he releases the ankle he'd so expertly caught to wrap my leg around his waist.

"Thorne," I whisper, unable to stop the name from leaving my lips, for it's his fingers I'm imagining between my legs now, sliding over my slick entrance—

"Oh."

Thorne's voice has me biting back a squeal. I freeze, my eyelids flying open to find Thorne hovering over me, completely nude, much like he'd been in my imaginings. Or is this still my imagination? Stars above, *please* let this be my imagination.

His hair is mussed, dark strands falling over his forehead. He blinks at me a few times, then utters a bashful, "Good morning."

Shit. What is this? Dream or fantasy? Is it ever just fantasy between us?

Before I can find out for sure, the sound of my bedroom door opening has me yelping in surprise once more. This time I pull the covers over my head and force all thoughts of passion from my mind.

Minka's voice calls out from the other side of my blankets. "Good morning, Highness."

Her words echo Thorne's—who is, thankfully, nowhere to be seen—sending my heart skittering. The sound of curtains being drawn open follows, and I do all I can to even out my breathing, gather my composure, and pretend I wasn't just seconds away from pleasurable release over thoughts of my enemy.

AFTER BREAKFAST, I HEAD FOR THE GALLERY WITH MINKA. SHE struts beside me in her feline form, while I'm dressed in the pink ballgown. Where last night I decided to wear it to potentially impress Monty, today I'm wearing it simply because I want to. I'm not at all looking forward to seeing the bastard, but I feel a renewed sense of control this morning. A different sort of determination.

I'm done playing his game. I'll do whatever I can to fulfill my bargain with Thorne and break my family's curse, even if I must negotiate my own betrothal with Lord Phillips. I'll use threats if I have to. My magic if I can. I'll use whatever dark and underhanded methods I have at my disposal to see this through, but I won't stand for humiliation at Monty's hands. I'll humor the asshole. I'll let him think I'm still playing his game while I wait for his father to return, but I'm playing my own now.

I'm not doing anything I don't want to do.

We reach the gallery, and I take a fortifying breath before crossing the threshold. Not just to prepare myself to deal with Monty, but to see Thorne too. If he's even here. I don an easy grin and enter. The gallery is a long rectangular room with plush carpeted floors marked with pedestals of statues, vases, and other displays. Its high walls are bedecked with portraits and several seating areas are arranged throughout the room. Thorne and Monty stand at opposite ends of the gallery, postures tense as they stare at the artwork lining the walls. I have a feeling neither of them are truly *seeing* what they stare at, and I wonder if they fought this morning, or if the tension is merely residual from last night.

Thankfully, the room is host to more than just the two men. Angela circles a pedestal featuring a sculpture of a water nymph, rendered in such lifelike detail that the folds of its skirt seem to flow like a stream.

Monty notices my arrival first. "Highness," he says with a dimpled smile. There's no remorse in his eyes, no embarrassment over what happened last night. Only his stiff arms betray his unease.

Thorne slowly turns to face me. I hold my breath and wait for any sign that what happened this morning was real.

That I drew his dream form into my bed. He gives me nothing but a curt nod, which provides the slightest relief.

Monty saunters my way, but I head straight for Angela. The only person in this room—save for Minka, of course—that I feel even remotely comfortable around. Her expression brightens, and she meets me at the center of the room.

"I was so sad to hear Miss Dervins left last night," she says, her smile tinged with worry, "but seeing you makes it all better."

"Save your sorrows, Angela," Thorne says. "Cosette doesn't deserve them."

She frowns at him. "You say that, yet neither you nor Brother will tell me why."

Monty speaks next. "You should simply trust us when we tell you your friendship with her is better left discarded."

"Yes, but *why*?" Angela glances from Monty to Thorne. Neither says a word.

A furrow knits my brow. Have they not said a word to Angela about Cosette's true motives? I recall Thorne telling me that Angela is too kind to see through her friend's ruse—that Cosette is only friends with Angela to remain close to Monty—but wouldn't she understand the situation if someone simply *told* her? Well, if they won't do it...

Her lips pull into a tight line, and I can tell she's frustrated.

I offer her my arm. "Shall we take a turn about the room?"

Her expression softens and she links her elbow with mine. "Oh, yes, let us admire the art. Thorne's collection is stunning. Not half as stunning as your ballgown, of course. You look incredible, Highness."

My cheeks flush. I'd nearly forgotten about my elegant state of dress. "Thank you."

She leads the way, guiding me over to a wall of landscape paintings. Minka follows, then circles our ankles when we stop to admire the art. Angela emits a joyful gasp and crouches before the cat. "You brought your lady's maid!"

Minka eyes the girl with feline suspicion, then turns to the side, presenting her flank. "You may pet me if you like. I'll even allow you to pick me up if you don't drop me."

Angela wastes no time, scooping Minka into her arms and nestling her to her chest. "I'm so honored you've forgiven me."

Minka closes her eyes and begins to purr as Angela strokes her fur. We move on from the landscape paintings to assess a series of glass sculptures in the shape of tiny pixies. My chest squeezes as I'm reminded of my three teachers.

I sidle closer to Angela and cast a glance around us, ensuring Thorne and Monty aren't too close. Thorne remains where he was, while Monty paces the wall behind us. Keeping my tone nonchalant, I say, "You seem quite fond of Miss Dervins, even though Mr. Blackwood and your brother disapprove of your connection with her."

"I am fond of her! I don't understand why everyone dislikes her so. She and Brother used to be such good friends."

Friends, not lovers. Does she not even know Cosette and Monty once courted? "Is that how the two of you became acquainted?"

"Sort of. We struck up correspondence after I started boarding school. She wrote to me, knowing I must be lonely being away from my family. She's been my only true friend since."

"Your *only* friend?"

Her expression sinks. We move on to the next display, a wall of still-life paintings, and she releases a heavy sigh. "I haven't had the best of luck making friends at boarding school. I'm at the top of my class and I come from one of Earthen Court's most prestigious human families. I thought these things would make me popular, but they haven't. Instead, the girls treat me coldly."

"I'm so sorry."

She dons a grin that doesn't reach her eyes. "That's why I'm happy I have Miss Dervins."

My chest tightens. Stars, no wonder Thorne and Monty have kept quiet about Cosette's treachery. The girl has no other friends, and she's clearly being bullied at school. How would she feel if she discovered her only companion has interest in her brother instead of her? I thought I'd be brave enough to tell her the truth, but it turns out I'm just as weak as the two men when it comes to Angela's feelings. So instead, I give her a different truth. "You have me now. And...and Minka."

Minka shifts in the girl's arms. "I do like you much better now that you aren't throwing me in puddles."

Angela chuckles. "I'm so glad. And I'm honored to have your friendship too, Highness. After you marry my brother, we'll be even closer. You'll be my sister."

Against my will, the smile slips from my face. While I want to be Angela's friend, the reminder that I'll be marrying her brother takes away all the pleasantness I felt a second before.

She moves on to the next group of paintings, pointing out one to Minka that features three playful kittens. Meanwhile, my feet remain rooted to the spot. A rebellious fire burns inside me, the same I felt when I first heard of my surprise engagement. I don't want to do this.

I *don't* want this.

My gloved fists curl tighter as I remind myself that this

aversion, this burning dread, is exactly what it takes to break the curse on my family. Yet the fire remains. It burns brighter. Stronger.

"You look beautiful." Thorne's deep whisper empties my mind and sends a shudder up my spine. I angle my head over my shoulder and find him standing just behind me. "That's not one of the dresses I bought for you."

"No, it isn't," I say, doing my best to keep my voice even. "It's from one of my teachers."

"It suits you."

"Thank you."

My eyes rove over the still-life paintings but my focus is narrowed on his proximity, the heat of his nearness. It reminds me too much of what happened this morning.

"I trust you slept well," he says, voice still lowered to a whisper.

I stiffen. "Indeed, I—" My words catch in my throat. I didn't sleep well at all, so I can't say I did. "No, I didn't get much sleep."

"A shame." He steps beside me, his shoulder nearly brushing mine. If I leaned only a fraction of an inch, my bare arm would caress the fabric of his jacket.

I remain perfectly still.

His face turns toward mine and I feel his gaze scalding my profile. "At least you had the comfort of pleasant dreams."

My heart climbs to my throat. I meet his eyes and find the taunting smile playing over his lips, the dark gleam in his eyes.

Glittering hell. That wasn't a fantasy this morning. It was *him*.

He leans in closer and whispers, "I hope you were able to finish." Then he strides away to another art display, leaving me burning yet again. This time not with rebellion. Instead, it's a place where anger meets desire.

Clenching my jaw, I move in the opposite direction, toward Angela. We continue our turn about the room, assessing the art, though I barely pay attention to any of it. It's impossible with the feel of Thorne's incessant gaze on me, distracting me from everything else. He remains on the opposite side of the room, moving when I do, orbiting me and the empty space between us, never closing the distance. He may be avoiding me after our brief chat, but he never fails to meet my eyes when I glance at him over my shoulder.

I almost forget Monty's presence entirely until he says, "This is thoroughly boring." I find him lounging in a chair beside a pedestal displaying a blue-and-white vase. He slumps in his seat, one leg thrown over the arm of the chair.

"This was your idea," Thorne says.

"The location, perhaps, but we aren't playing anything."

Thorne shoots Monty a meaningful look. "Maybe no one wants to play with you anymore."

He straightens in his chair. "That's no fun. Well, I can fix that. This calls for a private chat with the princess and Thorne. Sister, dear, will you give us some privacy? The kitty cat too."

Dread forms in my stomach. What does this private chat entail? Is it part of today's game? Or...does he perhaps want to discuss what happened last night?

Angela's shoulders sink. "I suppose, but I can't speak for Minka. She's the princess' lady's maid. Surely she can't leave her lady unchaperoned."

Minka turns in Angela's arms to give me a questioning look.

I glance from Thorne to Monty and back again. If this

really is about last night, I suppose I can hear Monty out. Maybe the idiot will have the decency to apologize. Not that it would change anything between us.

"It's all right," I say to Minka. "I'll speak alone with Mr. Phillips and Mr. Blackwood."

"Very well." Minka leaps out of Angela's arms, shifting into her seelie form by the time she lands on her feet. She rises on two legs, smoothing out the ruffles on her black-and-white dress. "I'll make tea. It's going to be very, *very* good tea, so you better be finished with this private conversation by the time I return. Come, you can help me." She says the last part to a wide-eyed Angela, who seems enthralled at having seen her shift.

I suppress a grin. It seems Minka's feline sass is invading her persona in seelie form too. But my momentary amusement fades as soon as I'm left alone with Monty and Thorne. The two men face me. Thorne's expression holds the same wariness I feel inside.

Monty stands and puts his hands on his hips. "Let's play the next game, shall we?"

"Game?" I echo.

"Yes," he says, eyes twinkling with mischief. "It's time to play the kissing game."

35

BRIONY

"K issing game?" Thorne and I say in unison.

"The most important game of all," Monty says. "I must know whether my future bride is an adequate kisser. Otherwise, you might end up kissing like...like that." He points to one of the largest oil paintings gracing the nearest wall. Angela and I didn't linger over that section of the gallery when we made our rounds, as the paintings were rather dark in subject matter—scenes of war, brutal hunts, and depictions of monsters. But now I assess the piece in question and find a terrifying winged creature with bulging eyes devouring a human body.

I slide my gaze back to Monty, a glare burning on my face. "I'm not kissing you."

Monty's head snaps back. He stares at me for a moment before his lips curl into a crooked grin. "I like seeing that fire from you. An essential element for my future wife, but do save it for your demonstration."

"I said I'm not—"

"She's not kissing you." Thorne strides over to Monty with slow yet forbidding steps. "Remember who you're talking to. She's a princess, Monty."

He rolls his eyes. "It won't be on the lips. I know better than to request such a vulgar act from a royal. Besides, I never said she was kissing *me*."

My pulse quickens, my eyes flashing toward Thorne. His are already on me. I look back to Monty. "You don't mean..."

Monty tilts his head in a way that he probably thinks is cute and coy. It isn't. "Why do you think I wanted to play this game with the two of you alone? You didn't think I requested an audience so we could air our darkest indiscretions, did you? That's not how human high society operates, Rosey. Better get used to it if you're so determined to marry into this world of false smiles and platitudes."

There's a bitter edge to his words, one that makes me wonder if there's a layer to him that I've yet to see. Even Thorne looks surprised, brow furrowed as he studies his friend.

Monty waves a dismissive hand. "I'm getting off topic. We're here to play a game. The kissing game. I want to see how well Princess Rosaline can use those lips of hers, but— as you learned during our dancing game—I like to watch more than participate. So...go on. Show me what you can do."

I've never seen Thorne so tense. His breathing so shallow. "You don't have to do this," he says through clenched teeth.

He's right. I don't have to do this. I promised myself as much this morning when I decided I wouldn't put any effort into Monty's game anymore or do anything I don't want to do.

But as I take in Thorne's posture, a dark thrill stirs inside me. He's...flustered.

Well, that's what he gets for having done the very same to me earlier.

It's my turn for revenge.

On swift feet, I close the distance between us, place one hand on his shoulder, and stand on my toes. His breath hitches as I plant a soft kiss on his cheek. He's still frozen in place by the time I step back. I give him a triumphant grin, but it falters as I realize how rapidly my heart races, how warm my lips are where they grazed Thorne's flesh.

Monty releases a groan. "No. Gross. That was so boring."

Thorne shakes himself from his stupor. "She did what you asked."

No, I think to myself. *I did what I wanted to do.*

"That's not what I asked," Monty says. He runs his hands through his curly hair in an agitated manner until his expression brightens. He gestures toward the chair behind him. "I've got it! Sit down, Thorne. Rosey, sit on his lap."

"His lap?" There goes the smooth composure I held when I kissed Thorne's cheek.

Thorne shakes his head and starts toward the door. "This is ridiculous. I've had enough, Monty."

"Have you? And here I thought you wanted to help me and the princess find our happily ever after."

Thorne pulls up short and rounds on his friend. "I never said that."

"Yet you've been so accommodating," Monty says. "Why stop now?"

Thorne's eyes meet mine. I feel a strange pulse between us, and it isn't the desire that has ignited inside me. It's a neutral energy, one that seems to tug Thorne closer. Only when Thorne returns to us and slumps in the chair does the tug disappear.

I realize then what that pulse was. It's the magic of the bargain we made. Monty may have been taunting Thorne with his words, but he's right. Thorne and I made a bargain, and he is bound by his promise to ensure my marriage to Monty proceeds as planned. With fae magic, intent and belief are everything. If Thorne thinks playing this game will aid our task, then he has no choice but to participate. Refusing will compromise the terms of our bargain.

I know I shouldn't revel in Thorne's current state of helplessness, but as I watch him shift awkwardly in the chair, eyes pinned on me, my earlier thrill returns. In this moment, he's at my mercy. Stars, does that feel exhilarating.

"Now, Rosey, sit—"

I march over to Thorne before Monty can finish and plant myself in his lap. Not because Monty wants me to. This isn't about him at all. Monty may think he's in charge of this game, that it's between him and me, but Thorne is the one I'm playing with. This is yet another round of *who can make the other flustered*, and I've never been more certain of a win.

Thorne's posture goes rigid as he leans into the backrest. I pretend not to notice as I straighten my abundant skirts, smoothing ruffles and leaning over far more than necessary. I keep my shoulders thrown back, ensuring my breasts strain against my bodice as I adjust my position in his lap.

"Yes, beautiful," Monty says, his voice an unwelcome intrusion. I don't bother looking at him as he continues. "That's the position I'd like you to demonstrate your skills in. Now, rules. No kissing on the lips. We've already addressed how vulgar that would be, but I do want to see some passion. Woo me. And you can't touch her, Thorne.

Seeing your hands on her will spoil the fantasy for me, so try to move as little as possible. But I want you, princess, to touch him."

"She can't—" Thorne's voice sticks in his throat as I angle myself toward him and place a hand on his chest. The other anchors against the backrest. From the corner of my eye, I see his hands curl around the wooden armrests of the chair, his grip so tight his knuckles turn pale. His discomfort is so delectable I can almost taste it.

Still, I can't say I'm entirely comfortable right now either. My heart thuds so hard my entire body trembles to the beat. But the hand pressed to Thorne's chest, palm splayed over the gold silk of his waistcoat, reveals his chest pulses even heavier, faster.

"I'll watch from here," Monty says, his voice barely above a whisper. Whether he realizes how little I want to hear it right now or if he's merely enraptured by the view, I know not. Nor do I care. This is *my* game. *My* win. My object of desire and revenge.

I am going to destroy Thorne Blackwood.

Keeping one hand on his chest, I slowly slide the other from the backrest to behind his neck. I hold his gaze and let my thumb drift down the column of his throat until it settles over the raging pound of his pulse. My lips quirk to tell him I *know*. I'm fully aware of how unsettled he is, how vulnerable. Inch by inch, I bring my lips to the corner of his jaw and lightly press a kiss. His chest hitches, and I feel his heartbeat slam against my palm. I trail my lips up the side of his face, then alight another kiss on his cheekbone. Pulling back slightly, I watch his eyelids flutter closed. I dig my fingertips into the hair at the nape of his neck, pulling slightly.

"Fuuuuck," Thorne utters, the word more of a breath than anything, too quiet for Monty to overhear.

I'm nearly giddy with satisfaction, my blood sizzling with a pleasurable heat that radiates from my head to my toes. It tingles my skin, radiating from every pore. The air grows thick with it. Or...no, it's my magic. Darkness falls around us, and my favorite meteor shower devours the walls of the gallery. It's the same thing that happened when Thorne and I danced, but I don't try to suppress it this time. What does it matter when I'm the only one who can see it?

I shift my position in Thorne's lap and lower my mouth to his jaw again. This time, I part my lips and trail the tip of my tongue along his jawline until I reach his ear. There I pause to whisper, "In reply to your earlier statement, no, I wasn't able to finish."

He shudders and I press my final kiss to his earlobe, ending it with a graze of my teeth. In one graceful move, I release him and slide from his lap.

My meteor shower dreamscape dissolves, returning the daylight and the walls of the gallery. And—to my great displeasure—the sight of Monty. It was easy to forget he was here while I was tormenting Thorne, but now his dimpled grin is impossible to ignore.

His eyes are wild with delight. "That was fantastic. Yes. Exactly what I wanted to see. That touch at the end with the meteor shower—"

My heart leaps into my throat. "You saw that?"

"Oh, was I not supposed to? Well, regardless, it set the scene for a lovely kiss. I wondered if you took after your mother, but I've never heard of a succubus who could cast illusions outside of dreams. It has me curious what other magical feats you can accomplish when fueled by desire."

I blink at him. No one has ever seen one of my dream-scapes before. Only Thorne, and that's because he's a subject I've framed. Could I have...dragged Monty into a dream? No, that's not possible. I never framed him.

But that means...

I remember what my mother said about succubus magic. How arousal in her subjects isn't necessary but does strengthen her abilities.

I look back at Thorne, slumped forward in his chair, elbows propped on his thighs. The way he hangs his head makes him look...drained.

Stars above. Did I...evoke arousal in him and...drain his energy somehow? That's what the darkest tales of succubi always suggested. And if so, did I use that energy to make a more powerful dreamscape—one others could see?

"As impressive as that illusion was," Monty says, pulling me from my thoughts, "that's the evidence that impresses me more."

I frown, following his line of sight. At first I think he's talking about Thorne—who still hasn't lifted his head—but then I notice one of the wooden armrests of the chair. It's... splintered. Right where his hands had been curled.

Monty chuckles. "Such violent reactions, Thorny. And you still owe me a cup."

"Fuck off," Thorne mutters.

"Will do. I assume you need a moment to...recover. Well, I'll leave you to it." Monty saunters toward the door, then pauses at the threshold. Turning back to face me, he says, "It would be a shame to spoil that kiss with one from me, so take this instead. You won that round." He presses a kiss to his fingertips, then flutters them at me in a wave. With that, he leaves me alone with Thorne.

I face him, my heart sinking with guilt. He still won't look at me, won't lift his head. My gaze roves to where he broke the armrest, and my guilt deepens. In the moment, I relished his torment, his desire, but now...

Swallowing my pride, I utter a curt, "I'm sorry."

Finally, he straightens in the chair. I expect him to look pale, sickly. Instead, his eyelids are heavy, his cheeks flushed. With a long sigh, he meets my eyes. "For what?"

"I didn't mean to drain you. My magic has never done anything like that."

He frowns. "Drain me? What are you talking about?"

"Didn't I...use some strange magic on you?"

He chuckles. "Whether you did or did not, I don't think *draining* is the right term."

"Well, what happened then? Why were you slumped in the chair like that?"

He rises to his feet and takes a step toward me. "Do you need me to spell it out for you?"

I lift my chin. "Maybe. I'd like to know whether I should feel bad for you or not."

"Why would you feel bad in the first place?"

I gesture toward the broken armrest. "I clearly made you feel uncomfortable."

He holds my gaze, a smirk playing over his lips as he absently runs a hand over his jaw. Right where I kissed. "It wasn't discomfort that made me do that. At least not the kind you're imagining."

"Then what kind was it?"

My pulse ratchets up as he slowly closes the distance between us, but I force myself not to react. I know what he's doing. He saw my moment of weakness—of doubt—and he's using it to get back at me. I won't let him. This is *my* win. Mine.

Once he reaches me, he places his forefinger under my jaw, lifting my face higher. With his thumb, he caresses my chin, just under my bottom lip. "The kind of discomfort that makes it hard for a man to stand afterward. The kind that—should you ever make me feel it again—I won't want you to stop."

He releases my chin and strolls away, hands in his pockets. As soon as he's gone, I take his place in the chair. I grip the armrests, still warm from Thorne's touch, and brush my fingers over the place where the wood splintered. My sense of triumph returns. Now that I know my magic didn't drain Thorne—only used his desire to forge a more powerful dreamscape—I can release my guilt. And even though he made a good comeback at the end with those tantalizingly seductive words, I still feel like the victor.

The feeling remains even after Minka returns with Angela, and we enjoy the tea Minka brought with just the three of us. It isn't until Mr. Boris finds us and hands me an envelope that my good feelings falter. I excuse myself from my companions and open the envelope in the empty hall outside the gallery. I expect it to be from Monty, announcing our next game, but a quick perusal of the letter's contents proves otherwise.

> *Little Briar,*
> *One more week until I must collect your family for the catacombs. That's truly all I can give you.*
> *Best of luck,*
> *Nyxia*

My heart sinks, my stomach hollowing out along with it. Her words serve only as a reminder, not a surprise, for I knew I only had one week left of the two she allotted me.

Still, the reminder is sobering indeed, for it marks the very day my wedding is supposed to proceed.

The event that will fulfill my bargain with Thorne.

Break the curse, just in time.

Save our families.

It's why I'm here. It's the reason I put up with so much of Monty's shit. And with today's win—one I earned when I was no longer trying to play with him—I'm closer than ever to succeeding.

If I win one more game, he'll be bound by the rules he agreed to. He'll have to beg his father to reinstate our betrothal. And if I don't win one of the final two games, Lord Phillips is due back in a matter of days, and I'll take the issue up with him. I *know* I can convince him. I *know* this wedding is within reach.

I should be thrilled.

I should be exhilarated.

So why do I feel like my lungs are going to burst?

36

BRIONY

That night I find myself battling sleep—or maybe it's the one battling me. Whatever the case, I can't relax. Can't shut off my mind, no matter how much I toss and turn in bed, and for different reasons from this morning. Instead of the desire that plagued me before, now it's the unheard ticking on an invisible clock, one that draws me closer and closer to my goal. Dread burrows deep inside me, a sharp and murky emotion that I haven't been able to shake since receiving Nyxia's letter.

Mr. Boris was strangely quiet afterward when we returned to the girls in the gallery to finish tea. Not that he's normally loud. It's more that his silence seemed heavy, etched in the stiff lines of his formal posture as he stood by the door. After Angela left, and it was just me, Mr. Boris, and Minka, I asked him if something was wrong. All he said was that my impending sacrifice was weighing on him. Minka's countenance fell too then, and she muttered something about enjoying her unseelie form as much as she can now, for soon she'll be disallowed from donning it again.

Now as I lay in bed, their words echo back to me, weaving through others. Like what Thorne said about the catacombs, how my parents sought to burn them down, just to put an end to his family. How Mr. Boris all but confirmed it, saying he'd heard the rumors. I remember him insisting my parents must have had a good reason to do such a thing, but he never gave me one.

Then there's what Thorne said about my parents when we argued after the race.

You don't have to do anything to earn their love.

You are enough exactly as you are.

Your efforts are wasted on them.

I argued back, and I remember every word, every ounce of conviction I felt.

It doesn't matter because I love them.

The words rang true in my heart and...they still do. Of course they do. Nothing has changed since then, so why...

Why do my legs flinch as if they're desperate to run? Why can't I forget that my family forbade Minka from shifting into her feline form after she made one mistake? Why does Mr. Boris' sympathy over my sacrifice pierce my heart? Why do I feel so sick whenever I imagine the catacombs burning, coffins filled with my family's rivals—but innocents too? Thorne's youngest sister, who would be the same age as Angela, and all the other banshee clan children who might be under the sleeping spell.

Something sharp and fiery wends its way through my veins—anger. For *them*. For Thorne. For a family that isn't my own. My mind fills with images of his mother and sisters choking on powdered iron from a grenade my kin threw. The screams Thorne heard. And even before that, when that same cousin used his magic to lift Morgana's veil and forced Thorne to see his mother's face, enacting the curse my family placed upon him.

Melting his eyes.

Stars, his...eyes.

My lungs constrict, and I bolt upright in bed, forcing the images away. I rub my hands over my face as if that can banish my dark thoughts. What's wrong with me? Why am I focusing on my family's wrongs when they've received the same treatment?

I tell myself this, but no matter how much I try to dwell on what's happened to me and mine, no matter how I try to recall the terror Thorne inflicted upon me at my birthday party, I can't find the same spark. I feel...empty now. Hollow.

Pushing back the covers, I slide from the bed and turn on the bedside lamp. The small clock on the nightstand reveals it isn't yet midnight, while the illumination from the lamp shows my legs are still clad in stockings. I glance down at myself and find my torso is still wrapped in my corset as well.

The slightest relief unravels within me. No wonder I couldn't sleep. I was so distracted by my thoughts before bed, I never finished undressing. With a mirthless chuckle, I do so now, loosening the laces of my corset and unhooking the closures. My ribs and lungs expand, and I gather in a fortifying breath. I toss the corset on the bed and am about to remove my stockings and garter when my attention snags on the lace hem of my chemise. The one Sister Spruce gifted me.

Longing plummets my heart, and I run my fingers over the lace, then the soft pale blue muslin. Stars above, I miss my teachers. My glade. My friends and fellow students. I even miss the time I thought I'd be a governess. My heart ached for a family I didn't remember, but it was a simpler time. One of smaller hopes and dreams.

Now the fates of two families rest upon my shoulders, as does the stability of the seelie Lunar Court throne.

Everything hinges upon me.

My actions.

My choices.

My sacrifice.

My marriage to Monty.

Pressure tightens my lungs, and this time I can't blame it on my corset. Shaking my head, I stride over to my wardrobe and open the doors. I kneel at the base, seeking the bag stuffed in the corner. It's mostly empty, aside from one gray dress and the sparse items upon it. Calm warmth fills my chest as my eyes fall on my tattered fan, the one I used to dance with in my glade. I extract it from the bag and unfold it, a sad smile on my lips as I study the dance steps illustrated on one side, ones I've long since remembered. Turning it over, my gaze follows the blue floral pattern, faded after so long in my care.

I fan myself with it and can almost smell the breeze in my glade.

Why didn't I cherish my glade more? Why did I think of the convent as a prison? If anything, *this* is a prison. Not Thorne's manor but the bargain we made. The marriage I must enter. The sacrifice I must make.

I bite the inside of my cheek and close my eyes, fighting to trade my growing anxiety for something else. Anything else. Images flash behind my eyes—the memories I've framed. Several flip by before I see my party in the convent kitchen, a moment of joy frozen in time. Then comes my first ballet, then the meteor shower.

Then...Thorne. Standing in the Starcane field, his hands planted on his hips—

I shake him from my mind and return to the meteor shower.

I release a slow exhale and open my eyes, finding my surroundings have been replaced with falling stars. Where the wardrobe should be, instead stands the railing of the convent's rooftop balcony. I shift to the side and lean into the balustrade, a calming sense of support. Even though I know in reality it's simply the door of the wardrobe I'm resting against, it doesn't matter. I'm safe here, in my mirage. Free from my worries. My anxieties.

At least I should be.

I shouldn't feel such a sharp pain piercing my chest, such warm tears trailing down my cheeks. They continue to leak from my eyes, even when I close them. Even when I clutch my fan to my chest, desperate to force back the sob that builds there, growing, climbing, clawing its way up my throat—

"What's wrong?"

My eyelids fly open, and I find Thorne crouched before me.

And he is, of course, shirtless.

Glittering hell, why am I constantly pulling him into my dreamscapes lately? And why is my mind so debauched? I curse under my breath, but it snags on the emotion that remains trapped in my throat. It leaves my lips in a pathetic whine.

Thorne's lips pull into a frown, and he lifts a finger toward my face. I hold my breath as he brushes my cheek, gathering a tear on his fingertip. His eyes narrow at the moisture there. Then he swipes his thumb over the edge of my jaw, where more tears hover, waiting to fall.

That's when I realize...

His touch is too firm. Too warm. Too real.

Which means...

I bite back a squeal and leap to my feet, my paper fan falling to the ground. My dreamscape melts away but leaves Thorne perfectly intact. He rises slower than I did, his eyes never leaving mine. I back up a step. "Why the hell are you in my room?"

His voice comes out smooth. Calm. "You didn't answer when I knocked."

"Why were you at my door?"

"Why were you crying?" His eyes dip to my jaw, where his fingertips brushed mere seconds before. His gaze turns hard, cold, punishing. Like he's holding a vendetta against the tears he wiped away. I realize he isn't wearing his spectacles. The absence of his lenses paired with that expression makes me feel vulnerable, bared before him—

Heat floods my cheeks as I recall my state of undress. I resist the urge to cover myself, for that will only draw attention to my flimsy chemise. "That's none of your business," I say through my teeth. "This may be your manor, but you can't just waltz into my room in the middle of the night. What if I was..."

"Naked? Pleasuring yourself?" His cold stare dissolves as a smirk forms on his lips. It's a far more comforting sight than that fierce look that had me feeling naked just moments ago. He tilts his head to the side. "Dearest nemesis, let's not fret over things I've seen before."

My blush deepens with a spark of rage. I thrust out a palm to strike his arm, but he catches my wrist and tugs me a step closer.

He bends down slightly, bringing us eye to eye. Again, I wish he was wearing his spectacles, if only to provide a barrier between me and the heat of his gaze. "I was worried about you."

I swallow hard. "Why?"

He releases my hand, and I manage not to stagger back. "You kept tugging at me," he says.

"Tugging?"

"I could feel you grasping for me, again and again, over the last several minutes."

I didn't think my cheeks could burn any hotter. "What are you talking about?"

"Your magic was trying to drag me into a dreamscape, which tells me you were losing control. And it wasn't the fun kind, like this morning." His lips quirk once more, and it takes all my restraint not to try and hit him again. Before my anger can grow too much, his expression turns serious. "I knew that meant you were troubled, so I was worried."

I cross my arms. "And then you barged into my room? Shirtless?"

"I knocked first."

"I didn't say you could enter. And you still haven't told me why you aren't wearing a shirt."

"You woke me up," he rushes to say. "When your magic tugged at me, you pulled me from sleep. I...I wasn't thinking clearly. I just came to check on you. You're clearly fine, so I'll take my leave."

As he turns toward the door, my chest constricts, and I find my feet moving before my mind realizes what I'm doing. I take a step after him, but my foot nudges something on the floor. Glancing down, I expect to find the fan I dropped, but instead...it's a rectangular floral-printed box. It wasn't here before, nor did it come from my wardrobe.

I lift my gaze to Thorne's retreating back. "What's this?"

He releases an aggrieved sigh, then turns halfway

around. Staring at the far wall, he says, "Something I thought might cheer you up."

"You had the presence of mind to bring something to cheer me up...but not to put on a shirt."

"Just open it." Thorne's posture has turned stiff, his tone clipped. Whether he's angry or embarrassed, I can't tell. "Do you want me to leave?"

I should say yes. I know I should. But I'd be lying if I did.

Perhaps it's just that I don't want to be alone right now. Whatever the case, I don't want him to exit that door.

Feigning indifference, I retrieve the box from the ground and say, "You can at least stay while I open it. That way I can ensure it isn't a bomb—" My teasing words stick in my throat as I remove the box's lid and glimpse its contents.

I'm frozen in place as I stare down at the pink silk tucked inside tissue. I brush aside the delicate paper and find a pair of dancing slippers, adorned with long silk laces, each shoe decorated with a single rosette. "What...what is this?"

"A gift."

"But why? When...when did you get these?" My heart hammers when Thorne's gaze meets mine, the frantic rhythm heavy and unfamiliar. I take in the way he stands so stiffly, still half turned away from me, head angled over his shoulder as he watches me sidelong.

His throat bobs before he answers. "I bought them when we went shopping at Bartleby's. They were supposed to be your wedding gift."

My stomach sinks, and I feel my expression fall with it. "A wedding gift," I say, tone flat.

"I thought they would cheer you up from whatever upset you've been dealing with tonight." He looks away from me and runs a hand through his hair. My eyes follow the wayward strands that fall around his face, baring the rounded curve of his ears, his nape, before settling above his bare, ink-covered shoulders. He brings the hand over his jaw, rubbing it absently. "Clearly it didn't work. I...I should go."

Again, my feet move instinctively after him as he takes a step toward my door. "I like them," I blurt out. "I really, really like them."

He halts and glances over his shoulder at me. His lips pull into a smile that doesn't reach his eyes.

I know my own is unconvincing as I try to mirror his grin. "It's just...you brought up my wedding." My lungs tighten all over again, and I force the rest of the words from my mouth. "That's the very subject that has me feeling out of sorts."

He turns fully around, then slowly closes the distance between us. "Come on," he says, voice barely above a whisper. He gently tugs the gift from my hands and sets it on the ground. Then he grasps my palm and pulls me into the main room of my suite. It's so dark, I can hardly see a thing as we cross the floor. Only when he brushes aside a curtain does the moonlight illuminate our surroundings. He's brought us to a door leading to a balcony I've never explored.

"Where are you taking me?"

He turns the handle and pulls me onto the balcony. His lips curl, his smile more genuine now. "We're going to see the stars."

37

BRIONY

With his hand still clasped around mine, he faces me and extends the other in an inviting gesture. I arch a brow, glancing between the open hand, the balcony we stand upon, and the sky above us. As he suddenly shifts into his unseelie form, I start to understand what he meant by *taking me to see the stars*. My eyes widen, taking in the expanse of wings that have sprouted from his back, the horns that now curl from his head. "You want me to fly with you?"

"Yes," he says.

"To see the stars."

"Yes."

My gaze drifts to the muscled planes of his bare chest, and my stomach tumbles. "Why?"

"I figured you could use a new dreamscape."

I pull my hand from his and fold my arms. "I can see the stars just fine from here."

"Yes, but not like you can see them from up there." Mischief plays around his mouth, but not the taunting kind. There's a softness to it that almost makes me want to accept his offer. But to do that, I'll have to step into his arms, let him hold me, let him fly me who knows how damn high. Some strange thrill flips inside me, but it's muted by trepidation.

He speaks again. "It will be worth it. Trust me."

I scoff, an automatic response. "Trust you?"

His countenance falters, the softness I glimpsed a second ago now edged with uncertainty. He steps back and leans his backside against the balcony's balustrade, hands perched upon the railing. His wings fold in and settle against his back, but he doesn't shift back to his seelie form entirely. "You're right," he says with a sigh. "That was poorly worded. You have no reason to trust me."

Guilt sinks my heart. I argued with him more out of habit than sincerity. I'm more flustered than anything, and this time he doesn't seem aware of it. This doesn't feel like one of our games or our taunting flirtations. This is something else.

Which sparks a question in me. "Why do you care, Thorne?"

He lowers his brows. "What do you mean?"

"I mean, why do you want to cheer me up in the first place? Why do you care whether I'm hurt or sad? I can understand why you saved me from the horse during the race, for if I die or am gravely injured, our bargain will be compromised. But cleaning my wounds after I fell in the garden, buying me dancing slippers because you know I love to dance, gifting them to me early just because you thought I needed cheering up—none of that matters to our bargain." I take a step closer to him, and he stiffens. "So why do you care?"

"Do I need a reason?" His voice is low, deep, barely audible over the quiet of the night.

"After what we've been through, I need a reason. *I* need to know why you care when there's nothing in it for you."

He huffs a dark laugh. "I care *because* there's nothing in it for me."

"What does that even mean? Is it guilt? You apologized for what you did to me. Is that why you're doing this? Out of some false sense of compensation?"

"I do feel guilty for what I did. It pained me to hurt you even while I was doing it, and it didn't abate after. I hate myself for what I did. I hate the methods I used. I cannot make excuses because I don't deserve to be seen in any other light than how you see me. But that's not why I care about you."

"Then why?"

He pushes off from the balustrade and takes a step toward me. Several feet of space separate us, but even the inches that he's closed make me feel warmer. He holds my gaze as he speaks, each word pointed. Deliberate. "I care because you deserve to be cared about, exactly as you are. You don't have to earn that. You just have it. My care is yours."

My pulse thrums at his words, my chest tightening. Something warm and peaceful threatens to unravel inside me, but it's too wrapped in brambles. Too guarded. I retreat a step back. "We're supposed to be enemies. You're supposed to hate me."

"Well, I don't, and it doesn't matter what we're supposed to be." He runs a hand over his face. Then, eyes distant, he speaks. "Before all this, we were friends. Or something like it. We may have thought we were merely the substance of dreams, but we danced. Talked now and then. Enjoyed each other's company, and I'm not making an innuendo this time. Even now, after the hurt I caused you, and in between our fights and teasing, I still feel the same. That here and now, we don't have to be Vintarys and Rosaline. We don't have to wear the masks our families have designed for us. We can be Thorne and Briony. Just as we are."

My heart thrills at how he says *Thorne and Briony*. That warmth threatens to flood my chest once more. I nibble my bottom lip. "Is it really that simple? That we can just...be who we are, regardless of the pasts and our familial ties?"

"I don't know, but I want it to be." His gaze slides to mine. "What I'm trying to say is...I don't know what will happen after this is all over. Whether we go our separate ways or manage to end the rivalry between our families by some miracle. I just need you to know—no matter what happens—that you never have to earn anyone's care. Not Monty's. Not your family's. Not mine. No one's. You deserve to be cared about. You, my enemy. You, my friend. You, the girl who haunted my dreams. You are worthy as you are in every form."

I can no longer hold it back. The warmth spills from its cage in my chest, devouring the brambles that had kept it locked away. It sends my heart thudding, my breaths sharpening. My knees are almost weak with it, but I try to keep it from showing on my face. I'm not ready for that. Not ready for Thorne to know how deeply his words have moved me. Not ready to admit what I've yet to name—the honey-sweet feeling that fills my heart.

I breathe in a slow intake of midnight air and state the only thing I'm willing to confess. "You do too, Thorne."

He arches a questioning brow.

"You deserve to be cared—"

"I don't."

I narrow my eyes. "You do. If I do, then so do you, and you just have to accept that. Got it?"

He tightens his jaw, lips pursed.

I step closer to him, chin lifted, and poke him in the chest with my forefinger. "I said, *got it*? You aren't a tool for vengeance. You weren't born to be used. You were born to live, same as the rest of us. You're a baker, a villain, and a pain in the ass, and you deserve to be—" I almost say a word that rose so naturally to my lips, but I stop myself. Not because it isn't true, but because...it's frightening. Vast. Overwhelming. So I repeat the safer term we've already used, with another poke to the chest. "Cared for."

He studies my face, his expression hard. Empty. Finally, it breaks with a crooked grin. "All right," he whispers. "I'll accept that."

I return the smile. "Good."

"Now," he says, extending his arms and wings, "will you let me take you to see the damn stars already?"

My breath catches. I'm still wary about his invitation, but after the sweetness of our conversation, I find a budding excitement in me as well. I've never seen the stars from anything higher than the rooftop balcony at the convent. This isn't something I can pass up. Swallowing back my fears, I wade through the mire of my hesitation, and close the remaining distance between us. "Take me, then."

His throat bobs as he looks down at me. Then, in a graceful motion, he crouches slightly, lifts me behind my knees and back, and hefts me into his arms. My own encircle his neck, tightening as he takes a leaping stride onto the railing. His wings spread wider, and moonlight catches on the glint in his eyes. I glance at the garden two stories down, my stomach turning as I realize we're about to be even higher. Before I can change my mind, Thorne bends at the knees and leaps off the balcony.

I bite back a scream as his wings catch the air, my arms going even tighter around his neck. His chest rumbles with laughter, and if I weren't so horrified right now, I'd punch him for finding amusement in my terror. Thorne's wings continue to beat the air, lifting us higher and higher. I don't dare look down and have now shifted my face into the crook of his neck, but I can still tell we're gaining altitude. After a few terrifying minutes, I begin to get used to the feel of Thorne holding me, of the air snatching tendrils of my hair, of my stomach lurching as we fly higher and higher. Not once do I feel Thorne's grip loosen, and the flight is far smoother than I expected.

Soon our momentum shifts and Thorne whispers into my ear, "We're here."

I lift my face from his neck and find darkness all around. There's no sign of the ground, but that's probably because I refuse to look down. Instead, I stare straight over Thorne's shoulder, certain I just might pass out if I discover how high we've flown. The sight of his wings rhythmically pulsing in the air to maintain our place in the sky interrupts my line of sight, but it serves as a comfort too. He's still flying. We're steady. We're safe.

"Look up," Thorne says.

My eyes find his face first. His chin is lifted, gaze pinned directly overhead. Slowly, I allow myself to see what has him transfixed.

My heart stills.

Overhead the black sky is awash in tendrils of vibrant

color, the same hues as my meteor shower memory. Rippling waves of pink, blue, green, and purple snake across the dark canvas, dancing amongst the multitude of stars. "What is that?"

"That's an effect of three courts' atmospheres colliding," Thorne explains. "From here, we are witnessing the place where the Earthen Court meets Wind and Solar. The differing climates and air pressures create this effect."

"It's beautiful."

"Yes." The word comes out with a breath, and I realize Thorne's gaze is on me now. I can feel it burning against my profile. He clears his throat. "Do you want to capture it?"

I slowly shift my attention from the display of color to Thorne. "Capture it?"

"As a dreamscape."

I glance back at the sky, and yearning fills every inch of me. "I do, but...I need to use my hands, and I can't let go." Just thinking about it has my stomach lurching. My arms reflexively tighten around him again.

"Sure you can," he says, and I squeal as he shifts my weight. Keeping one hand firmly behind my back, he tugs my thigh until one leg is on each side of him.

"Thorne!" I clamp my thighs tight around his waist, circling it fully with my legs. Only now do I again recall how little I'm wearing. With his trousers so low on his hips, the thin muslin of my nightdress is all that separates our bare flesh. My next words come out breathless. "What are you doing?"

"You're more secure this way. Keep your legs tight around me, and I'll keep my arms around you. You can lift your hands and capture the sky as your dreamscape."

So badly do I want to do that, but what he's suggesting is

madness. I can't release my hold around his neck. There's no way!

"You're safe, Briony."

"How do you know?"

"Because," he says, "I will never let you go."

That sweet warmth returns to my chest, softening the edges of my fear. Why do his words sound like they hold a dual meaning? And why do I so badly want to hear them?

He squeezes me tighter, as if to remind me where his arms are. "I'll never let you fall. You can let go, but I won't."

My breaths come out shaky, but I feel emboldened by his assurance. Lulled into the safety of his arms. Clenching my legs even firmer around his waist, I slowly begin to untangle my arms from around his neck, one inch at a time. I expect to feel unsteady as I release him, but I remain in place, as secure as I was when I had him in a death grip. My hands settle upon his shoulders, my final resting place as I gather my nerve.

He gives me an encouraging nod.

With all the bravery I can muster, I tilt my head to the sky and lift my arms overhead. My lower half remains pressed against Thorne, bound tightly in his arms, his waist locked between my legs. Safe, just as he promised.

An exhilarating thrill ripples through me. A sense of freedom I've never felt buzzes inside my veins, my blood. I know I released my hands to frame the sky, but I'm finding far more enjoyment in simply feeling this free, this wild. Seeing my hands thrust out toward the wash of undulating color is almost too intoxicating to bear. I wonder if this is how Thorne feels when he flies.

He says nothing as I stretch out wider, taller, my head thrown back with the widest grin I think I've ever worn. Finally, I take my thumbs and forefingers, shaping a rectangle over the glorious vision overhead. I blink. And the memory is mine.

It's almost agonizing to pull my gaze away from the sky, but I soon find an equally beautiful sight. My eyes find Thorne's, and his face is transformed, his smile as wide as mine, his irises flashing with the multihued light reflected from the celestial canopy above. His gaze isn't on the sky, though; it's on me, drinking me in. I slowly draw my arms back down, resting them on his shoulders. His wings continue to pulse the air, making his muscles flex beneath my palms. Wind whips around us, stealing strands of my hair to tangle in the breeze, sending his dancing around his face.

Stars above, he's beautiful.

Really fucking beautiful.

His smile shrinks, turning hesitant. Shy.

I lace one hand behind his neck, clawing into the hair at his nape, while the other cradles his jaw.

His eyelids grow heavy, throat bobbing. "Briony," he whispers.

I caress the stubble on his jaw, his chin, then round the lobe of his ear, the very place I kissed this morning. "What?"

"You're giving me that kind of discomfort again."

My smile turns sly as I'm reminded of what he said before he left me in the gallery. "Am I?"

The pound of his heart slams against me, echoing mine. "You know what I said about it."

"Yes."

"I don't think you recall."

"Oh, I do," I say, lowering my head. With my position high on his waist, I hover above him. I slide my forefinger from his jaw to under his chin, forcing his face higher, until our lips are mere inches away. "You said if I ever made you feel this discomfort again, you wouldn't want me to stop."

His grip tightens on me. "Exactly," he says through his teeth.

"So I won't." Lowering my lips, I brush them softly against his cheek.

38

BRIONY

He hisses a breath as I plant the kiss on his cheek, then another beside his mouth. It's his lips I want to claim, but I resist. After the game in the gallery, this feels safe. An extension of the torment I took pleasure in delivering him. I can't help but feel if our lips meet, something will change between us. I'm not sure what that change is, but I want it. Yearn for it. And I want him to be the one to make it.

I pull back and study his face. His lips are parted, eyes half closed. I lower my face again, this time to his neck. Brushing my lips over his collarbone is still not a true kiss. Nor is the way I drag my tongue up the length of his throat or the way I press my mouth to his temple.

I run the hand still buried in his hair down his neck, between his shoulder blades, sliding it against the skin between his still-beating wings. With a gasp, he pushes me tighter against him and buries his face in my neck. His lips caress the space beneath my ear, but it still isn't a kiss. He drags his mouth across my shoulder, rounding its curve and making the sleeve of my chemise slip lower down my arm.

Still not a kiss.

I pull back, taking in the desire etched clearly over his face. My nightgown slips lower, baring the top of my breast. I hold his gaze, making no move to adjust my top. Instead, I arch my back, letting the muslin bare me completely. He bites his bottom lip and I curl mine, daring him with my eyes.

What are you going to do, Thorne?

He lowers his mouth to my clavicle.

Still not a kiss.

He brushes his lips over the top of my breast, his tongue flicking over the generous mound of my flesh.

Still not a kiss.

I arch into him, and he closes his mouth over my nipple for all of a second before releasing it. A gasp escapes my lips at the momentary pleasure.

But it still isn't a kiss.

Frustration, lust, and desire burn every inch of me, inside and out. I tilt his chin again, bringing our lips level, our eyes locked. Why is he resisting me? Does he too sense that a kiss—a real kiss, not a tease, not a game—might change things between us? Does he not want that?

Stars, I don't even know why I want it, but I do. So badly do I want this change. I want him to kiss me. I want him to seek me for once. Since I'm constantly pulling him into my dreams, calling to him with my emotions, I want him to come to me this time. Just so I know this isn't all in my head. That this desire goes both ways.

I know it does. Without a doubt.

But I want him to show me.

I press our foreheads together and close my eyes.

Maybe I'm getting carried away.

A slow, shaking sigh escapes his lips, his breath brushing the very place I want him to kiss. "We can't do this."

My heart sinks, making my blood go cold.

But he isn't finished speaking. "In the sky. Right now." His words are clipped. Sharp. Emitted between uneven breaths.

Hope sparks inside me. I pull back a few inches, enough to see his eyes again. "Right now? What do you mean right now?"

A seductive smile curls his mouth. "If I was used to the feel of your hands on me, I could control myself. But I can't fly and kiss you at the same time. I can't touch or be touched by you too long. We'll plummet to our deaths."

I arch a teasing brow. "I thought you said you'd never let me fall."

"Which is exactly why we're landing."

Before I can prepare myself, Thorne's wings go still and we begin to plummet. I squeal, securing my arms around his neck once more. His chest rumbles with laughter against mine. Our momentum shifts, gathering speed. Soon I'm no longer squealing but laughing with him, drinking in the thrill of my stomach dipping, still tingling with desire, still aching for that kiss.

This time, I don't try to avert my gaze from our surroundings. I take it all in. The sky, those tendrils of color growing fainter the farther we dive, the ground rising up to meet us. Soon the silhouette of the manor comes into view, but Thorne slows down before we reach it. His wings beat the air slower, heavier, and we drift down to a plush lawn beside a lake. His feet hit the earth with grace. I, on the other hand, expend far more effort in disentangling my legs from around him.

Once I gather my bearings and secure my feet beneath me, Thorne takes my hand and leads me closer to the lake, where a gazebo sits near the shore. I vaguely recognize it from our ride the other day. I'd only seen it from afar then, but now I enter the charming structure of white wood draped in climbing ivy, its domed ceiling illuminated by a cluster of bright-green bugs. Or sprites, perhaps. They flutter overhead, then dart away to the lake's edge as I step beneath the roof. Two wicker chairs and a lounge decorate the inside, covered in an array of plush pillows. The sound of the lake rippling with gentle waves provides an enchanting lullaby alongside the chirp of crickets and other nighttime critters skittering about the lawn and the forest beyond.

"It's beautiful here," I say, turning around to face Thorne.

He stands outside the gazebo, his hands braced overhead on the outer beam of the roof. His wings and horns are gone, and while part of me is disappointed to see those beautiful wings hidden, I suppose he's used to banishing his unseelie form whenever it's no longer needed. My eyes skate over his wide chest, muscles flexing as it pulses with his sharp breaths. I drop my gaze to the low rise of his trousers, the tantalizing V between his hips. I'm once again entranced by his beauty, his seductive allure.

But why isn't he approaching me? Why is he still outside the gazebo?

His dark gaze is locked on mine, and there's something predatory in his eyes. Something dark and thrilling that I want to explore. That I want to tease out of him.

"Briony." The sound of my name mingles with the lapping of the lake, the rustle of the breeze. I nearly shudder. "Do you want me?"

"Was it not obvious up there?" I say.

He gives no reply, only studies my face, my shoulders, still bare from where my chemise slipped, then down to my stockinged legs. The veins in his forearms flex, as if he's gripping that ceiling beam with all his might. It reminds me of what he did to the chair when I kissed his ear.

"Why are you hesitating?" I ask. I don't want to say the rest, but I have to ask. "Is it because of...my engagement?"

He lowers one hand from the ceiling beam to run his hand over his jaw. I watch the trail of his fingertips as they graze his bottom lip, wishing I could replace that hand with my tongue. When he speaks, his voice is husky. Gravelly. A tone that has my stomach tightening. "A good man would care that the woman he desires is practically engaged to someone else. That she's prepared to marry that person. An honorable man would refuse to touch her until her ties with the other party were thoroughly severed."

My pulse quickens. Will he ask that of me? Ask me to dissolve our bargain and end my unwanted betrothal to Monty Phillips for good? A weight lifts off my shoulders at the thought.

"But," Thorne says, his seductive grin returning, "I am neither good nor honorable. I will have whatever of you you're willing to give me. Even if it's fleeting. Temporary. Stolen. If that's what you want. If you truly want me, say so and I will give myself to you, in any way you desire."

"I want you," I state without hesitation. My body thrums with my conviction. Stars above, I want him. Someone who is mine. My choice. My desire. Bargains, curses, and family rivalries aside, I want him. My baker, my villain, my dance partner, my friend, my enemy. All of that. I want *him*. "I need you, Thorne."

He removes his other hand from the ceiling beam now.

In just a few long strides, he reaches me, one hand cradling the back of my head, the other splayed against my lower back. I collide with him as he presses his lips to mine, hard and demanding. Angling my head, I allow the kiss to deepen. I part my lips and feel his tongue sweep against mine, hungry and searching. My legs tremble at the feel of him kissing me—*finally* kissing me—and I turn my weight over to him, letting him support me, lift me, and lay me on the cushion-strewn floor of the gazebo.

My back settles into one of the cushions, and Thorne lowers himself over me, tugging the hem of my chemise higher to allow him to occupy the space between my legs. I wrap my thighs around his waist, much like I did in the sky. His lips leave mine to trail over my cheek, my jaw, and this time it doesn't feel like a tease. This time it's simply an extension of our kiss, an illustration of the passion burning between us.

His mouth paints every inch of my skin that my chemise bares, and when he reaches my breasts, he tugs the gown lower, greeting each mound with a sweep of his tongue. Then lower once more, freeing my stomach. I arch my back with every kiss he lays over my skin, then my hips as he pulls my chemise the rest of the way down.

He settles lower, trailing kisses over my garter, then to the lace at the top of my stockings. With a flick of his fingers, he unhooks the silk from the garter and slides my stockings down one leg, then the other, replacing every inch he bares with a kiss. He pulls down my garter and silk underwear next. My heart slams against my ribs as I lie fully naked before him. He sits back on his heels, eyes sweeping over me. "You're stunning, Briony Rose."

I lift myself from the cushion and rise to my knees before him. A sudden self-consciousness comes over me as I bring my hands to his chest, trailing my fingertips over the inked designs of coiled scales. This is so different from anything we've done before, even in *that one dream*. Then, we refused to touch, only watched each other's hands. But now he's solid beneath me. Real. We know one another— the good parts and the bad, our pasts, our identities—and we still delight in the other's touch.

A groan rumbles in his chest as I slide one hand down the front of his torso, then lower until I cup the length straining against his trousers. Leaning closer, I press my lips to his, capturing another groan. His tongue sweeps in as one hand palms my backside, the other rising up my waist, then over my breast, to tease my nipple with his thumb. I pant against his mouth and slide my hand beneath the waistband of his trousers. He leans back, shifting his position until his legs are beneath me and I'm straddling his hips.

Together we tug his trousers down, finally freeing the full length of him. He remains seated upright as I slide my aching center over him, gasping as he fills me. We pause, and he presses a long, gentle kiss against my lips. "I meant it, Briony," he whispers against my mouth. "When I said you were perfect, I meant it. Whether we're fighting or fucking, stones, you're perfect. You're everything. Exactly as you are. I love—"

My heart leaps at that word.

"I love everything about you," he says, softly, slowly. "I love the way you argue. The way you laugh. I even love the way you hate me."

"I don't hate you," I whisper.

"And I love that."

The warmth in my chest unfurls entirely. I open my mouth, but I'm not as brave as he is. Not as ready to put words to the feelings in my heart. I want to tell him that I love everything about him too. I don't love that he hurt me, but I love that he admits to his wrongs. That he takes responsibility for them without making excuses, without trying to justify his darkest actions. I love that he cares about me. That he protects me. That he feels these things for me, even though we should be enemies.

But I can't bring myself to say the words, and he doesn't ask me to. Doesn't demand I say them back. I love that about him too. Instead, I pour all my tangled feelings into another kiss. Finally, we start to move again. I rock my hips, and he moves with me, filling me deeper, igniting a fire both inside and out. He grasps me tight against him, his face buried in my neck. Ecstasy buzzes through me as I throw my head back, eyes half open. For a moment, I'm startled to find not the ceiling of the gazebo overhead, but an ink-black sky streaked with pink, green, blue, and purple.

I know what's happening—our arousal is fueling my magic—and it doesn't give me pause. Instead, it doubles my desire. Triples it. And Thorne seems to feel it too. We waltz beneath my dreamscape, our bodies writhing in tandem. Pleasure builds, higher and higher, and my illusion grows brighter. The rippling tendrils of color no longer hover above us but instead weave all around, dancing over our naked flesh, reflecting in Thorne's beautiful eyes.

His lips part with a final moan, and I swallow it in a kiss, my release unraveling with his. The last vestiges of pleasure undulate between us, rippling like the colors that flow around our bodies. And even after we're still and spent, the dreamscape doesn't fade. It remains as bright as the warmth in my heart, the emotions flooding my soul.

39

THORNE

riony's dreamscape remains around us for at least ten minutes before fading away. Without a stitch of clothing on my body, much less a pocket watch, I count the passage of time in heartbeats, not minutes. For all I know an hour has passed and has simply felt too short.

In the wake of our pleasure, we've rearranged the pillows, propping them against the side of the lounge to create a makeshift seat. Neither of us has the energy to sit upon the lounge itself or in either of the chairs, so I recline half upright against the pillows and Briony reclines against me, her back to my chest, the top of her head just under my chin.

I inhale deeply, breathing her in. She smells of sweat-slicked skin and mountain air, perhaps something sweet and floral too. It's a scent that was always missing from the dreams we shared, but now it fills my senses. *She* fills my senses. The feel of her flush against me, the softness of her hair, the sound of her breathing, now mellow after the hard panting, the tantalizing whines and moans I elicited from her. I can hardly believe she's here at all.

Like this.

With me.

I've held myself back all this time. Because of our families. Because of Monty. And most of all, because I don't deserve her. But after we talked about deserving to be cared for and she bullied me into accepting that the principle applies to me too, my resolve to resist her crumbled. And when she stated she wanted me. Needed me.

I stiffen against her at the memory. The way she looked when she said those words, full lips parted, chest heaving, chemise slipping from her shoulders...

A sound, almost like a growl, rumbles in my chest, but I try to pretend I was simply clearing my throat. Briony angles her head to meet my eyes. My lips curl in an idiotic smile. How can they not when she looks at me like that? No animosity, only the sweetest hint of taunting.

"What is this place, anyway?" she asks. "Your secret love-making lair? Is this where you take all the women you try to seduce?"

The words sound nonchalant but there's a sharp angle in the line of her jaw, the slight narrowing of her eyes. Is she...trying to ascertain whether I have other lovers? I could answer her honestly, but where would be the fun in that?

"You say *try*, but I have a one hundred percent success rate at seducing every woman I've brought here."

Her nostrils flare. With a huff, she starts to sit, but I encircle her waist and pin her in place. Bringing my lips beside her ear, I whisper, "Because you're the only woman I've ever brought here, Briony Rose."

She stiffens, then relaxes against me once more. I keep my arms around her waist and begin drawing circles with one hand over the soft curve of her stomach. Her skin pebbles beneath my touch. "Why would you tease me like that?"

I kiss the top of her head. "Why wouldn't I? You think just because I've had your body, I no longer want your ire? I meant it when I said I love the way you hate me. Even when that hate isn't hate. Even when it's just a spark of your beautiful anger. I still intend to treasure every bit of rage you fling my way."

"Well, good, because I have plenty to spare where you're concerned—when you tease me." She adds the last part in a rush which tells me the first was at risk of being a lie. "So what is this place *really*?"

"When I was younger, it was more of a playhouse," I explain. "Father and Alina gifted it to me as a place to get away when I needed to be alone. If I felt my magic flaring and needed to shift, I could come here. As a young boy, that wasn't uncommon, especially when my emotions got the better of me. Grief. Longing. Simply aging out of adolescence. There used to be curtains lining the outside, so I could safely shift without anyone on the estate seeing me. I still utilize it for that purpose, for the servants are used to avoiding this area by now. When I want to fly, I come here first and shift far from the manor."

She angles her head again to look at me. "You shifted at the manor tonight, though."

I smile down at her. "Yes, but that was an emergency."

"An emergency," she echoes with a scoff. "Me being sad was an emergency?"

"It was, and I knew you'd change your mind if I made you come here first. The only way I could get you up there with me was if I stole you straight from your room. I was right, though, wasn't I? It was worth it."

"Yes," she whispers, draping an arm behind her to caress the side of my neck. "For more reasons than the view."

My chest pulses with a sensation so soft and bright, it's almost painful. I want to flip her over until we're chest to chest and kiss her again. I want to bury myself in her and make her moan in ecstasy.

But I'm still holding back. I know I can't get carried away. I know I can't love this moment—this thing between us, whatever it is—too much. Obstacles remain. Our bargain. Our families. Her wedding.

Fury ripples through me, tensing my muscles. I find my fists curling, so I force my hands to relax, force my fingers to splay over Briony's stomach once more and resume drawing circles over her skin.

She shudders. "You said I'm one of the very few who's seen your unseelie form. Is that true? Have you truly no friends who know the truth? What about...lovers?"

The hesitation in her tone has my lips curling wickedly. She truly is interested in my romantic exploits. I suppose my earlier answer wasn't enough to sate her curiosity. This time I deliver my reply without teasing.

"I have no lovers at present, Briony, and every courtship I've had before this has been short-lived. I've never felt right lying about my past, especially when I knew the day would come—be it five years or a hundred—when my family would awaken and I'd have to merge my identities. I didn't want to be loved for someone I wasn't, and I've never trusted anyone enough to divulge my secrets. As a result, no past lover has ever known the truth about me."

"That must have been lonely."

"It was, especially after my father died, leaving only Trentas to know the truth."

"That was the dragon who allied with Morgana, right? The fae everyone thinks is your true father?"

"Yes, and I don't see him often anymore." Dread forms in my gut. There's something I should tell her, but I fear it will spoil the sweetness of the moment. Still, it must be said. "That will change after we break the curse. I'll see Trentas again and...so will you."

She tilts her head to cast me a questioning look.

I release a sigh. "He'll want to challenge your father to the throne as soon as he knows there's a chance he'll win. And I...I told him when that would be. I sent a missive after we made our bargain informing him that he'd have a chance to challenge your father after your marriage to Monty Phillips."

My heart hammers, each beat laced with guilt, with fear, as I wait for her response. Will she push away from me? Grab her clothing and storm back to the manor on her own? Tell me this was all a mistake?

Her expression is unreadable as she studies my face. Finally, she averts her gaze forward again. I wait for her to sit upright, to stride away, but she settles heavier against me instead. "That makes sense," she says, her tone resigned if not a touch disappointed. "That's an essential part of our bargain. Our task must benefit your family as well as mine. As Morgana's ally, that applies to Trentas too. Of course you told him."

I wrap my arms tighter around her waist, hugging her to my chest. I want to tell her I'm sorry, that I hate the divide that stands between us like a knife, wielded by others, and handed down to us too. But an apology feels flimsy against the transparency we've shown each other. The truth is, I wasn't sorry when I sent the letter to Trentas. Guilty, yes, but I'd felt equally as guilty for withholding more information from Trentas. And even now, even with my feelings for Briony growing with every heartbeat, outpacing the loyalty I feel to Trentas, I still believe the seelie Lunar Court throne would be better served by a new ruler.

In my heart of hearts, I oppose Horus Briar. I oppose his neglect of humans and seelie fae. I oppose his plot to burn down the catacombs and my family with it.

I oppose Briony's father.

I oppose the family she's so desperate to be accepted by.

Stones below, why must it be like this? Why must *Briony and Thorne* also be *Rosaline and Vintarys*? Why must we be the Briars versus the Lemurias? If either of our families saw us like this, knew we cared for each other enough to kiss, make love, hold each other...what would they do? What would Briony's family do? Rage at her? Disown her?

My blood runs cold as truth splinters my heart.

They can *never* know about this.

"You once said something about not honoring your father's dying wish," Briony says, rousing me from my unpleasant thoughts. Not that my father's death is any better of a subject. "What did you mean by that?"

My muscles tense as I consider whether to answer her question. I don't even remember confessing this to her in the first place...

No, I recall. I briefly mentioned it on our way to my estate.

I told you not to pity me. Were I deserving of it, I wouldn't have sought vengeance on your family. I would have honored my father's dying wish.

"You don't have to tell me," she says quickly. "It's just... you seemed to consider it a reason for why you weren't worthy of care. After what we talked about on the balcony tonight, I...I just want to know."

I hang my head, burying my face in her hair. "It was six months ago, shortly after the first attempt to destroy the catacombs."

Briony stiffens in my arms. She knows what I'm referencing, despite me calling it *the* attempt and not *your parents'* attempt.

"Father took ill around then. I knew he was sick, but I didn't think he was ill enough to die, so I focused on my own problems. I was full of rage, craving revenge, desperate to protect my entombed family. When he asked me to promise him not to seek revenge, I denied him, having no idea it would be the last conversation we'd ever have."

She shifts in my arms, laying sideways against me so she can see my face. Spreading one hand over my chest, she softly brushes her fingertips over my collarbone, tracing my tattoos.

"After he died and I realized that request he'd made of me was the last I'd ever get, I grew angrier. At myself, at...at your family. That was when I decided to put my all into revenge, if only to prove that the heartache I caused my father in his dying days was worth it."

Nausea turns my stomach. I've never said those words out loud. I've never even admitted them to myself, but they're true.

Briony laces her arms behind my neck and pulls me in for a soft kiss. The press of her lips is like a balm on my soul, one I wish I never had to let go of. I angle both our bodies until we're laying on our sides, arms wrapped around each other. She ends our kiss but keeps her forehead pressed to mine. The way we lay like this, not kissing, our naked bodies tangled not in sex but comfort, truths hanging in the air between us, feels more intimate than any erotic act. It feels like it will break me and heal me all at once.

I close my eyes, relishing the feel of her breath warming my lips. "Tell me about your favorite ballet again."

She emits a light chuckle. "Why? I've told you about it so many times. Now that I know my dreams of you were shared, you can't pretend you didn't let me talk your ear off time and time again."

"I liked the sound of your voice. I liked the way you smiled when talking about something you loved. I still do, so humor me."

She gives in, going on about her first trip away from the convent, her first time attending a ballet, her stay in the city of Lumenas and all the times she snuck from her lodgings to investigate other forms of dance. The sound of her talking about dancing is the most beautiful thing in the world, almost as soothing as the feel of dough beneath my hands. The smell of sugar. Briony Rose is a confection, a blade, and a beauty all rolled into one, and I want nothing more than to devour her. Her sweetness as well as her sharp edges. Everything.

She finishes her joyful rambling, and we fall into silence. I close my eyes, trying not to consider how long we've been out here or the fact that we must return to the manor before dawn.

"I want to dance again," Briony says, her voice muffled as she buries her face against my chest. "For so long I dreamed of meeting my family. I fantasized that they were upper-class citizens, which would mean I'd get to debut in society. I'd attend dances in elegant private ballrooms, or even in a public assembly hall. Instead, my hand was auctioned off before I knew I had a family, and to a man who hates to dance."

My chest tightens at her reference to Monty. I stroke the back of her hair. "There is still dancing in your future,

Briony. Married women can accept dances from partners who aren't their husbands. In fact, that's the norm in society. As a princess and wife of an aristocrat, you'll be expected to honor respectable figures with dances." I try to say all this without an edge to my voice, but I'm not sure it works.

"I know," she mutters.

I pull back, forcing her to meet my eyes. I swallow hard before speaking. "And...and you'll have me. Whether it's a stolen dance at a ball, a masquerade where we can evade our families' disapproval, or tucked safely away in a dream-scape. I'll always dance with you."

Her expression hardens, matching the rebellious fire that burns inside me. I hate every word I just stated, speaking about a future where we'll remain on opposite sides of that sharp-edged divide. Where she'll be someone else's wife. Does she hate it too? And if so, is it for the same reasons?

The hard look leaves her face, and she averts her eyes from mine. Gently pulling out of my grasp, she gives me a sad smile. "We should head back to the manor, shouldn't we?"

"Yes," is all I can say, even as my heart screams *no*. That we should stay here a little longer. Maybe even after dawn. Maybe we shouldn't part at all. Maybe we should dissolve our bargain, and choose each other—

I bury those words in my heart, reminding myself of ones she said.

They're my family.

There is nothing more important to me than them.

I could never ask her to choose me.

Never.

Once we finish dressing, I shift into my winged form and gather her to my chest. In a final act of selfish bliss, I take my time flying us back, circling over the manor far longer than necessary, simply enjoying the warmth of her body, the trust she's given me. Then we make our descent and I land us on her balcony. In silence, she walks me to the door that leads out to the hall. In silence, I pull her to me and press a long, lingering kiss to her lips. In silence, I convey the truth I cannot say, written in the pressure between our mouths, the sweep of my tongue. It secretly states that I love her. That I've deeply and completely fallen for the girl that should be my nemesis.

That even though I'll never ask her to choose me, I'll choose her.

I'll choose her over revenge, over the feud that threatens to break us, over the name I was born with, over the family I'm supposed to be loyal to.

I'll choose *her*.

And I'll do anything it takes—sacrifice everything, even my own heart—to ensure she gets the happiness she desires.

40

BRIONY

The next morning, I awaken with the certainty that no bed has ever felt so cold. Or so empty. I slept well for once, my slumber deep and dreamless after being so thoroughly sated on a physical level, so emotionally full. Last night, I was content with the passionate kiss Thorne left me with before he returned to his room, but now I can't help feeling the absence of him all around me. Waking up alone makes me wish he'd never left my chambers. That he'd stayed with me through the night. But the deeper that wish grows the more I recall why he didn't.

Because we can't be seen together like this.

Furthermore, *we* were never supposed to happen in the first place.

I turn onto my back and press a hand over my heart, seeking regret or shame. Surely what we did last night was merely a tryst—the natural culmination of the tension that has been building between us, some poisonous concoction of desire and hatred. But even as I try to convince myself that's the case, I only grow more convinced it isn't.

Last night wasn't a mistake. Or a superficial meeting of our bodies. It wasn't just anger or pleasure that drove me into his arms.

It was him.

Thorne.

That same soothing warmth I felt last night settles over me, and I find myself missing him all over again. Yet beneath those pleasant feelings are darker ones I don't know what to do with. Ones that remind me I'm supposed to be marrying Thorne's friend.

Rage ripples through me, burning my blood and expelling me from my bed. I march over to my wardrobe just to give myself an excuse to stomp my feet across the smooth wood floor. It helps soften some of my ire, as does the distraction of dressing myself. Minka normally aids with the process, but she's yet to come to wake me. By the time I hear her enter the door from the outer room, I'm outfitted in a cream blouse with leg-of-mutton sleeves and a sage green skirt. Even though I know the sound of approaching foot-steps are Minka's, I can't stop the traitorous quickening of my pulse and the futile hope that it's Thorne who's entered my suite.

I try not to let my disappointment show when my lady's maid strolls into my bedroom. She's in seelie form, yet even her humanoid manifestation bears whiskers, and they twitch now as a sign of her disapproval. "You got dressed without me."

"Sorry," I say, giving her a forced smile. "I woke up early and couldn't stand being idle. You may help me with my hair."

She beams and follows me to the vanity. I settle upon the

chair as she takes up the brush and begins running it through my tresses. In the mirror, I catch sight of her amber eyes going wide as the brush snags on a tangle. "What happened to your hair, Miss Rose? It's a disaster. It wasn't this tangled last night."

The blood leaves my face. "Oh! I..." Shit, I can't lie. Nor can I confess to my late-night flight or the lovemaking that knotted my golden strands. "I went out on the balcony last night. The wind mussed my hair."

There. Two true statements.

"Well, this is one situation where my cat claws may work better. Perhaps we should shear these knots straight off." She chuckles but her expression falls. "I'm merely joking, Highness. I really shouldn't shift into my unseelie form too much more. Once you break the sleeping spell and we return to the palace, I'll need to stay in seelie form."

I frown, studying her fallen face in the mirror. "Is there a chance my parents will have a change of heart? I'll do what I can to convince them you deserve a second chance. I can tell you really enjoy being a cat."

She grins but it doesn't reach her eyes. "That's very kind of you, Miss Rose."

I nibble my bottom lip as she continues brushing my hair. A question brims in my mind. Finally, I ask, "Do you enjoy working at the palace? For my parents? Aside from forbidding you from shifting, do they treat you well?"

"Oh, they pay me very well," she says. I can't help but note that she said *pay* well instead of *treat* well. "And I do enjoy working at the palace. I love being in charge of tea and wine service. The position is highly coveted, so I am quite wealthy for a servant. I wouldn't make even half as much working at a public house or restaurant."

Discomfort writhes inside me as she continues to brush

out my hair. She's said nothing about my parents as employers, only that the pay is enviable. I feel just like I did last night before Thorne came to check on me. It seems he succeeded in cheering me up after all, for only now do I feel the full weight of my burden crashing down upon me, my anger over the sacrifice I already agreed to make.

I fold my hands in my lap but they quickly form fists.

Minka steps back, my now-smooth hair half pinned up while the rest tumbles around my shoulders. It's the same way she styled my hair during the dancing game when I wore the dress Thorne chose and waltzed with him in the parlor. The memory makes me smile. I may not have been willing to acknowledge it at the time, but even then Thorne was my object of desire. It was his reaction to the dress I relished, his partnership in our dance I treasured.

"When did you get these lovely shoes?"

I turn to find Minka crouched before my wardrobe, assessing the pink silk dancing slippers Thorne gifted me last night.

"Oh. Those. They're...dancing slippers. For dancing."

"Yes, I know that, but when—"

"Would you mind fetching my breakfast, Minka?" I give her my sweetest smile. "And your best cup of tea?"

Excitement flashes over her face and she forgets the slippers at once. "Of course, Miss Rose. I'll brew the absolute best cup of tea!" She skips out of my room, and I retrieve the shoes from the floor. My heart flutters as I'm reminded once more of Thorne's sweet gesture. I can't believe he bought these when we were shopping at Bartleby's without me knowing.

My heart aches as I fight my growing need to run to his room, knock on his door—

That very sound echoes from the main room of my suite.

My pulse rackets as I realize...it's too soon for Minka to have returned. Besides, she wouldn't have knocked. I try to smother my excitement, my anxiety, my hope, but my arms tremble with it as I shove the shoes inside my wardrobe. Then I all but run from my bedchamber, through the sitting room, and to the door.

It's Thorne. It has to be Thorne. It—

I fling open the door.

It isn't Thorne.

It's Monty.

I smother my second bout of disappointment for the morning with a too-wide smile. I'm sure it looks more like a sneer. "Mr. Phillips."

"Good morning, princess," he says flatly, not even bothering to humor me with a smile. He's dressed in brown trousers, a white shirt, and a cream waistcoat, but every article is either wrinkled or improperly buttoned. His hair makes him look like he just rolled out of bed, though I suppose it always has that quality. Before I can say anything else, he barges over the threshold and strolls into my sitting room like he owns it.

I remain by the still-open door, my fingers resting on the handle. "To what do I owe—"

"Close the door, won't you, Rosey?" He slumps onto the divan.

I clench my jaw. I'm still not fond of that nickname. "My lady's maid is fetching my breakfast. It wouldn't be proper to be alone together."

Placing his arms behind his head, he settles further onto the floral-patterned upholstery. "Aren't you bored of our game?"

"I'm not sure bored is the right word."

"Let's end it."

My interest sparks. Does he mean end the game? Or end...*us*?

"You're one more point away from winning," he says. "I originally stated we'd play seven games, but if you win the next, there's no reason to play another. I've received word that Father is coming home early. He'll arrive first thing in the morning, so...let's just end our game here. With one final play. An easy win."

A slow and heavy thud pounds in my chest, a rhythm of dread and hope. Half my heart rages at the thought of entertaining even one more game. The other reminds me that this is what I came to do. Marry Monty. Break the curse. If this game's win is as easy as he says, I won't have to negotiate with his father. It will be over. I'll have won.

I'll have lost, a small voice says inside me, and with it comes a flash of Thorne's face in my mind's eye.

No, won, I argue back, picturing my parents rising from their enchanted sleep, their eyes brimming with happy tears when they see me—their hero, their savior. The girl who broke their curse and saved their throne, their reputation, and their finances all at once.

I wait for my pride to swell, for my resolve to strengthen...but it doesn't.

Still, I swallow the dryness coating my tongue and force myself to speak. "All right. One more game."

"First," Monty says, "close the door."

My hands shake as I do as he said. I'm still determined not to play along if he asks me to do anything I don't want to do, but...this could really be the end. The fulfillment of my bargain with Thorne.

Thorne.

Thorne.

His name echoes in my heart, an almost painful resonance.

I secure the door and slowly turn to face Monty. He sits upright on the divan, lips curled in a glowing smile. If I didn't dislike him so much, I'd find him incredibly handsome. His curly blond hair, those dimples that form when he grins, his roguish appeal. But try as I might, I only see an enemy.

An obstacle.

A treacherous roadblock that stands between me and what I truly want. I shudder as I realize a terrifying truth—that he's not alone on that hateful divide. Beside him stands my family.

My blood runs cold.

Since when did my family become an obstacle? They're supposed to be my goal. My happiness. My deepest wish. Yet if they're the divide...then what's waiting for me on the other side? What is it I truly want, if not them?

"Let's play our final game," Monty says, pulling me from my thoughts. He pats his knee. "Sit on my lap and kiss me the way you kissed Thorne yesterday."

I blink a few times as I reconcile his words.

The way...I kissed Thorne.

Visions of our lovemaking flood my mind. My stomach takes a dive before I realize that isn't what he means. He's referring to the kissing game in the gallery.

My pulse calms. "You want me to...kiss you."

He nods. "On the lips, of course, so not exactly the way you kissed Thorne. Today I want to participate, not watch. You understand now why this is an easy win. Kissing you back will automatically secure your win of the game."

Dread. Hope. Dread. Hope. The two emotions flare in

tandem, tangling in my stomach like a vile poison. I take a hesitant step back. "Are you trying to trick me?"

He holds up a hand. "I swear to you in a binding vow, if you kiss me right now, on the lips, with even a fraction of the passion you showed during our game yesterday, I will marry you. I'll ensure our wedding proceeds as planned. We'll leave at once to Sandalwood Manor to finish preparations for our nuptials. We'll greet my father upon his return, and I'll have him draft a new contract. It won't require your father's permission, only yours. We'll have our wedding in the chapel six days from now, and you'll have this marriage you've worked so hard for."

I study his face, seeking any sign that he's being disingenuous. "Why are you making this so easy? This game was your idea."

"I told you, I'm bored of it. Besides, is it so hard to believe I've simply fallen for you?" He winks.

"Yes," I say.

"Well, you're right about that. I haven't fallen for you, but I'm done playing. So come. Take the win you deserve."

My body trembles with the weight of my heartbeat, my burden, my sacrifice, my hope. All I have to do is kiss him and my marriage to him is secure. The salvation of my family guaranteed, in every way from the sleeping spell to their debt and their reputation.

I planned this.

I forged the terms of this bargain.

I coerced Thorne into joining me in this plan.

Everything we've aimed for is within reach. All I have to do is sacrifice my heart, my hand, my future, and marry a man I don't love. All I have to do is choose my parents. The family I yearned for my entire life.

All I have to do is *not* choose myself.

My needs.

My heart.

"No." The word escapes my lips with almost violent fervor.

Monty tilts his head in a coy manner. "Why? You don't want to marry me?"

"I don't."

He squints at me, his expression taunting. "Let me guess. You're in love with someone else, aren't you?"

The word *love* sends my heart skittering. I fold my arms over my chest as if that can hide the truth he's trying to unearth. "My feelings are none of your business, for they don't involve you."

He throws his head back in a bark of laughter. His shoulders sink with something like relief. "Good girl," he whispers.

I blink at him, taking in the sudden ease that melts over his posture. Where he normally seems lazy and careless—a contrived countenance—there's something far less forced about it now. I narrow my eyes. "Is this another game?"

"The real game," he says, rising from the divan. "The only one that mattered all along."

"What are you talking about?"

Hands in his pockets, he saunters over to me. "I hope you realize I've been on your team all along."

"I can't imagine that's true," I say through my teeth.

He chuckles. "My methods may be cruel, and I apologize for that, but I think we can both admit they're effective. Tell me, do I make a good matchmaker? I daresay I'll be disowned and in need of a job once I tell my father I won't be marrying you. Perhaps I should take up the match-making trade."

His words pierce my mind, sending it reeling. Is he suggesting...

No, he couldn't be.

He couldn't have done all this to get me and Thorne to...

"Speak plainly, Monty," I say, voice quavering with suppressed rage. "What was the true purpose of this game you've played with me?"

"Oh, come on," he says, lowering his voice. "You and I were never the ones playing."

"Then who was?" I ask, though I know the answer. I have all along.

Monty is silent for a few moments. When he speaks, his tone is more careful than I've ever heard it. "Thorne is my best friend, Highness. I know him better than he knows himself. He thinks he's hidden his true nature from me, but he isn't the only one with secrets. I admit, I proposed our game merely for entertainment, but all it took was one conversation with Thorne to discover the latest secret he was hiding."

His talk of Thorne's secrets makes me wonder what exactly he knows. Has Thorne been hiding his identity less thoroughly than he believes? It isn't my place to ask, though I am curious about one thing. "You say Thorne is your best friend, but he seems to hate you. And you don't seem to care."

"Thorne's hate is as warm as his love. You know that by now, don't you? I'm happy to have his hatred, for he's hated me most loyally. Protectively. It was time I repaid him in the only way he deserved."

"What way is that?"

His grin widens. "Torment." With that, he strides to my door. I stare at his back, my mind burning with questions.

Did he truly do all of this, annoy me and Thorne to no end, to try and get us to fall in love? Could he truly be so scheming? So...maddeningly brilliant? And how much of his devil-may-care attitude is real?

As he reaches the door, I realize I might never know. But for the first time, I consider that Monty Phillips may be more than meets the eye. Whether that's a good or bad thing, I haven't a clue.

"Wait," I say, racing after him, a final question burning my tongue. "You get to choose your bride now. Who are you going to wed? Cosette?"

He pauses, turning to me with an apologetic look. "No, not Cosette. Yet I can now genuinely apologize for my behavior the other night. I know you caught us. I don't want to explain or excuse what I did, but...I can say I'm sorry. That was repulsive of me, whether I was the object of your affection or not."

What the hell? Who is this man? "If not Cosette, then who will you marry?"

"That's easy. No one."

"Won't your father be angry?"

"Spectacularly. I meant it when I said I'll soon be disowned and in need of a job, but fret not. Once I'm booted out of the family, the Phillips fortune is in good hands with Angela as heir. Oh, and I do hope you'll stay friends with her, even though we won't be marrying. Surely you'll find it easier to befriend her without an unwanted marriage to my ugly mug souring the friendship. Am I right?"

I'm still so shocked by this turn of events I can hardly find my words. "Yes, I'll...I'll be her friend," I manage to say.

"Good. Well, I must be off for the scolding of a lifetime. You, meanwhile, should talk to Thorny-boy. Go put him out of his misery. He's baking again." He winks and reaches for my hand. I tense, expecting him to bring it to his lips. For a moment I fear he truly has tricked me, that he'll secure my final win with a kiss—but no. He simply grasps my palm in a firm handshake. "Goodbye, Princess. Thank you for playing."

41

BRIONY

I stare at my bedroom door for several long minutes, unsure how to feel now that Monty is gone. Half of me is elated. Free. Exhilarated by my bold choice to refuse my unwanted engagement. But the other half of me curls into a dark pit in my stomach, wailing a chilling refrain of *what have I done?*

I know what I've done. I've chosen myself and my wants. Yet I've also made it impossible for me and Thorne to fulfill our bargain. The terms were clear: I was to marry Monty —*specifically* him—and Thorne was going to help me. Now that I've rejected Monty...

No. I still haven't made it impossible to break our families' curses. Thorne has insisted from the start that there are better, easier ways. I was the one who demanded our bargain terms. Not only did it align with the timeline Nyxia gave me, but it carried the assurance that my parents would forgive me. Trust me. Be proud of me.

Thoughts of Thorne fill my mind's eye. Of his lips

pressed to mine, his hands roving over my flesh, the way we held each other after the expenditure of our passion. My chest tightens as I acknowledge how fervently my parents would disapprove of such a union. What will they do when they found out I rejected Monty for...for—

I shake my head. There's only one thing I can do now. I have to dissolve my bargain with Thorne. It's over, and I won't change my mind. After that, we can figure this out together. Can't we?

My heart leaps as I race from my room, my feet flying down the halls as I head for the kitchen. Monty said Thorne was baking, which means that's where he'll be. My heart warms with every step. A sense of safety, of fierce protection draws me forward, and I know I will find that with Thorne.

A smile stretches my lips by the time I push open the door to the kitchen. Unlike the last time I was here, alone with Thorne after midnight, the room swarms with a bustle of activity. A cook tends to boiling pots on the stove while servants fill plate-laden trays with pastries, fruit, and sausages. I'm surprised Minka isn't here, for she left to fetch my breakfast. I'd be more curious, however, if my attention wasn't stolen by the figure standing at the worktable—the very same spot he was when he tended my wound. His hair is tied back in the gorgeous style I've seen only once, and his spectacles are perched upon his nose. Before him sits a muffin tin, and he's halfway through filling it when his eyes meet mine.

He freezes, batter dripping off the edge of a wooden spoon. His throat bobs and uncertainty flashes over his face. Then his expression thaws, his lips curling into a soft, almost shy smile.

I feel a similar one form on my face. It is a little awkward seeing him for the first time after our time together last night, but the feeling isn't uncomfortable. Something inside me tells me to treasure this awkwardness, the way my heart pounds heavier as heat floods my cheeks. The way he slowly sets down the bowl of batter and takes a careful step toward me, his eyes never leaving mine.

Quiet fills the room as the kitchen staff notices us. "Five minutes, please," Thorne says to the room at large, his tone kind. With that, the cook and servants file out, leaving us alone. The sound of boiling pots mingles with the pound of my heart, the hitch of my breathing.

"Briony," Thorne whispers. His hands curl at his sides, and I wonder if he's trying not to reach for me. The same instinct buzzes down my arms and through my palms. I want to pull him to me, taste his lips, feel his strong arms, but...there are things he needs to know first. Subjects to discuss.

"Thorne," I say, and my mouth stretches into a wider smile. I've half a mind to simply blurt everything out, that I rejected Monty, that I release him from our bargain, that we must find another way to save our families, and most of all that I—

That I...

I exhale a slow breath. My final confession terrifies me.

Can I tell him how I feel?

Can I even trust my feelings?

Can I let myself feel this way about him?

I try to summon my rage over his hurtful actions...but it's gone. There's a fierce conviction inside me that knows what he did was wrong—that using our cursed bond and tricking me into putting my family to sleep was deplorable—but something warmer, softer has outgrown every darker feeling I've had for him. It blooms from the dances we shared in my dreams, from the conversations we had, from the way he's defended me with Monty and his game, from how he rescued me from the runaway horse, tended my wounds, teased me, held me, kissed me. From the dancing slippers he gifted me. From the flirtatious game we played of *who can make the other flustered.*

From the way my heart melts in his presence.

The way my chest opens fully for the first time.

No, this isn't something I can simply blurt out. This is something to handle with the tenderest care.

I take a step closer to him. The warmth of his proximity nearly has me undone as everything inside me begs to wrap my arms around his neck.

Soon.

"To what do I owe the pleasure this morning?" Thorne asks, his lips quirking slightly at the word *pleasure*.

Inhale. Exhale. I can do this.

"I just played my final game with Monty," I say, doing my best to keep my voice steady.

His expression goes blank. "Oh?"

A satisfied thrill goes through me at the subtle break in his voice. I know I shouldn't delight in tormenting him now, not with such sweet feelings warming the air between us, but I can't resist. A sliver of darkness just might be inherent to my nature. As I believe it is with Thorne too.

"I thought there were supposed to be two more games," he says, regaining his composure.

"Monty was bored. He gave me a final game to play. One that would automatically result in my win if I participated."

His jaw tightens. "What game?"

I tilt my head slightly to the side. "He asked me to kiss him the way I kissed you yesterday."

"And did you?" Each word is clipped. Sharp. I can tell

he's trying with all his might to remain nonchalant yet failing miserably.

"No." I step even closer and slowly lift a hand to his torso. It trembles as I rest it over his heart. He intakes a sharp breath, his chest pulsing a frantic tempo against my palm. Finally, I drop every ounce of teasing, taunting, tormenting, and infuse my tone with sincerity. Locking my eyes with his, I say, "I can't kiss him the way I kissed you. I can't kiss anyone like that, because...the way I kissed you is just for you."

"Briony." He steps closer, his heart thudding faster as he cradles my cheek with his palm. His gaze sweeps down to my lips, then back to my eyes. "What does this mean?"

A delightful terror runs through me, but I'm ready now. "It means I—"

The sound of the door opening has me jumping, my words lodged in my throat. Thorne and I whirl around to face the interlopers.

Mr. Boris and Minka rush in, paying no heed to the private moment they interrupted. As I take in Minka's pale cheeks and the way Mr. Boris wrings his hand, my irritation turns to fear.

"Highness," Mr. Boris says, tone laced with panic, "we've received a letter from Nocturnus Palace. There's trouble."

$$\sim$$

I STARE AT THE HASTILY SCRAWLED NOTE IN MY HANDS, willing it to say more than it does. Yet no matter how many times I read it over, I fail to glean the clarity I seek. I scan it once more anyways, reading each word slowly.

Miss Whitney is missing. Our Majesties' secret state of cursed sleep is now compromised, and the truth is circulating. We need someone who can lie at once. Princess Rosaline, please advise.

—Mr. Ferdinand

Cursing, I crumple the letter in my hand. Thorne takes it from me and reads it for himself.

"Who is Miss Whitney?" he asks.

Mr. Boris looks at me before answering. I give him a nod. "Miss Whitney is the only half-human servant who attended Her Highness' birthday dinner," he says, "and was therefore the only fae who could lie for us. She was left in charge of maintaining the story that our king and queen traveled with the princess for her wedding. If she's missing, we can assume she may have been captured by spies, likely to coerce someone at the palace to tell the truth."

Minka makes a startled sound. "I hope she isn't being tortured. Miss Whitney is too gentle for that!"

"Don't underestimate her," Mr. Boris says. "She's a slow loris in her unseelie form. Her bite is venomous, dangerous even to fae. It's more likely that she's being kept captive while her captor tries to trick someone at the palace into giving them intel."

"I don't understand," I say. "Who would seek the truth in the first place? Who would challenge such a believable story? We made sure only trustworthy servants were left in charge at the palace. Everyone else was given a paid holiday."

Thorne runs a hand through his hair. "Trentas," he says under his breath.

My eyes widen. "You think Trentas captured Miss Whitney?"

He meets my gaze briefly, his expression brimming with guilt. "He's the only one who would have reason to suspect something is amiss at Nocturnus Palace. I only told him that he'd be able to challenge your father to the throne after your wedding, but..." Throwing his head back, he closes his eyes and releases a heavy breath. "Fuck."

A spike of betrayal spears my heart, but I can't truly blame Thorne. He did exactly what was in his right to do—using the benefit of our bargain in a perfectly reasonable way. Still, I can't stop the panic that claws at my chest. I was supposed to have another week to figure this all out. To find another way to break the sleeping spell. I haven't even told Thorne I rejected Monty yet.

"When do you think the letter was sent?" I ask.

"It was delivered by messenger bat overnight," Mr. Boris says, "so I assume the trouble began yesterday."

"Let's go," Thorne says, racing from the kitchen. I belatedly follow. "We'll head for the palace now."

I quicken my pace to reach his side as he storms through the halls. "Will we even get there before the situation escalates? It's twenty hours by train."

"We aren't taking the train." He storms into the drawing room and exits the door that leads to the back garden.

"Then how will you get there?" Mr. Boris asks, following hard on our heels along with Minka.

As soon as we're outside, Thorne stops in place. His leathery wings appear out of nowhere, as do his horns, making his answer clear. "We're going to fly."

I catch sight of nearby movement—a gardener staring

open-mouthed at his employer's unseelie form. His sheers halt mid-snip over the topiary he was trimming.

"Thorne," I say through my teeth, giving him a pointed look. "Everyone can see you right now."

"It's too late to care," he says. "We need to hurry or everything you've fought for could be at an end. Come. We'll make it to the palace by nightfall. If it's Trentas we're dealing with, I'll talk to him. If it's someone else, I'll lie, just like I bargained to do."

"But—"

He steps closer to me, eyes burning with a fierce quality that's almost terrifying. "I will make this right, Briony. I will do anything it takes to fix this for you. Just...trust me."

Calm settles over me, the edges of my panic smoothed under his dark ferocity. We can do this together. We can fix this, deal with whatever problems have arisen at the palace, and ensure we still have plenty of time to break the curse. "I do trust you," I whisper and step into his arms.

"Are you sure about this, Highness? You're going to...to fly? With *him*?"

I encircle Thorne's neck in my arms, and he lifts me against his chest. "Yes."

Minka's lips curl into a pout. "Can I come? Perhaps if I were a cat—"

"I'm sorry," Thorne says, "but I can only take Briony. I will bring her back safely once we've dealt with the threat."

Mr. Boris wrings his hands. "Do you really trust him?" he hisses from the corner of his mouth.

I meet Thorne's eyes and run my thumb over the back of his neck. "With all my heart."

Mr. Boris releases a resigned sigh. "Please don't drop her. If you do, I'll...I'll find you and tear you limb from limb with my teeth."

"And I'll gouge out your eyes with my claws," Minka says in a chillingly pleasant tone.

Thorne smiles down at me. "I already assured Her Highness that I'll never let her go."

My heart tumbles in my chest. Even more so as he springs into a jump, his wings gathering a gust of air and launching us high into the sky. I cling tight to him, my face buried against his neck, his arms secured around me, as we fly to face whatever awaits.

PART FOUR

SO
CURSED

42

THORNE

The sun dips low toward the horizon by the time we near Nocturnus Palace, the hazy cast of the Lunar Court atmosphere blanketing our surroundings in warm pink and purple tones. We pass over forests, lakes, and cities at a dizzying speed—even for me. My wings ache from constant flight, my arms nearly numb as they keep Briony secure against me, but I didn't dare stop or rest. Not until we sort out whatever trouble has befallen Briony's home.

Whatever is happening, I know it's my fault. It has to be. I never should have sent that missive to Trentas after Briony and I made our bargain. Why was I so hasty? I knew he was eager for an update after I told him I was enacting my plan to put the Briars to sleep, but I could have made him wait just a little longer. Yet I was worried he'd do something hasty if I left him out too long.

And now he has, but it was *because* of my correspondence with him, not my avoidance of it.

Now everything Briony cares about is at stake.

The towering spires of Nocturnus Palace come into view, the amethyst walls and gilded crenellations sparkling under the waning light of the ever-descending sun. I finally allow myself to slow my pace, my wings beating in gentler intervals as we begin to lower toward our destination. I bring my lips close to Briony's ear. "We're about to arrive."

She untucks her head from under my chin, where she kept her face shielded from the relentless wind. I, of course, am used to such an incessant barrage. My skin may look the same in my unseelie form as it does in my seelie, but it grows tougher when I shift. Demons were made to fly. It is one of the few things humans are right about when it comes to the many misconceptions they have about my kind of fae. Yet, as we draw even closer to the palace and I catch a glimpse of what troubles await, I feel like a demon in the darkest sense. For I must bear responsibility for what lies below.

Briony releases a startled gasp, a sound that sends shards of pain to my heart. I keep us suspended midair, directly over the palace lawn—or what used to be it. Now it's a field of scorched earth, glowing embers, and wild brambles that erupt from the soil. Upon this field, several figures are locked in combat, sending snarls, growls, and shouts to ripple through the air. Two kitsune with balls of flame hovering over their tails—one orange and the other blue— exchange vicious bites. Another fight involves a pair of fae who look mostly human in their seelie forms, engaged in a brawl of fists and daggers. Spectators circle the field like vultures, awaiting their chance to join the brawl.

I can tell just by looking at them who they are—leaders of the factions who've been desperate for the throne ever since Horus Briar claimed it twenty-one years ago. Figures who've been thwarted by Divina Briar's magic and the protocols required to challenge a monarch. The fact that they're fighting now tells me they know about the king's condition. They know there's no one to hear their challenges. No one to refuse them. No one to set an appointment and order them to come back later, as royal custom demands.

This is their chance to claim the crown.

Stones below, I can't imagine how much deadlier this would be if it were the unseelie throne that was open for the taking. This is bad enough.

And yet...where the hell is Trentas?

I scan the lawn, but as a shadow falls over us, I realize I should have scanned the skies first. A black dragon with slitted yellow eyes soars overhead. As he passes, Trentas meets my gaze, a challenging look on his scaly face as his attention shifts to Briony in my arms.

"Is that him?" she asks, voice quavering. "The dragon who raised you?"

"Yes," I say through my teeth. Trentas averts his gaze, then soars down to the lawn below. I follow in his wake, but I don't land near the fight like he does. Instead, I veer closer to the palace. As we approach, I discover a wall of tightly woven brambles has been erected around the palace, which I assume was constructed by palace guards, ones with earthen magic. It isn't a perfect solution, for anyone with the power of flight could land on the roof and invade. Then again, I suppose the challengers have no reason to invade. They must know the king and queen are incapacitated. Their goal isn't to seek out the current monarch or destroy the palace; it's to determine who will cross that wall of brambles as the new ruler.

"What do we do?" Briony asks, her voice laced with panic. "This...this is chaos."

"I know." Guilt and rage infuse my tone. "I must talk with Trentas and get him to back down. You should check on your family."

She nods, her motions jagged. We cross the wall of brambles with ease, though I keep my senses keen in case any airborne attacks try to counter our approach. An arrow whizzes toward us from one of the battlements, and I dodge it just in time. Shit. Of course they can't see I'm carrying their princess. I pick up speed, dodging another arrow as we fly to the opposite side of the palace. Lucky for us, there seem to be very few archers or soldiers present to protect the palace, for we reach a vacant battlement unscathed. Though if the palace were properly staffed, perhaps there wouldn't be a bloodbath on the lawn.

I gently set Briony on her feet, and she slowly unlaces her arms from around my neck. Her limbs must be burning from clinging to me so tightly for the last several hours, but she doesn't fully release me. Instead, she lays her palms over my chest. "Thorne, what can we possibly do about this?"

I gently cup her cheek and lower my lips to hers in a soft kiss. "I'll take care of it. All we need is time. I'll convince Trentas to give it to us."

She nibbles her bottom lip, her body tense. I can tell she's fighting to say something—or not to—but I don't know what it is. Is she hiding something? Did something happen? I recall the conversation we were in the middle of when her servants interrupted us.

I can't kiss him the way I kissed you.

My pulse quickens, but this isn't the time for soft confessions. "Go check on your family. I'll find you once I've spoken to Trentas."

With a deep breath, she gives a reluctant nod. I step away and launch into the sky. We keep our eyes locked as she moves to the door that leads into the palace. She hesitates, then finally tears her gaze from mine and enters the palace.

As soon as she closes the door behind her, I soar back over the wall of brambles in search of my first father figure.

I FIND HIM NEAR THE ONGOING MELEE. NO LONGER IN HIS dragon body, Trentas leans against a tree in seelie form, half hidden by shadows as he watches the fight. Only the faintest blush of sunset remains on the horizon, leaving the burning trees and shrubs dotting the ruined lawn as the primary light source.

Trentas doesn't bother looking my way as I approach. He simply crosses his arms over his chest, a humorless smile stretching his lips. He's dressed in a long black coat threaded with violet embroidery at the hems and sleeves—an elegant fae style not often seen in modern fashion. The tips of his pointed ears show through his strands of long black hair.

This is my first time seeing him in person since the day he brought me to Edwyn Blackwood. Seeing him now, I'm struck by how young he looks. When I was a child, he looked ancient, but now we look nearly the same age. With his long black hair and dark eyes, it's easy to see why everyone believed we were related by blood. Still, no matter how young he looks now, I find myself intimidated in his presence. He's always been a force to be reckoned with, and I've respected him all my life. Even after I built a far warmer relationship with my birth father, I never forgot my respect for Trentas. I cherished his part in my life so much that I inked my loyalty to him onto my skin.

Now, for the first time, I must defy him.

"Vintarys," Trentas says in greeting, finally deigning to look at me as I stand before him. There's no warmth in his expression, only reprimand. It cuts like an iron dagger to my heart. This is the first time we've seen each other in fifteen years, and he looks at me like I'm the greatest disappointment of his life. For a moment, I feel like the child version of me, eager for his approval, his pride. That need to change the way he sees me crawls up my skin, compressing my lungs—

Then I realize...this is exactly how Briony feels now. About her family. This wretched feeling, this dark desperation, is what drove her into this bargain with me.

And I've already decided to choose her. To reverse what I made her do. To ensure she never has to feel this way again.

If that means taking this awful feeling upon myself, casting a divide between me and the fae I looked up to, then I will. I'll take Trentas' resentment and burn with it. Reflect it back to him. Just because I respect him doesn't mean I must obey.

I breathe out slowly and meet his gaze without falter, silently conveying I'm not the little boy he pretended to sire.

Trentas shakes his head with a mirthless laugh. "So I was right. I knew there was something strange going on. You finally succeeded in fulfilling your mother's mission, yet you're working with *her*."

"I never told you I succeeded," I say, my fingers curling into fists. Hearing him refer to Briony with such venom sets my blood boiling, strengthening my will to defy him.

"No, you said I'd have a chance at challenging King

Horus after the princess' wedding, and you refused to answer any of my correspondence thereafter."

"I've been busy."

"Doing what? At least tell me your actions are all part of your revenge. Tell me you're not trying to protect the girl. Tell me there's a reason why her family isn't in the catacombs yet."

I curl my fingers tighter. "How did you find out?"

"I was suspicious. My spies hadn't seen the king and queen in days and word had spread that they'd left for the princess' wedding. Yet my Earthen Court spies hadn't seen Horus and Divina there either. I came to investigate myself and found a dining room full of lifeless bodies."

Shit. So he truly knows everything. "What are you doing now? What is all this?" I gesture toward the combatants.

"The factions are fighting over their right to claim the throne. We all deserve a fair shot, so here we are."

"You're stirring chaos."

He pushes off from the tree and burns me with an icy stare. "I'm establishing my reign. One that should have been mine from the beginning. This court has suffered from Horus' neglect long enough. I will be the seelie king the people deserve, and that starts with fairly engaging with my challengers now. I will let them choose their victors, and then I will defeat them one by one until there's no question that the throne belongs to me. Unlike Horus, I won't have my right to rule constantly questioned. I will prove myself now."

Stones, I know he's the right ruler for the throne. I know this court needs him, but I can't let him take away what Briony deserves. "I need more time, Trentas. I told you about the princess' wedding for a reason. You weren't supposed to challenge her father until after she's married."

"Why?"

I clench my jaw, unsure if I should tell him the truth. Could he use it against me and Briony? Or will it get him to understand? Fuck. What other choice do I have?

"The princess and I made a bargain."

He narrows his eyes. "Explain."

"She found a way to break the sleeping spell on both our families. She learned the truth from Nyxia herself. Waking our families hinges upon this wedding, which won't take place for another six days. Back off. Call off the fighters. Once Briony is married, Divina Briar is bound by a bargain with the king to cease using her magic on challengers to the throne. No one will ever be subject to her manipulations again."

Trentas assesses me in cold silence. Then, hands clasped behind his back, he takes a step closer. "You know damn well Morgana would rather sleep for one hundred years than wake to find her son has allied with the enemy."

I take a forbidding step forward of my own, holding my ground. "I don't care."

"Well, I do. You may have lost your principles, Vin, but I haven't. You say you want time? You have until the melee is over. If Horus awakens by then, I'll call the factions off, and we'll wait for this wedding to take place before we challenge him according to protocol."

"Horus won't wake *until* the wedding takes place."

"Then that is only good news for me."

"Morgana won't either," I say.

"I've said my piece on that subject."

My blood races with rage, surging through my arms, my hands—

"Do you want to fight me, Vin?" His lips curl in an amused smirk. "I have loved you like a son my entire life, but I will fight you if that is your wish. But first I request that you step back and remember your place. Remember the name you were given, the purpose imbued upon your birth."

A flicker of guilt sparks inside me, but I recall what Briony said to me. "I wasn't born to be a tool for revenge."

"You weren't born to be with *her* either," Trentas counters.

Alarm ripples through me. Are my emotions truly so transparent?

"You're in love with her," he says, voice flat.

"That's none of your concern."

"It is when your misplaced priorities threaten decades of effort. I've been fighting for this throne ever since Horus took it and made a mockery of the seelie fae. You know I'm the best candidate as king. You know I'll serve the court a thousand times better than Horus ever did."

I do know. I always have. But...

Briony fills my mind. My heart.

Trentas may be the king I support most, but not at the cost of taking away Briony's family. Of destroying her relationship with them. Of losing that pride and respect that means so much to her.

Trentas continues. "You're doing all of this to wake your families, but what happens after that? Your feelings for the princess will matter none. Neither family will approve of a friendship between you, much less a courtship."

Again, he's right. But I'm not doing all of this for a future with her. I'm doing this for *her* future.

It's all for her.

Yes, my family stands to benefit from our bargain, but that has become second to Briony. My mother and sisters could awaken but there's still a chance they're already dead.

That the iron grenade that destroyed their lungs before I enacted the curse continues to plague them. That waking will only end in their tormented final breaths. Even if they wake hale and whole, I've already made my decision.

To choose Briony.

She has a chance at the happiness she's always wanted. I made a promise to her that I would do whatever it took to get her family back. While my human blood allows me to lie, making a promise to a pureblood fae is as good as a binding vow. Even if I hadn't said those unbreakable words *I promise*, I'd still be determined to see this through.

For her. Always for her.

"We're done talking about this," Trentas says, striding to the ring of fighters without giving me a second look.

My shoulders drop, muscles uncoiling. I know what needs to be done.

Briony and I have a bargain to fulfill.

She must marry Monty.

43

BRIONY

My family is exactly how I left them. Before I sought out Thorne to coerce him into joining our bargain, I aided the palace servants in ensuring my family could rest as comfortably as possible. Where they once were strewn in deathlike poses, bodies slumped, hands empty, they now lay on makeshift cots, each pair of hands resting over their abdomens. As for Uncle Bobbins, the featherless rooster—a lidérc, mother had said —he simply lays on his side upon the now-clean table.

I circle the sleeping bodies, noting that their current positions aren't any less chilling than they'd been when haphazardly sprawled. At least this will provide a much more comfortable waking.

If they ever awaken.

If it isn't already too late.

I settle upon the floor near the head of the table where my parents' cots rest side by side. Gingerly, I reach for each of their hands, settling my palms over flesh that is neither warm nor cold. My eyes sweep over my father's form, then my mother's. I can't help remembering the joy of our first meeting. My mother's enthusiasm and nonstop chatter. My father's shy grin and pats on the head. I've since learned darker facts about my family, but there remains a deep well of affection for them. One that weighs heavy with grief.

"I'm sorry," I whisper to them, voice trembling. "I couldn't save your throne."

Only silence echoes back. There's not a hint of breath stirring the air. No thudding heartbeat but my own. Not even the servants standing guard outside the closed dining room doors make any noise, which leaves my apology ringing empty. Unheard. Hollow.

I study my mother's round cheeks, too pale in her slumber. I remember the warmth of her arms, the giddy excitement in her letter. My heart sinks as I recall the words that once filled me with so much pride. So much conviction.

You're the Briar family hero.

My marriage to Monty meant so much to her and my father. While I can't regret the choice I made, I do dread their disapproval once they find out I rejected him. Because they will find out. They will awaken. I'll make sure of it. Thorne and I will find a way. Even if they wake without a throne or a marriage alliance and with a mountain of debt. Even if they wake, remembering me as a traitor, a weapon wielded by the enemy. They will, at the very least, awaken.

I'll need to be satisfied with that.

The question is...will that be enough for my family too?

The same terror I felt earlier after I rejected Monty returns, screaming in my mind. *What have I done? What have I done?*

I chose myself, I tell the voice.

I deserve to choose myself.

The reminder only softens my sorrow the slightest bit. I suppose it will take time to come to terms with all of this. "I'm sorry," I say again, swallowing the lump in my throat. "I can't be the hero you wanted me to be."

"You can." Thorne's voice has my heart leaping out of my chest. I hadn't heard his approach, but I find him emerging from a partially open door—likely from the servants' hall. He's still in his unseelie form, his horns visible, his wings folded against his back. His expression is hard, lips pursed in a tight line. He extends a hand to me. "Come. We're going to find Monty. Let's settle our bargain."

I frown at his open hand. "What are you talking about?"

"We are going to find Monty right this minute. I will drag him by the ear to a twenty-four-hour chapel if I must."

"No, Thorne," I say, rising to my feet without the aid of his extended palm. I'm too afraid if I take it, he'll whisk me away before I've had the chance to explain. I wanted to tell him in a different way. A heartfelt way. But my earlier attempt was thwarted by Mr. Boris' news. "We aren't getting married. I never finished telling you, but I...I lost the game. On purpose. I rejected him. It's over—"

"It's not over. I won't give him a choice."

I narrow my eyes. Why isn't he listening? "It's. Over," I say punctuating each word. "It's over because I chose for it to be. We aren't completing our bargain. I will not marry him."

Thorne's expression breaks, a tormented edge pulling at his lips and the corners of his eyes. "This is your last chance to wake your family before Trentas takes their throne."

"I thought you wanted him to take the throne," I say, regretting the bitter note that creeps into my voice.

He runs a hand over his face. "I do, but not like this. Not in a way that compromises your standing with your family."

"We'll find another way to wake them," I say.

"No, you were right from the start. This is the only way you get everything you want."

Anger laces through me. "You're wrong. This isn't everything I want. And why do you keep talking about our bargain and how it benefits *me*? Why are you focused on what you think I want? Do your wants not matter? Or do you *want* me to marry Monty?"

"No," he says through his teeth. "Every part of me recoils —rages—at the thought of you together. There is nothing I want less than that. Which is why our bargain still stands to succeed—"

"Thorne Blackwood," I say, holding his gaze. "Vintarys Lemuria, and every name you've ever gone by, I hereby release you from our bargain and consider every term null and void."

He steps back, frozen in place as if I've slapped him. I wait for some grand sign that our bargain has ended, some indication that our magical agreement has been terminated, but all I feel is ease in my lungs. Relief in my muscles.

Thorne's voice comes out stifled. "Why did you do that?"

"You know why I did that. I did it because, above everything I want and crave, there's you. I want you, Thorne." I take a deep breath, prepared to say the words I left buried in my heart. Words I wanted to convey with warmth and not anger. But my anger for him is as warm as my love, so I suppose this will have to do. I take a step closer to him, reaching for him. "Thorne, I—"

"Don't." His voice barrels into me, seizing my tongue and rendering it immobile. At first, I think it's merely surprise that sticks my words in place...but the chill running down my spine says otherwise. He speaks again. "Don't say it."

Icy hot betrayal carves a line through my heart.

He's using the cursed bond between us to command me.

Now that I've dissolved our bargain, he's no longer bound to the terms that forbade him from using it. Tears brim in my eyes. "How could you do that to me?"

"Because we're out of time. There's only one thing left we can do. One last way to break the curse right now."

I wish his words inspired hope, but the sorrow filling his face crushes all potential. "What way is that?"

"We'll let each other go."

My blood runs cold. "What are you talking about?"

"I'll command you to forget about me. You will sacrifice your memories of me—your feelings for me—and remember me only as an enemy that you made a temporary alliance with. You'll forget you ever dreamed of me. This will be a singular task we'll accomplish together. A sacrifice neither of us wants to make but benefits both of our families."

Panic surges through me. He can't be serious. I throw my hands in the air. "How will that benefit either of our families?"

"Forgetting me will save your family from strife and scandal." His voice is empty as he speaks. "You'll be free of your attachment to me, of a union your parents would never approve of. In turn, my family will benefit as they would have in our original bargain. Without me in your heart, you'll have no reason to reject Monty. You'll wed him as planned and your mother will be bound to her vow to stop interfering with challengers to the throne. Trentas—even Morgana herself—will have a fair chance at defeating your father."

I release a cold, humorless laugh. "You can't possibly believe I'd still marry Monty. I won't, even if you force me to forget my feelings for you. Then the benefit to your family will be null, and the curse won't break."

His throat bobs. So badly do I want to wrest from him that emotion he's swallowing down and force him to confront it. To honor it.

"Neither of us can know for sure," he says. "Our previous bargain was equally as uncertain. So long as there's a chance that the perceived benefits can come to fruition, the curse will break."

Fuck. He really is serious. "Why do you suddenly care so much? You're the one who told me I'm better than my family. That my desire for their approval was wasted on them. And you..." I do all I can to rein in my panic, my anger, and speak with candor. "You're the one I want to be with."

His lips curl in a sad smile. "I'll never be enough to fill the void of family."

"That's not true—"

"You've yearned for them all your life."

"Yes, but—"

"I saw your face just now when I entered the room. I heard the grief in your tone when you apologized to your mother. You looked as heartbroken as you did when your parents first fell under the spell. That was my fault and so is this. I can reverse it all, and I will. I promised to do whatever it took to bring your family back. I'm beholden to that vow."

Tremors rack my body. I'm desperate to speak, to convince him to abandon this awful plan, but every word I've said to reel him closer has only pushed him farther away. Finally, I make a final bid for his heart. "You also promised you'd never let me go."

He shakes his head. "I never said the binding words *I promise* when I told you that. And while it wasn't a lie when I said it, it will henceforth remain the most treacherous untruth I've ever told."

He steps closer to me, and I tense. My tone turns desperate. Pleading. "Don't do this. If you do, you will prove yourself crueler than I've ever given you credit for. I will hate you—"

"I know." He reaches for my hand and places it on his chest. "I will take your hate and hold it close to my heart."

"You'll be a true demon in every sense of the word. A monster."

"Yes," he whispers. "I'll be the villain so you can be the hero."

"I don't want to be the hero anymore!" I shout, tears streaming from my eyes. "I want to be with you."

He inches closer, lifting a hand to wipe a trail of moisture from my cheek. "That's what makes our sacrifices so achingly perfect."

"Thorne—"

"I won't let you tell me you love me," he says, pressing his forehead to mine. His heart slams against my palm. "But let me say it once to you. I love you. I have ever since you were nothing but a dream. And I continued to love you when you were revealed to be my enemy. I loved you when you annoyed me. I loved you *because* you annoyed me. Briony, I love you with every inch of my soul, and I want you to keep that somewhere deep inside. I want your heart to remember that you were loved. That you deserve love still. But everything else, I want you to forget."

His words gouge my heart, a pain so vast I nearly crumple beneath its violence. But I don't crumple. I don't fall. Instead, I stand taller and meet his eyes with defiance. "I won't," I say through my teeth, curling my hands over the front of his shirt. "Command me all you want, but I will find a way to defy you. I will claw my way back to my memories. I promise I will dig them from the depths of my mind, my heart, my soul with everything I have—"

"Please do." He presses his lips to mine in a hard, unrelenting kiss that tastes of salt, broken promises, and the bitter tang of goodbye. Mingling with that is a hidden sweetness, one of chocolate cake, stolen glances, and taunting games. Of tended wounds, dancing slippers, and protective embraces. But the words he speaks against my mouth burn like venom. "It's time to forget, Briony Rose."

44

BRIONY

onfusion blankets my mind. For a moment, I don't know where I am. What I'm doing. My chest heaves with a broken sob while tears stream down my face without reason. Am I...crying? Pain pulses at my temples as I try to arrange my thoughts, but motion steals my attention.

I blink at my surroundings. The dining room at Nocturnus Palace sharpens into view, the space dark save for the moonlight streaming through the windows. A body shifts on a cot, stirring with slow, heavy movements. That must be the motion that drew my attention, but what are these cots? Who are these bodies?

My memories return in a rush of images, some vibrant, some hazy or out of order. I remember my birthday dinner, reuniting with my family before that, and being betrayed by Thorne—

Thorne.

Why would I call him that? The man is no better than a

stranger, so his proper name is Mr. Blackwood. He was tasked with bringing me to my parents, then to my fiancé, but at my birthday dinner...

Another layer of memory peels back.

Shit. That's right. Mr. Blackwood is also Vintarys Lemuria, the enemy of my family. And he...he forged a bond with me, one that allowed him to make demands of me, to control my actions, even my memories. I remember being ordered to draw the cake knife on my father, then the terror in my parents' eyes.

My parents!

I stare at the bodies with fresh awareness and realize my parents are the ones lying before me. My mother was the figure who'd begun to stir. I fall to my knees at her side, gathering her hand in mine. As I do, more memories fill my mind, of me slicing the underside of Mr. Blackwood's jaw—

An unsettling guilt fills my heart at the thought.

Why the hell would I feel guilty over cutting Mr. Blackwood?

The repercussions play out in my mind's eye next. The way my family crumpled in place around the dinner table. Nyxia's visit and explanation of the sleeping spell.

Relief flows over me, at least where my guilt is concerned. I wasn't regretting hurting Mr. Blackwood but what drawing his blood caused. I regret what I did to my family.

My mother's eyelids flutter open. I squeeze her hand tighter and settle in closer as her gaze rests on my face. Her round cheeks are pale, but the slightest hint of a rosy hue begins to color them. She tilts her head to the side, wincing as if the motion jars her senses. Finally, she speaks, the sound a tired rasp. "Rosaline? Is...is that you, lovey?"

"Yes, I'm here."

She lifts her head, and I help her sit. Shuffling sounds rustle around us as my aunts, uncles, and cousins begin to stir as well. My father releases a tired grunt, but he still hasn't moved.

"What's...happening?" Mother asks, casting a squinted glance around the dining room. "Why..."

I don't have words to explain so I wait for the memories to return to her on their own. Meanwhile, I hold her hand and brace her back, in case her strength falters. I see the exact moment when recollection dawns. Her eyes widen slightly, pupils dilating to swallow her blue irises.

"Right," she says under her breath. With a jolt, she tugs her hand from mine, her gaze landing on my face with renewed terror. I flinch at the sight, and darker feelings emerge. A spark of resentment flickers in my chest, along with a sobering flood of new memories, all hazy and out of order.

Minka and her feline form.

My parents' attempts to burn down the catacombs.

My unwanted engagement to Mr. Phillips.

The last memory unravels yet another layer, and I recall a bargain I made with Mr. Blackwood, then a game I played with Monty Phillips. Both feel more like a dream than a clear memory, as does me rejecting my fiancé and quitting the game. I can't help feeling like I'm missing something amongst these hazy recollections.

Pain strikes my temples as I try to gain more clarity than that.

My mother rushes to her feet, stealing my attention back to her. "Where is he?" she asks, eyes wild. "Where is Vintarys?"

"He's not here. It's been..." I close my eyes, sifting through my murky understanding of the passage of time.

Finally, I sort out enough to finish what I started to say. "It's been over a week since you fell under the sleeping spell."

"A week?" she echoes. "We...we've been asleep?"

"Then how are we awake?" My father's deep voice has me whirling toward him. He pushes off from his cot, his beady eyes sweeping over the room. "How did this happen?"

My heart slams in my chest as I realize I don't have an answer for him. Not a clear one, at least. I remember making a deal with Mr. Blackwood, that he would help me marry Mr. Phillips and break the curse. I remember rejecting Monty in favor of my own wants.

But what were those wants?

Did I truly reject him for the sake of freedom alone?

And if so, how did we break the curse?

Something bright and warm pulses inside me, but it feels muffled. Muted. I envision the warmth growing claws, slashing out at whatever binds it...

"Answer me, Daughter." Father's stern tone has my spine going rigid. He rises from his cot and hauls me to stand with him. His grip isn't rough, but it isn't gentle either. From the corner of my eye, I find several of my other family members waking, standing, turning their attention to me and Father. "Tell me what happened."

"I broke the curse," I say.

"How?"

"I...I don't remember." I filter through my memories once more, trying to glean exactly what I was doing before my family awoke, but all I can remember are the tears that streamed down my cheeks, the sob that broke from my chest when I first found myself standing here.

Then another flash of memory emerges. A wall of brambles around the palace, a ring of fighters, and a dragon soaring in the sky overhead—

"Father, you have to stop the fighting. I tried to keep the sleeping spell a secret while I worked to break the curse, but someone found out."

No, not just *someone*. A dragon named Trentas.

The fae who raised Mr. Blackwood when he was a child.

A child whose secret name was Vintarys.

A child who listened to his mother's and sisters' screams as they suffered from an iron grenade.

A child whose eyes melted from his sockets because of a trick played by one of my family members.

Rage funnels through me, a protective fire that confuses me more than anything else. Why do I feel so angry on Mr. Blackwood's behalf?

I shake the question from my mind and return to the topic at hand. "There are factions outside who are preparing to take the throne in your absence. They need to see you're alive."

The doors to the dining room swing open, and a pair of guards rush in. They must have finally heard the commotion. "Majesty," they say in unison, bowing at the waist as soon as they catch sight of my father.

He clears his throat. "Does my daughter speak the truth? Are there challengers to the throne at the palace?"

How could he ask if I'm telling the truth? He knows I can't lie.

"Yes," one of the guards says. "They will be forced to disband if they know you're awake and still in possession of the throne."

Father nods. "Then I must go at once. Divina." He turns to my mother. I expect him to say something else, but he only gives her a pointed nod. She gives one back, her eyes flicking briefly to me.

I frown, unsure what to make of that exchange.

Father stalks out of the room, flanked by the two guards, while my awakened family members blink around the room in confusion. Some sink into vacant chairs while others rub their temples. A few seem to have gained their bearings already and eye me with keen looks.

Looks that aren't at all comforting.

"Lovey," Mother says in a sing-song voice. She lays a gentle hand on my arm. "You said you don't remember how you broke the sleeping spell. Are there other things you don't recall?"

"Some," I say. "My mind is hazy right now. Breaking the curse must have affected me too."

Her lips pull into a pout and she gathers me in a hug. "My poor girl."

Emotion rises in my throat as she softly brushes her hand over my hair. While I'm still tense from these confusing events, I feel some relief too. Comfort in being hugged so tenderly by my mother.

Stars, this is my *mother*!

I've been so distraught over my confusion that I haven't had a chance to revel in the beauty of this moment. My plan worked! My family is awake. My father's throne is saved. And my mother—the woman I've always wanted to meet, whose love and pride and approval I've always hoped to gain, even when I thought there was a good chance I was an orphan—is here before me. Hugging me.

She squeezes me tighter. "My dearest Rosaline, I'm so sorry you've had to suffer. This is all Vintarys' fault. When he's dead—"

"Dead?" I pull back slightly, just enough to catch the narrowing of Mother's eyes.

"Does that concern you, Rosaline?"

I open my mouth but don't know what to say. Mr. Blackwood's death shouldn't bother me in the slightest. We forged an alliance to break the curse, but...

Pink dancing slippers flash in my mind, but the image is gone before I can make sense of it.

"Vintarys must die." Mother's voice takes on a chilling tone. "He has a power over you that we cannot allow him to wield."

She isn't wrong about that. While I'd assumed my individual curse—the one that binds me to iron if it touches my flesh—would break along with the sleeping spell, I seem to recall Mr. Blackwood insisting that wasn't the case.

But when did he say that?

I remember a runaway horse...

Wings that wrapped around me...

"Until then," Mother says, "you are a danger to us."

"What—" My voice cuts off in a shout as hands encircle my forearms, wrenching my arms from around my mother and tugging them behind my back. A glance over my shoulder shows a pair of my uncles standing just behind me. They must have crept from the table while my mother was hugging me. My face whips back to her. She now stands a few feet away. Her expression brims with pity but she makes no move to get my uncles to release me. "What are you doing?"

"I'm sorry, my love, but we don't know what demands Vintarys left you with."

"He helped me break the curse."

She arches a brow. "He helped you? Why?"

"Both of our efforts were required," I rush to explain. "It was the only way. He benefitted because the spell would break for his family..." My words die in my mouth as I realize they are the worst ones I could say.

She purses her lips so tightly they almost lose color. "Are you saying the Lemurias are awake now too?"

I give a wary nod.

"And you haven't a clue what you did to wake us up?"

A jerky shake of my head.

She huffs. "Well, until Vintarys is dead, we can't know what he might make you do. He could have ordered you to slaughter us in our sleep this very night."

"He didn't," I say, and every part of me hums with the truth of my words. I don't know how I know, but I am certain he's done nothing to hurt my family since my birthday party.

"We will hunt him down and end his life. Now that the sleeping spell is broken on both families, we can fight Vintarys, Morgana, and all the Lemurias in earnest. We can shed their blood without repercussions. The mahrts will defeat the banshee clan once and for all."

"No!"

Mother's eyes widen. She angles her head to the side. "No? Oh, my poor girl. This is so much worse than I thought. He truly does control you now, doesn't he?"

"That...that's not it."

"Then what is it?"

I open my mouth but my words won't come. I can't explain the warm fluttering in my chest, nor do I know what it means. In my mind, I know Mr. Blackwood is my enemy. I know our bargain was forced upon him and he only agreed for his own benefit.

But in my heart...

My heart can't bear to hear any threat against Thorne.

Mother gives a sharp nod to my uncles, the same she exchanged with my father before he left. "Take her to the tower."

45

THORNE

hree days have passed since Briony and I broke the sleeping spell, and only now can I safely say my mother and sisters survived. While the rest of my relatives—all twenty-seven who consider themselves Lemurias or members of Morgana's banshee clan—have awoken and left the catacombs already, the three I care about most remain behind, tended to by healers. At first, I was certain they were dead. That the sleeping spell had done nothing but preserve their already-lifeless bodies. Despite my worst fears, the fae physicians assured me the iron had left their lungs over the last fifteen years of slumber and that enacting the sleeping spell was the sole reason they survived. Only this morning did my youngest sister wake. Then my eldest. Two hours ago, Morgana opened her eyes.

Thank the All of All the Lunar Court royal catacombs fall under King Franco's care. Were Horus Briar a better king, he'd be responsible for them, for matters of death and the preservation of bodies are more traditions favored by humans and seelie fae. But if that were the case, my family would have been dead long ago. Or the physicians sent to attend them now would secretly murder them instead of help.

Stones, I'm thankful my mother and sisters woke at all. It's my one consolation, the sole flicker of light in the otherwise dark shroud that has fallen over me. The only comfort I've allowed to soften the fissure in my heart and the self-hatred that has been my constant companion since I left Briony at Nocturnus Palace. But even the comfort of my family ends today. For there's one last sacrifice I must make for the woman I love.

I stand outside my mother's makeshift room in one of the numerous stone hallways of the catacombs, waiting for her current guest to leave. I haven't seen or spoken to my mother since she regained consciousness, yet Trentas managed to beat me to it.

Shifting closer to the open doorway carved into the stone wall, I strain my ears to make out their conversation. Their voices are too low to catch more than a word or two. *Retaliation. Revenge. Justice.* Still, it's enough to tell me that— despite breaking the curse—the feud between the Briars and the Lemurias is as strong as ever.

A dark feeling hollows out my gut. I know what I must do next, but I doubt it will put an end to the rivalry. I just hope it's enough to secure what Briony values most. She's my choice, and I'm seeing this through to the end. Even if it costs me everything.

Morgana and Trentas lower their voices further, but I catch my name amongst their whispered tones. I'm certain Trentas will relay everything he knows, including how I tried to thwart his attempt at taking the throne. Yet true to his word, as soon as Horus Briar showed his face, proving he was still hale and whole and in full possession of the crown, Trentas left, as did all the other factions. Now I suppose he must wait to see if the promised wedding takes place.

The thought sours my stomach. Stones, I hated saying those words to Briony, about her having no reason to reject Monty without me in the picture. I don't know if there was any truth to what I said, but I had to twist my intent to serve the magic that would break the sleeping spell. If I didn't state some benefit for my family, the curse wouldn't have broken.

But I did.

And the curse did break.

Shattering my heart along with it.

Impatience ripples through me, making my wings twitch. They beg to spread out, to fly, to do anything but wait in this eerily quiet hall. I fold them tighter down my back.

It's been strange staying in my unseelie form, not having to hide my wings or horns. I haven't left the catacombs since arriving three days ago, so I've yet to glean whether my dual identities have become public knowledge yet. I'm still not certain how I'll handle that.

The steady drip of water catches my attention, its sound drowning out the whispers I'm trying to overhear. I frown at the opposite wall where rivulets of moisture trail down the dark stone and drip from the ceiling. Such streams aren't uncommon in the underground tunnels that comprise the catacombs, but this one's presence is quite inconvenient. Though, if there wasn't moisture, there wouldn't be light, as the only source of illumination comes from the clusters of bioluminescent mushrooms sprouting from the walls.

I shift even closer to the doorway, but my shoe nudges an unseen rock, sending it skittering down the silent hall.

The whispers cut off. Trentas speaks at a normal volume as he says, "It seems you have a visitor, Morgana. I'll check in on you later."

Footsteps sound, then Trentas emerges from the room. His eyes find mine at once, and he delivers a stern look. I'm about to brush past him when he grabs my arm. Keeping his voice low, he mutters, "Be careful what you say to her. She is just as fierce as ever, but she is still your mother and loves you dearly. Do not break her heart. Remember who you are."

I pull back and lock my eyes with his. We're the same height and we appear the same age. I stand tall, uncowed by his reproach, silently conveying that which I don't say—that my respect for him will always remain, but I will not return to the role I once had. I can no longer be his subordinate, his foster son.

"I know exactly who I am," I say, each word delivered with the unyielding strength of my resolve.

His eyes widen slightly and he releases me.

I leave Trentas in the hall and enter the room. It's slightly darker than the hallway, with only one cluster of mushrooms to light the modest space, but I keep my eyes on the ground nonetheless. "Are you veiled, Mother?"

"Vin! Is that really you?" Her voice is weaker than I remember it, which must be due to the iron she inhaled. My chest constricts at the thought. "Yes, my dear, I'm veiled. Come. Let me get a proper look at you."

I lift my eyes and find her sitting upright on a narrow cot, dressed in a plain black robe. Her long dark hair hangs limp around her shoulders while a lacy black veil obscures her face. A face I'm cursed never to look upon.

She pats the cot and I take a seat next to her. My chest tightens as I take in how small she looks. How frail. Was she always this tiny? When I was a boy, she seemed to tower over everyone, her bearing so strong and demanding. I angle my body toward her, unsure if I should greet her with a hug like I would have when I was small. It doesn't feel natural, so I do nothing. She makes no move to reach for me either.

"You're grown, Vin," she says, her voice quavering with emotion. "I hardly recognize you. Have you seen your sisters yet?"

"Yes, and they didn't recognize me either. They were frightened of me, so the physician asked me to leave." That does pain me, though I try to keep it off my face. It makes sense that such a rift would form between me and my siblings after all this time. The last time they saw me, I wasn't much older than them. Now I'm a man grown. Meanwhile, the girls hardly understand what's befallen them.

"They'll come around," Mother says. "It will take all of us much work to reestablish our lives after fifteen years of slumber."

"Indeed it will," I say, my words weighted by the confession I must soon make.

She must hear the hidden edge in my tone, for her own grows sharper as she speaks next. "Trentas tells me I have you to thank for breaking the curse before our hundred-year term of slumber. He also said your methods were questionable. I'll give you the benefit of the doubt and trust that your choices were made in favor of your family, regardless of having allied with the enemy."

"I'm going to stop you right there, Mother."

"Do not interrupt me," she says, each word punctuated with venom. I now recall exactly why she seemed so large before. Despite her stature, she was always a formidable creature. She still is.

But I am no longer hers to command.

She speaks again. "We'll need you and your ability in the coming days. Trentas tells me you managed to put the Briars to sleep, so I trust you've learned of the meaning behind your name. You'll use that to—"

"Morgana," I say, the word hard and unforgiving on my tongue.

She flinches back. Not once have I called her anything but Mother. "Vintarys—"

"No, not Vintarys. I cannot be Vintarys for you any longer."

Silence. Then, "What are you saying?" The quaver in her voice would pierce my heart if it weren't already broken for another reason. Even so, I know what I do next will hurt her. It will widen the divide the last fifteen years already wedged between us. Between me and the siblings I once loved as deeply as life itself.

"I wish I could wait until you were fully recovered to say this. I wish I didn't have to hurt you while your wounds are still fresh." Every word I say is true. Stones below, I know I'm going to break her heart, and she's already had a lifetime of pain. She's known so much cruelty at the hands of the Briars. Yet she never rose above it. Instead, she met their darkness with equal darkness. Turned their own cruelty back at them. While I understand her hatred, her rage, and agree much of it is justified, I can't serve as a weapon of revenge anymore.

She scoffs. "I don't have to listen to this. Go. Come back when you're ready to—"

"No, Morgana. You will listen. This is of the utmost importance."

"More important than your family? More important than your own mother? What kind of son are you?" Despite her sharp words, her outward fire, I can see the hurt in her hunched shoulders, hear it in the pitch of her voice.

I gather one of her hands in mine and give it a squeeze. My eyes dart over her veil, and I wish I could see her face beneath it, if only to ensure she's looking at mine. That she can see the sincerity in my expression. "I will always love you and my sisters. I've loved you fiercely. But there's someone else I love who aligns with my future. With the person I want to become. So...I'm leaving the banshee clan."

She pulls her trembling hand from mine. "Why would you—"

"You would use me against Princess Rosaline, and I will never hurt her again."

"We need you, Vin. We're so close to seeing justice. We're so close to overthrowing Horus' reign—"

"I don't care, Morgana." My voice is firm yet gentle. "You may have named me for the sake of revenge, but I will not take part in it."

She shakes her head. "Trentas was right. I didn't want to believe his suspicions, but he was right, wasn't he? This great love you speak of...it's the princess."

"Yes," I say without hesitation. "I love her with all that I am. If you would cease the rivalry with the Briars, I could love you equally, but you won't. Which means I must choose. I choose her." My lungs expand with my words even as I watch my mother shrink back. What I say next will add insult to injury, but she must know the truth. "Let me make things clearer. If you do anything to try and hurt her, I will stand against you. I will fight you."

"Foolish boy," she hisses, her voice threaded with tears. "The two of you can never be. Your love is cursed. The Briars won't allow it."

"It doesn't matter what anyone allows or doesn't allow. I

don't need to be with her to love her. I will protect her even if I never see her face again."

"I don't know you," she says, and I watch as moisture drips from under her veil. Each drop is like a knife to my chest, but it's a pain I relish. A pain that severs darkness from my heart. Frees me from a burden I never should have been forced to carry. Her voice trembles with rage, with hurt, with heartache. "You're no son of mine—"

"No, I'm not." Another stab to my chest. Another release of my burden. Then, with a deep breath, I state the words that will drive the final wedge. Make the final cut. "I hereby reject the Lemuria name and renounce my place in the banshee clan. I deny all affiliation with the name Vintarys Lemuria. I swear that I am not Vintarys Lemuria and never will be again. I release all bonds of bloodline, family, and magic that are attached to said name, both past and present, and will henceforth be known only as Thorne Blackwood."

Another layer of release blossoms in my chest, making me breathe deeper than I ever have. It may simply be relief, but I hope it's more than that—that it marks the end of my cursed bond with Briony. Now that I've rejected the name Vintarys, I'll never be able to command her again. Her family will have no reason to distrust her because of me.

But buried deep inside is an additional hope.

That rescinding the name I was given will undo even the demands I made in the past.

And perhaps free the memories I forced her to forget.

Morgana trembles, head lowered, her fists curled at her sides. She sniffles, and I'm once again struck by how small and frail she is. Half of me begs to hug her. Comfort her. But I made my choice, and I don't regret it. Now I must make peace with having hurt the woman who was once my mother.

"Go," she whispers, her voice caught on a sob. Then louder. "Get out!"

I rise from the cot and give her a deep bow, the final act of deference I'll ever deliver her. It's a wordless gesture, thanking her for having loved me in the only way she knew how. A love tangled with revenge. A kind of love I fully understand even as I reject it.

I leave the room, turning my back on the woman who gave birth to me, the family I cherished, fought for, and drew blood for. With every step, I feel lighter, shedding layer after layer of the burden I was born with.

No more.

Never again.

I take no more than two steps into the hallway before I find Trentas lurking in the same spot I vacated minutes before. I can't blame him for spying on our conversation when I did the very same thing to him. Nor do I care that he knows what I did. I meet his eyes and stand before him, daring him to confront me.

He crosses his arms. "I should kill you for hurting your mother like that. For leaving the family."

"You can try." My fingers flinch at my sides, ready to fight him should it come to that. But I know his threat is empty. Trentas may seek to become Seelie King of Lunar, but he has no legal power now. Nor does my mother. Both are merely citizens, just like me, and their standing in society pales against mine. Killing me would be a punishable offense, one that could compromise Trentas' chance at the throne.

Besides, as furious as he is with me, I don't think he truly wants to hurt me.

His posture eases, as if he too has come to the same conclusions. "I truly loved you like a son, Vin—Thorne."

I'm surprised by his correction of my name. I didn't expect him to acknowledge my choice. "If you ever knew love at all, you'd understand why I'm doing this."

He studies me through slitted lids. "Is this truly the path you want?"

"Do you even need to ask?"

His expression turns thoughtful, curious. "You've changed. And I don't just mean since you were a boy."

"I know."

"Because of her."

"Briony," I say, unwilling to leave her unnamed. Unspoken.

He tilts his head, curiosity still etched in his face as if he's seeing me for the first time. The analytical assessment shows me a side of him I haven't seen before. Or if I have, I don't recall it. "I suppose you're right about me. I haven't known whatever flavor of love you've tasted. I wonder what it's like."

Pain. Pleasure. Joy. Agony. I say none of this out loud.

He clears his throat and his stern expression returns. "My spies have heard no word that the marriage between the princess and Mr. Phillips will take place."

My heart pulses a traitorous rhythm. One of hope I don't deserve to feel. "Why would you tell me that?"

"Because you assured me I'd have my chance at facing King Horus after the wedding. That Divina Briar's magic would no longer be an obstacle."

I give him a cold smile. "If you overheard what I said to Morgana then you know that's no longer any concern of mine."

"You may have left the clan, but do you honestly believe Horus deserves the throne?"

"Of course I don't. I still support you as king, but I will

not condone anything that harms the princess. What I said to Morgana applies to you too. If you hurt her—if you so much as threaten her—I will fight you. I am not above ending your life if it comes to that."

Trentas lifts his chin, assessing me once more. Then he uncrosses his arms and lowers his voice. "Then I'll tell you one last thing my spies have discovered. The king and queen have locked the woman you love in a tower."

Fiery shock ripples through me, sparking a wave of fury so hot it sears my blood. "They locked her in a fucking tower?"

Trentas gives me a cold smile. "Perhaps Lemurias aren't the ones you should be threatening with violence."

I don't know why he's told me this. Whether he's trying to help me or manipulate me into confronting his enemies, I know not. It doesn't matter. My feet fly beneath me, every beat of my heart calling Briony's name.

46

BRIONY

For three days, I've been stuck in this tower room, all the while marveling that someone used to live here. Not just anyone either, but the changeling who served as my decoy. I'm sure of it. I know because at first look, the tower room appears fit for a princess. While the room itself is small, the furnishings are fine. There's an elegant bed with silk sheets and pink brocade blankets, a wardrobe filled with flowing dresses, and a gilded vanity. The single window in the room provides a convincing look for winged spies at a bedroom made for comfort. A lovely living space for a coddled, cloistered princess.

But that benign depiction is a lie.

For this room is all there is in the tower. There are no additional chambers like my suite at Blackwood Manor. There isn't even a modern bathroom, just a chamber pot behind a dressing screen and a daily jug of lukewarm water for bathing. The single door is locked at all times save for three daily intervals when I'm given a tray of food, and the window opens to a long drop to my death should I seek to exit through it.

There's no denying that I am a prisoner.

Which means so was the changeling that lived here before me. There are signs of life everywhere. A discarded dress left at the edge of the bed, a hairbrush with strands of hair tangled in the bristles. I was disturbed enough when Mother first mentioned having kept a decoy in a tower, but now I'm filled with ice-cold dread. While I want to believe she was released, spirited away to safety after I was found to be at the convent, it's more believable that she was executed to keep silent about the role she no longer needed to play. Though there is one last possibility.

She could have escaped.

If that's the case, I wish she'd left some clue as to how. I glance around the tiny room, seeking any sign that it's possible. A hidden key in the cracked porcelain vase? Empty. A letter tucked into one of the drawers of the vanity? Also empty. I've practically turned this room upside down in my search for freedom—for what the hell else am I to do with my time?—to no avail.

Which leaves me with my current plan. With a sigh, I fall back on the bed, upon blankets that still carry the scent of someone else's skin. Then, closing my eyes, I summon my inventory of stolen memories. A guard's scowling face appears in my mind. Dark eyes, indigo hair, pointed ears. Then I move to the next image, another guard, this one with brown hair, enormous black eyes, and long white whiskers like Minka's.

My heart tightens at the latter. I haven't a clue where she and Mr. Boris are right now. Have they returned to Nocturnus Palace? Are they serving my parents again? Or are they still waiting back at Mr. Blackwood's manor? I

assume they followed by train after Thorne and I failed to
return by air—

A shiver ripples through me as I recall that lengthy
flight, my body cradled in Mr. Blackwood's arms. Why did I
ever agree to such an arrangement? I remember being
worried over the news that trouble had befallen Nocturnus
Palace, but what in the stars possessed me to trust Mr.
Blackwood enough to fly with him? Shards of broken
memories flash in my mind, of how tightly I was nestled
against him, the sound of his heart pounding against my ear
like a lullaby...

No, that can't be right. Thorne and I were only allies. We
hated each other. Everything we did over the last week was
meant to break the sleeping spell, nothing more. In fact,
what's happening now is his fault—my missing memories,
my parents' distrust, my captivity. It's all thanks to *him*.

So why does my heart ache like I've lost something treasured? Why does it feel so empty, yearning for a fullness I've
never experienced?

I shake the question from my mind and return to my
assessment of the guards I've framed. But as I study the
features of the third subject, I'm forced to admit that what
I'm doing now isn't any less unsettling than my conflicting
thoughts about Mr. Blackwood. My entire plan with the
guards hinges upon something I have no explanation for—
the fact that I know, without a doubt, that if I frame a single
subject and capture their likeness as a memory, I can pull
that person into a dream and leave them paralyzed.

That's how I plan to escape. First, I must capture the
likeness of every guard on rotation outside my room. There
are four, and they seem to change at random. The only time
I see them is when they allow a servant to enter with my
meals. Once I have all four framed, I'll make my escape,

paralyzing whichever guard opens the door. Then I'll steal his key, lock him and the servant inside, and rush to freedom. What happens after that will be a risk and a gamble, for the palace is no longer as short-staffed as it was the night of my birthday dinner. Every glance outside my window reveals archers and sentries perched on the battlements. The servants who bring my meals are ones I've never seen before.

Still, risk or not, I'm doing this.

A chill runs through me at my own conviction. How am I so certain my magic will work like I imagine? I remember my mother insisting that I share her same power as a succubus, and I distinctly recall finding proof that that is the case. Yet the proof evades me whenever I seek it. Furthermore, I know my power is different from my mother's. Where she can only operate while she's sleeping, I can only control this magic during daydreams.

But how in the name of the stars do I *know* that?

I return to my study of the guards' likenesses, mentally flipping through them one after the other and back again until I'm sure I have them memorized. I'll need to act fast, for it only takes seconds for the servant to enter and set down my meal tray before scurrying back out. Which means I must recognize the guard, summon the correct image in my mind, and cast a daydream, all in that handful of seconds. And I still have one more guard to frame.

I flip through the three images once more for good measure, but as I finish, I accidentally move to another memory, one that precedes the guards. I've stumbled upon it a few times now, and it's yet another thing that defies all reason. It's an image of an inky sky awash with glowing light, rippling with streams of stunning color. Every time I look upon it, my chest aches with loss and longing, craving something I can't recall.

Tears prick my eyes, and a wave of frustration crashes over me. Who or what do my tears concern? Why do I feel this ache whenever I glimpse this image? What the glittering hell am I missing from my mind?

My fingers tighten into fists as I let my consciousness flit over the vacant spots in my memories. I know I'll find the same resistance I always do when I try to see past them. Every attempt to remember what I've forgotten ends at a mental wall, an insurmountable slab of stone that prevents me from delving further. I expect to find that same wall now, but...

The stone is gone.

I'm so startled I bolt upright. With my eyes unfocused, I assess the voids once more, this time with renewed determination. My stomach flips as I confirm I was right. Where once there was an unrelenting wall, there's now merely a curtain of hazy black. The hollow spots remain, but they no longer feel lost to me. I shift my attention back to my memory of the colorful night sky. It remains as perplexing as ever, but as I fill my mind with that image and focus on the yearning in my heart, something gives way. The thinnest layer of the veil that covers my comprehension lifts, and the image seems to move in my mind, just a fraction. I pour my attention deeper. Open my heart further. Peel back another layer. Another.

Inch by inch, the image shifts, no longer merely a still frame I've captured. Slowly, it's becoming a true memory. As I peel back yet another layer, the vision moves. My view shifts, leaving the colorful display above and lowering down, down, inch by imaginary inch, until the tops of horns come into view. Then steadily beating wings. Black hair with a widow's peak. A forehead.

My heart pulses.

I know it's him, even before I see his dark eyes. Even before my mental gaze falls upon his smiling lips. Lips the memory version of me...wants to kiss.

The sound of my door opening drags me from my vision with violent force. My chest heaves with a gasp as I attempt to gather my bearings.

"Face me," demands a male voice. "Hands in your lap."

I do as I'm told, following the same order I'm given every time the door opens. Sit at the edge of my bed. Face the door. Hands in my lap. Like I'm a damn criminal.

A servant enters the room with my lunch tray and hurries toward the small tea table where my previous tray rests. But she isn't who I should be looking at. I banish lingering thoughts of that night sky—and Thorne's lips—from my mind and remind myself of my current objective.

Escape. Freedom. My plan.

My gaze snaps to the guard. He's the fourth and final one I need to capture. He's the shortest of them, with beady eyes, a layer of dark fur covering his skin, and a head of short gray hair. The contrasting colors and patterns of his fur and hair make me wonder if he's a honey badger in his unseelie form.

I lift my hands—my arms still trembling from the shock of uncovering a partial memory—and form a rectangle with my forefinger and thumb. I quickly frame it around the guard, and blink.

There. Captured.

His eyes narrow. "Hands down, Highness," he barks, showing a mouth of pointed teeth.

I give him a coy grin and lower my palms to my lap. "Of course."

The servant gathers up my empty breakfast tray, leaving the new one behind, and rushes from the room. With a final glare, the guard closes the door. The sound of the key securing the lock follows. I grit my teeth, realizing I still haven't discovered where on their person the guards keep the key. They never leave it showing while the door is open. So that is yet another thing I must do while my subject is paralyzed. Search their body for the key. It can't be too far, for the guards are always quick to lock the door as soon as it's closed—

A rattling sound draws my attention. I glance around my room, unsure of where it's coming from, until I notice a shift of movement on my tray. With careful steps, I approach the tea table, eyes locked on the silver domed lid that covers my dinner plate. More rattling and scratching as the dome scrapes against the porcelain plate. Then a clear yowl as it launches off the tray and crashes to the ground. I freeze in place, staring at the black-and-white creature sprawled on my plate, one leg extended where she must have kicked the lid away.

Her name rushes from my lips. "Minka?"

"Thank the night," she says, tiredly rising to all fours. "I'm so glad you didn't eat me."

I blink at her. "What are you doing here?"

She hops off the tray and onto the floor, circling my legs with a purr. "You have no idea what I went through to get served as your lunch."

I scoop her up, and she nestles against me, clearly distressed. "Yes, but...why?"

She pulls back to look at me with her wide amber eyes. "We're here to help you escape."

"We?"

"Mr. Boris too. We took the first train here, but when we arrived yesterday, we found out what happened. Thankfully, Mr. Ferdinand spoke to Mr. Boris before the king and queen found us."

I tilt my head. "Mr. Ferdinand?"

"Mr. Boris' brother."

Ah, she must mean the other fox with the bow tie.

"So," Minka smashes her face into mine in a very feline way, "we're here to help you!"

Emotion clogs my throat. I've grown so fond of Minka and Mr. Boris, but they never expressed any definite loyalty to me, especially in terms of defying my parents, but what they're doing now...

"Thank you," I say, hugging Minka a little tighter.

"Nope, I'm done." Minka flees my grasp and lands on the floor. "Now, let's go over the plan. We'll escape when your dinner arrives. Mr. Boris will be waiting at the bottom of the stairs, and he'll see that our way ahead is clear. Since the guards don't know I'm here, you'll distract whoever opens your door while I attack. I've never attacked anyone, so I'll have to do my best. I do think I can claw his eyes out, which is really all we need."

The ease with which she says the last part is unsettling, but something surfaces in my mind. An almost-memory. The knowledge that this isn't the first time I've heard her threaten someone with an eye gouging.

I'll gouge out your eyes with my claws.

Like with my sky memory, a layer peels back from this one. Then another.

I see Thorne's smiling face. *I already assured Her Highness that I'll never let her go.*

Pressure strangles my lungs.

I remember. Not everything, but I do recall *that*. He said he'd never let me go, and he said it before that too. It was during my still-hazy memory of that colorful sky.

Realizing Minka is talking again, I rouse myself back to the present. "—the guards keep your door key tied to their wrist, hidden just under the sleeve of their cuff—"

"You know where they keep the key?" Hope pulses in my chest.

"Of course. We planned well, Miss Rose."

A smile curls my lips. "Then there will be no need for clawing anyone's eyes. I too have a plan."

I convey what I intend to do. Now that I have all four guards' likenesses captured, I'll be able to paralyze whoever opens my door during tonight's dinner service. And with Mr. Boris waiting for us, prepared to clear the way ahead, I won't have to worry as much about the rest of my escape.

With the help of my friends, I'm getting the hell out of here.

47

THORNE

My reconnaissance of Nocturnus Palace tells me I'll have no luck reaching Briony by air. I give the palace a wide berth as I seek any weakness to the palace's defenses, its blind spots. But even from here, I can see just how focused the sentries and archers are, keeping their eyes to the sky, as if they expect me. Or perhaps it's Trentas they're keeping watch for. Either way, it poses a threat to my plans. I circle the palace several more times, then retreat to the woods just outside the walls, landing in the shadows of the trees.

My heart races with impatience, but I wait for night to fall. As soon as the sun sets, I launch into the sky once more and survey the palace. Stony hell. The sentries remain as alert as ever, the battlements lit with torches to illuminate even the darkest spaces between the towers.

Shit. I don't even know which tower Briony's in. I can assume she's being kept where her decoy once resided, but I only know about the changeling's tower from previous correspondence with Trentas regarding intel from his spies. Which means I'll need to search for the correct tower before I have any chance of freeing her. Yet if I fly within range of those battlements, I'll get shot down.

That leaves me only one option.

I'll need to walk straight through the palace doors and lie through my teeth.

My stomach turns. There's an equal chance I'll get killed on sight, but it's a risk I'm willing to take. Steeling my resolve, I circle back to the woods, and cross the palace walls near one of the many gardens. From there I make no secret of my presence, do nothing to mask the sound of my footsteps. Instead, I stroll directly onto the path of a trio of guards on patrol. They freeze at the sight of me, hands flying to the hilts of their swords.

"Still your hands," I say, voice bellowing, "or Princess Rosaline dies. Unless you want her death on your conscience, grant me an audience with the king at once."

BRIONY

It's agony waiting for dinner to arrive. I'm so anxious that I don't touch the food that arrived with lunch. Not that there was much left with Minka having taken the place of my entrée. My stomach is a roiling mess and my nerves even more so. All I can do is watch day turn to night and practice casting dreamscapes with increasing speed. I dare not practice on any of my subjects in case they catch on to my abilities and jeopardize our plan, but Minka lets me capture her likeness. She's amused by my magic and marvels at my different dreamscapes. By sunset, I'm fairly confident I can

paralyze a subject in approximately five seconds. That's
plenty of time.

Right?

The turn of the key in my door silences me and Minka.
We exchange a nod. I take a seat at the edge of my bed,
getting into the position the guard will order me to take
upon entry while Minka pads over to the far wall. Still in her
unseelie form, she crouches near the door. Her slitted pupils
grow large and round as the handle turns. Her rear shifts
back and forth as she prepares to pounce.

Not to claw the guard's eyes out, as I've had to remind
her several times during our planning sessions, but to
steal the key. That's her duty while I have the guard
paralyzed.

The door swings open.

"Face me, hands in your lap," says a tired voice. I'm
already seated, so I make a show of splaying my hands over
my thighs. Meanwhile, I assess the guard, identifying him as
the one with indigo hair.

The servant hurries in, dinner tray in hand.

Breathing deep, I cast a dreamscape only I can see—one
I framed just hours ago, depicting this very bedroom.

The servant sets down my dinner and exchanges it for
the lunch tray.

I summon a vision of the blue-haired guard in my
mind's eye.

Blinking, I pull him into the daydream.

"Now," I say to Minka.

A clatter of dishware. Then a yelp from the servant.
While the servant has been excluded from my dreamscape,
I can still hear her, and her alarm tells me Minka must have
made her move.

The dream version of the guard frowns, oblivious to

what's happening outside the dreamscape. His eyes widen as he notes the servant's absence. "Where the hell—"

"I have to go now." I rise from the bed and approach the guard. "You will have to stay here. You as well, though I do apologize." I say the last part in the direction where I heard the servant drop her tray.

"You aren't going anywhere," the dream-guard says. His hand flies to where his sword should be, but of course, I've made sure not to include it in his dream form. A memory tugs at my mind, one still buried beneath a haze. It's clear enough to tell me I can control what people wear or don't wear.

The *don't wear* part stands out the most. Followed by a tantalizing recollection of inked naked flesh...

This is the worst time to uncover lost memories, so I force it away. Funneling all my attention into holding the guard in place, I brush past him and out the door. My vision grows faint and vertigo seizes me as I fight to maintain the dreamscape. It's a challenge considering I'm now standing on the other side of the threshold in reality yet remain in the bedroom inside the dreamscape. That's what happens when I dream. My dreamscapes move with me. I cannot exit one without freeing my subject too. This is again something I'm not sure how I know, but I'm starting to suspect it has every-thing to do with Thorne Blackwood. My increasingly persis-tent emotions. The memories that have begun to surface.

The dream-guard whirls to face me but halts. With how my dreamscape has shifted with me, I appear to be standing before my bed once more. He blinks a few times then shakes his head. "Sit down," he orders through his teeth.

"No."

The sound of the door slamming secures my victory, followed by the scrape of the key in the lock. With a gasp, I release the dreamscape and find Minka standing before me in her seelie form. A wide grin splits her face, and she tugs the key from the now-locked door. Muffled voices call out from the other side, followed by the slam of a fist.

"We should hurry," Minka says. With a shudder, she shrinks back down to her feline form and sprints down the stairs. I follow her down the dark stairwell, lit only by the occasional sconce. Thankfully, the frantic voices of the trapped servant and guard don't carry far. Though I suppose if they think to call outside the window, they may be able to draw attention. My heart climbs high in my throat as we reach the bottom of the staircase. I expect other guards to round the corner any moment—

"Oh, thank the All of All." I'm both startled and relieved at the familiar voice. Mr. Boris, in his fox form, pads into view from around the next corner. He rushes to us. "You did it. You really did it."

I'm so happy to see him I have to keep myself from scooping him up and squeezing him like I did Minka. Mr. Boris isn't nearly as affectionate as she is, so I doubt that would go over well. Instead, I settle on a simple, "Thank you, Mr. Boris."

"Unfortunately, I didn't have to claw anyone's eyes out," Minka says.

Mr. Boris' muzzle pulls into a fox version of a grimace. "*Un*fortunately? Minka, dear, I daresay you have the strangest priorities. Now, come along. I've learned everything I can about the guards' rotations. The path should be clear enough."

He starts off down the hall and Minka and I follow, keeping our steps swift yet quiet.

"All we have to do is get you out to the garden," Mr. Boris says, his deep voice pitched with mild panic. "There's a portion of the fence you can climb over without being spotted. Though I haven't a clue how we'll be able to get you to climb such a high wall—"

"That's a problem for later," Minka says. "Let's just get outside."

We reach the end of the next hall. Mr. Boris orders us to hold back while he investigates the way ahead. My heart riots in my chest every second that he's gone. Finally, he peeks at us from around the corner. "It's clear."

Our journey continues in much the same way. Proceed. Pause. Proceed. Pause. Stars, I haven't a clue how close we are to our destination. I was hardly of sound mind when the guards hauled me to the tower, and when I arrived the night of my birthday dinner, I was too overwhelmed by the sheer size and splendor of the palace to grasp its layout.

We reach a narrow staircase, one I assume is reserved for servants based on its lack of adornment. With one side open save for its oak railing, I feel exposed. If anyone walked by now, they'd spot us. I wish I'd brought a cloak or something to mask my appearance. Though it isn't exactly inconspicuous to wander around in a cloak either. In fact, such an obvious disguise would scream *Greetings, I'm suspicious.*

Mr. Boris must be as apprehensive as I am, for he guides us down the staircase one step at a time, our pace agonizingly slow. My feet beg to run, but I hold back. Just one step. Then the next. Then the—

Movement shoots past the bottom of the stairs, a guard rushing down the hall at the bottom. I freeze, my pulse speeding. But the guard pays us no heed. Nor does the one who follows.

"That's odd," Mr. Boris mutters.

"That they didn't see us?" I whisper.

"No, that they're here at all. This is the servants' hall that leads to the west gardens. Guards don't patrol here, though the western barracks are in the direction they came from."

"Is that bad?"

"Well, those two did just run toward our destination." Mr. Boris paces on the stair, a worried whine humming in his throat.

"I'll go see what's happened," Minka says, and pads down the stairs.

"It's dangerous," Mr. Boris hisses.

She cuts him an irritated look. "I am stealth incarnate. Do not doubt me." With that, she slinks the rest of the way down the staircase and rushes down the hall.

Mr. Boris and I retreat up the steps, keeping close to the wall to evade the notice of any other guards who might follow after the first two. The wait sends my stomach roiling, my already ragged nerves fraying further.

"Why are you doing this for me?" I whisper, eager for a distraction.

"Hmm?" Mr. Boris glances up at me before returning his attention to the hall below. "You mean why am I helping you escape? I took on the duty as your bodyguard, and you have yet to dismiss me."

A small smile forms on my lips. "Technically, I appointed you as my butler, remember?"

"Yes, well, I took it upon myself to act as your bodyguard, Highness. I will not let you down now."

"What about your standing with my parents? If they find out you aided my escape...I fear what they'll do to you."

He's silent for a few moments. Then, "I have no intention of getting caught, Highness. Nor will I serve them if this is how they treat you. I...I have always respected and obeyed them, even trusted that the darker rumors about their actions were untrue. But this is where I draw the line." He glances over his shoulder. "I'm very fond of you, Highness. I have no children of my own, but...but I think this might be how it feels to have one. I cannot let harm come to you. Once we escape, I hope you'll allow me to remain in your service."

Tears prick my eyes. Mr. Boris cares for me...like a child of his own. We aren't related by blood and yet he's the one protecting me where my parents are not.

Is this what family truly means?

Is this what it's been all along?

"I have good news and bad news." Minka appears on the stairs before us, making both me and Mr. Boris jump. Stars above, she really is stealth incarnate.

"What's the good news?" I whisper.

"While there are plenty of guards down here," she says, "they are distracted. If we're quiet, we can skirt behind them and escape to the garden without being seen."

"And the bad news?" Mr. Boris asks, his tone brimming with trepidation.

Minka tilts her head in a questioning look. "Well, this might be good news too, come to think of it. I suppose it depends how Miss Rose feels about her former enemy-turned-ally-turned...whatever they became after that."

My heart skitters. She must be referring to Thorne. "What do you mean?"

She angles her head toward the end of the hall. "That's the reason the guards are so distracted. They've captured Mr. Blackwood."

48

THORNE

My demand for an audience with the king is granted, but instead of being escorted into the throne room where a proper audience would be held, I'm taken just beyond a plain door that leads from the garden to the palace. A servants' entrance, based on its innocuous appearance and almost-hidden location. We enter a dim narrow hallway that confirms my assumptions, and the guards order me to halt once we pass an empty corridor. The placement is strategic. Servants' halls. Windowless. A corridor behind and before us, allowing reinforcements to enter from both sides should the guards need them. The perfect place for an unseen execution.

The guards surround me in a circle, their swords pointed at my neck. I stand with controlled calm, my hands folded behind my back just under my wings, chin lifted as if to aid their desires to sever my head from my neck.

"Don't move," one of the guards shouts.

"I wouldn't dream of it," I say with a wink. Everything

inside me rages at being surrounded like this. I'm desperate to break free, to storm the palace and search for Briony. But I have a plan. One that requires a lot of risk and just a little more patience.

After what feels like a too-quiet eternity, footsteps sound from the hall ahead, and I see the king and queen sweep toward me, flanked by several guards. Horus' small black eyes narrow on me, his gray lips pulling back from his serrated teeth. "What is the meaning of this threat on my daughter's life?"

"Speak," Divina shouts, even though my lips were already parted in preparation to do exactly that.

My eyes lock on the king's. I keep my voice even, steady, ignoring the circle of blades that still surround me as I deliver my calculated lie. "The princess will stop breathing by midnight unless I counter the command and revoke it in person."

Divina's eyes widen, her cheeks reddening with anger while Horus goes a shade of pale gray. "When did you issue this command?" the king asks.

"It was merely a failsafe I put in place at her birthday party. One that would prevent her from speaking against me if she's ever imprisoned by her family."

The lie pinches my heart. I would so much rather tell the truth—that I never gave such a horrendous command. That I no longer have the power to command her at all. That I gave up my birth name, my affiliation with the Lemurias, to rid us of this dangerous bond.

But they would never believe that. Why would they? I've managed to deceive them once before. They may not know the full truth of my half-human parentage, but they must suspect I can lie. It's better to tell one they'll believe.

"I know you love your daughter," I say, "so let us make a

bargain. Release her from the tower, promise to never lock her up again, and I will revoke every command I've ever made of her and promise never to command her in any way for as long as I live."

The king and queen assess me in icy silence.

Finally, Horus speaks. "Why? You are our enemy. If we refuse this bargain, our daughter will die, and your family will have another tally against us in their revenge schemes. So why offer this bargain at all?"

I bristle at how easily he speaks of his daughter dying. Though I suppose I spoke smoothly of the same topic. Is his indifference a bluff like mine is?

"Answer the question," Divina says through her teeth.

I release a heavy sigh. It's time to weave truth into my lie. To bare my heart.

"Because I'm in love with your daughter."

BRIONY

Thorne's words wrench my heart, halting me in place. He's too far down the hall for me to see him, what with the dim lighting and the guards surrounding him, but his voice...

Stars above, that voice. Those words.

I know I shouldn't stop. I should move. Flee. I'm so close to freedom. All I have to do is round the corner of this corridor and sneak down the next. After that, it's a short sprint to the garden door. This is my chance while the guards and my parents are distracted. While all eyes are on Thorne.

My enemy.

The man responsible for my current plight.

That's what my mind says, at least. My heart is another matter. It swells with warmth at his words, stripping more and more layers away from that dark veil clouding my memories. I cling to the wall at the corner of the dark hall. Minka nudges my ankle, silently prompting me forward.

But I can't move.

As the warmth spreads from my heart, shearing back more and more layers of that veil, memories flood my mind. They strike me one after the next with dizzying force, completely out of order. My knees tremble, and I clasp the wall tighter. It's all I can do to keep from sliding to my knees.

My memory of the colorful night sky spreads out from beginning to end. I see Thorne's beautiful smile in full, one I only glimpsed briefly earlier today. Then I recall the gazebo. The feel of his lips on mine. I remember the dancing slippers, the kissing game. I recall the first time I ever saw him, standing in the Starcane field at the convent. How I captured his likeness in a frame. How I dreamed of him often in the two years since.

And *that one dream.*

Stars, that dream.

Then him cleaning my wound in the kitchen.

Him making me flustered again and again.

Him stealing my heart.

Everything collides, shifting into place in my mind. Finally, my most recent lost memory surfaces. Of him commanding me to forget I loved him. Of him putting my happiness before his own. And his confession.

I won't let you tell me you love me.

But let me say it once to you.

I love you.

A sob rips through me, one woven with sorrow and rage.

I smother it down and catch my breath, heaving lungfuls of air as tears leak from my eyes.

"Highness," Mr. Boris whispers, eyes darting between the hall that leads to our escape and the distracted guards.

"I'm not asking for your blessing," Thorne says. His voice carries down the hall, sending warm shivers down my arms, my spine. How could I have forgotten how much I love the sound of his voice? "I'm asking you to treat her well. To love and trust her the way she deserves."

"We must go," Mr. Boris says, eyes pleading. "This is our best chance."

"Unless..." Minka stares up at me with her head tilted to the side. "Was I right, Miss Rose? That this is bad news?"

I give a shaky nod.

"Very well." Minka lifts a paw, claws extended, and gives me a questioning look. "Eye gouging?"

"What? No?" My voice is a rough whisper. "The two of you run to freedom. I..."

Stars, what *do* I intend to do?

My father's voice echoes down the hall. "If we kill you, your control over my daughter ends. The sleeping spell is broken, which means we can shed your blood to our heart's content without repercussions."

My heart slams against my ribs. I straighten and push off the wall. My feet move before my mind knows what I'm doing.

"Try me," Thorne says, his voice like a growl.

Then comes my mother's voice. "Kill him."

The guards surge inward. I catch sight of wings splaying wide from within the ring of soldiers. They knock a couple aside, but there are too many more surrounding him.

Rage and terror spark a fire in me, igniting something bright and warm and terrible—my magic. I reach for it, drawing it up. I don't know how it will help or if it will, only that it's all I have.

And I'll use everything at my disposal to save the man I love.

"Stop!" The shout emerges from my lips as my magic surges outward. The colorful night sky blankets the hall, melting the walls and absorbing the floor until we appear to be floating midair. Based on the sudden shouts that erupt from the guards, the way they stumble back, steps uneven... they can see it too.

I have no time to marvel at that. No time to think of anything else as I shove my way past the terrified soldiers and plant myself in front of Thorne. Firm hands grasp my shoulders, but as they whirl me around, I see they belong to him. His wings splay out wide, knocking more guards off their feet.

"What the stony hell are you doing here?" he asks, voice strained with either worry, fear, or anger. Perhaps all three.

I shrug from his grasp. "What does it look like? The question is, why are *you* here?"

"I came to rescue you."

"I already saved myself, you idiot."

Something tugs at my skirt, and I find Minka climbing up my skirt until she's perched on my shoulder. She scoffs. "Oh, did you now?"

"I had help," I amend.

Thorne surges back suddenly, pulling me with him. A blade cuts the air just above my head, missing us by mere inches. Thorne's wing slashes out, and one of the taloned joints at the end of his wing slices through the guard's throat in a spray of blood.

"Stand down," comes my father's bellowing voice. "Now!"

The hall goes silent, aside from the grunts of the dying guard. I turn away from Thorne, but his arm encircles my waist, pulling me close to him. Minka hisses from her perch on my shoulder, while something presses against the front of my legs. It's Mr. Boris, and his teeth are bared at the king and queen. My parents stand frozen, colors flashing over their faces, painted by my illusion. Father's hand remains outstretched in a silent order for his guards to remain at ease while Mother stares at me as if she's never seen me before.

"Rosaline." Father's voice trembles. His shoulders visibly hunch, lips pulling into a frown. Is that guilt I see twisting his features? "You...you shouldn't be here."

"Yes, I suppose you liked me better in my tower," I bite back.

"That was for your own protection," he says. "Now get away from that vile beast and we will end this once and for all."

"No."

Irritation flashes over his face. "You don't know what you're doing right now. You're under the influence of his power over you."

"I'm not, Horus." He flinches back at me calling him by his first name. Not Father. Not Papa. "Yes, he's made commands of me before, but in this moment I am acting of my own free will. If you come near us, I will fight you. I will freeze every one of your guards in place—"

"And I will claw their eyes out," Minka says.

"And I...I will bite." Mr. Boris' voice is far less confident.

Mother's eyes go wide. Then a slow smile spreads over her lips. She gestures toward the dreamscape-laden ceiling. "Lovey, are you doing this?"

"I am."

Her face brightens with joy, an obscene expression when one of her guards lies dying in a pool of blood near her feet. "You're a daydream succubus? Rosaline, that's the most fantastic news—"

"Oh, now you see value in me?"

She frowns as if she can't comprehend the venom in my words.

Darkness and warmth mingle in my heart, a vicious concoction that has tears pricking at my eyes. "I loved you so much," I say, voice quavering. "Even as strangers, I loved you. You were my family, and I wanted to give you everything. Yet you gave nothing back."

Mother moves closer, stepping over the dead body of her guard as if he's nothing more than a fixture on the floor. Mr. Boris barks a warning, and she halts her progress. Her soft smile remains on her face. "That's not true, Rosaline. We've always loved you. We looked for you for years. You know this."

Thorne's grip around my waist tightens the slightest fraction, as if to remind me he's here. Holding me. Protecting my back. I sink into his touch, turn some of my burden over to him as I utter words I've suspected all along. "Let me guess, Divina. You didn't start looking for me until after you promised my hand to Lord Phillips' son."

Her smile falters. "That's hardly relevant. If I say I've always loved you, then it must be true."

I shake my head. "Your love may be true but it's less than I deserve."

"Don't speak to your mother like that," Father says. "We're your family. Your blood."

"Blood, yes. But family?" I swallow the lump in my throat. "I never realized until now, but I've known family all my life. My teachers at the convent were my family, as were my friends and peers. It only took a matter of days for Mr. Boris and Minka to feel like family. And now...Thorne is as good as family too, because he's the future I choose."

He stiffens behind me. My name leaves his lips in a whisper. "Briony..."

"Yes, you asshole," I mutter, angling my head to meet his eyes. "I remember everything. Did you not believe me when I promised to claw my way back to my memories?"

A crooked smile forms on his mouth, but his gaze is dark. Intense. Like an oncoming storm, both beautiful and deadly at once.

I force my eyes away from his lest they distract me from the matter at hand. "I have a few choice words for you," I say under my breath, "but we'll talk later."

"Rosaline, please," Mother says, "enough with this nonsense. If you truly want to keep Morgana's boy as your plaything, we'll make a bargain. Just step away from him and we'll talk this through."

"No. We aren't bargaining. You have only one choice, and that is to let us walk out of here unharmed. Me, Thorne, Minka, and Mr. Boris. We're leaving and you're letting us go. Refuse, and I'll destroy you. I can do more than cast pretty illusions." The words almost sear my tongue. While they're true, I can already feel my hold over my magic slipping. I'm not sure I can react fast enough to frame and capture each guard that surrounds us, should they resume their attack.

"You cannot threaten your family like this," Father says, teeth bared.

"If that were true, you wouldn't have set such a stunning precedent with me."

"You cannot threaten your *king*."

I arch a brow. "Is that who you are to me then? It's up to

you. Are you my father or my king? Am I your beloved daughter or someone to subjugate?"

He holds my gaze, and for a moment he looks nothing like the kind, bashful man I met at my dinner party. Then his expression softens, and that same guilt I glimpsed earlier returns to his face. "I'm your father, Rosaline, and you are my cherished child. I never wanted to hurt you. Everything I've done has been to protect you."

"I believe you," I say, for I'm sure his intentions were pure from his point of view. That doesn't mean I agree with them. My voice comes out hollow. "I don't hate you, nor do I like you. Maybe there's hope for us in the future, but that starts with you letting me go."

Father's beady gaze darts from me to his guards. Soon I'll know the truth about him. Would he rather risk my life and save his pride? Is he more concerned with keeping me under his control, more invested in revenge, than he is with my happiness? My wants?

"Horus," Mother says in a sing-song voice. "Why are you hesitating?"

He purses his lips.

Mother's expression flashes with rage as she rounds on her husband. "Let them go, Horus!"

His gaze whips to Mother's, surprise tugging his mouth. "Divina—"

"She's our daughter. What is there to think about?"

He shakes his head as if coming out of a daze. His shoulders tremble. "You...you're right. Rosaline...go."

I nearly take off at his words, but I know better than to take a step before I've secured a binding vow. "Promise me you will let us leave unharmed and unpunished. Swear that you'll send no one after us, that you'll release me, Minka, and Mr. Boris from all obligations as your subjects. That you'll let Thorne walk free with us."

Father does as I've requested, stating each term, his voice quavering over every word. Mother chimes in with an eager, "I swear to every term too."

With that, Father waves at his guards and they step away, sheathing their swords and filing along the wall. I study my parents for a few silent moments, seeking any sign that I've left too much room in their promise. Father watches me with a tortured expression while Mother dons another one of her out-of-place smiles. Finally, Thorne takes my hand in his and folds his wings down his back. Minka lets out a last hiss at my parents, and we collectively turn down the hall and make our way toward freedom.

"Rosaline," Mother calls, and my back stiffens. Her footsteps don't follow, only her too-sweet voice. "We'll see each other again, lovey! I'll write to you. I'll be a better mother, I promise."

Her words do nothing to my heart. If she wants me to believe that, she'll need to do more than write a few pretty letters. I swallow my reply and quicken my pace. Hand in hand with Thorne, I leave my family behind and exit with those who feel far more deserving of that term.

49

BRIONY

As promised, no one shadows our retreat as we rush outside to the garden. Once we're several yards from the palace, Thorne turns me to face him. "We should fly. I want to get you away from here before anyone has a chance to change their mind."

"Good plan," Mr. Boris says before I can answer. "Get Her Highness off palace grounds. Minka and I will climb the western wall. We can reconvene at Blue Moon Lake. Do you know it?"

Thorne nods.

"Don't drop her or I'll kill you," Minka says sweetly as she launches off my shoulder. Together she and Mr. Boris sprint for the wall.

A shudder of apprehension ripples through me now that I'm alone with Thorne. I haven't had a chance to fully reconcile my recovered memories, and he and I have...a lot to talk about.

He seems to feel the same trepidation, as he stares down

at me with a furrowed brow. Then, extending a hand, he asks, "May I?"

"Yes," I say, stepping closer. He crouches down, lifting me beneath my knees and back. I encircle his neck with my arms and rest my head against his chest, lulled by the sound of his heart, the familiar scent of his skin.

How could I have forgotten this?

Splaying his wings out wide, he leaps up, and we shoot into the sky. We fly in tense silence, and once I feel our momentum shift, I realize our flight is almost at an end. My pulse quickens. While I know we need to talk, I almost wish our journey was longer, if only to give me time to gather the courage I'll need to say what I'm prepared to say. But my wish isn't granted, and too soon we land on the grassy shore of a small lake surrounded by towering trees. No wonder Mr. Boris suggested this sheltered location to reunite at.

Thorne sets me on my feet, every move slow as he releases me with clear reluctance. I stand facing him, hardly daring to meet his eyes.

"I'm so sorry." His voice is a strangled whisper. "For everything I—"

"No," I say, lifting my eyes to meet his. I clench my jaw, grinding my next words between my teeth. "You shut up and listen now. I told you I had a few choice words for you, and I meant that. I have exactly three."

His throat bobs, but he says nothing, ready to accept whatever vitriol I spit his way.

I tick each of the three words off on my fingers, a glare burning in my eyes. "I. Love. You."

∽

THORNE

I blink at her a few times, not daring to believe what my ears heard. "What?"

She props her hands on her hips and steps closer, angling her chin to keep her eyes locked with mine. "I thought I'd get to say that with kindness, but instead I have to convey it with anger because I'm *so* mad at you."

"You have every right to be," I rush to say. I'm still reeling from her declaration.

"Damn right I do," she says. Then her shoulders sink and some of the tension leaves her posture. Her eyes release mine and she lowers her face. Her forehead lands on my chest.

My fingers burn to touch her, to hold her, but I'm not sure whether she wants my embrace or to rail at me more. I will not touch her until she's ready for that. I will not try to smooth this over with caresses and kisses. What I did to her —stealing her memories, breaking the sleeping spell—may have felt like the right thing to do in the moment, but it ended up putting her in danger. It pitted her against her family when my binding promise to do whatever it took to wake them was supposed to bring them together.

What I did was wrong.

Fuck, have I ever done anything right by her?

I fight back my roaring urge to hold her and keep my hands at my sides.

"But this is fitting for us, isn't it?" she whispers against my chest. "Love and anger entwined. Stars, I love you so damn much but I hate what you did."

My heart slams against my ribs. "I love you too, Briony."

She lifts her head and grasps the front of my shirt in her hands. "Don't ever command me again. I won't ask you to make a bargain like you tried to make with my family, but—"

"The cursed bond is broken," I say. "I revoked my birth name and left the Lemurias. I am no longer Vintarys. The meaning of my name isn't *iron* anymore, which means you cannot be bound by me. My name is Thorne Blackwood. *Only* Thorne Blackwood."

Her eyes go wide. "You left your family?"

I nod. "It was the best way to set you free from my power over you."

"Oh." Her hold loosens around my shirt as her brow knits into a furrow. "Why aren't you touching me?"

My chest tightens at the question. "I didn't want to until you were ready. Until you've lashed out at me in all your rage."

"Why?"

"Because as soon as I touch you, I won't be able to let you go." My fingers flinch, eager for the feel of her. "So until you've given me all your hatred like I deserve, I'm keeping my hands to myself."

Her expression softens with a coy smile. She slides one hand up my chest, then behind my neck. The other caresses my collarbone, sending a shiver down my back. "You're out of luck there, Thorne," she says, voice soft. "I'll never be done being angry at you. I'm sure you'll enrage me a thousand times more after this. But that doesn't lessen my love. I love you, Thorne. I love you in all my anger. All my rage. All my passion. I love you fiercely."

Her words pierce my heart, but not with pain. With warmth. With...hope. Do I dare accept that? "You know I don't deserve you, right?"

She narrows her eyes. "You don't get to decide that. I do. And I've chosen you."

"You've chosen me over your family. Will you come to regret that?"

She scoffs. "You've got some nerve assuming I'm doing all of this for you. I left my family for *me*. Got it?" Her hand leaves my collarbone to prod my chest with her forefinger. It reminds me of when she did the same thing when we stood on her balcony before I took her to see the stars. She said something similar then. That I deserve to be cared for and have to accept that as a fact.

A layer of darkness melts beneath the increasing warmth in my chest. "Got it."

She splays her hand over my heart and squints at me. "You didn't leave your family just for me, did you?"

I know the right answer. That I left them out of a sudden awakening to my family's wrongs, that I realized she was right about both our families being corrupt. But the truth is, if I hadn't met Briony Rose and fallen in love with her, if she hadn't so deeply changed me in ways she doesn't yet know, I would be with my family still. I would have no reason to doubt them or my place in the clan as a tool for revenge.

I left my family to save Briony.

I'm not sure what that makes me. A good man would have stood against my family long ago and never would have done what I did at Briony's birthday party. An honorable man would have stuck with my family at all costs, holding promises of family and duty over matters of the heart. But as I've already surmised, I am neither good nor honorable. Nor do I have any intention to be on a grand scale. All I want is to be a better version of myself. The one Briony sees. The one she deems worthy of forgiveness, of love, and to stand at her side.

I don't know what kind of man I am, and I honestly don't

care. A liar, a lover, a villain. I'll be all that and more. For her.

"Yes," I say, lying in a way that isn't at all a lie. "I left my clan entirely for me."

"Good," she says, wrapping both arms behind my neck. "Then kiss me already."

My lips crash into hers, my arms tugging her against me. She angles her head to deepen the kiss, her tongue sweeping against mine with desperate need. Stones, I love her. The taste of her anger. The softness of her affection. I relay this with every caress of my lips, every breath I exhale against her mouth.

The sound of rustling grass has us stilling in each other's arms.

"Should we come back later?" Minka's voice says from somewhere in the grass beyond the lake's shore.

Briony's lips leave mine, but she keeps her hands on my chest. A shy smile curves her sensuous mouth. "That's all right," she says with a sigh, and we partially turn to face the two heads that peek above the tall grass, one feline, one vulpine.

"I see you've made up," Minka says.

Mr. Boris lowers his head. "I admit I didn't fully see this coming. Did I miss something?"

Minka's tone is pandering as she says, "I'll explain later. You don't understand because you aren't a romantic."

He scoffs and whirls to face her. "I...I could be."

Minka arches her back. "Don't look at me, I'm not interested."

"I didn't say I was!"

"You should be. I'm very cute."

"I...well, yes, I know you are! But I'm more mature than you."

"I'm three hundred years old! I'm older than you by two decades!"

"Then...why do you act like a child?"

Briony chuckles as the two continue to bicker back and forth. Then, shifting in my arms until she's facing me fully again, she asks, "What happens next?"

A ripple of anxiety rushes through me as I realize I don't know the answer. I may have left the Lemurias, but that doesn't mean there won't be repercussions. My birth identity will most likely still get out. I have no doubt Morgana will do whatever it takes to regain her standing in society, and that will probably draw attention. The public is even more brutal when it comes to gossip and invading private matters than it was before the Lemurias fell under the sleeping spell. I wouldn't be surprised if her return from slumber spreads through every paper across the isle.

The same goes for Briony's parents. Word of what happened at Nocturnus Palace the night Trentas sparked conflict amongst the contenders to the throne will spread, as will tonight's events, to at least some degree. Briony and I both stand to become fodder for gossip.

But as she reaches for my neck and runs her fingers over my nape, all my worries melt away, burned by that ever-expanding warmth that glows in my chest.

"I don't know," I finally say, "but whatever happens next, we'll face it together."

Her lips curl in a smile tinged with sadness. She too must realize that the path ahead may be littered with at least a few obstacles.

"We will," she whispers and plants a soft kiss over my lips.

Mr. Boris' mocking tone shatters the moment. "As intrigued as I am by your *lesson in love*, Minka, this is hardly the time or place. We should make haste from the Lunar Court at once."

Minka huffs and turns her back on Mr. Boris. "I have to agree."

I hold back a laugh and take a step back, lacing my fingers through Briony's. "Shall the four of us head home then? If we walk quickly, we can catch a late-night train downtown."

Her eyes widen at the word *home*. Then her expression melts into the most achingly beautiful smile. "Home. Yes. Let's go home."

EPILOGUE

ONE YEAR LATER

BRIONY

Music spills from the horn of my phonograph, flooding the room with a beautiful melody. "One, two, three, one, two, three," I repeat with the beat, sweeping through the room alongside the dozen giggling girls. They dance with invisible partners, much like I used to do in my glade. The smallest girl trips over her feet. I catch her before she falls and help her synchronize her steps with the song. "One, two, three, one, two, three. Light on your feet. Now turn."

The children follow my instruction, but the dance lesson is more like play than anything. Their grins tell me each girl is enjoying herself, their happy faces illuminated by the glittering night sky I've cast over the parlor at the convent.

Over the past year, I've learned I only need strong emotions to cast dreamscapes that others can see. While arousal certainly works, as I discovered with Thorne the first time it happened, and anger, like it did when I came to his defense at Nocturnus Palace, I find love and joy are equally as strong. Minka has told me I should hone my ability and apply it in some impressive way, but I find this suits me far better—using it to make the students at the Celesta Convent School for Girls smile.

The waltz comes to an end and I exchange the cylinder on my phonograph for another. A new song begins to play, one with an exuberant beat. The girls immediately begin bouncing on the balls of their feet in anticipation of the gallopade. It always seems to be a favorite. I guide them into the frolicking dance, skipping side to side, then turning. The corners of my lips stretch wide, and my dreamscape grows even brighter.

I catch sight of a figure standing at the edge of my illusion. It's Sister Marsh, and since I can only see half of her, I assume she's peeking through the doorway from outside the hall. Her usually stern lips are pressed into a tight smile as she watches the joyful display. Our eyes meet, and she gives me an approving nod before disappearing back into the hall.

When I first visited my former teachers to deliver my proposal—that I'd volunteer at the convent once a month to teach dance lessons to the girls—I thought Marsh would be the most difficult to persuade. But she agreed before I said another word. What she did balk at was my request that the girls be allowed to wear colorful dresses during the lessons. She eventually conceded that they could wear colored pinafores over their gray dresses, but they all needed to be the same color. That sparked a war between Agatha and Spruce as they fought over blue and pink. I didn't see how their argument ended, but I assume it was in some magical mishap, for by the time I returned for my first lesson, each girl was outfitted in a pinafore splattered in haphazard blotches of both colors. The children were thrilled, and though the final result was a bit messy, it fulfilled Marsh's term that they all be the same color.

I'm out of breath by the time the lesson comes to an end, as are all the girls, but a little fatigue isn't anything cake can't cure. After the girls hand over their pinafores and we store them away for next time, I lead them into the kitchen where a two-tiered cake rests. It's from Blackwood Bakery, of course, for I wouldn't dream of visiting the convent without a gift from Thorne.

Spruce and Agatha greet me with warm smiles and kisses on the cheek before doling out slices of cake. Tilly, the little white bunny fae who was always so fond of me when I was a student, climbs upon my lap. A pang of nostalgia strikes me, but it's a pleasant sort of pain. I glance around the room filled with both familiar faces and new. Lina, of course, is absent, as she has returned to her parents. I was able to get her address from my teachers, and we've been exchanging letters. As she'd so smugly declared a year ago, she snagged a husband by the end of her first social season. We plan on reuniting at Blackwood Estate when she and her husband come to visit next month.

Dorothy is absent as well, as she officially took her vows as a sister and is likely tending the Starcane fields right now, but I'll be sure to visit her before I leave.

As soon as we finish the cake, it's time for hugs and tearful goodbyes. It's always hard to leave the convent, for these girls and my teachers are very much my family. But I have more family waiting for me elsewhere and much to look forward to at home.

～

HOME HAS BECOME A REVOLVING LOCATION, AND TRAVEL HAS become a staple in my life. With so many bakeries under Thorne's care—and the stringent expectations that go with said care—I find myself staying in a new city for at least a week out of every month. This week, *home* means the city of Lumenas. It's a lengthy train ride from the convent, despite being in the same court, and I don't arrive until the following evening. The bright lights of the city greet me as soon as I step off the train platform. I hail a hansom cab and give the coachman the address.

Our progress is slow, the streets crammed with other horse-drawn carriages and even the occasional automobile. That's no surprise, for Lumenas is a city famed for its busy nightlife. Music blares from every corner while street performers crowd the sidewalks, drawing curious spectators.

I fell in love with this city back when my three teachers took me and the other older girls to see the ballet. I grew even more enamored when I stayed here an extra week for the bridal pageant I participated in. And I love the city still. It is that love that convinced Thorne to open his newest branch of Blackwood Bakery here, despite this being the absolute last place he wants to be.

I chuckle to myself as I watch brightly lit marquees and storefronts pass my window. Thorne may have changed quite a bit since we first met, but he's still fond of his long stretches of silence and reading his broadsheets uninterrupted. I do my best to give him that time and not pester him with conversation. It is a challenge, however, for I still don't like being bored. More than that, I still very much enjoy annoying him.

My cab finally rolls to a stop on one of the quieter streets in the city. Here only a few of the storefronts are lit, as most others are closed for the day. I pay the fare and enter the front door beneath a sign that reads *Modest Minka's*. The room is dark and moody, lit by strings of glowing bulbs that hang from the ceiling. The scent of fae wine and ale fill the air, along with the sound of raucous laughter. The public house is crowded, but I spot Minka in her feline form strutting across the long countertop at the far end of the room.

Near the bar, I see a familiar figure slumped on a stool, his curly blond head bowed as he nurses an overfull cup of ale. What the hell is Monty doing here? While his and Thorne's relationship has begun to improve over the last year, we don't see him often. Not as often as we see Angela, whom we visit at least monthly. After being expelled from the Phillips family, Monty had to debut in the workplace. I hear he now has a job in journalism or publishing. Still, he seems to be in quite a mood, and I'd rather not provide an ear for his problems. That's what *Modest Minka's* is for.

I'm about to scurry into the kitchen before Monty can spot me, but curiosity draws my eyes back to the bar. Upon the counter rests a long row of tumblers filled with some golden liquid. Smaller glasses containing a different liquid are interspersed between the larger ones, balanced on the cups' rims. I pause, wondering what in the name of the stars Minka is up to. It doesn't take long to find out, for she saunters over to one end of the row, bats the first tiny glass with a paw, and sends it tumbling into the larger glass. Her actions have a domino effect, as the rest of the tiny glasses fall into the next cup over, one after the other. The patrons cheer and gather up the strange cocktail. Minka catches my eye and greets me with a meow. I smile back and make my way toward the kitchen. Just when I reach the door, Mr. Boris rushes out. He's in his seelie form, a rag in his hands. He brightens when he sees me. "Oh, Highness! I mean...Miss Rose. You're back."

"I am."

"How were the children?"

"They were—"

"Oh, night above." Mr. Boris stomps away, a horrified look on his face. I follow him with my eyes to where he frantically wipes up a spilled drink at a table of particularly inebriated patrons. Why he chose to work at Minka's pub is beyond me, for his nerves don't seem cut out for such a boisterous atmosphere. He'd probably be more suited to working for Thorne at the bakery.

I catch him flashing a glare at Minka, who's already lining up another row of glasses, but I know there's no malice in the look. In fact, I'm starting to suspect there might be tenderness growing between them. I know an adoring glare when I see one.

I enter the kitchen, and the sound of frivolity is cut in half. The kitchen is large and dimly lit, a space shared between *Modest Minka's* and *Blackwood Bakery*. It's an oddly efficient pairing, with the bakery only open in the morning and afternoon and the public house opening after nightfall. I cross the kitchen to the door at the back, pausing when my eyes land on the small shelf that hangs next to the door, one designed for organizing letters. I find the compartment reserved for me holds a single envelope. I lift it from the shelf and find my name scrawled in a familiar script. Conflicting emotions tighten my chest as I see my mother's name as the sender.

We've exchanged several letters over the last year, and while I wouldn't call our relationship warm, I can tell she and Father are trying. After finally losing the throne to Trentas—thanks to the debt my family was never able to scheme their way out of—the Briars have had to reenter society from the bottom up. I haven't seen them in person since I left the palace that fateful night, and I won't until I'm certain they are worthy of a true relationship with me. If they manage not to fall back into organized crime, I might give them a chance.

I return the envelope to its shelf, resolving to read its contents later, and scan the compartment reserved for Thorne's letters. It's empty, but I wonder if he's had any recent correspondence from his mother or sisters. Morgana has succeeded in reclaiming a place in society, especially with the support of Trentas, the new Seelie King of Lunar. Like my parents, she too has attempted to make amends with Thorne. Neither of our families have engaged in violence, so there's hope yet that the feud is at an end. Regardless of anyone else's efforts, Thorne and I are committed to discarding our birth names and keeping the identities we've chosen. The new lives we've built.

Thoughts of Thorne have my heart fluttering and I can't wait a moment longer. I open the door and enter the dark storefront of the bakery. There I find Thorne behind the counter, stocking the display case with crescent bread.

He turns at the sound of the door opening and greets me with a soft smile. "Welcome home."

Stars, I'll never get tired of that sound. The word *home*. The sight of him. He's in his seelie form, his horns and wings nowhere to be seen. Though he no longer has to hide his past affiliations with Morgana and the Lemurias, he claims horns and wings make for tedious baking, so he saves his unseelie form for times when he gets to fly. His hair is tied back the way I like it, while his spectacles lie on the counter, unneeded in such a dark room. I stroll to the front of the counter and prop my bottom on the countertop.

He sets down his empty tray and wipes his hands on his apron. Eyes narrowed, he stands before me. Though he's trying to look serious, his smirk betrays his efforts. "Briony, what did I tell you about sitting on the counter?"

I bat my lashes. "You said don't sit on the counter unless I want to be your meal." I adjust my long skirt and widen my legs ever so slightly, delighting in the way his throat bobs. I know he remembers exactly what followed after he said those words. It was the first time he showed me some rather impressive talents with his tongue.

He steps between my parted legs, leans in, and frames my hips with his hands as he plants them at the edge of the counter. "That was one time and in our private kitchen. This is a storefront. You're in violation of the health code."

"Oh, that sounds serious," I say, leaning slightly closer. "Perhaps you should punish me."

We stay frozen like that for several beats, neither touching nor kissing nor breaking eye contact. This game of ours never ends. It seems we never tire of trying to make the other flustered.

"I can think of something." His whispered voice has my stomach tightening. One of his hands slides off the edge of the counter, circling behind me. He leans in closer, closer, and I brace for him to touch my backside—

He doesn't.

Just when I think he's about to kiss me, his face bypasses mine, and he leans across me. When he pulls back, he has a plate in hand, a mischievous glint in his eyes.

I release a gasp. "Damn you, Thorne."

He nods. "I won that round. Now, try this."

I open my mouth to argue, but he presses one of the plate's contents to my lips. I should be offended that he shut me up with sweets, but I see this as another opportunity.

Without fully taking the morsel from him, I flick out my tongue and caress the chocolatey confection, holding his eyes the entire time. The flavor is rich and tinged with cherry. I release an exaggerated moan. "That's good," I whisper.

His jaw tightens, and I know I have him.

I extend my tongue again, this time fully taking the confection. He's about to lower his hand when I catch his fingertip between my lips, licking the remnants of chocolate that had melted on his skin.

"Briony," he utters, voice thick with want.

I withdraw my lips and finish chewing my chocolate. "That was my win."

He blinks a few times, then his sly grin is back. "I wouldn't be so sure."

"Why is that?"

"Because my play wasn't finished yet. You haven't looked at the plate."

Frowning, I glance down at the porcelain dish. Three more chocolates lie on the plate, surrounding a small gold ring. At the bottom of the plate are cursive letters piped in chocolate to spell out *Marry me*.

Something giddy bursts in my chest, and I purse my lips against the emotion that bubbles in my throat.

"Are you laughing at me?" Thorne asks.

I cover my mouth with my hand but there's no hiding my laughter now. "I'm sorry, it's just...this is a bit...ridiculous. And you're not a ridiculous man."

"Which is exactly why I did it this way." He smiles until his eyes crinkle at the corners. "You like ridiculous things."

I stare down at the cursive letters, tears of joy mingling with my mirth.

He releases a mock sigh and starts to pull the plate away. "I suppose you don't want it—"

"I do! Give it." I extend my left hand, which trembles as I watch him lift the ring from the plate. Then, taking my palm tenderly in his, he slides the ring onto my finger. It's a circlet of gold carved with vines and roses.

With his other hand, he lifts my chin with his forefinger, forcing my eyes to his. His gaze is so earnest, so serious, my heart takes a tumble. "Will you marry me, Briony Rose? Will you accept me, exactly as I am, as your husband?"

More tears glaze my eyes. How did he know this was in my heart? That I've begun yearning for this next step between us? He knew marriage was a sore point for me last year. After almost being forced into an unwanted union, I wasn't sure I'd ever want to participate in such an unnecessary ritual. But so much has changed since then. I've learned to trust. To love. To understand the meaning of family. It's all come down to choice. I've chosen who I call family. Who I call friends. I've chosen the man I love. And this next step in our lives, once a choice that was thrust upon me, is now one I want to take with all my heart.

I also realize what this means for him. Accepting his own worth has been an obstacle, and it's taken him time to fully grasp that he's worthy of me. The fact that he's proposed—and the way he did it, asking if I accept him exactly as he is—shows that he's finally moved past that once-painful hurdle.

I wrap my arms around Thorne's neck and pull him close. My emotions burn brighter, surging out of my control and pouring from me in an unintentional burst of magic. The dimly lit bakery is swallowed by a dreamscape. I know exactly which one it is without even looking. The dark sky awash in vibrant hues encircles us, making it seem like we're floating midair. Nostalgia pangs me in the sweetest of ways. The first time I saw this sky, my feelings for Thorne were new. Terrifying. Now they've grown and matured, shifting into something stronger and more beautiful every day.

"Yes, Thorne Blackwood," I say, watching as his face flashes with the undulating colors waltzing through my illusion, "I'll marry you."

He presses his lips to mine. The taste of chocolate and cherry mingles between us, along with the promise of yet another new beginning. A new game. A new shape for our love to take.

"I won that round, right?" he mutters against my mouth.

Laughter fills my heart, dancing in my chest like butterfly wings. "Yes, my love. I suppose you did."

NOT READY TO LEAVE FAERWYVAE?

WHAT ABOUT MONTY? Whether you loved him or hated him, you might have an inkling that the roguish Monty Phillips is more than he seems. And I'm not done with him yet! He's coming with me to my next series set in Faerwyvae, *Fae Flings and Corset Strings*. He'll be tormenting another couple in the first book in the series, *A Rivalry of Hearts*, before he gets his own happily ever after in the following book.

Fae Flings and Corset Strings is a series of standalone adult fantasy romcoms. If you can't get enough of Faerwyvae and love the banter and heart-pounding romance of my *Entangled with Fae* books, you will love this new series too!

If fairytale retellings are your absolute favorite, worry not! More books in the *Entangled with Fae* series are coming, and if you haven't read them all, there are plenty more for you to enjoy.

You can also take a trip to Faerwyvae's past with *The Fair Isle Trilogy*, which takes place twenty-three years before *A Dream So Wicked*.

ALSO BY TESSONJA ODETTE

ENTANGLED WITH FAE - FAE ROMANCE

Curse of the Wolf King: A Beauty and the Beast Retelling

Heart of the Raven Prince: A Cinderella Retelling

Kiss of the Selkie: A Little Mermaid Retelling

— And more —

FAE FLINGS AND CORSET STRINGS - FAE ROMCOM

A Rivalry of Hearts

—and more—

THE FAIR ISLE TRILOGY - FAE FANTASY

To Carve a Fae Heart

To Wear a Fae Crown

To Spark a Fae War

STANDALONE FAE ROMANCE NOVELLA SET IN FAERWYVAE

Married by Scandal

PROPHECY OF THE FORGOTTEN FAE - EPIC FANTASY

A Throne of Shadows

A Cage of Crystal

A Fate of Flame

YA DYSTOPIAN PSYCHOLOGICAL THRILLER

Twisting Minds

ABOUT THE AUTHOR

Tessonja Odette is a fantasy author living in Seattle with her family, her pets, and ample amounts of chocolate. When she isn't writing, she's watching cat videos, petting dogs, having dance parties in the kitchen with her daughter, or pursuing her many creative hobbies. Read more about Tessonja at www.tessonjaodette.com

instagram.com/tessonja

facebook.com/tessonjaodette

tiktok.com/@tessonja

twitter.com/tessonjaodette

Printed in Great Britain
by Amazon

43111852R00290